Never
Say
Never

By Nicole Edwards

The Alluring Indulgence Series

Kaleb

Zane

Travis

Holidays with the Walker Brothers

Ethan

Braydon

Sawyer

Brendon

The Club Destiny Series

Conviction

Temptation

Addicted

Seduction

Infatuation

Captivated

Devotion

Perception

Entrusted

Adored

The Dead Heat Ranch Series

Boots Optional
Betting on Grace
Overnight Love

The Devil's Bend Series

Chasing Dreams
Vanishing Dreams

The Devil's Playground Series

Without Regret

The Sniper 1 Security Series

Wait for Morning
Never Say Never

The Southern Boy Mafia Series

Beautifully Brutal
Beautifully Loyal

Standalone Novels

A Million Tiny Pieces

Writing as Timberlyn Scott

Unhinged
Unraveling
Chaos

Never Say Never

A Sniper 1 Security Novel

Book Two

Nicole Edwards

Nicole Edwards Limited
PO Box 806
Hutto, Texas 78634
www.NicoleEdwardsLimited.com
www.slipublishing.com

Never Say Never*: A Sniper 1 Security Novel* is a work of fiction. Names, characters, businesses, places, events and incidents either are the products of the author's imagination or used in a fictitious manner. Any resemblance to actual persons, living or dead, or actual events is purely coincidental.

Cover Image: © Burmakin Andrey | 123rf.com (man with gun - 27241746), © Opas Chotiphantawanon | 123rf.com (art gallery - 37592641), © Nicole Edwards (background image)
Cover Design: © Nicole Edwards Limited
Editing: Blue Otter Editing **www.BlueOtterEditing.com**

ISBN (ebook): 978-1-939786-49-4
ISBN (print): 978-1-939786-50-0

Romantic Suspense
Male/Male Romance
Mature Audiences

Table of Contents

BREAKDOWN OF THE KOGANS AND TREXLERS

Below is an outline of the families within this series.

THE TREXLERS (from Sniper 1 Security)
Parents: Bryce and Emily
Children: Ryan/RT (33), Colby (31), Clay (28), Marissa (26), Austin (24)

THE KOGANS (from Sniper 1 Security)
Parents: Casper and Elizabeth
Children: Conner (33), Hunter (31), Trace (28), Courtney (26)
Grandchildren: Shelby (Conner's daughter)

BRYCE'S YOUNGER BROTHER'S FAMILY:

Parents: TJ (Bryce's younger brother) and Stephanie
Children: Tanner (25), Kira (24), Evan (23), Dominic (22)

THE ADORITES (from Southern Boy Mafia)

Parents: Samuel and Genevieve
Children: Maximillian (29), Brent (27), Ashlynn (26), Aidan (26), Victor (24), Madison (22)

PROLOGUE

Three years ago

"What the hell were you thinking?" Ryan yelled, unable to contain the anger that surged through him as he stared back at the man who was responsible for nearly getting two of Ryan's enforcers killed in recent days.

Kevin's answering stare was blank, lacking any emotion whatsoever.

"You blew their cover and damn near got Trace and Z killed! Why the *fuck* would you do that?"

Still no answer.

Ryan thrust his hands through his hair, tugging hard on the shaggy blond strands as he turned on his heel and paced away from Kevin, hoping to keep from wrapping his fingers around the man's throat and...squeezing.

How could someone be so fucking reckless? So careless? So goddamn stupid?

It was almost as though Kevin didn't give a shit that he'd fucked up so epically. That was one of the main reasons Ryan had held off on having this conversation until today—four days after the shit had hit the fan.

Unfortunately, he couldn't put it off any longer or he'd likely do just that.

"Are we done here?" Kevin asked, his tone hard.

Ryan turned to look at him, stunned by how uncouth the man was being. "No, we're not fucking done here, *Kevin*. Were you *not* thinking? Did you not consider what the hell you were doing? The lives you were putting in jeopardy?"

When Kevin didn't respond, Ryan had to hold back the frustrated groan that wanted to break free. Not sure what to say or do, Ryan walked behind his desk, but he didn't sit down. He couldn't. There was too much anger built up, too many emotions tearing him in a million different directions. Disappointment, fear, frustration. Incredulity. A fucking ton of incredulity.

"Look," Kevin began. "I've got shit to do. So if you're done ripping me a new one, we can talk about this at home later."

Ryan stared back at the man standing before him, a man Ryan no longer recognized although they'd been dating for the better part of three years. He'd met Kevin in this very same building nearly five years ago when Kevin had come to work for Sniper 1 Security.

"No, we won't," Ryan countered hotly. "I... Fuck! I don't even know what the hell to say to you right now."

"Don't say anything," Kevin told him, a hint of concern echoing in the words. "Let's talk when you calm down."

"That's the thing, Kevin. You don't fucking get it. I won't calm down. You almost got two people killed."

Kevin's usually pale skin heated, his cheeks turning crimson. "I did what I thought was best. Are you sure you're not just pissed because it was Trace and Z?"

"What the hell does that mean?" Ryan squared his shoulders and faced off with Kevin. "It wouldn't've mattered who the hell it was."

"Are you sure about that?" Kevin snapped, his green eyes glittering with menace. "I've seen the way you look at Z. You've got a hard-on for the guy. Even I can see that."

"You don't know what the fuck you're talkin' about." Ryan knew this conversation was going nowhere, but leave it to Kevin to turn it around on him. For the three years they'd been dating, Kevin had grown more and more insecure with every passing day. He was jealous, so much so that Ryan had heard a few offhanded comments from others recently. It was clear that Kevin had allowed emotion to interfere with his ability to do his job and he could no longer be objective. That or... Holy fuck. "Did you do this on purpose?" Ryan took a step closer. "Did you fucking blow their cover because you're jealous?"

"*What*? No!" Kevin's gaze dropped to the floor, a clear sign of guilt.

"Christ. I can't believe I didn't see this before." Ryan paced away from Kevin, fury causing his hands to shake. He suddenly didn't want to be in the same room with him.

"See what?" Kevin retorted, his voice louder this time. "You can't see a goddamn thing, RT. You're too busy worrying about your precious career, your stupid job, this *stupid* company. You don't give a shit about me at all, do you?"

Ryan stared at Kevin in disbelief. Three years. Three fucking years he'd given to this man, trying his best to make it work despite their differences, despite Kevin's jealousy, his anger, his short fuse. "This is my company, Kevin! Those people"—Ryan stabbed his finger toward the door—"are my employees. I owe it to them to be worried about their safety."

"*Them*? What about *me*?" Kevin yelled. "Aren't you the slightest bit worried about *me*?"

"Of course I am." Ryan couldn't believe they were having this conversation. It was one they'd gone round and round about many times before. Kevin would never be satisfied with the fact that Ryan had to worry about someone other than him.

They continued to stare at one another, and during those interminably long seconds, Ryan felt his world crumbling around him. Not that he hadn't been anticipating it. For the last few months, he'd been trying to find a way to break things off with Kevin. He'd given the relationship everything he had. But now he no longer had anything left to give.

Kevin's face fell, his anger seeming to subside. "We can talk about this later tonight."

"No, Kevin, we can't," Ryan told him. "There's nothing more to discuss. I'm meeting with Bryce and Casper again this afternoon after I talk to Z. They'll be making the decisions going forward."

"What does that mean? Decisions? Are you firing me?"

Ryan didn't answer. He wouldn't know until he spoke to Bryce and Casper in a couple of hours, but yeah, if they gave him the choice, Ryan would be cutting Kevin loose today. From his job. From Ryan's life. He couldn't stand to look at Kevin anymore. The man standing before him damn sure wasn't the same one Ryan had fallen in love with so long ago.

"You don't need to do anything rash," Kevin stated, a hint of concern enhancing the words. "Give me a chance to make it up to you."

"To *me*?" Ryan couldn't believe what he was hearing. "This isn't about *me*."

"It never is, is it?" Kevin countered hotly. "I'm the one who's at fault. Always me. You can't even accept responsibility for the arguing, the fighting, the...alienation."

"What. The. Fuck. Are. You. Talking. About?" Ryan couldn't hold back any longer. He was being buried under the emotional overload, anger resonating, churning into something much more potent.

"I know you've been pushing me away, RT. That's what you do. You push everyone away. And yes! Maybe that's why I did it. I'm sick and fucking tired of you paying attention to everyone else. Maybe I need some attention. Did you ever think of that?"

Ryan stared at Kevin, shock and horror coalescing as his worst fears were realized. If he hadn't misunderstood— and he really didn't think he had—Kevin had just admitted to setting Trace and Z up.

It must've registered with Kevin what he'd said, because his eyes widened. "I didn't mean that," Kevin backtracked. "It wasn't my fault. I swear to you it wasn't my fault. Look, it won't happen again. We can work this out, RT."

No, they couldn't, but Ryan couldn't even say that much. He merely pointed toward the door.

"Don't kick me out, RT. Don't make me go. You owe it to us to listen, to be on my side."

Ryan swallowed hard, studying Kevin's face. He'd given the last few years of his life to this man, and it had all come down to this. "There is no more us," he told Kevin as gently as he could, which honestly wasn't much. He wished they'd been able to keep this topic separate from the discussion at hand, but it was inevitable. As it was, Ryan had managed to keep his distance from Kevin, speaking to him only in the office or on the phone, but it hadn't been easy.

"No. Hold up. You don't mean that," Kevin sputtered.

"I do. It's been over for a long time. This was just the last straw."

"RT, please. Don't—"

Raising his voice to be heard over Kevin's continued tirade, Ryan said, "We're done here. Now get out of my face."

For the first time since the incident on Monday, Kevin appeared almost apologetic, but Ryan knew better. Not once during any of the conversations he'd had with Kevin had he ever said he was sorry—fault or not. And he never would. It wasn't like Kevin to accept responsibility for his own actions.

Kevin turned toward the door, and Ryan was grateful.

Unfortunately, his hope that Kevin would walk away disappeared when, with his hand hovering over the knob, he turned back. Ryan's stomach churned, anger and hurt merging into a potent mixture of hatred and disgust.

"I'll give you some time to cool off. We can talk at home later. I'll stop by."

"Don't bother," Ryan answered. "I don't have anything more to say to you."

"RT. Come on, you can't be ser—"

"Get outta my face." Dropping into his chair, Ryan glared up at Kevin. "Go!"

When the door closed behind Kevin, Ryan sighed, dropping his head into his hands. How had things gone so horribly wrong?

He had to go talk to Bryce and Casper, figure out what their next steps were. As much as he wished it didn't have to come to this, he knew that firing Kevin was the only way this could play out.

And in order to get on with his life, the final decision couldn't come soon enough.

Zachariah Tavoularis had no idea why he had been called into the office on a Friday afternoon, but here he was, trying to smile as he limped through the nearly empty space toward the offices in the back. After the week he'd had, Z wanted nothing more than to put his feet up, relax, maybe have a beer or two. Specifically, he wanted to give his right foot a rest since he was pretty damn sure he'd broken his big toe in the skirmish that had ensued just four days ago.

Damn. Had it only been four days? It seemed like a hell of a lot longer than that.

After the fiasco that had nearly cost him his life, Z had been treated for the stab wound in his shoulder, but he'd kept his trap shut about his toe. No reason to get everyone more fired up than they already were when there wasn't anything that could be done about it. When the shit hit the fan around this place, things got messy, and Z didn't want to add to the strain he could already feel.

Rapping his knuckles on RT's door, he waited until he was called to come inside.

"You wanted to see me?" Z asked, peeking his head in the door.

RT was sitting at his desk, his brow furrowed, his mouth a hard, thin line. He didn't look happy at all.

"Yeah. Have a seat," RT instructed, nodding toward the empty chair across from him.

He suddenly wished he could be anywhere but there. As it was, he'd spent the last four days thinking about the shit that had gone down and the fact that he'd been hung out to dry by one of his own. Having gone deep cover for months inside a drug cartel in order to unearth a missing wealthy businessman, Z and Trace had been lucky to escape alive. Fortunately, they had, but it damn sure hadn't been easy. Despite being set up to take a fall, Z and Trace had still managed to extract the man they'd been hired to find from the cartel's clutches.

Barely.

No thanks to that bastard Kevin Fischer.

Not wanting to rehash the incident, because the more he thought about it, the angrier he got, Z attempted to redirect the conversation before RT had a chance to steer it in that direction. "I already gave the details of what happened to Casper," Z informed RT, trying not to limp too much although his toe was throbbing like a motherfucker. Probably would've been best not to stuff his foot into his boot, but riding his motorcycle without it hadn't been an option.

So here he was, lowering himself into the chair in RT's office.

"How're you doin'?" RT asked, his eyes sliding to Z's shoulder.

"Oh, that?" Z smiled, peering down at his shirt sleeve, which was hiding the white bandage that still covered the three-inch-deep gash in his arm. "Just a scratch."

Z got caught up in RT's crystal-blue gaze for a moment, unable to look away. Although his body's untimely response wasn't exactly appropriate considering Z worked for RT, he couldn't help but be attracted to the man. Hell, he'd been harboring what he'd regarded as a slight crush on the guy for the better part of the last five years, maybe longer. Not that it mattered, because once RT had started dating Kevin, Z had done everything in his power not to think about him.

Most of the time it had worked.

Okay, *some* of the time.

"Are you really okay?" This time RT's question sounded less business-like and more...personal.

What Z wouldn't give for RT to care about him. Well, on a level other than employer to employee, that was. There was no doubt that RT cared about all of the enforcers who worked for Sniper 1 Security. He made that abundantly clear.

"I'm great," Z lied. "Just chillin', waitin' for my next assignment."

"I think you should take a coupla weeks off," RT said, leaning back in his chair and crossing his arms over his thick chest, his biceps bulging from the movement. "Recuperate. Acclimate to the real world once again."

Z locked his eyes on RT's face once more. "Nope. Not necessary." The last thing Z wanted was downtime. He needed something to keep him busy, and his job provided the perfect excuse not to sit around and dwell on all that had happened over the past year. Things were just beginning to stabilize—as best they could, anyhow—and he had no intention of upsetting that precarious balance that had become his life.

"You sure?" RT inquired.

Without hesitating, Z answered with, "Positive. Why? Is that why I'm here?" Z glanced around mainly because looking at RT was making his body hum to life in a way that was definitely inappropriate but couldn't be helped. "'Cause you coulda done this over the phone, ya know?"

RT shook his head. "I called you in because I wanted to talk about Kevin. I met with him a couple of hours ago."

Oh, shit. The absolute last person Z wanted to chat with RT about was Kevin. Hell, he'd prefer to talk politics or religion—both subjects he generally considered completely off limits—rather than discuss the fucking douche that RT had hooked up with.

Z had never disliked anyone as much as he disliked Kevin. The guy was a first-rate dickhead who considered himself high and mighty because of the fact he was sleeping with RT. A point Kevin always made sure to relay.

There were a few comments Kevin had made over the years that Z was sure he'd never forget.

Don't forget who you're talkin' to. Remember whose bed I keep warm at night. That makes me practically in charge.

I don't want to have to tell you that I can call the shots, but I will. If I see you lookin' at RT like that again, I'll make sure he cans your ass. After all, I do pull most of the strings with him.

I'm the one he eats his meals with, the one he's fucking every night. You'd be wise to remember that.

Yep, first-rate prick.

Rather than share his feelings on the subject, Z steeled his expression, waiting to see what RT had to say.

"We have no choice but to terminate his employment," RT explained. "I spoke at length with Casper and Bryce a little while ago, and they agree. What Kevin did…?" RT shook his head in disbelief. "It's unforgivable. We're just damn lucky no one died."

There was that. The man their client had hired them to find had been lucky as fuck, and it had cost Z the "scratch" on his arm and a near miss with a few bullets. The wealthy businessman who'd been kidnapped by the cartel had been delivered home to his wife and kids, and for that, Z was grateful.

But Z was pretty sure the failure of the mission—at least on Z's and Trace's parts—had been Kevin's intention in the first place—to get Z and Trace killed so he could swoop in and save the day. The guy had always been volatile, but ever since his relationship with RT had become rocky, Kevin had grown more and more unstable. On more than one occasion, he'd accused Z of wanting to fuck RT. It never mattered what Z said to defuse the situation, Kevin had never believed him.

"I hope you're not expectin' my input," Z stated. He did not want to be part of this. It was up to the big dogs as to what they did to Kevin. Whether they fired him or reprimanded him, that was their choice, not Z's.

"No, I'm not," RT assured him, leaning forward and resting his elbows on the desk. "I just wanted you to know that I take this seriously. The welfare of my employees is important to me. I can't sit by and let Kevin get away with this."

Z couldn't say he wasn't happy with that decision. If Kevin had gone so far as to try and get Z and Trace killed because he was jealous, there was no telling what he was capable of.

Shrugging as though it didn't matter one way or the other, Z got to his feet.

"I'm sorry this went down the way it did," RT said, standing as well.

"It wasn't your fault," Z replied, looking directly into RT's eyes, wanting the man to realize he meant those words. RT was the type to take everything on himself, even the irresponsible actions of a man like Kevin.

"It'll get better from here," RT said, smiling, though it was obviously forced. "I promise."

Yeah, well, Z wasn't so sure RT could ensure that, but Z wasn't going to disagree. After all, Z didn't hold RT responsible for any of it. He was only human; there was no way he could've seen this coming.

"Smooth sailing from here on out," Z replied with a smile as he moved toward the door.

"Why're you limping?" RT asked as Z placed his hand on the doorknob, anxious to put some distance between him and RT. When the man showed his softer side, he only enraptured Z more, and that wasn't necessarily a good thing.

"Huh?" He didn't bother to turn around.

"You're limping. Is somethin' wrong with your leg?"

Peering at RT over his shoulder, Z smiled. "Cramp."

RT's eyes narrowed, and Z knew his boss didn't believe him, but he wasn't going to go into detail. The man had enough to worry about as it was.

"See you on Monday?" RT asked as Z opened the door.

"Monday." With that, Z left, feeling the heat of RT's gaze trailing him as he did.

As he hobbled out of the office, he had to wonder whether or not Kevin's termination would also mean the end of his relationship with RT. It shouldn't matter to Z, but for some strange reason, it did.

ONE

Three years later – August

"Today. Got it." Kira tapped out something on her iPad before looking up at Ryan once more. "Who do you want me to call in?" she asked, her easygoing drawl polite and to the point.

Ryan Trexler stared back at his cousin, trying to hide the underlying urge to offer her a bit of advice. The dress she wore seemed to be more skin than fabric. Today's outfit was some off-the-shoulder, puffy black-and-white number combined with dangly earrings, cowboy boots, and a hell of a lot of flesh. Rather than advise her to broaden her shopping to departments that utilized more fabric, Ryan shook his head. Getting Kira to change her style now was like trying to convince Jayden that bright colors were banned in the office.

If only Ryan could keep guys like Decker Bromwell from noticing his cousin, then Ryan wouldn't give a shit what Kira wore. Since that would likely never happen, he had to remember to keep his opinions to himself. Her fashion sense had nothing to do with her ability to get the job done, and he wasn't the type of employer to enforce a dress code. They had more important issues to worry about.

Despite her taste in clothing, Ryan was grateful for Kira's no-nonsense manner. It made getting down to business that much easier for him. And on a day like this one, when an impromptu meeting was the most critical thing on his to-do list, Ryan appreciated it all the more.

Answering her original question, Ryan said, "Clay, Conner, and Z."

After keying something else into her iPad, Kira gifted him with a beaming smile as she eased toward the door. "Got it, boss. I'll shoot them a message telling them to be here by three." Kira disappeared, closing his office door behind her.

"Thanks," Ryan muttered to the space Kira had just vacated, casting a sideways glance at his watch. Two twenty. That'd give him just enough time to put the details together for the briefing before the others arrived, and then it'd give the four of them enough time to get in place by sundown.

A few quick keystrokes on his computer and Ryan printed four copies of the details that the parents of the missing girl had provided him with yesterday when they'd called seeking Sniper 1's assistance. He could still hear the father's fear for his daughter; Mr. Dumont's anxiety had seeped through the phone, leaving Ryan desperate to help the man find his missing child.

Ryan added the extra notes from the recon he'd done last night, and ten minutes later, after tossing each set into its own file folder, he was ready.

Tucking his laptop along with the additional files beneath his arm, he made his way down the narrow hall that led to his father's office. Rapping his knuckles on the closed door while staring at the silver and gold nameplate that read **BRYCE TREXLER**, Ryan waited until his father's booming voice announced for him to come in.

Opening the door, Ryan stuck his head in but didn't bother to join his father inside. "I'm meeting with Clay, Z, and Conner at three. We'll be in the conference room."

Bryce Trexler, one of the two owners of Sniper 1 Security, nodded. "You need me there?"

"Only if you wanna be," Ryan said.

Out of a deep respect for the two men who'd built Sniper 1 Security from the ground up, he continued to keep Bryce and Casper involved in the goings-on when he could. For the most part, Ryan had taken control of the business dealings while the original owners contemplated what to do with the downtime they could see in their future. Neither man had yet to take the fully retired plunge, so Bryce and Casper simply did what they were used to doing...they came into the office every day. And Ryan continued to include them.

"Casper and I'll meet you in there."

"Thanks." With that, Ryan left his father to his own devices and then ventured into the empty conference room across the hall. He flipped on the bright fluorescent lights and set his load on the far side of the long table, farthest from the door.

Less than a minute later, the heavy clomp of booted feet announced the first arrival, which turned out to be Ryan's younger brother. The guy could be quiet as a mouse when he wanted to be, but all other times, Clay Trexler seemed to make as much noise as possible. Ryan had never understood why that was, but he didn't care enough to question it, either.

"What's up, boss man?" Clay bellowed, his thunderous voice echoing in the glass-enclosed space.

Ryan turned in time to see a slightly disheveled Clay—complete with shaggy blond hair, white tank top, and tattered blue jeans—flop into one of the fifteen high-back leather chairs circling the table. Without an ounce of propriety, Clay propped his feet up on the conference table while he tapped something on his phone.

"Kira said you wanted to meet."

"In half an hour," Ryan informed him, tethering his laptop to the power cable poking up through the grommet in the center of the table. He'd been going nonstop since that morning, nearly draining the battery.

"Make a note then, 'cause I'm early. I know how you are about punctuality," Clay mumbled. "I'll prob'ly need to borrow some of these extra minutes at a later date."

Of course he would. Clay wasn't the most adept at being on time.

It was true, Ryan's biggest pet peeve was timeliness, followed closely by proficiency, and his agents were well aware. If someone couldn't arrive on time or do the job to the best of their ability, he expected to know so that he could prepare accordingly.

In his line of work, these things were critical.

Especially on days like today.

Ryan spared his brother another cursory glance before he pulled up the information he needed and briefly scanned the contents once more to ensure he had everything.

"When'd you get back?" Ryan asked Clay as he searched the online folder for the picture of their client that he would use for the meeting.

"Half an hour ago. I was in the elevator when I got Kira's text."

"You up for this?" Ryan knew that Clay had recently completed a two-week-long assignment and likely needed to get some sleep.

"Yep," Clay announced, not looking up from his phone.

A rumble of laughter outside the room had Ryan's head swiveling in the direction of the door. Not that he needed to look to know whom the flirtatious bellow belonged to. The distinct intonation of Zachariah Tavoularis's voice was something Ryan would likely never be able to ignore. Though he was doing his damnedest to on a daily basis.

A few seconds later, Z waltzed into the room, filling the doorway with his massive frame, a huge grin plastered on his too handsome face. Telling himself not to, but doing it anyway, Ryan took a moment to take Z in. From his disheveled dark hair, the black T-shirt plastered to an extremely sculpted chest, down past his narrow waist, thick thighs, and then, finally, stopping on the enormous black shitkickers Z wore.

Why he continued to torture himself, Ryan would never know, but his body hummed to life from that quick perusal. It was enough to remind him that looking at Z wasn't conducive to business. Especially when he needed to keep his head in the game.

With a fist bump, Z acknowledged Clay. "What's up, bro?"

"Nada. You?"

"A little of this, a lot of that." Z smirked. "You know how it is."

Clay grunted, dropping his feet to the floor when Z slid into the seat next to him.

Ryan could feel the curiosity in Z's silent inspection from across the table, but he turned his attention to his computer screen.

"Afternoon," Z finally greeted, sounding slightly more formal, although his amusement wasn't masked, when he spoke to Ryan than when he spoke to Clay.

It wasn't because Ryan was his boss that Z did that, though, and Ryan was well aware of that fact. They'd been working together for far too long for Z to treat Ryan any differently than he had Clay, boss or not.

No, Z wasn't overly polite because of Ryan's status within the company; Z merely liked to give Ryan a hard time whenever possible. That was just one of his many ways.

Instead of responding, Ryan nodded in acknowledgment.

"We waitin' on someone else?" The deep tenor of Z's voice rattled along every one of Ryan's nerve endings. Again, like every time Z spoke, Ryan ignored his body's traitorous response.

"Conner," Ryan said simply, pushing to his feet. "We've got fifteen. I'll be back in a minute."

Unable to sit in the same room with Z for that long and pretend to be busy when he wasn't, Ryan opted to head down to the coffee shop. It'd give him some time to gather his thoughts, and a chance to put some much-needed distance between him and the man who'd been plaguing his every thought for the last few months.

Years.

Great, now his subconscious was arguing with him.

Fine, he'd been plagued with thoughts of Z for the last few *years.*

Hell.

By the time Ryan returned, Conner Kogan had graced them with his presence, along with Conner's father, Casper, the other owner of Sniper 1 Security. That meant the only one who hadn't arrived on time was Bryce, but Ryan wasn't going to wait on his father. He'd catch the man up on the details later.

"Thanks for gettin' here so quickly," Ryan told them, tapping one of the keys on his laptop to wake it up and then taking his position at the front of the room. The information reflected on his computer screen flickered to life on the wide screen behind him, and Ryan ducked out of the way.

"Desiree Dumont," Ryan began without preamble. "Fifteen years old, five foot three inches tall, one hundred thirty pounds, blonde hair, blue eyes, just completed her freshman year of high school. Her parents last saw her Wednesday morning before she left to go to a friend's house. They expected her back for dinner, but she didn't show. They received a text from her Wednesday afternoon letting them know she was fine. Nothing since. After dealing with the police, her parents contacted us yesterday asking for our assistance."

"Kidnapping?" Clay inquired, his full attention on the screen, dark blue eyes narrowed.

"Yes and no," Ryan replied, briefly tracking Bryce's casual movements as his father joined them and proceeded to take one of the seats beside Casper. "It appears Desiree was with her nineteen-year-old boyfriend, Bill Hendricks, a two-bit drug dealer—specializing in Ecstasy—who she's been dating for over a year. I got the information on the boyfriend from the dad, including the license number of the kid's car. I checked with Detective Jacobs; he said they found the car in a ditch on Wednesday night." Ryan sighed at the same time Conner growled. "The boy was in it. Fatal gunshot wound to the head."

"Does the girl know?" Conner asked.

"Don't know for sure. Not sure how she could've missed it, though," Ryan told him truthfully. They didn't even know whether the girl was still alive, but on a positive note, according to his source, the last time she'd been seen, she'd been a little worse for wear but still breathing. "I did some recon yesterday, talked to a couple of my sources in the area where Desiree and Bill'd last been seen. Looks like an internal issue with a local gang. The boyfriend was killed for sampling the merchandise rather than selling it. Owed a couple grand. The guys who took him out grabbed the girl with the plans to ask for a ransom as a way to recoup their costs."

"Did they?" Z queried, his steady gaze scanning the picture of the young girl on the screen behind Ryan before sliding back to Ryan's face.

"Not yet, according to the parents. My source—she's reliable only because these guys jilted her on her last visit to them—told me they're holding the girl for now."

"Your source? Hooker?" Conner inquired.

Ryan nodded. "I've got the address of the house Desiree's bein' kept at. Based on the information, there'll be three males there tonight. All armed, though more than likely high after dark. I want us to go in and get her out."

Clay spoke up. "Tonight?"

"As soon as the sun goes down."

Clay, Conner, and Z nodded, all eyes focused on Ryan.

"Clay, you're the driver, so you get the van. Conner and Z, meet us here at eight thirty. We'll get in, get her out, and then we'll call it in. The cops can clean up the mess."

"Why not let the police handle the extraction?" Casper asked.

Ryan had expected the question. It wasn't that Casper thought getting the cops involved was necessarily a good idea, but the older man preferred asking questions to ensure Ryan had thought the situation all the way through.

"I don't want these assholes alerted that anyone's coming. We've got a better shot of getting her out without the cops."

Casper nodded. No one else said anything, but the sound of papers shuffling could be heard as they skimmed the information in the file.

"Y'all with me?" Ryan glanced between the five men at the table. "Questions?"

Again, nothing.

"I want a sit rep as soon as you're outta there," Bryce informed them, getting to his feet. "And be careful."

A round of grunts echoed in the small space, and a minute later, Ryan was the only one in the room. He released a heavy breath and steeled himself for what was to come.

Later that night

"On my signal, Z, you'll go in." RT's commanding declaration came in crystal clear in Z's earpiece.

Standing at the northwest corner of the ramshackle little house, his back pressed against the rough bricks, Z patiently waited for the go-ahead. As with any mission, everything except for the plan faded from Z's mind. He wasn't worried about the lack of moonlight that kept his surroundings effectively hidden from his view, the steady pelting of rain hitting his face and pinging off the metal shed a few yards away, or even the sticky heat washing over him from the humid summer night.

No, his comfort wasn't factored in. The only thing that mattered was getting inside the trashed-out drug house and grabbing the girl who'd been snatched right out of her boyfriend's twenty-year-old piece-of-shit Buick on Wednesday night. Z didn't know if the girl had been aware of the true danger she was in, or if she was even up to speed on the fact that her boyfriend—a bottom-feeding X dealer—was dead. Although, Z somehow doubted the kid's murderer had bothered to shield her innocent eyes from the grizzly scene.

One could only hope.

The sound of knuckles rapping on a door echoed in Z's ear, followed by Conner's gruff tone. "Pizza!"

Z couldn't make out the mumbles that erupted inside the house, but he could hear movement.

"I said I got your fuckin' pizza, bro. Open the goddamn door."

Okay then. Leave it to Conner to get right to the point. The man's temper had been flaring bright and hot for quite some time now. Tonight was proof.

"On three, Z," RT stated calmly.

Z took slow, measured breaths and listened as RT's rumbling voice counted down slowly. On one, Z slipped around to the back of the house, lifted his foot, and aimed the sole of his size-fifteen combat boot at the weathered doorknob, effectively breaking the door and sending it flying open and crashing into the wall. From inside, he heard the sound of glass smashing, people yelling. While Conner and RT created a distraction, keeping the kidnappers otherwise occupied, Z eased inside, aiming his Sig in front of him as he scanned his surroundings, the wet soles of his boots squeaking on the worn, yellowed linoleum flooring that was peeling up from the concrete beneath.

Good Lord, the place was disgusting. And it smelled as bad as it looked.

There were dishes and trash piled high on the chipped and broken kitchen counters. The refrigerator in the corner, with its broken handle and dented door, rattled loudly. A cheap metal card table sat in the corner, propped on two boxes because it was missing a leg, an ashtray in the center, overflowing with cigarette butts.

Didn't look like these guys knew how to manage their drug money all that well. Clearly no budget for a housekeeper.

With his back to the wall, Z made his way through the kitchen and toward the room where the girl was supposedly stashed.

"Get on the ground!" RT and Conner both yelled at the same time, their words reverberating off the thin walls in the other room.

"What the fuck, man? I thought you said you had pizza!"

"Oh, shut up. And don't fucking move or I'll shoot your fucking foot off," Conner added, the man's fury reverberating like a bass drum at a rock concert. Z couldn't imagine what Conner was feeling. Considering the guy had a fourteen-year-old daughter of his own, Z could only assume this hit a little too close to home.

"I said get the fuck down, you dumb ass!" Conner again.

More yelling ensued, this time from the occupants of the house. There were three of them, they'd been told. All armed but likely getting complacent due to the late hour, or perhaps from the pot that had left a cloying scent lingering in the air.

Definitely dumb asses.

The intel they'd received came from a prostitute who'd been doing business out of the same house in recent weeks. Seemed she had a conscience. That or she knew that RT's request for information hadn't been a request at all. Regardless, to hear RT tell it, it hadn't been difficult to get her to talk. Turned out, the asshole drug dealers had stiffed her on her payment, and she was out for a little revenge of her own.

Z was heartbroken over the lack of ethics between bad guys. Shame.

Glancing into the living room as he passed, Z nodded to RT, who was pinning a tall, floppy-haired white guy down on the floor with his foot centered in the guy's back.

Continuing down the hall, Z kept his back turned to the wall. He peeked into two other rooms—first, a small, yellow-tiled bathroom with a cracked sink and a dirty shower curtain, and then a small bedroom, with a set of grungy twin mattresses tossed onto the floor with a flurry of clothes. Both empty, except for the dirt and disarray.

And finally the last door. Closed, as the nightwalker had said it would be.

Z didn't bother reaching down to try the knob. The padlock attached to a cheap brass hinge was proof that the door wouldn't open. Good thing about dumb ass bad guys, they didn't realize that kicking in the door and breaking the hinge from the jamb was as simple as smiling for the camera.

With little effort once again, Z turned and slammed his shoulder into the door up near where the lock was securing it closed. The wood cracked easily, but he hadn't expected any less. At six foot seven inches, two hundred forty-four pounds, getting through a flimsy interior door wasn't difficult for Z.

When the door flew inward, he immediately took stock of everything in the room. The girl—a mere kid—sat huddled on a grimy mattress, her hands tied behind her and her terrified cries muffled by the duct tape covering her mouth. A cheap brass lamp—sans the shade—sat on a small plastic table on the opposite side of the room, casting a golden glow over her and her meager surroundings. She looked like hell, but that tended to happen when kidnapped by thugs. The fifteen-year-old had been missing for two days and likely hadn't seen a shower, or even a bathroom if the smell was anything to go by, during her lengthy stay in the shithole her captors had stashed her in.

"I'm here to get you out," he informed the girl, ducking his head to avoid hitting the doorjamb as he stepped into the room, keeping his voice low, reassuring. After kicking a discolored pillow out of the way—weren't they fucking sweet, thinking of her comfort?—Z leaned down and gently pulled the tape from her mouth. "If you keep a lid on it and don't knee me in the...well, you know...we'll be outta here in no time. Cool?"

Her panicked blue eyes widened, but she nodded.

When it was clear she was going to cooperate, Z jerked his chin upward, a signal for the girl to get up.

She stood slowly, her eyes scanning Z from head to toe, then back again. He dwarfed her in size, which seemed to frighten her all the more. Tears streaked a trail of dirt over her cheeks, and snot ran down over her chapped lips. Yep, she was a mess.

Her feet weren't bound, which was a good thing. Z didn't have time to untie her, especially since they would possibly have to resort to plan B due to the wrought iron bars covering the window that trapped them inside the house. His big-ass foot wasn't going to get them out of there quite as easily if walking out was no longer an option.

Conner's irritated grunt sounded from outside the room, but Z didn't leave the girl. His job was to protect her until they could get her out of the house. "I said, stay the fuck down!"

"The girl! They're tryin' to get the girl!" one of the drug dealers hollered.

"You get a medal for bein' perceptive. Now get on the floor, fucker," Conner grumbled.

Something—or more likely someone—slammed into the wall outside the room, and another thud sounded when they hit the ground.

"I got them, Con," RT growled bitterly. "You help Z. Let's get outta here."

"Fine, but you better keep your eye on this squirrely bastard," Conner affirmed, followed by a muted grunt, this time not from Conner. If Z had to guess, Conner had given the bad guy a gentle nudge before leaving his ass on the floor.

"Shit!" RT yelled. "Don't fucking move!"

That didn't sound good.

Silence followed, and Z waited for direction, keeping his eye on the girl while footsteps sounded from the hall. He knew people did crazy shit when they were scared—he'd been shot at, stabbed, and yes, kneed in the family jewels during more than one rescue attempt—and he didn't care for surprises.

Z sidestepped the garbage on the floor and stuck his head out into the hall. There RT stood, holding a gun in each hand, one aimed toward the kitchen, the other into the living room.

"Problem?" Z asked.

"Fucker's in the kitchen."

As though making his location known, a gunshot erupted from that direction.

"Fuck. Get down!" RT yelled.

Great. So much for plan A. RT's hostages were split, and one was trigger happy, which greatly diminished their likelihood for a cakewalk rescue.

"Back door's blocked, Z." RT's voice sounded in his earpiece and from only a few feet away. "You and the girl'll go out the window."

"Roger that." Z headed for the window, not bothering to tell RT he could toss the girl over his shoulder and walk out the front door with her. Where was the fun in that?

"Bars," Z reminded them via the com link as he yanked the cheap plastic blinds down, letting them crash to the floor.

"Con! I can't see him," RT called. "Get to Z."

"Ten four."

Less than a minute later, the sound of someone rapping on the glass outside the window had Z looking down to see Conner frowning up at him, talking to him via the transmitter. "I need one minute. Get the girl away from the window," Conner insisted, the man's blunt tone broadcasting in Z's earpiece.

Conner Kogan had been tasked with blowing the bars from the window if plan A didn't work out—Conner's suggestion, of course—and the man's gift with explosives, a skill he'd picked up in the military, had apparently come in handy once again.

Z grabbed the girl and pulled her into the narrow closet with him, keeping her shielded by his own body since the bifold doors were hanging from the track, unable to offer them any cover. "Go!"

While he waited, Z listened to RT instructing the remaining bad guys to zip-tie themselves, his words clipped but steady. A couple of minutes later, a series of small explosions resounded, sending wood shards and glass flying into the room. The girl squealed, but she didn't try to run.

"Let's go!" Conner yelled, sticking his head in the window once the smoke cleared.

Z grabbed the girl, lightly shoved her toward Conner, and waited as the other man pulled her to safety.

"RT, need help?" Z questioned, turning to peer into the narrow hall.

"All good in here," RT answered breathlessly. "Keep your eyes open out there. On my way now. See you at the van."

With that, Z followed the rest of the plan to the letter, slipping out the window behind Conner and the girl, checking for the AWOL bad guy before darting through the backyard, then catapulting himself over the chain link fence into the alley. He took off running in the pitch-blackness, carefully dodging the trash cans and other debris in the narrow space between backyards.

Two minutes later, he was hopping into the van with Conner and the girl while Clay Trexler sat behind the wheel, ready to make tracks. Z held his breath, counting down from ten...*nine, eight, seven...six...shit...five...* The air escaped him in a rush of relief when RT jumped in the van, slamming his hand on the seat and telling Clay to go.

"Stop to have coffee?" Clay teased as he threw the van in drive.

"Nope. Just knock out the escapee. Don't want to do a half-assed job."

Z chuckled.

Conner was on the phone with the police, calling it in, and before they exited the alley, RT was dialing the girl's parents to let them know she was okay.

"Everyone good?" Clay asked from the front seat. "Well, you know, aside from the bad guys?"

Z peered at the girl. She was still crying, her chest heaving with her sobs as she huddled in on herself in the backseat. Alive, yes. How well she'd fare after this ordeal was yet to be seen.

"As good as can be expected," Z told him.

Conner glanced back, then met Z's gaze. It was obvious the guy wanted to say something, but thankfully he kept his parental advice to himself.

A handful of minutes later, they were on the highway, making their way back to Dallas, another successful extraction completed.

TWO

With the long day now behind him, going home and crashing was the first thing that crossed Ryan's mind. Unfortunately, he knew that wasn't going to be an easy feat. It never was. His body was exhausted, but the rest of him—namely his brain—hadn't yet received that news flash.

First of all, the adrenaline spurred by the op was surging through his veins, his muscles still tense, heart rate slightly elevated, all leaving him restless. As he saw it, he had two choices: go to the office, drown himself in work until his eyes crossed and he couldn't stand upright, or offer to take the guys out for a beer. As he thought about the endless amounts of paperwork that awaited him—something he didn't look forward to doing on a good day, much less on a Friday night—he figured the beer was the more reasonable choice.

After they had delivered the terrified teenage girl back to her distraught, yet relieved, parents and briefly discussed her getting treatment for her injuries as well as counseling, Clay had turned the van in the direction of the Sniper 1 Security office, where they'd met up earlier. The trip back had been dull, especially bearing in mind the showdown at the drug house—and even that had been relatively simple, all things considered. In the van, Ryan had made a quick call to his father, letting Bryce know the mission was a success and that he'd share the details when he saw him next.

Now, as Ryan slid out of the passenger seat of the nondescript black van, waiting for Conner, Clay, and Z to follow, he glimpsed the four sport bikes lined up in a row along the concrete wall of the parking garage. What he wouldn't give to hop on his motorcycle and hit the open road. It didn't matter that it was closing in on midnight. The need for some quiet time to clear his head clawed at him, but he shoved it away. There was too much shit to do.

"I'm headin' home," Conner said gruffly. "See y'all later."

That was Conner. Never mincing words.

Ryan knew better than to try and coerce Conner into going out for a beer. The guy hadn't been in a sociable mood as of late. Not that anyone could really fault him for his less-than-stellar attitude. It'd been nearly two years since Conner's wife had been murdered, leaving them all with a hole in their hearts but, most importantly, leaving Conner's and his fourteen-year-old daughter Shelby's lives irrevocably shattered.

"See ya Monday," Ryan told Conner.

Conner nodded as he pulled his helmet over his head. Less than a minute later, he was roaring out of the parking garage at high speed. Ryan, along with Clay and Z, watched him go.

"Y'all wanna get a beer?" Ryan offered coolly, still staring out into the night, suddenly not really in the mood for going out after all but not looking forward to paperwork *or* going home to an empty house, either.

"Not me, man," Clay answered. "I've been up for twenty-four hours. You didn't even give me time to take a nap. I'm ready to crash."

Ryan nodded at his younger brother, then turned to Z.

That sudden, overwhelming desire he'd been battling for longer than he cared to admit hit him square in the chest as his gaze slid over the big man. Z was dressed in all black, and his presence sucked all the oxygen from Ryan's lungs. The man looked hot enough to...

Head in the game, Trexler.

There was no doubt about it, Z was the bane of Ryan's entire existence. There was something about him that Ryan—no matter how hard he tried—simply couldn't ignore. Not that he'd ever acted on his physical reaction to the man's proximity, but he'd sure as hell wanted to.

And with each second that ticked by, that desire was getting harder and harder to disregard.

There were plenty of reasons *why* Ryan needed to stay away from Z, mostly due to the fact that, for all intents and purposes, Ryan was Z's boss, his employer. As of a year ago, Ryan had stepped in to take over Sniper 1 Security so that Bryce and Casper could officially retire. Thirty-five years running a company was a long time for anyone, and Ryan didn't blame them for wanting to spend less time at work and more time with family.

As far as Ryan was concerned, business was business and personal was personal. The two didn't cross. He'd learned that from personal experience, life lessons, and all that shit. Thanks to the debacle that had disrupted his life for months, Ryan knew a relationship that crossed those lines wasn't worth it.

And if that wasn't enough to deter Ryan from giving in to the craving that nagged at him, there was also the fact that Z was a playboy. The man, without shame, spent his nights with different men, choosing not to settle down with anyone. For as long as Ryan had known Z—all ten years and counting—he'd never known the man to have a serious relationship.

Never Say Never

Since Ryan's sister, Marissa, had married Trace—Z's closest friend—Ryan knew more about Z's extracurricular activities than he cared to. Due to the fact that Z lived on the first floor of the converted warehouse that he and Trace had bought years ago, and Marissa and Trace lived on the second, his sister had firsthand knowledge of Z's comings and goings. To hear his sister tell it, Z was never home.

"I'll get a beer," Z accepted now, smirking at Ryan as though he knew exactly where Ryan's thoughts had detoured.

Knowing he couldn't recant his offer or he'd risk giving away his desire to keep a safe distance between the two of them, Ryan nodded once. Their relationship was strictly business, and he had to keep reminding himself of that fact.

"Meet me at Rick's?" Ryan suggested.

Rick's was a local bar that catered to cops. It was a place that the Sniper 1 Security team had been known to frequent. Considering it was just a couple of blocks away from the office, the trek was quick and easy.

"Sure thing."

Without another word, they both mounted their motorcycles and tore out of the garage.

By the time Ryan was walking into the bar, he was fighting an overwhelming sense of anxiety. The more time he spent with Z, the harder it was for him to pretend that there wasn't an inexplicable chemistry between them. After having endured a couple of weeks in Coyote Ridge—Z's hometown—on a stalker case for one of Z's friends and the friend's famous country music singer girlfriend, Ryan had found himself being pushed to his limits. But somehow— honest to God, he had no fucking idea how—Ryan had managed to resist the temptation that was Zachariah Tavoularis.

Barely.

But he certainly had to make a conscious effort.

Could've been the fact that Ryan hadn't gotten laid in... Well, fuck... It'd been months now. His hand wasn't doing it for him these days, either, but he used work as an excuse as to why he couldn't take the time to date.

Truth was, he didn't want to date. He didn't want meaningless sex, either. He was tired of all the bullshit, and at thirty-two, he was beginning to believe that was all he could expect out of life. Didn't help that work seemed to be his one and only priority.

Ryan planted his ass on one of the rickety stools at the bar, subtly glancing around the room, noting every single person and their location—something that was second nature to him. The place wasn't as busy as it would be later, but there wasn't a shortage of bodies, either. Rick's was already filled with cops and a handful of cop groupies, all surrounded by booze, the clack of pool balls, and the steady drone of conversation—but that wasn't unusual for a Friday night. Cops wanted to blow off some steam after a difficult week as much as the next guy, and though Ryan wasn't one of the good boys in blue, he'd established some rather strong relationships with the Dallas police department, hence the reason they opted to frequent the place.

"Two Coronas with lime," Z told the bartender when the older man sauntered over, a gap-toothed grin splitting his weathered face.

Hoping not to appear too conspicuous, Ryan stole a glance at Z. The guy's dark hair was tousled, a stray lock hanging over his forehead while the rest spiked on the top. Z had previously kept all of his hair short; however, now only the sides and back remained relatively close to his scalp. His mocha-brown eyes scanned the room, his prominent chin jutting out, and the corded muscles in his neck strained slightly as he did.

Ryan had to jerk his eyes away when Z turned back toward him.

"How's…uh…Brendon?" Ryan asked, trying to make casual conversation despite the nervous energy flowing through him. It was so unlike him to let anyone get to him, but Z did so without effort.

"Good. No more issues with the stalker," Z replied in his signature laid-back Texas drawl. "Oh, and his twin's 'bout to get married."

"Yeah? They settled on a date?" Last Ryan had heard, Braydon Walker—the twin Z was referring to—and his long-time fiancée, Jessica Prescott, hadn't settled on a wedding date.

"They did. Bray originally said they'd wait till Sawyer got married in December, but he's an impatient one. They're tyin' the knot on the twenty-second."

"Of *this* month?" Wow, that seemed fast. That was… Holy shit. That was next weekend.

"Yep. Oh, and I know it's late notice, but they invited you."

Ryan peered over at Z, studying him momentarily. "Really?"

Z laughed. "Yeah. You act like that's crazy or somethin'. You're responsible for takin' down the stalker. Why wouldn't they invite you?"

"Whoa there. No, *you* get credit for that one, not me. I was merely there to help out."

"Right." Z grinned. "Since I learned from the best, you still deserve the credit."

Ryan wasn't sure what to say to that.

"And before you make up some excuse about not bein' able to go, I checked with Jayden. Your schedule's free."

Great. And now he didn't even have an excuse.

Glancing down at the bowl of peanuts in front of him, wishing like hell he had his beer already, Ryan nodded.

"Is that a yes?" The incredulity in Z's tone was thick.

"Yeah," he told him. "I'll go."

Ryan had met the Walker clan—a group of good ol' boys who happened to own a risqué sex resort in their small town in central Texas—back when Z had requested Ryan's help for the stalker case. But the brothers' business sense hadn't been all he'd been impressed with.

Spending two weeks in the small town had given Ryan the opportunity to get to know the brothers, but he'd mostly chatted with the eldest Walker, Travis. Ryan had been somewhat inspired by the fact that Travis had managed to successfully establish his own form of gay marriage in a state whose government, at the time, had still been stuck in a much different (translated to *repressed*) era.

Travis's younger brother Ethan and Ethan's husband, Beau, had also made it work, even with the many obstacles that had plagued their relationship in the beginning. Turned out, Ethan had received some sage advice from Travis, who had successfully gone into a committed ménage relationship with his husband, Gage, and their wife, Kylie.

According to Travis, there were ways to get around everything, and if you wanted something badly enough, it didn't matter the lengths you had to go to in order to get it. One thing Ryan had learned about the Walker brothers was that when they wanted something—and accepted that fact—they simply went after it, not taking no for an answer.

"When're you goin' down there?" Ryan questioned nonchalantly, not bothering to look directly at Z.

"Thought I'd head back on Friday. Wanted to spend some time with my brother this time."

"He's comin' home?" That surprising news had Ryan's gaze returning to Z briefly.

"Got back a week ago." Z grinned, the dimple in his cheek winking.

"And your sister?" Ryan asked.

Z's smile widened as it always did when he talked about his baby sister. "She's still truckin' along."

"Is Jensyn comin' home at all this summer?"

It was no secret that Z was incredibly proud of his brother and sister, and for good reason. From what Ryan had been told, Z had been eager to go into the military after high school until he'd learned that a congenital defect—a hole in his heart that had been repaired when he was three—had kept him from doing so. Instead, Reese had opted to follow in his brother's unrealized dream—only slightly modified—by going directly into the Air Force before the ink on his diploma was dry. As for Jensyn...the woman was pursuing her doctorate in psychology at Stanford and still had another year or two to go.

"For a couple of weeks, yeah. She agreed to try and make it down next weekend, if she can. That way I can see them both."

Ryan had met Z's sister only once, but he'd seen Z's younger brother, Reese, a few times over the years. The kid—six years younger than Z qualified him as a kid in Ryan's eyes—had been finishing up his eight-year stint before he returned to the civilian world. At one point, Z had even mentioned the possibility of Reese coming to work for Sniper 1. Ryan had told him to have his brother come see him when that time came, if Reese was truly interested.

Looked like that conversation might be happening in the near future, something Ryan looked forward to. As far as enforcers went, Z was top-notch, and no doubt his brother would be as well. Z was the no-holds-barred type of operator. Nothing mattered except for the mission, and his loyalty to their family was unprecedented. It was something Ryan truly admired in the man.

Among other things.

It was easy to admit to admiring Z's work ethic, but Ryan wasn't about to cop to liking the guy's dark hair or his inquisitive brown eyes, his squared jaw, or the incredible breadth of his shoulders, or—a big point—Z's wicked sense of humor and upbeat attitude.

Nope, not admitting it to anyone, not even himself.

When the bartender handed over their beers, Ryan took his and attempted to pass money over, but Z beat him to it.

"You can pick up the tab next time," Z told him.

Ryan met Z's intense gaze, a million thoughts running through his head. Not a single one of them appropriate.

The idea of going out with Z again, just the two of them... It was something he knew he couldn't think about.

No matter how much he wanted it.

One of Z's favorite pastimes was to get RT riled up. It was a hell of a lot easier to do than one might think. These days it seemed Z could throw RT for a loop simply by being in the same room with him. Or less than a foot away, as was the case now.

There was no doubt in his mind that RT was attracted to him, and considering the feeling was definitely mutual, finding ways to shake RT up was amusing Z to no end. Mainly because it was evident that RT was fighting the attraction between them. Had been for a while now.

Only because of the debacle with Kevin a few years back that had changed RT's perspective on things did Z keep his distance. If it weren't for that jackass RT had been seeing, Z would've staked his claim long ago. Or tried, anyway.

Unlike RT, Z wasn't fighting his attraction to the other man. He was quite comfortable in his own skin, didn't mind the fact that he was transparent when it came to the way he lived his life. He considered that one of his strong points. Didn't mean there hadn't been lovers in his past who had thought the opposite. Turned out some guys enjoyed being in the closet, but not Z.

For reasons such as that, Z was still single at thirty-one, and he'd come to one final conclusion: when he did finally settle down, it was going to be with a man who was proud to be with him.

One of the reasons Z enjoyed RT's company was the fact that RT wasn't in the closet. He was openly gay and had been for as long as Z had known him. He merely pretended not to be interested in Z although most people could see right through him. However, despite Z's many attempts, RT had never given in to the flirting, which was why Z had considered doubling his efforts as of late.

"Any plans for the weekend?" Z asked RT, focusing on the sexy man sitting beside him, pretending not to notice the way RT continued to steal glances when he thought Z wasn't looking.

That was RT. Subtle but not.

Z had never been into blonds, but there was something about RT that just did it for him. The short, golden hair, rounded jaw, those crystal-blue eyes and perfect plump lips that were made to wrap around a man's... Yep, just looking at the guy could give him a hard-on that wouldn't quit.

"Work," RT told him, sipping his beer as he faced forward, his back hunched slightly.

"You should take a day off, ya know?" Not that RT would listen to him. He really did work too much.

Distinctly avoiding the question, RT answered with, "What about you? Hot plans this weekend?"

Z smirked behind the lip of his beer bottle. "Not sure I'd call 'em hot, but sure, I've got plans." Same plans he'd had every weekend for the past four years.

Not that he intended to share the details with RT or anyone else, for that matter.

Knowing RT would derail the conversation soon, Z helped it along. "I heard you had some visitors the other day. Someone askin' about that ATF agent." Keeping in mind where they were and the ears that were likely listening, Z kept the details vague when asking the question. He'd heard that one of those alphabet agencies was looking into the disappearance of the ATF agent who'd hired someone to kill RT's sister earlier that year. Z doubted the man would be found, considering he'd been offed by a ruthless mafia boss and had likely been shredded in one of the many landfills Max Adorite owned.

"Protocol," RT said, his gaze sliding from side to side slowly before he added, "And as of right now, we're in the clear."

Z nodded, letting the subject drop.

Before he could launch another question at RT, a firm hand landed on Z's shoulder, causing him to turn carefully. Most people knew not to touch Z without his permission, but there was one man...

"What's up, Z-man?"

Yep, that one.

Z rolled his eyes as he caught sight of Jefferson Smart, one of his...exes. About a year ago, they'd engaged in a brief affair that had fizzled after only a couple of weeks. Z was fairly certain that no one knew of their romantic past since Jefferson was so far in the closet he couldn't even see the fucking clothes. Which was the main reason Z had lost interest. That and the fact that Jefferson called him Z-man. Seriously.

Jefferson peered over Z's shoulder at RT. "Hey, RT. How's it hangin'?"

RT grunted. RT wasn't a fan of Jefferson, mostly because, according to RT, the guy overplayed the alpha card, his way of pretending he wasn't spending his nights with some dude buried balls deep in his ass.

"What was that?" Jefferson said with a high-pitched chuckle. "To the left and below the knee? I know the feelin', man."

For fuck's sake.

"Good to see ya, Jeffy." Z purposely used the name Jefferson hated, one that he'd told Z a former lover had given him. "We're talkin' business, so…"

"Right," Jefferson said curtly, his eyes darting around them as though the entire room had been eavesdropping, ready to pounce on the queer when he turned around. "Later."

"Where were we?" Z asked, turning back to the bar and purposely brushing his arm against RT's.

"Drinkin' beer," RT replied, quickly putting space between them. "In silence."

Z chuckled. "Right. 'Cause I do silence so well."

"You should try it sometime," RT muttered.

It didn't look like the night was looking up. Another attempt to get close to RT had failed, though Z knew that when all of his attempts were added together, he was making progress. RT might not think so, but Z knew better.

It was only a matter of time before this thing between them ignited, and no amount of water would be able to put it out.

Z was just waiting for the opportunity.

Until then, he'd simply have to hone his patience.

THREE

One week later – Friday

Coyote Ridge was the same as it had been four months ago, when Ryan had last visited when they'd come to assist Brendon Walker apprehend Cheyenne Montgomery's stalker. Only this time, instead of being in stealth mode, trying to draw out a man intent on hurting Cheyenne, everyone was getting ready for the big event on Saturday— the wedding of Brendon's twin brother, Braydon.

The pulse of the town was certainly more upbeat. Excited even.

Having grown up in Dallas, Ryan found it interesting to sit at a table in the small diner and hear bits and pieces of conversation at the surrounding tables, all talking about the event. Not something Ryan was used to, that was for sure.

"I can't believe he's finally tyin' the knot."

"What I can't believe is that they're all gonna be married soon."

In a small town, everyone knew everyone else, just like the saying went, and Coyote Ridge was no exception. And they knew Z, as well. He was somewhat of a celebrity, in Ryan's opinion. When the waitress had been taking their drink order, she'd briefly reminisced about high school, and a couple of other people had stopped by the table to say hello, welcome him back, tell him how great it was to see him.

Ryan wasn't sure he would've survived in the microscopic bubble that wrapped around this place. He much preferred the big city. A lot more anonymity.

They'd just received their drinks when a boisterous voice sounded from behind Ryan.

"Well, how the fuck are ya?"

Glancing over his shoulder, he saw a familiar face walking toward them, dark eyes locked on Z. Before another word was said, Z was on his feet, his burly arms wrapped around his brother, hands pounding each other's backs as they said their greetings.

When the two broke apart, Z smiled. "Reese, you remember RT?"

"Of course I do." Reese held out his giant hand. "How are ya, man?"

"Not too bad." Ryan got to his feet and shook Reese's hand. "You're lookin' good."

Reese tugged at his T-shirt, white teeth flashing as he smiled. "Ain't I? It's the hometown air. Does wonders for the complexion."

Reese Tavoularis was as outgoing and laid-back as his brother, with the same quick smile and wit. In fact, the two men looked so much alike, if it hadn't been for the apparent difference in their ages, they could've probably passed as twins. Reese was just as tall as Z but without so much of the bulk. He was leanly muscled, with the same dark hair, but his eyes were several shades lighter than his brother's.

The two men took a seat. Z squeezed Reese's shoulder once before releasing him. It was clear that Z had missed his brother. Ryan could understand because his job took him away from his siblings time and time again, but he was lucky enough to see them more often than not.

"What's it like to be home?" Z asked Reese as he reached for his tea glass.

"A little surreal. Not sure I'm ready for this." Reese situated the plastic utensils on the paper napkin, spacing them perfectly before noticeably realizing what he'd done.

"Settling back in?" Ryan asked.

"Yeah." Reese's smile appeared slightly more forced than a moment ago. "You'd think it would be easier than it is. It takes some getting used to, not having the structure I'm so familiar with. Not to mention, I've got too much time on my hands."

Ryan looked at Z, not sure where to go with that. Thankfully, the waitress chose that moment to come back and take their order, her smile radiant when her eyes landed on Reese. After the three of them placed their order and the flirtatious woman stopped running her fingers over Reese's closely cropped dark hair, they resumed their conversation.

"Have you given any thought to what we talked about?" Z asked, his question directed at his brother.

"The job, you mean?" Reese glanced at Ryan briefly, then flicked his gaze back to Z.

Z nodded, taking a sip of his tea, his big hands making the glass look smaller than it was.

"I have," Reese said solemnly. "A lot, actually." Reese's gaze darted over to Ryan once more. "And keep in mind, I'm not goin' off any assumptions that it would've been a done deal or anything." His attention returned to Z. "But I kinda like it here."

Ryan tried to hide his confusion. He wasn't sure what the two men were talking about.

"So not interested in movin' to Dallas, huh?" Z appeared disappointed, but it was obvious he was trying to hide it.

That was when Ryan figured it out. Z had been hoping Reese would come work for Sniper 1 Security so he could see more of the guy.

"Not yet," Reese admitted, shifting when the waitress set his glass of water in front of him.

"What're you gonna do for work?" Z asked, his worry for his brother's financial stability evident in his tone.

"I've actually got two interviews," Reese said, his grin widening. "One with Jared Walker. I ran into him a coupla days ago at Moonshiners. He said he was lookin' for someone to help out at Walker Demo."

Z looked interested. "And the other?"

"Jared's cousin CJ owns his own construction company. He's lookin' for a foreman. They told me one way or another they'd have somethin' for me. Oh, and if I want, they're lookin' for another volunteer at the fire station."

"That's great," Ryan said when Z didn't speak. "Not back a week and you've already got two jobs lined up."

"Is that really what you wanna do?" Z asked, his tone solemn.

Reese studied Z for a minute, the two brothers clearly communicating on a different plane than the one Ryan was on. Taking a sip of his tea, he glanced around the diner, suddenly uncomfortable with this family conversation. Had it been a topic Ryan could contribute to, he might've thought differently.

"It is. Momma's still got the house down here. I'm gonna stay there, take over payments until I figure it all out."

Ryan discreetly looked at Z, wondering what he'd say to that. It was obvious Z wanted to have Reese closer to him.

"Well, if that's what you want…" Z's mouth turned up in a huge grin. "Then I'm fuckin' happy for you, bro. That's great."

Reese looked slightly off-kilter, and Ryan knew how he felt. Sometimes Z threw him for a loop, too, without even trying.

The food at the diner had been the closest thing to home cooking that Z had had in quite some time. For the most part, he stuck to a clean diet that consisted of a lot of grilled chicken and vegetables, though he did give in to his craving for pizza at least twice a month. But his favorite— country fried chicken, corn on the cob, and fried okra— wasn't something he could've passed up if he'd wanted to.

Since he didn't come back home to Coyote Ridge often, Z tended to let go a little more than usual. And twice a year at most wasn't enough for him to worry. But damn, it was good to be back there. Like the last time, there was a sense of nostalgia that came with being in his hometown. He'd missed the place, and though he could never imagine himself living there now that he'd expanded his horizons outside the small town, that didn't mean he didn't have fond memories.

And of course, seeing Reese. That made it all the sweeter. His visits with his brother had been intermittent at best over the last decade. Between Z moving to Dallas right out of high school and then going to work for Sniper 1 shortly thereafter and Reese going into the Air Force, they hadn't exactly had a lot of time to hang out. In fact, Z missed seeing his brother and sister.

Sure, they still indulged in the normal sibling rivalries like they'd done as kids, but these days, their interaction was mostly limited to text or email. The three of them had tortured and annoyed one another the way most siblings did from the get-go, but they'd always been close. They talked several times a week just to keep up with all that was going on with one another, but they were all busy, making getting together much more difficult. Still, Z had made a promise to himself four years ago when...

"Hate to put an end to the party, but I've gotta head out," Reese said, pulling Z from his thoughts as he surged to his feet and reached for his wallet.

Z placed a hand on Reese's arm as he stood. "I got this one. You can buy next time I'm in town."

Reese grinned. "It's damn good to see you, man."

Giving his brother one last hug, clapping him on the back a couple of times before pulling back, Z tried to ignore the disappointment that came with not being able to see his brother more often. He'd been hoping that they'd have more time to spend together now that Reese was back in the civilian world, but he would never let on to Reese. Z was content just to know he was back for good.

"We're headin' over to Moonshiners," Z told Reese. "You wanna join us?"

"Wish I could, but I've got somethin' to take care of." The smirk on his brother's face told Z he was referring to a woman.

"Well, don't let me hold you up." Z turned to RT. "You ready?"

RT nodded, then offered his hand to Reese. "If you ever change your mind about a job, give me a call."

"Will do," Reese said, obviously not expecting RT to make that offer.

After Reese left, Z flagged down the waitress, paid for their meals though RT complained the whole damn time, insisting that he could pay for himself.

"You can buy me a beer," Z told him as they walked out of the restaurant.

"That I can."

If Z had been expecting a lengthy conversation, he was sorely disappointed, because the drive from the diner to the bar took less than five minutes and contained fewer than three words between them. Not that he'd expected any less from RT; the man had been rather quiet since they'd left Dallas early that afternoon. Quiet and fidgety.

"You ready for this?" Z asked as they headed toward the doors to Moonshiners.

"As ready as I'll ever be."

Opening the door and stepping inside was like taking a trip back in time, only the people there weren't stuck in the time warp. They'd all aged like the wood planks lining the walls, but other than a few more wrinkles, maybe a couple of gray hairs, it was the same chaos that he'd encountered whenever he'd come to the bar back when he used to come home to visit his parents.

A couple of whistles sounded as people acknowledged their arrival. Z offered a couple of chin jerks in response as he made his way to the bar.

"Hey, man," Braydon Walker greeted, tilting his beer bottle in Z's direction. "So glad you could make it."

"Wouldn't've missed it," Z told his friend, offering his hand. "I never figured you'd find a chick who'd feel sorry enough for you to marry you."

"Whatever it takes," Braydon said, placing his arm around Jessie and pulling her close. "RT. How's it goin'?"

"Good as can be expected," RT replied from a few feet away. It was clear to Z that he was attempting to keep his distance from Z—which was only a little disappointing.

"Hey, Z. RT," Jessie said sweetly. "Y'all want a beer? They're on us tonight."

"I won't say no to that," Z replied.

While Braydon turned to tell Mack, the bartender, their order, Travis Walker appeared, shaking both their hands, followed by Travis's brothers Zane and Ethan. The next thing Z knew, he was being led in one direction while RT was led in another, conversations exploding left and right as the party got underway.

Before he got pulled toward the back of the room, Z turned to glance back at RT, surprised to find the man staring back at him.

Not that that lasted long. RT was, of course, still RT.

Subtle but not.

FOUR

"How's the business goin'?" Travis asked as he steered Ryan toward a booth near the front of the bar.

"Busy," Ryan answered.

"That's a good thing, right?"

"Of course." Ryan smiled as they approached Travis's wife, Kylie, and their husband, Gage. "Good to see y'all again."

"Same here. Have a seat." Gage motioned toward the opposite side of the table as he slid his other arm over Kylie's shoulders and pulled her close while Travis grabbed a chair.

Flipping it around backward, Travis straddled the seat, placing his elbow on the table. Ryan didn't miss that Travis's other hand disappeared under the table, likely resting on Kylie's leg, if he had to guess.

"We weren't sure you'd be able to make it," Travis said.

Ryan knew he could always be called back to work at any time, depending on the case, but he didn't need to tell Travis as much. The man ran a multimillion-dollar resort, so he understood. "I'm glad I could."

"How's Z doin'?" Kylie asked, peering toward the back of the room, where Z had been pulled away by his friends a few minutes before.

"You know Z. Nothing gets him down."

Gage smiled. "Seems he's quite interested in you."

Knowing better, Ryan still turned to glance in Z's direction. He thought for sure he'd be busted stealing a look, but Z was paying him no attention.

"And you're quite interested in him," Kylie noted.

Ryan's head snapped back around to face her. He was about to fire off a rebuttal, but her smile silenced him.

"Leave the poor man alone," Travis injected. "He's in denial."

Ryan snorted.

"I concur," Gage added.

"Why's everybody gangin' up on me?" Ryan questioned, unable to hide the smile.

"Seemed like the thing to do." Travis took a sip of his beer. "Has your ol' man retired yet?"

Ryan shook his head. "I expect it to be soon, but he's havin' a hard time lettin' go."

"I can imagine that would be hard," Kylie said. "When you do what you love, it's not easy to walk away."

Ryan would have to agree with her. At this point in his life, he couldn't imagine ever walking away from Sniper 1. His only sense of fulfillment came from the company he'd devoted his life to. Ever since he'd been young, he had wanted to take over the family business, and here he was, getting ready to do just that.

"Conner still not interested in taking over?" Travis asked.

When Ryan had been there last, he'd opened up to Travis more than he'd opened up to anyone. The guy was perceptive and smart and quick to offer advice if warranted. Ryan honestly liked the guy.

"He hasn't come around yet," Ryan told him. He didn't bother adding that he didn't expect Conner to ever want to take on a leadership position within the company, though it was his birthright. The fact that neither Conner nor Hunter was willing to step up had been a point of contention for Ryan, though he attempted to keep his thoughts to himself.

"What about Hunter?" Gage asked. "He back from wherever he disappeared to?"

"He came back briefly for Trace's wedding," Ryan told him, "but he's off again. I expect him back in the next couple of weeks."

"Any chance he'll want to take over?" Kylie inquired.

"Doubtful." Seemed everyone was dealing with their personal issues these days. Everyone but Ryan, who continued to shove his as far down as he could so that he didn't have to. Unlike Conner and Hunter, Ryan preferred to bury himself in work in order to forget the fact that his personal life was lacking. Not wanting to get into the details, Ryan changed the subject. "How's the baby?"

Kylie's eyes lit up, a beaming grin on her face. "She's gettin' so big. She'll be one in just a few months."

"Y'all gonna have any more?"

"We're tryin'," Gage answered with a mischievous smirk. "Every chance we get."

"Where're y'all stayin tonight?" Travis inquired, shaking his head but grinning like a fool.

"Don't know yet. All the hotels in the area are booked," Ryan said before thinking his answer through. When Travis's dark eyebrows shot up, he knew instantly that he should've kept his mouth shut.

"We've got a few rooms available at the resort still. You and Z have a standing invitation, any time you want," Travis said.

Ryan was trying to come up with a response to that, but the thought of staying in a hotel with Z not only tied his tongue but it sent a surge of heat surging through him. So rather than reply, he settled for taking a drink.

"Well, that settles it then," Travis said with a grin. "I'll make a call. Y'all want one room or two?"

Ryan felt his face flame, but he managed to say, "Two. Definitely two."

"Right." Travis offered a knowing wink, then grabbed his cell phone.

Shit.

"What're you doin' over there? Contemplatin' the meanin' of the universe?"

Pulled from his thoughts, Z plastered a smile on his face as he looked up to see Ethan Walker and Ethan's husband, Beau, standing directly in front of him.

"Actually, I was tryin' to figure out how this place was still standin' after all this time," he offered with a smile. Truth was, he was thinking about RT and the fact that they hadn't yet found a place to stay for the night. He was wondering whether or not he'd get lucky and there would only be one hotel room in the entire county and he'd get a chance to spend the night with RT.

Not that he was going to tell Ethan that.

"Mind if we sit?" Beau asked, nodding toward the two empty chairs at the table.

"Not at all." Z welcomed the company. And the distraction. He wanted to avoid spending the evening lost in his own thoughts when he had the opportunity to spend it with friends.

Now, sitting at a tall table at the back of Moonshiners—the small bar hadn't changed at all in the years he'd been gone—Z was ready for the activities to commence. He'd called up Brendon when they'd crossed the county line a few hours ago, and his childhood friend had mentioned they'd be heading down to the bar to celebrate before the big day tomorrow.

They hadn't been lying, either. This was a party if Z'd ever seen one. And true to form, the Walker family knew how to celebrate, bringing people in from all over, cramming them all into the one-room bar.

The place was packed from wall to wall with people, most of whom Z recognized but hadn't had any contact with in at least ten years. Didn't look like tonight was going to be one to catch up and reminisce, either, but he was okay with that. Z figured that had a lot to do with some of the familiar faces who had arrived a few minutes ago. Not only was Cheyenne Montgomery—the West Texas Princess who was up for a CMA this year—there with Brendon, but Cooper Krenshaw and Dalton Calhoun, two other country music sensations, had also graced the small town with their presence, and everyone seemed to be captivated by their celebrity guests.

The beer was flowing almost as smoothly as the conversation.

Tilting his beer to his lips, Z scanned the room, looking past the people he'd grown up with until his gaze centered on one man in particular.

Ryan Trexler.

Watching as RT sat at a table with Travis and Travis's wife, Kylie, and their husband, Gage, he couldn't take his eyes off the man. For the first time in what seemed to be ages, RT was smiling, laughing even. But without a doubt, RT was avoiding Z at all costs.

The only thing that could've possibly made the night better would've been if RT hadn't been doing his best to avoid him. Dinner had gone well, but they'd had Reese there to entertain them with his war stories, as he referred to them.

It wasn't until Beau clapped him on the back that Z realized he'd once again retreated into his own head and Ethan had since abandoned them.

"What's up, man?" Beau asked, his words slurring slightly. "It's good to see you."

"Not much. You?" Z studied Beau briefly. Being that he was so big, Z was used to being the biggest guy in the room (unless his brother or father was there), but next to Beau Bennett, he didn't feel like a complete abomination. With maybe an inch on the guy, Z was inclined to believe Beau might've had a few more pounds of muscle on him than Z did. But not much.

Still, it was interesting to see people look their way, some doing a double take.

Beau's head turned toward the other side of the bar. Z followed his line of sight, his gaze coming to rest on RT once again.

"Did you hear?" Beau's eyes lit up. "Ethan and I got married."

Z's eyebrows darted down. "A while back, I heard."

"No. Recently." Beau's grin widened. "Well, back then, too, but…" Beau peered around, seemingly looking to see if anyone was paying attention. "Shh, you can't tell anyone."

"Tell them what?" Z couldn't hide his confusion.

"We went to the justice of the peace and got married. The real deal."

It finally dawned on Z what Beau was talking about. Though the couple had had a traditional ceremony, their marriage hadn't been legal in the state of Texas, but now that same-sex marriage was legal in all states, they must've taken the plunge.

"Congrats, man," Z offered.

"Thanks." Beau beamed with pride. "I'm a lucky guy. So what's up with your man?"

Z choked out a laugh, the quick subject change surprising him. "Don't let *him* hear you say that."

"Why not?" Beau's eyebrows darted down in confusion.

"Because he's my boss, not my man."

"Really?" Beau looked across the bar. "Someone might wanna tell him to stop ogling his employees then."

"He's oglin' me?" Z's eyes were locked on RT now, wanting desperately to see what Beau was seeing.

When Z turned back to look at Beau, the guy's grin was wicked, which meant he knew exactly what he was doing.

"Man, you're easy."

"Thanks."

"More beers," Ethan announced when he arrived back at the table, his timing impeccable. "What're you up to?" he asked Beau suspiciously.

"Nothin'," Beau answered innocently.

Ethan smirked at Z. "He's tryin' to play matchmaker, ain't he?"

Z didn't respond, simply tilted his beer to his lips and chugged half the bottle.

"Better be careful," Beau said in a mock whisper. "You get drunk and your boss might take advantage of you."

If only he were that lucky.

"Quit," Ethan commanded with a smile. "Speaking of bein' careful...how many have you had?"

"Not nearly enough," Beau joked. "But don't worry, I'll let you take advantage of me no matter how much I drink."

Ethan's smile slipped slightly, his eyes scanning those around them. Z knew that Ethan wasn't as open as Beau, but from what he'd heard from Ethan's brothers, he was coming around. If Z had to guess, that was likely all thanks to Beau.

But it was interesting to see Beau so tipsy. He was a big guy, so a few beers shouldn't have gotten him quite so inebriated so quickly.

"How many shots did you have with Cheyenne?" Ethan asked, still studying Beau.

"A few."

Ethan glanced over to Z. "Chey seems to think she can outdrink him despite the fact he's got a foot and a half and probably a hundred fifty pounds on her."

"You should try pickin' on someone your own size," Z joked.

Beau's eyes narrowed, his smile widening. "Good call." Lifting his head high to see over the others, Beau shouted, "We need some shots over here!"

"No, we don't," Ethan said quickly, laughing. "I swear I don't know what's gotten into him."

Z downed the rest of his beer and noticed that people were beginning to circle their table.

"Oh, hell yeah!" Zane Walker hollered. "Z's gonna try to outdrink Beau, y'all!"

Actually, that hadn't been Z's plan at all, but as his gaze met RT's across the room, the other man quickly looking away as though he'd been caught committing a crime, Z figured what the hell.

Never Say Never

He didn't have anything better to do.

FIVE

So the night wasn't going *exactly* as Ryan had planned.

Okay. Amend that. The night wasn't going *at all* as he had planned.

If he was honest with himself, things had started to unravel on the drive down from Dallas. Three hours in an enclosed space with Z wasn't something Ryan looked forward to, but then again, he wasn't much for inserting himself into a situation that offered so much…temptation. Being that close to Z, listening to the seductive tone of his voice as Z rambled on and on about nothing and anything, hearing him sing—which surprisingly he was quite good at— and laugh and be witty and funny and… Well, it had left Ryan a little anxious when they'd finally arrived in Coyote Ridge.

It hadn't helped much when they'd hit town to find out that all the hotels in the area were booked solid, mostly due to Braydon and Jessie's wedding tomorrow. He'd actually been trying to figure out what they were going to do about accommodations for the night when Travis had informed him they had plenty of available rooms at the resort.

Alluring Indulgence Resort.

A *sex* resort.

Ryan hadn't known what to say, which Travis had taken as Ryan's agreement, and now here they were.

To make matters worse, they'd had to get a ride with Zane and V—V was one of the designated drivers for the evening since she was pregnant and all—because Ryan and Z, as well as Zane, had imbibed a little too much.

So, after checking in at the front desk, handing over his credit card to cover both rooms because Z was nearly passed out in a chair nearby, Ryan had managed to help Z up to his room with every intention of sneaking out as soon as the door opened.

Why he was still there... Well, because he apparently wasn't good at resisting temptation no matter how bad for him it was.

After unceremoniously dumping Z onto the bed, Ryan took a step back, needing to put as much space between them as he could.

"Don't leave," Z muttered, rolling onto his back on the huge king bed that took up a majority of the room.

"I have to," Ryan explained. "I've gotta get some sleep or I'll be useless tomorrow."

"Sleep here," Z whispered, his eyes open and focused on Ryan's face.

For an instant, Ryan could almost believe Z was stone-cold sober.

"Go to sleep, Z," Ryan instructed, walking over to the bed.

His intention had been to pull the blanket over Z and wait until he passed out, but in the next instant, he was no longer on his feet but rather on his back, and Z's mouth was covering his.

Oh, fucking hell.

Warning bells clanged loudly in his head, telling him this was a bad idea. Very bad.

Alcohol and Z did not mix well.

But the man could kiss.

Maybe it was the fact that his inhibitions were lowered thanks to the alcohol, or possibly because he hadn't had sex in… Fuck, he couldn't think about that now. Whatever it was keeping him pliant beneath Z's big, beautiful body, Ryan couldn't pull himself away, couldn't convince his fight-or-flight instinct that this was a time for flight.

Instead, Ryan found himself lost in the kiss.

Z's mouth was warm and supple and quite skilled for a man in his current state, which made it damn near impossible for Ryan to think straight. He only made matters worse when his arms wrapped around Z's neck—involuntarily, he was sure—pulling him closer as he thrust his tongue into Z's mouth.

He could taste the beer Z had had, along with a hint of licorice from the Jeigermeister shots he'd been downing most of the night in an attempt to outdrink Beau Bennett—which he'd done, surprisingly. Not that Ryan agreed that had been a good use of Z's time, but it had been hard to argue when Z had been in such a good mood.

When Z's hand snaked beneath Ryan's shirt, he tried to pull away, but even he had to admit the attempt was only half-assed. He wanted Z to touch him, to taste him, to give him everything he'd dreamed about for the past few years.

"Ryan," Z moaned, lifting his head and staring down at him. "I've wanted to do this for so long."

Before he could argue, push Z away, make some excuse as to why they shouldn't do this, Ryan pulled Z back down to him, crushing their mouths together as his hands slipped beneath the T-shirt Z wore. He kneaded Z's strong back, pulling him close as Ryan switched their positions, rolling them over so that Ryan was in charge. Grinding his cock against Z's through the denim of his jeans only exacerbated his need, making him desperate.

71

Then Z's hands were fumbling with the button on Ryan's jeans, popping it free while Ryan lifted his hips, giving him better access. He should've jumped off the bed and headed to his own room, but he couldn't bring himself to do it. And he couldn't even blame the alcohol, because Ryan hadn't had more than a few beers over the course of the four hours they had been at Moonshiners.

When Z's big fist wrapped around Ryan's cock, he groaned aloud, the pleasure making him light-headed.

"Fuck," he whispered as he drove his hips forward, pushing his cock into Z's hand. "Don't stop."

"I don't plan to," Z said, peering down their bodies to where his hand was jacking Ryan's dick.

When their eyes met once again, Ryan could see the need in Z's eyes. He wanted this, but Ryan knew they shouldn't. No matter how good Z's touch felt.

"Don't overthink this," Z insisted, rolling them so that Ryan was flat on the bed once again, Z's feet touching the floor as he leaned over Ryan and…

"Sonuvabitch!" Ryan's head tilted back, his hips driving forward as Z took his cock into his mouth, sucking him to the root. "Z… Fuck… Oh, fuck…"

Ryan could hardly catch his breath. The pleasure assaulted him, the equivalent of being hit by a jet plane at warp speed, knocking the air from his lungs as his eyes crossed.

"You like that?" Z asked, his mouth relinquishing Ryan's cock briefly.

"Yeah," he groaned.

Understatement. Of. The. Century.

Z's tongue laved the underside of Ryan's dick, sending shockwaves of sensation through him. He wanted more; he wanted everything…and he knew he wouldn't be able to stop this.

So, for tonight, Ryan put himself in Z's capable hands.

And tomorrow he would worry about the consequences of his own actions.

Z couldn't help but wonder whether he was awake or dreaming. He wasn't nearly as intoxicated as he'd been an hour ago, but he had kept that tidbit of information to himself. As much as he wanted to get his hands on RT, he'd figured pretending had been the best way to get RT to relent.

And relent he had.

Working RT's dick with his lips and tongue, Z pushed him closer to the edge, the man's moans making Z's cock throb behind the zipper of his jeans. RT was fucking beautiful. His cock exquisite, long and thick, curving slightly to the left. Z wanted to suck RT for hours, to memorize every ridge.

While he continued to blow RT, watching the sensual expression contort his handsome features, Z managed to remove RT's jeans and boots, along with his own. There was no way in hell he was allowing this moment to pass him by. If RT was willing—and he definitely was—then Z was going to make his move. He'd fantasized about this for far too long.

Standing tall, Z yanked his T-shirt up and over his head before joining RT on the bed once more, kneeling between RT's legs as he claimed his mouth. RT's kiss was quite possibly the most intense thing Z had ever felt in his life. It might appear they were about to embark on a memorable one-night stand, but for Z, it was so much more than that.

Forcing RT's shirt up, he managed to get him completely naked, settling over him once more and ravishing his mouth, his hand sliding through the golden silk of RT's hair while he held him still to stake his claim.

"I want you," Z whispered, trailing his lips over the rough stubble on RT's cheek. "So fucking bad."

"Condom," RT replied, his fingers tightening in Z's hair as he held Z's head. "In the bag."

Z did his best not to show his surprise. He'd fully expected RT to put a halt to this before they made it that far. Z had been mentally preparing himself for rejection when RT came to his senses, something he was ridiculously good at.

Rather than wait for that to happen, Z crawled off the bed once more, retrieving a condom and a small packet of lube from RT's bag. If he'd been thinking clearly, he would've asked RT why he was prepared, but at this point, Z really didn't give a shit. The fact that he was meant RT had been anticipating something, which gave Z hope.

For fear RT would change his mind if given too much time to think, Z ripped open the condom, but before he could cover himself, RT sat up and took the rubber from his hand.

There was a brief standoff—their eyes locked—and Z fully expected RT to change his mind. When RT got to his feet, Z braced himself for the inevitable rejection.

"On the bed," RT instructed, nodding toward the mattress as he rolled the condom over his erection, then coated his cock with a generous amount of lube while Z took a seat on the bed and continued to watch him, stroking his own dick as he did.

Z wanted to look at RT when RT took him this first time, to make sure RT was with him the entire time. So rather than flip over onto his stomach, Z reclined back, then placed both feet flat on the mattress, opening himself up for RT.

When RT's lubed fingers probed his asshole, Z groaned, eager for more. "Oh, fuck. That…feels…good."

RT's eyes locked on Z's while Z bucked his hips toward the intruding digits. Truth was, Z hadn't anticipated being on the receiving end, but he wasn't big on logistics. Being with RT was all that mattered at this point.

"You wanna feel me deep inside you?" RT inserted two fingers, scissoring them and making Z gasp. A little maneuvering and…

"Fuck!" Z's hips bucked off the bed when RT ground his skilled fingers against Z's prostate.

Seeing RT so intensely focused, combined with the mind-numbing pleasure of RT's fingers expertly fucking his ass nearly sent Z over the edge. Rather than make a spectacle of himself, Z closed his eyes briefly, trying to stave off his release. "More. I need more."

Thankfully RT was on board with that plan, because he planted one knee on the bed, forced Z's knees back toward his chest, and brushed the head of his dick against Z's puckered hole.

"Fuck me," Z pleaded.

RT gave him what he asked for, pushing against him until his thick cock breached the tight ring of muscles. Z sucked in a breath, the immense pressure a promise of what was to come.

"Damn, you're tight," RT groaned, forcing himself deeper while Z held his legs to his chest, opening himself more.

"Relax for me, Z," RT whispered. "Feel me."

Oh, he was feeling him, all right. Every single glorious inch of him sliding into his body, grazing delicate nerve endings until Z's breath was rushing in and out of his lungs.

"Not gentle," Z begged. "Fuck me hard, Ryan."

RT's eyes widened, and Z figured he was a little thrown off by the fact Z used his full name, but he didn't take the time to think about that. Being filled by RT was even better than he'd anticipated, and Z had years of fantasies to compare it with.

"You're so fucking tight." RT forced himself deeper, until he was filling Z completely.

RT brought his body over Z's, resting his hands on the mattress, while his shoulders pushed against the back of Z's thighs, folding him damn near in half. Z didn't have time to think about the discomfort of the position, because RT retreated slowly and then drove into him, pulling a strangled groan from Z's chest.

"Too much?" RT questioned.

"God, no. Fuck me. Hard."

From Z's position, it looked as though RT couldn't have held back if he'd wanted to. And Z...well, he finally had RT right where he wanted him. This was so much better than the numerous fantasies he'd had—most of them about RT succumbing to the pleasure beneath him. But this worked, too.

"God, you feel good," Z moaned. "So fucking good.

Pulling RT's head down, Z sought his mouth with his own, licking his tongue past RT's lips while RT continued to drive his hips forward, pulling them back while Z took everything the man was willing to give him. RT fucked him deeper, harder, faster until the kiss was nothing more than a few attempts of their tongues touching. Pulling back, RT placed his hands beneath Z's knees and pounded into him over and over, faster.

"Ryan…fuck…"

"Stroke your dick," RT ordered. "I wanna watch you come."

They were both coated in sweat as RT continued to impale him over and over. Z couldn't tear his eyes off RT, watching the way he focused on Z's face. It was more than he could take, but he managed to hold back long enough, clinging to the razor-sharp edge, not wanting to go over without RT.

When it became clear that RT was hell-bent on waiting him out, Z couldn't hold on any longer. Crying out, he continued to stroke his cock until his orgasm crashed through. With his eyes locked with RT's, Z let himself go, cum spurting over his chest.

"Oh, fuck, that's hot," RT exclaimed, his cock pulsing in Z's ass moments before he exploded, still buried deep inside Z.

When RT was finished, he removed the condom, glancing around as though seeking an exit. Not wanting him to think too hard about what had just happened, Z got to his feet, took the condom, then disappeared to the bathroom to clean up and dispose of the condom. He left the door open so that he could keep an eye on RT. He knew if he left the man alone long enough, he'd be the one to disappear.

Never Say Never

He returned a minute later with a warm washcloth, which he'd intended to use to clean RT, only RT stole it from him, doing the honors himself. It wasn't lost on him that RT wasn't looking at him. For now, Z pretended not to notice, not wanting to think about what this all meant.

Instead, he grabbed the washcloth when RT was finished and tossed it toward the bathroom, climbed into bed with RT, and pulled him into his arms.

And for the first time in a long time, Z slept without so much as a single dream.

SIX

The following morning, Ryan had awoken long before the sun, surprisingly sated—more so than he'd been in years. However, the instant his eyes had opened, he'd realized his mistake.

There, in the bed beside him, was Z, sleeping soundly and so very naked. A vivid reminder of what had happened the night before. It had only taken Ryan one minute before his brain registered that he needed to get the hell out of there.

So he had.

He'd run out of there and right to his own room, taken a shower, and tried to pretend that he hadn't fucked up royally. He'd fucked Z. Never mind the fact that it'd been mind-blowing, quite possibly the best sex Ryan had ever had. He'd still allowed it to happen, and fraternization at work was something he didn't allow. Not for himself, anyway. Not anymore.

He couldn't care less what his employees did, but Ryan had already experienced hell on earth the last time he'd been so foolish. He had no intention of repeating history.

No fucking thank you.

Now, as he sat at a white-linen-covered table with several others he hadn't met, Ryan tried to enjoy the reception. Braydon and Jessie's wedding had been damn near perfect, and the party afterward was moving along nicely. As much as Ryan wanted to enjoy himself, though, his mind couldn't seem to let go of what had happened last night with Z.

Every single time he looked at Z, Ryan remembered the way it had felt to be lodged deep inside him, relentlessly fucking him while Z had watched him so intently, giving himself over to Ryan without question.

Yep, he'd fucked up. He'd single-handedly undermined his own rules, and though something deep down inside him yearned for another round with Z, another chance to get close, to experience that connection he'd felt, Ryan knew it could never happen again.

And now he had no idea how to reverse the damage he'd done. The only positive was that Z seemed to be pretending it'd never happened. Whether or not that was for Ryan's benefit, he didn't know.

"Hey, man," Braydon greeted, dropping into the empty seat beside Ryan. "I wanted to thank you for comin'."

Ryan ignored the fleeting mental image of Z that rattled him when he processed the word *coming*.

"Sure. No problem. Beautiful wedding."

"I also wanted to thank you for what you did for my brother."

Ryan nodded. He didn't need thanks. The job had been pro bono, something Z had offered, and Ryan had merely tagged along. That was the kind of guy Z was, always willing to lend a helping hand to those he cared about. It was only one of Z's many altruistic qualities.

"Y'all stayin' till tomorrow?" Braydon inquired, his attention shifting to the center of the room, where Z was currently dancing with Cheyenne Montgomery.

Ryan watched the pair, smiling to himself. The woman looked so freaking tiny next to Z.

"Naw," Ryan answered. "We'll be headin' back later tonight." Ryan held up his glass of water. "No overindulging for me tonight."

No need to, he told himself. He'd learned the effects even a few beers could have after last night.

"Well, we're headin' out, too. Eight-day Caribbean cruise, though I have no intention of even seein' the water if I can help it."

Ryan smiled because he was supposed to. It wasn't that he didn't like Braydon. Quite the opposite, actually, but he felt like a fraud being there. He'd originally come to Coyote Ridge because Z had asked him to accompany him on a job. Then the wedding invitation had been extended, and Ryan felt it would've been rude to decline. Yet this trip had altered the course of his life, and he still wasn't sure what the fallout would be. Not until he and Z addressed the gigantic elephant in the room would he even know what to expect.

"Well, I'll get outta your hair. Thanks again for comin'. Y'all be careful on the drive back."

"Congratulations, man," Ryan offered along with a handshake.

Braydon shook Ryan's hand, then disappeared across the room once again, leaving Ryan alone once more. Feeling a set of eyes on him, Ryan scanned the area around him only to find Z staring back at him. He was no longer dancing, instead talking to Beau Bennett while casting repeated glances in Ryan's direction.

Why the fuck did Z have to be so handsome? So funny? Witty? Hot? Sexy? God, the adjectives kept coming, and Ryan knew it was stupid to continue to think about Z. Nothing could come of this. It'd been a horrible—although incredible at the same time—mistake, and the best thing for both of them would be if Ryan pretended it had never happened.

Yep, that was exactly what he was going to do. Forget that last night's tryst had been the best sex of his entire life. Forget that being with Z had made him feel whole for the first time since...

Nope, not going there. No need to dredge up the past. It was behind him.

And now, if he was lucky, in a few hours when they were back in Dallas, this would be behind him as well.

Z had known since the moment he'd gone to sleep with Ryan in his arms that the euphoric feeling he'd been overwhelmed with wasn't going to last.

But Z was all right with that.

Sort of.

No, he wasn't looking for happily ever after. Not at this point in his life. He had too much shit on his plate, too many responsibilities. Too much he wanted to do. And according to his friends, he wasn't supposed to be *that* guy, the one who wanted something more than one night. After all, it had been Trace—Z's closest friend—who had started those rumors in the first place.

Not that Z cared. He was here to have a good time, to celebrate his friend's wedding, to enjoy a little time away from work. Although he considered himself the luckiest man on earth when it came to what he got to do for a living, he appreciated a break. It made working that much sweeter, and he'd been going nonstop for so long he was having a hard time even remembering the definition of fun.

Which would likely explain what had happened between him and RT last night. Z didn't have an ounce of regret. Far from it, actually.

Did he want more? Abso-fucking-lutely.

Would he push it? No.

That wasn't Z's style. It was clear by the way RT had been avoiding him all day that he wished last night had never happened. And for that reason alone, Z had been giving RT the space he so obviously needed, pretending that his world wasn't turned upside down and backward.

"You cool, man? You look a little…preoccupied," Brendon asked when he joined Z on the edge of the dance floor.

"Fantastic," Z said, ensuring his tone matched the word.

"They look happy, don't they?"

Z watched Braydon and Jessie dancing, the two of them smiling at one another as though they were the only two people in the room.

"They definitely do."

Brendon turned to face him. "Jared told me he talked to Reese earlier in the week. Wants to hire him on."

Z nodded. "Reese told me."

"I told Jared if it were up to me, I'd hire him on in a heartbeat. Told him if he waited too long, CJ was gonna snatch him up, so Jared called him this mornin' and offered the job."

"Yeah?" Z was torn between being happy for his brother and saddened by the fact that, by his brother landing a job, that last little bit of hope Z had that Reese would end up in Dallas fizzled out.

"He accepted. Starts Monday. He'll fill in while Bray's on his honeymoon."

"Good deal."

"Bray said you're headin' back after this. You gonna see Reese before you go?"

"Probably not," Z replied. "We've gotta get back."

Not that there was anything pressing to go back to, but Z knew RT would be anxious to put more space between them. And the only way to do that was to get back to life as normal.

Cheyenne approached them, gifting Z with a smile before turning her attention to Brendon. "You said you'd dance with me."

"I did," Brendon confirmed before looking at Z once more. "It was good to see you, man. Don't be a stranger, hear?"

"I'll do my best. Take care of my brother, would ya?"

Brendon grinned, allowing Cheyenne to lead him onto the dance floor. "You got it. Be safe on the trip back."

Z watched as Brendon scooped Cheyenne up into his arms, making her squeal, then scanned the room looking for RT. Once again, RT's gaze darted away quickly. Looking at him brought back all the memories from the night before, made him wonder whether or not he should've handled things differently.

Sure, it would've been nice to wake up with RT, to roll him over, slide deep inside him, and make love to him until they had no choice but to get ready for the wedding, but that hadn't happened. And Z couldn't change the past.

Not that he would.

Z wasn't one to live with regrets. He lived his life one day at a time. It was the only thing he could do. As he'd learned, things could change in the blink of an eye, and he wasn't willing to waste a second of it worrying about shit he couldn't change.

So, for now, he would bide his time, wait for the right moment, because, like last night, Z was fairly certain it would come along. What had happened between him and RT wasn't supposed to be limited to only one night. Maybe RT hadn't felt it, but Z had. It had been so much more than sex.

But Z knew when to back off, and based on the unhappy gleam in RT's glittering blue eyes, now was one of those times.

SEVEN

Two weeks later – Monday morning

Ryan should've been tired when he walked into the Sniper 1 offices early Monday morning, but he wasn't. Or maybe he was and he'd simply gotten used to the feeling after two weeks of practically no sleep. Thanks to the incident with Z when they were in Coyote Ridge, he couldn't sleep anymore aside from a couple of fitful hours here and there. His conscience weighed on him, making him crazy, fearful that tomorrow Z would decide to tell Trace or Marissa or, hell, *anyone* what had happened between them.

That didn't stop Ryan from going on with life, but it sure as hell didn't make sleep any easier than it had been prior to that night. But it was Monday morning, time to get a new week started, and here he was, the first to arrive, as was usually the case. Granted, it had always been his choice to come in before anyone else had bothered to roll out of bed. That was his nature—work, work, work, then work some more. On top of that, he'd adopted the motto: early to rise, late to bed.

Regardless of how much sleep he'd managed, Ryan enjoyed that first hour or so of every morning in the office to himself. It gave him time to get things in order, sort out his thoughts, and have a cup of coffee or two.

This morning he'd stopped by Percolation—the coffee shop on the bottom floor of the building they worked in—and chatted with Ally, the sweet little owner, for a minute before heading up.

Now that he was there, the steady hum of anticipation churned in his veins. He was eager to get the week started, to get his mind off things that were better left alone—namely Z.

After flipping on the main lights on his way to his office, Ryan hit the button on the electronic panel that would open the blinds throughout the building. In no time, the sun would drown out the fluorescents, but until then, there'd be something to see by.

All the desks were empty, as were the other offices as he maneuvered down the narrow hall. Once he'd unlocked his office door, he set his coffee cup and his laptop on his desk, hit the power button, and eased into his chair. While he waited for the machine to boot up, Ryan glanced out the window, admiring the dimly lit concrete jungle that grew around him. Sometimes he wished for a more scenic view; other times, like now, the never-ending rows of buildings didn't bother him. It was familiar. Comfortable even.

And today was a new day.

When he was turning back around to face his computer, he noticed the bright yellow Post-It note that had been taped to the phone on his desk.

Important assignment. Let's talk first thing Monday.

It was written in his father's short, block-lettered handwriting, but why the hell would Bryce leave him a handwritten message? It wasn't the Stone Age anymore; they had things like email and text messaging and no longer needed to resort to using…pen and paper.

After entering the password on his laptop, Ryan pulled up his email. He scanned his inbox quickly. Nothing. With his curiosity piqued, Ryan grabbed his cell phone and punched in his father's number.

"Mornin'," Bryce greeted roughly, sounding as though he'd just crawled out of bed. "I'm on my way in. We'll talk when I get there."

"So you know why I'm calling," Ryan inquired.

"I assume you saw my note."

"Why not just send me an email with the details?" Ryan asked, leaning back in his chair and spinning around to look out the window again.

"Can't."

Ryan's eyebrows shot up into his hairline. The only reason his father wouldn't send an email with information would be if the assignment wasn't supposed to be documented. "Can you—"

"Ten minutes, RT. I'll be there then."

Ryan frowned when his father hung up, but he understood. He was merely curious, and his father got a kick out of testing his patience.

Twenty minutes later—not ten as his father had promised—Bryce strolled into Ryan's office, a cup of coffee in his hand and two-day beard growth on his jaw.

"Forget to shave?"

Bryce rubbed the golden stubble on his chin. "I'm testin' this whole retirement thing."

"Yet you're here."

"One step at a time, kid. One step at a time."

Ryan reached for his coffee and relaxed into his chair once again. "So what's up?"

"Casper's coming," Bryce told him. "He's in his office."

Casper *and* Bryce? First thing on a Monday? This should be interesting.

"You tell him yet?" Casper questioned as he trudged into the room carrying a cup of coffee and his cell phone.

"Did y'all ride together?" Ryan watched them closely. Since they all lived in separate houses scattered on a vast amount of land that they considered a compound, it wasn't unheard of for people to carpool, but Ryan got the feeling this was something more than an effort to save the planet.

"Yeah."

Leaning back in his chair, Ryan regarded them both suspiciously. "Okay, spill. What's goin' on?"

Casper's white-gray eyes darted to Bryce as though encouraging him to share the details. Ryan wished one of them would.

And then, half an hour later as he stared at the two of them, the conversation still turning in his head, Ryan wished they would've kept this assignment to themselves.

Based on what he'd just heard, it was going to be a very long day.

Z strolled into the office on Monday morning with a smile on his face. There wasn't a specific reason for the grin; it was just there. Could've been that he'd gotten nearly eight hours of sleep the night before, or perhaps because the sun was shining. As a rule, he didn't need a reason to smile; he simply tried to do it often. And coming to work on a Monday morning, to do a job he loved…well, that warranted a big fucking smile as far as he was concerned.

"Mornin', Z," Jayden Brooks—Sniper 1's receptionist—greeted, her cheery face lighting up as though he was someone important.

"Mornin', Glue," he replied easily, using the nickname they'd given her thanks to her ability to keep the office together. "How was your weekend?"

"Same ol', same ol'. You?" Her sweet smile caused her eyes to crinkle.

It was the identical conversation they had anytime he came in, and he didn't mind Jayden's friendly manner. Not that he intended to tell her—or anyone, for that matter—about his weekend. They'd all come to think of him as the playboy extraordinaire, believing he spent all his time naked with a different man each night. It was a reputation he didn't refute but one that he wasn't guilty of. If they knew the truth, they'd probably think he had a few screws loose. Which was why he kept his mouth shut when it came to his personal life.

"Not enough excitement. Which is why I show up here every week."

Jayden's light green eyes sparkled. "Smart man. And speaking of excitement"—her eyebrows shifted—"RT, Casper, and Bryce are waitin' for you."

"Me?" *What the hell were they waiting on him for?* Grabbing his phone from his pocket, Z checked to make sure he hadn't missed any calls.

Nope. Nothing.

"It just came up," Jayden explained, clearly picking up on his confusion. "They've been kinda quiet, just told me to make sure you found them when you got in."

Shit. He'd known that RT was acting weird for the past couple of weeks, ignoring Z, sending him on out-of-state assignments probably to put as much distance between them as physically possible. Not that any amount of space would make the memories of that night go away, but Z was obviously more accepting of what had transpired between them than RT was.

Then again, Z was hoping for a repeat.

Granted, that wouldn't likely happen if RT were going to fire him.

Surely not.

Fuck. He hoped not. What the hell would he do if he didn't have this job? Mall security?

Shit.

Z nodded and offered a brief wave to Jayden. "Then I guess I'm off. See ya."

Greeting others as he passed them, Z made his way to the offices on the far side of the building. Sniper 1 Security occupied the seventh floor, though Casper and Bryce owned the entire building, leasing out the rest of the space. The reception area and a small conference room, with their warm, homey décor, were made to invite clients to want to do business with them, but past the dark wood-paneled walls and chocolate suede furniture in the entry, the rest was relatively sterile. White walls and white-tiled floors were the extent of the decoration throughout. A bullpen with roughly twenty desks outfitted with computers, along with a break room, made up the majority of the floor, but on the far side were several offices—occupied by the big dogs of the company—and the conference room, where the agents would meet to be briefed on a case.

No one was in the conference room, nor were they in Casper's office, so he kept walking. Passing Bryce's office, Z noticed they weren't there, either, which meant...

"Oh, good, you're here," Casper said in an unusually chipper tone when Z stepped into RT's office doorway. "Come in and shut the door behind you."

"What's up?" Z questioned, glancing suspiciously from one man to the other as he did as Casper instructed.

"We've got an assignment that needs immediate attention," Bryce hurried to explain, as though keeping it a secret any longer was painful.

Z released a heavy breath.

"Somethin' wrong?" Casper asked.

"Not now, no," he told them. "So, urgent assignment, huh?" *Didn't all of their assignments require immediate attention?* Z kept the question to himself as he waited for someone to enlighten him.

"You and RT are goin' to Port Aransas," Bryce continued.

Hmm. The Texas coast. This was getting rather interesting already.

"Me and RT?" Z's eyes slid over to RT, whose blond head was bent down, his attention focused on his laptop.

While admiring him, Z noticed the man's broad shoulders tense. He fought the urge to fist pump the air at his good fortune. It'd been a while—the brief stint in Coyote Ridge notwithstanding—since he'd been on an assignment with RT. Z happened to know that RT had purposely kept them from working together even before The Incident— especially *alone*—and Z knew exactly why, but he'd never commented on it, waiting for an opportunity such as this to arise.

Z was nothing if not patient, and he'd learned over the years that dealing with RT required a certain amount of…skill. And patience. Definitely patience. Considering he'd had his eye on the guy for years, he'd merely been biding his time.

Good news… Looked as though his efforts were possibly about to pay off.

"The beach?" Z inquired with a smile, unable to mask the excitement sizzling in his veins. "Y'all are thinkin' I need a tan, right? I knew someone was gonna comment on it sooner or later."

Bryce laughed, as Z had expected him to. Casper merely watched him intently, a slight smile flirting with the corners of his mouth, but as usual, the older man fought it.

Those two were up to something; Z could feel it.

"Fine, I'll bite," Z continued. Leaning toward Casper, his smile widened. "They've got fishin' there, too, right? Get it?"

"Z," RT reprimanded.

RT's admonishing tone wasn't surprising. The guy was way too serious these days. Even when they'd been down in Coyote Ridge four months ago, after they'd taken down the obsessive stalker who had been antagonizing Cheyenne Montgomery for months, RT hadn't bothered to lighten up at all. His mood had only taken a darker turn since they'd slept together, and it was beginning to bother Z. A lot.

The way Z saw it, RT walked around like he had something stuck up his...

Okay, wait.

Nope, no freaking way. Z tried to ignore the lightning bolt of heat that jarred him at the thought of RT naked while Z was...

Damn it.

Definitely not the time or place to be thinking about *that*.

Focusing his attention on Casper and Bryce once more, Z resigned himself to getting through this conversation before he allowed his fantasies loose. "Fine," he said with an exaggerated sigh. "What's the assignment?"

RT reached for his iPad, then turned it around so that it was facing Z. The screen lit up, and Z found himself staring at…a painting?

"Man, I'm not much into art, but thanks for thinkin' of me," Z said instantly, frowning at the image.

"The painting was stolen."

"Really?" Z picked up the iPad for a closer look. "They coulda picked somethin' nicer than that. It's kinda ugly if you want my opinion."

"We don't," RT grumbled, his eyes never fully meeting Z's.

Ignoring RT's piss-poor attitude, Z said, "So, what's up?" Z was definitely curious now. "They stole the painting, took it to the beach for a relaxing vacation?"

"Not quite," Bryce said, getting to his feet and walking toward the window. "It wasn't the actual painting they were after."

"No? Then why steal the ugly thing?" Z stared at the screen, trying to understand why anyone would want something like that hanging on their wall.

"They snatched the wrong one," Casper told him, his voice gruff. "The one they took was a deliberate counterfeit."

"Holy shit," Z said with a whistle. "There're two of 'em?"

RT laughed. Finally.

Z met RT's crystal-blue gaze, another surge of heat vibrating through him, unlike anything he'd ever known before. Then again, he'd gotten quite familiar with the new version of lust he'd succumbed to. It was like lust on steroids, in fact. Whatever this was between him and RT, it was potent and powerful and off-limits as far as RT was concerned, and that intrigued Z more than ever.

Z had been with plenty of men in his life, felt different things with many of them, but nothing came close to the intensity of what he felt for RT. However, as much as Z wanted to pursue that lust, to grab RT, slam him up against the wall, and stake his claim on the man, he knew better. RT wasn't ready yet—*yet* being the key word.

Not for what Z wanted from him, anyway.

"The real painting contains a secret code."

"Seriously?" Z's head snapped over to Casper. "This is some high-tech shit? Why didn't you say so? Sign me up, I'll just head home and get my flip-flops."

"You don't own flip-flops," RT grumbled with a strained chuckle.

Nope, he didn't, but he'd buy a pair if it meant spending time at the beach. With RT. Instead of saying as much, Z smiled at RT, loving the way his boss looked away instantly.

Yep, this thing between them... It was high time they figured it out because Z had spent his entire life wishing for that cataclysmic awakening so many people found when they met their soul mate. And that night—two short weeks ago—though they'd both been a little intoxicated, was only the beginning as far as Z was concerned. He was looking for that person...the one who made you crazy enough to do stupid shit, to want stupid shit...like lots and lots of mind-blowing sex. And, you know, perhaps marriage and babies.

But mostly mind-blowing sex.

Z was pretty sure RT was that guy for him. And he was equally certain that RT knew it, too, he was just too damn stubborn to admit it.

EIGHT

Ryan did his best to ignore Z, but it wasn't easy. As serious as this mission was, he knew that taking Z along would keep it lively, if nothing else. Aside from entertainment... No, not entertainment. Aside from... Hell, at least Z was reliable.

Granted, it hadn't been his idea to include Z, but Casper had thought it would be a good idea. Bryce had instantly agreed. Why Z, Ryan hadn't figured out, because they could've selected from pretty much anyone at this point. Clay, Conner, Colby, Tanner, Decker, Trace, hell, even Hunter... They were all available, but Casper had picked the one man Ryan didn't trust himself to be alone with.

It wasn't as though he could tell Casper as much. He couldn't tell anyone. Especially since Bryce, Ryan's own father, seemed to think it was a brilliant idea. Ryan had to wonder if the two men knew something.

God, he hoped not.

Surely if they knew, they would've taken Ryan aside, reminded him of what had happened last time, advised him that this was a horrible idea.

No, looking at them now, Ryan didn't think they were aware of what had happened, but that didn't explain why they thought Ryan and Z were right for this job.

"When do we leave?" Z asked, his question directed at Ryan.

"As soon as possible. We'll take the bikes down there." It wasn't the greatest idea because a six-and-a-half-hour drive on a motorcycle wasn't the most comfortable way to travel, but that way Ryan didn't have to be alone in a car for an extended period of time with Z. He had a significant amount of self-control, but every man had his limits. Z was Ryan's limit, no doubt.

"Perfect," Z replied.

"I'll have Kira send your things ahead of you," Bryce informed them. "That way you'll look like two good ol' boys out for a little fun in the sun."

"Fun in the sun?" Ryan asked his father with a choked laugh. "Seriously? No one says that."

"I just did," Bryce retorted with a cocky grin. "We've acquired a house on the beach. It'll keep you close but not too close. Also, it'll provide the much-needed venue for a meet and greet."

"Meet and greet? Is that a fancy name for a party?" Z probed, his dark eyebrows downturned as though he was trying to unravel a mystery.

"In order to set up our covers, we'll have to show our interest in the art community," Ryan explained. "Big money, big parties."

"Aw, hell," Z muttered, speaking aloud what Ryan had been thinking when his father had originally told him the plan.

Bryce cleared his throat. "Once you're settled in, give us a call. We'll work out the logistics."

Ryan had gone over the details of the assignment multiple times already, yet he still hadn't mapped out exactly how it would play out. They were going in to protect a piece of art that was encoded with information that could prove to be detrimental if it landed in the wrong hands. Super spy shit, quite frankly.

But the mission wasn't what he'd anticipated in the beginning. Protecting the painting...relatively simple. What Bryce and Casper wanted...significantly more complex.

According to Casper and Bryce, their goal was actually to double-cross the guy who'd hired them, the one who wanted to protect the original painting at all costs. It was Ryan and Z's job to snatch the legitimate painting, hand it over to their contact at the Department of Homeland Security, and replace it with a fake—a *different* fake since the first one had apparently been stolen.

Simple, Bryce had said.

Uhhh...wrong.

The fact that the guy who'd hired Sniper 1 Security couldn't know that it was Ryan and Z who double-crossed him threw a wrench into the otherwise *simple* plan. Those details had yet to be hashed out, but with a six-and-a-half-hour drive ahead of them, Ryan had plenty of time to think.

If he could resist thinking about Z the entire way down to the Texas coast.

Hunter Kogan marched through the office, wondering where everyone was. He was about to go back up to the reception area and ask Jayden what was going on when the door to RT's office opened, and Bryce, Casper, and Z piled out.

"Hey," Casper said, looking surprised to see him.

"Hey," Hunter returned. "You two have a minute?"

Casper glanced over to Bryce, then both men nodded. Bryce went into his office, and Casper followed, so Hunter did as well. Closing the door behind him, he took a deep breath.

"Somethin' wrong?" Bryce questioned, taking a seat at his desk.

"No," Hunter told him. For the first time in a damn long time, nothing was wrong. Not entirely, anyway.

"You're not here to spring anything on us, are you?" his father asked.

"Like what?" Hunter wanted to see where Casper's head was.

Rather than answer, his father cocked his head in a manner that said, "Are you serious?"

Hunter eased into the chair beside Casper, ignoring the pain in his hip as he did.

"Whatever it is, I hope it's only good news," Bryce inserted.

"Depends on what you consider good news."

"Get to the point, Hunter," Casper growled, obviously not impressed with Hunter's stalling tactics.

"I'm ready to come back full time."

"So no more OCONUS assignments?" His father looked somewhat relieved as he asked the question.

OCONUS was the acronym for outside the continental United States, a term they all used thanks to their time in the military. Since Hunter had been previously on assignment in Greece—a cake job he'd taken in order to have some time to clear his head—he guessed it was appropriate.

"That's correct," he told Casper. "But no, I don't want to take over the company." Both Casper and Bryce had been pursuing Hunter to take over since Conner had balked at the idea, but Hunter wasn't suited for a desk job, even if it did require the occasional hands-on activity. He wanted to be in the field. It was the only way he'd be able to keep his mind from straying to things better left alone.

"That's good news," Bryce said with a relieved sigh. "RT and Z are goin' on an extended assignment, so the extra hands around here'll be good."

"Have you talked to Dani?" Casper inquired.

Leave it to his father to bring up the one and only subject that Hunter had no desire to talk about. It was Hunter's turn to extend the exasperated expression to his father.

"You're gonna have to deal with this sooner or later," Casper noted.

"Later," Hunter grumbled. Much later.

As though it hadn't been bad enough that Dani had bailed on him on their wedding day, the news she'd recently sprung on him had only exacerbated his anger.

"Have you talked to Max?" Casper asked.

"No." And he had no intention of talking to his brother-in-law. Hell, if it weren't for the fact that his sister was now married to the mafia boss, Hunter wouldn't want anything at all to do with that family.

"I know you're angry with Dani," Casper noted, "but the two of you need to get past this."

Hunter's anger ignited. "Get past this?" Launching to his feet, he stared back at his father. "She fucking lied to me about who she was. How the fuck do you get past that?"

The woman he'd wanted to spend his entire life with wasn't that woman at all. Turned out that Danielle Davidson was actually Danielle Adorite—Max's fucking cousin.

"Max got past it," Bryce added.

"That's not the same. He knew what Courtney was after when she came into his life. I had no fucking idea that Dani wasn't who she said she was."

Both men stared back at him, sympathy in their concerned gazes. Hunter didn't want their sympathy. He didn't want a damn thing from them or anyone else.

"Just give me an assignment as soon as you have one," he told them both as he walked to the door. "And it damn sure better not have anything to do with the fucking Adorites."

"Well, that didn't go quite the way I pictured it," Bryce told Casper as the other man stared at the door after Hunter's abrupt retreat.

His partner didn't answer immediately, and Bryce knew better than to push him. Bryce still wasn't sure what Casper's take on the whole situation was. He only knew that when Casper and Hunter had learned that Danielle Davidson—or, rather, Adorite—had appeared at Trace and Marissa's wedding, the outcome had been as far from what they had expected as it could possibly be.

The woman had left Hunter at the altar, sure, but according to her, she'd had good reasons. Turned out, she was an Adorite who'd been planted in their family by Max's late father, Samuel, in order to get dirt on Casper. From what they gathered, Samuel had been planning to take down the Kogans because Casper had dated Max's mother back in the day.

The whole situation was a convoluted, twisted heap of shit. Samuel had sent someone to spy on the Kogans, and Casper had sent his own daughter to spy on the Adorites, though neither knew of the other.

Fucked up was what it was.

But they were past that now. Since Danielle had come out with who she really was and what her agenda had been, Bryce thought the family had opted to forgive her. Evidently Hunter wasn't on board that train just yet.

A knock sounded and then RT stuck his head in. "Everything good in here?"

That seemed to pull Casper from his trance because he forced a smile and nodded.

RT glanced between the two of them suspiciously but then closed the door and disappeared.

"You still think this is a good idea?" Casper asked Bryce when they were alone again.

Good, another whiplash-inducing subject change. Just what Bryce needed.

Bryce had been pondering that exact question since he'd reluctantly decided to assign both Ryan and Z to the art case. Ever since he had received the call from Jericho Ardent, their new client, Bryce had been contemplating this very scenario, but it hadn't been until the ride into work with Casper that morning that he'd come to the final conclusion, thanks to a little encouragement from his friend.

"You don't?" Bryce asked Casper, getting to his feet and walking over to the window. "Think it's a good idea, that is?"

"I think you're too worried about it."

Bryce smiled, then glanced back at his business partner. "You think?"

"Yep," Casper answered casually, leaning back in the guest chair and pointing his amused expression at Bryce. Looked as though Casper had moved on from the subject of Hunter.

"I know why he holds himself back," Bryce muttered, thinking aloud.

"I assume we're still talkin' about RT here."

Bryce nodded.

"Because of Kevin?" Casper inquired.

He frowned. Kevin Fischer. To this day, Bryce still detested the guy for what he'd put Ryan through. And to think, if Bryce hadn't hired Kevin in the first place, it all could've been avoided. "That shouldn't have happened," Bryce replied.

"No, it shouldn't. But we can't change how people react," Casper said, his tone reassuring. "Kevin put a lot of lives at stake. We couldn't keep him on merely because he was dating RT."

Bryce fully agreed. Kevin had been an employee of Sniper 1 Security for nearly five years before they'd fired him for endangering the lives of his counterparts. The fact that he'd been dating Ryan at the time hadn't played into their final decision, but somehow Kevin had turned that around on Ryan. Turned out that Ryan and Kevin had been having problems, their relationship already on rocky ground, and RT had been about to break things off even before the disaster that had nearly gotten Trace and Z killed. Whether or not that'd been the reason Kevin had become such a loose cannon, Bryce still didn't know.

Nor did he care. What Kevin had done was unforgivable. It was luck that no one had been killed that day.

"He put Ryan through the ringer," Bryce said, though he knew Casper knew that already.

"Suing the company for sexual harassment'll do that to a person."

Yep, that'd been the kicker. The son of a bitch had turned things around and then sued Sniper 1 Security, claiming Ryan had lured him into an unreciprocated relationship. Luckily, they'd managed to beat that rap, but barely. Regardless, Ryan had been fucked up at that point, refusing to get close to anyone. Bryce assumed it was fear of the situation happening again.

"Z's not like Kevin," Casper stated.

Not by a long shot, but that clearly didn't matter to Ryan.

"This is a risk," Bryce said, turning to face his friend. "I'm not the type to play matchmaker, and certainly not with my own children."

"But...?"

Bryce sighed. His best friend knew him better than anyone. Well, anyone other than Bryce's wife, maybe. "Ryan wasn't going to give in any other way. And I've seen the way those two act around one another. They're like magnets, doing their best to keep from colliding. I thought for sure something would've happened while they were down in Coyote Ridge."

"Who's to say it didn't?" Casper inquired.

"RT's much too professional for that," Bryce said. "He learned his lesson."

"I wouldn't be so sure of that," Casper told him. "We can all agree that RT's hesitant, but those two... What's going on between them doesn't happen to everyone. Even if it did, they weren't on a sanctioned op. That was personal business they were taking care of."

"True," Bryce agreed.

Neither of them said anything for a moment.

Casper grunted, then got to his feet. "I think it'll be fine. They're both professionals. They know how to keep their business and personal lives separate."

Bryce nodded, moving to his desk and lowering himself into his chair. "Let's just hope Z can teach Ryan how to compromise. If not…"

"No harm, no foul." Casper laughed. "They're grown men. They'll figure it out or they won't. But maybe this'll keep the rest of us from being incinerated when we're in the same room with them."

Bryce smirked. It was true; there was some serious chemistry between those two men. Not that Bryce made a habit of setting his children up, but when it came to Ryan…they all knew the man had the willpower of a fucking saint.

Which meant he needed a little push.

At least once.

"Let's just hope it doesn't come back to bite me in the ass," Bryce told Casper as his business partner reached for the door handle.

"That's all we can do. And in the meantime…we need to figure out how to make this op successful. Those two are good, but without a plan, they're simply going to the beach for a vacation."

Casper had a point.

A very valid point.

NINE

The trip down to Port A was about as interesting as going to the dentist for a routine cleaning. Not a trip Z particularly cared to repeat unless absolutely necessary. After all, that was the same reason he made a trip to the dentist only once every six months. Necessity.

Six and a half hours, three stops for gas and food—and RT's surprisingly weak bladder—and they'd finally made it. Somewhat grateful to be standing on solid ground without the rumble of a powerful engine between his thighs (or his ass being numb), Z still found himself bursting at the seams with energy.

Perhaps it was the miles and miles of smooth, straight, open road that had given him the adrenaline rush. Possibly, hitting one fifty on the bike had spiked his blood.

Or...

It was because he'd spent the last half-dozen hours with RT's edible body directly in front of him while they hauled ass down to the Texas coast in order to pull off the impossible—but first they had to figure out how exactly they would accomplish that feat.

"This is where we're stayin'?" Z asked in disbelief after they'd dismounted their bikes, as he eyed the gi-fucking-normous monstrosity standing before him. Stilts kept it off the ground, but that didn't change how big the place was.

Beachfront house. Right. Looked more like a beachfront mansion. On steroids.

"It's the right address," RT confirmed, slowly ascending the steps and taking in their surroundings the same way Z was. "Is it me, or does this place seem a little...showy?"

"My thoughts exactly. But hell, I don't care what it is, as long as there's a comfortable bed for us." Z realized his mistake instantly. "Shit. I meant two beds," Z clarified. "*Two* comfortable beds."

Okay, it was official; he'd been ogling RT for far too long. His thoughts were free flowing right out of his mouth.

RT didn't even look at him. Luckily, Z didn't need a response to his clusterfuck of a comment, nor did RT, because he merely unlocked the door and stepped inside, leaving it open for Z to follow.

Once inside, Z released a long, slow whistle. "Holy fuck. Who chose this place?"

Beyond the bright entry and across the wide-open living room, past the wall of seamless, plate-glass windows was the Gulf of Mexico. Nothing but sand and ocean. Well, except for the crystal-clear infinity-edge swimming pool and the enormous veranda that separated the house from the beach.

Nice digs, sure, but what the hell were they supposed to do there? Act like a couple of frat boys partying it up?

Out of habit, Z made his way through the house first, fleetingly glancing in every room, making sure no one was there. No one other than them. Z wasn't big on surprises.

"All clear," Z told RT when they met up in the first-floor living area once again. Something across the room drew Z's attention, and he squinted to make out the pictures sitting on the mantel. "I thought this was a rental."

RT shrugged. "That's what Bryce said."

"Bryce?" Z clarified. "Your *father*, Bryce? The same man smiling like a loon in these pictures?" Z nodded toward the mantel.

RT walked over, picked up the picture.

"Either this place is more than a rental," Z told him, "or your pops has taken up modeling."

RT's smile barely registered, and though he conceded that much, he didn't respond.

"What's with the fancy shit?" Z finally asked, surveying the rest of the room. "Where'd your dad land this one?"

"Who knows," RT answered, seemingly just as stunned as Z. "He seriously told me it was a rental."

Rather than ponder the reasons for RT's father's misrepresentation of the place, Z opted to tour the house a little more thoroughly. After a quick pass through the oversized kitchen, the dining room, then back to the stairs, Z darted up to the second floor once again, surveying the rooms, taking in the detail this time. There were certainly two beds. Actually, Z had counted at least six amongst the four-thousand-square-foot non-rental.

Why was it that people thought it was cute to decorate the interior of their oceanfront property like...the ocean? Didn't they get enough of that shit out the window?

Someone had obviously cleaned out Pier 1 Imports on moving day. Evidently they lacked any creativity because everything was either blue or white. Well, except for the random seashells—seriously, that shit belonged outside— which provided a slight deviation of *pink* or white.

Oh, but the anchor was a nice touch.

Z rolled his eyes as he headed back downstairs.

"Six bedrooms, eight bathrooms, media room, game room, kitchen, dining room," Z muttered as he ticked them off on his fingers, talking to himself. He came to a stop at the bottom of the stairs. "Can't forget the wicked awesome outdoor living space." He took in the incredible view. "Rental. Right."

For some odd reason, he wanted to search for hidden cameras. "Why do I feel like I'm in an episode of *Lifestyles of the Rich and Famous?*"

And yes, as far as Z was concerned, it felt a little...stuffy, like the house was more for show than for comfort, although it sure as hell beat a cheap motel room with two full-sized beds. And by full-size, Z meant big enough for someone half his size.

After making his way across the main floor, Z headed out through the sliding door off the back, where RT was standing on the deck, staring out at the ocean, his forearms resting on the wooden banister that surrounded the area.

Beyond the deck, a huge sand dune separated the house from the beach. A narrow wooden walkway had been built across it to provide beach access.

"Not a bad view, huh?" Z muttered.

"I was thinking it was nice of them to carry the theme from inside the house out here."

Was that a joke? From RT?

Refusing to look as surprised as he felt, Z turned to face the house, propping himself against the railing.

"So while we're here," Z began.

"For an undetermined amount of time," RT added.

"Right. We're supposed to pretend to be interested in ugly fucking pictures—"

"Art," RT interrupted.

"If you say so," Z countered, glancing over at RT. "We're gonna party it up with the rich and seriously tasteless. Then we're gonna steal a painting that could've been nicer if a blind man with no arms had done it, replace it with an equally unpleasant fake, and get the original to DHS."

"Yep," RT confirmed.

"Sounds…" Shit. Z didn't know how it sounded.

"Fucked up?" RT suggested.

"Let's go with that." Crossing his arms over his chest, Z took it all in. The sand, the sun, the water. RT.

Yeah. He could complain all damn day if he wanted, but the truth was, he was pretty pleased with where he stood.

For the undetermined amount of time RT had referred to, Z got to spend some alone time with RT. Something he'd wanted for a long time. Something he'd honestly never thought he'd get after that one night two weeks ago when they'd shared the most incredible night together.

Yet here they were.

Ryan was beginning to sweat, and it had only a little to do with the blistering Texas sun but mostly everything to do with the man standing a foot away, looking every bit the badass that he was.

With his mirrored Ray-Bans covering his eyes, his biceps bulging beneath the maroon Texas A&M T-shirt he wore, and his dark hair blowing in the salty breeze, Z was damn near irresistible. The guy was in the best physical shape of any person—man or woman—that Ryan knew. And that was saying something considering the people Ryan associated with.

But Ryan didn't lust after any of the people he associated with. No one except for Z. Which was why he had to resist the irresistible. He didn't have much of a choice. After all, this was a mission, and he knew how Z handled missions. With unprecedented dedication to the end game.

And Ryan would do well to remember that.

Okay, that wasn't the only reason, but it beat all the others that Ryan had continued to remind himself of during the long drive down. He couldn't help remembering the night he'd been buried deep in Z's ass, fucking him hard and fast...

Not helping.

Needing a distraction, Ryan turned to Z. "Hungry?"

Z grinned, his crossed arms lowering, one giant hand coming down to pat his very flat, very chiseled abs.

End game, jackass.

"When am I *not* hungry?" Z questioned, turning his head and beaming at Ryan, giving him a glimpse of straight white teeth and a perfect dimple in his left cheek.

Fuck. "I saw a burger place back on the road we turned in from. Work for you?"

Z nodded.

Ryan could feel the intensity of Z's lingering gaze, though he couldn't see his eyes. He was suddenly grateful for his own sunglasses, praying like hell Z couldn't read his mind. This chemical reaction between them continued to burn bright and hot—hotter with every single additional minute they spent together.

Which was why Ryan needed to get through this assignment. Fast.

Twenty minutes later, they were pulling into a burger joint. The parking lot was overflowing with cars and trucks, people scattered about talking, laughing, only a few eating.

Parking their bikes on the sidewalk near the door, they headed inside, drawing only a little attention. Ryan figured some were admiring the bikes, and the rest...the rest were sizing up the giant of a man walking behind Ryan. Z was one of those people who others checked out. The sheer breadth of Z's shoulders was enough to cause people to do a double take. He wasn't just big, the guy was massive. Didn't matter, man or woman, adult or child, they admired him. He had that type of presence.

A bell clanged above the door when Ryan pulled it open, and more heads turned. A few welcomes from the staff behind the counter followed. The inside wasn't as crowded as the outside, which was surprising considering the heat of the day. Ignoring the stares, Ryan appreciated the chilly air of the interior, desperately needing something to cool him off.

The two of them went to the counter, ordered separately before finding a booth near the door. While they waited for their food, Ryan messed with his phone, checking in with his father and Casper via text, letting them both know that they'd made it. Bryce informed him that their things should be arriving at the condo in the next few minutes. According to his father, the jet had landed at Mustang Island airport a little while ago.

"So, what do we do first?" Z inquired, his gaze sliding from his own phone up to Ryan's face as they sat across from one another.

"Eat."

Z grinned and Ryan felt that strange eruption in his gut. It was lust, combined with...need. Following, a vicious heat infused his blood, snaking its way through Ryan's entire body. It was a phenomenon he'd gotten quite familiar with as of late. One he certainly didn't approve of.

So much for the air conditioning. He was not going to make it through this unscathed; he knew that now. Pep talks be damned.

"I got that part," Z replied casually, that sexy smirk making his dimple flash. "And then?"

"The art gallery we'll be staking out is in Corpus, not far from here. The big showing isn't until Saturday night. Figured we'd mingle with the locals, get the lay of the land until then."

"We're actually gonna *go* to this art gallery?" Z's tone reflected his disinterest.

"Affirmative. There'll be a small showing on Wednesday, and we're officially on the guest list. The client said he'd get us on the other list after he met with us. Vetted us, so to speak."

"Anyone tell you that you're a shitty date?" Z questioned, deadpan.

There was that fucking heat again.

"No, seriously." Z's dimple flashed. "I'm into guys who want to go to concerts, maybe catch a movie. Dinner's always welcome, too. But art... I'll pass."

Z knew how to lighten the mood. He kept the office laughing most of the time. If only Ryan didn't find that such an attractive quality in a man... Ryan had to admit, he wasn't immune to the guy's charm.

"Art virgin, huh? It only hurts the first time," Ryan joked, his blood heating from the innuendo.

Z's mouth widened into a full-fledged grin; his eyes darkened at the same time. "Ryan Trexler, are you offerin' to be my first?"

Oh, hell. This conversation train had officially derailed.

Glancing down at the table, Ryan shook his head, trying to get his brain to come back online. There for a second, he'd been on hormone overload. After a few deep breaths, Ryan finally lifted his head, meeting Z's dark stare. "We've gotta show interest in the art. Learn more about it, figure out how to replace the real thing with a fake," Ryan replied.

"Figure out how to *get* a fake," Z added.

"True."

"I think we should steal the original fake," Z told him. "That'd reduce the amount of work we have to do."

Grateful they'd gotten back on the initial discussion, Ryan nodded in agreement. "If we can find it." Z's idea wasn't a bad one, but it was dependent on whether they could locate the fake, which only added another unidentified aspect to the equation.

Z stared back at him as though processing his words. With a shrug, Z continued, "So what's this guy's name? The one we're working for but not."

"Jericho Ardent."

"Rich?"

"Loaded," Ryan said, setting his phone on the table and resigning himself to having to face Z directly.

"Old?"

"Nope," Ryan replied. "Thirty-one." Same age as Z.

"How'd he hear of Sniper 1?"

"Remember that gig last summer? We sent Clay and Decker down to Houston to keep an eye on the governor's wife for some charity event?"

"Sure." Z relaxed in the booth and spread his arms wide across the back.

Ryan did his best not to glance down to where Z's T-shirt lifted, showing a sliver of tanned skin and the dark trail of hair that dipped down into his jeans. Not thinking about where that trail led… It wasn't easy.

Ryan would need an ice bath by the time this was over.

"He's apparently friends with the governor," Ryan explained, forcing his eyes to Z's face.

"Good friends?"

"No idea," Ryan replied, leaning back when an employee walked up, delivering their food on two trays.

"Condiments?" the young woman inquired, a blinding smile transforming her pretty face.

Z waved her off with a devastating grin.

The man had a way with the ladies—even if he didn't sleep with them.

"We're good, thanks," Ryan told her, then turned back to Z when she skipped off. "The dossier I received on Ardent is slim. Not much information. Apparently the governor gave us a reference, and Ardent was impressed so he sought us out."

"So this painting, it's a big deal?"

"Yeah."

"Like *Da Vinci Code* stuff?"

Ryan smiled. Not only was Z intensely attractive, he was also smart.

"You read?" Ryan asked curiously.

Z nodded. "And write and wipe my own ass. How 'bout that?"

Oh, Lord. Ryan couldn't choke back the laugh that time, and it clearly pleased Z, because he paused, his burger halfway to his mouth, his eyes scanning Ryan's face, his cheeks lifting with his grin.

"Good to know," Ryan retorted. "And yes, this is *Da Vinci Code* shit. And it's not so much what was painted, though that does factor in. There's supposedly an electronic chip in the frame, which can be used to decipher top-secret information coded within the painting that could be detrimental to national security should it get leaked."

With his burger in his mouth, Z's eyes widened as he stared back at Ryan.

"No shit, man," Ryan confirmed with a chuckle before taking a bite of his own burger.

"Who painted this thing?" Z asked after chewing. "And how does one get national security secrets coded in something so ugly?"

"I'm not into art," Ryan admitted. "Don't remember the name of the painter off the top of my head. As for the information, from what I gather, the guy was a conspiracy theorist. Total whack job. Anyway, this guy's wife...she was CIA." When Z's eyes flared again, Ryan added, "Yeah. I know. Looks like they were either close and she divulged the information or he stole it. Not sure which. The painter and his wife are both deceased."

"How'd they die?"

"Murder-suicide. Ten years ago."

For a few minutes, the two of them ate in silence while they both pondered the information. Z's attention continuously drifted to the other customers in the restaurant. Watching Z, the way he worked, the way he saw things, it was fascinating. Ryan was almost certain he could ask Z what color shoes the man in the far left corner was wearing and he'd know.

Blue. With white laces.

The shoes.

After finishing both of his burgers and his fries, Z stole a couple of Ryan's fries, then pushed his own tray away, an inquisitive expression on his face. "So how do we get close to this guy?"

"We need to find something that we have in common with him. Or we need to fabricate it," Ryan explained.

"So what's he like?"

"Well, he's…" *Holy shit.* Before the words came out of his mouth, Ryan realized exactly why Bryce and Casper had suggested Ryan bring Z on this mission.

"He's *what*?" Z asked, leaning forward, his thick forearms resting on the table.

Ryan glanced up, meeting Z's eyes. "Bryce mentioned that we already had something in common with him, something that would be a way in."

"And?" Z asked, his eyebrows lifting with curiosity. "What's that? He own a motorcycle? Interested in security? Doesn't own a pair of flip-flops? What is it?"

Ryan couldn't believe he hadn't put two and two together earlier when he'd been scanning the information Bryce had provided him on Jericho Ardent. But it had been there, plain as day.

"I don't know what he's got in his closet," Ryan retorted, unable to disguise his own frustration with the situation. "No pun intended. But those aren't the reasons Bryce and Casper sent *us* down here."

Before Ryan had to admit the true reason they'd been paired up, realization lit up Z's face.

"He's gay," Z said. Not a question.

"He's gay," Ryan confirmed.

"And *what?* They think because *we're* gay that we're supposed to be interested? Or do they think there's a secret society of gays fornicating in art galleries? That we'll just be pulled into the fold because we don't fuck women?"

Ryan heard irritation in the other man's voice. No, there was no disguising the fact that Z didn't like the idea, based on the conclusion he'd obviously come to, but Ryan knew that Z hadn't thought it all the way through. Yet.

"Have you?" Ryan asked before he could stop himself.

"What?" Z looked as confused by the question as Ryan was for asking it.

"Fucked women?"

"Not once," Z said. "You?"

Ryan shook his head. He had no fucking clue how he'd managed to take this conversation off course again, but he was the only one to blame. Thankfully Z didn't expect him to expand, so Ryan chose not to say anything else.

"So, what's the plan then?" Z asked, sipping his drink through a straw.

Ryan tilted his head, lifted his eyebrows, and stared back at Z, waiting for him to put two and two together. It didn't take long.

"Holy fuck," Z said in a harsh whisper. "They want us to act like a couple?"

Ryan smiled; he couldn't help himself. As did Z, which startled him momentarily.

It wasn't because he actually liked the idea of pretending to be in a relationship with Z—because he really, really didn't—but he enjoyed watching Z figure it all out.

"Is that really it?" Z asked, his eyes narrowing. "Your ol' man wants you to hook up with me? I knew he liked me, but damn. This is a surprise. Think he'll invite me to dinner?"

Ryan ignored Z's teasing, tried not to think about the memories of that one night and what this new development might mean. "Honestly, I hadn't figured it out until just now. Had I known back at the office, I would've mentioned it to you. No way would I put you in that position."

Or himself, but he didn't add that part.

"I'm in," Z said quickly.

"*What?*"

"You heard me. I'm in." Z's gaze slid out the window briefly.

"I..." Ryan peered around the restaurant, desperately trying to think of something else. When he came up empty, he met Z's dark gaze once more. "I really don't think that'll be necessary."

"No?" Z looked disappointed. "What's your plan then?"

Fighting the urge to fidget, Ryan stared at his hands folded on the table in front of him. "I don't have one yet."

"Ah. Well, that's certainly better." Z offered a sexy smirk.

"I..." Ryan still had nothing.

"It's a good plan."

The hell it was, but Ryan didn't say as much. "I'm sure we'll figure something out. And it won't require...that."

119

"Well, you'd better think fast," Z said roughly. "'Cause if you don't come up with somethin' soon, we're goin' with that. Now let's get back to the house and figure out exactly how we make this work."

Ryan didn't need to figure out how to make it work. Z's suggestion was...remarkably simple, for the most part.

But there was one major problem.

The instant Ryan had to pretend to be Z's...boyfriend...he had a sneaking suspicion that it would all work out on its own.

And that wasn't necessarily a good thing.

TEN

Note to self: make more wishes on falling stars. And next time make them so that they include RT naked.

Leaning into the turn, Z followed behind RT, his full attention on the road as they accelerated onto the two-lane road that bisected Mustang Island. A quick head turn to both sides told him he was alone on the road, with the exception of the hot guy molded to his Aprilia RSV4 RF less than a car length in front of him. Once they were on the straightaway, RT gave his bike some gas, and Z followed suit. Within seconds, they were full throttle, doing ninety down the fifty-five-mile-an-hour road while Z's brain processed the information RT had relayed over lunch.

A couple.

Fucking A.

RT's words sounded in his head.

Had I known back at the office, I would've mentioned it to you. No way would I put you in that position.

Fuck that.

Z was game for any position RT wanted to put him in.

Sure, he wasn't all that thrilled with the idea of being pimped out, but he couldn't think of a better man to be pimped to. And if he could simply get RT on board with the plan, Ryan Jacob Trexler was—although pretend—going to be close enough for Z to put his hands on again. And there wasn't a damn thing RT could do about that.

Unless he intended to blow their cover. Which RT would never do, even Z knew that much.

Now, if only he could sell RT on the idea, he'd be home free. And that was a big *if*. After what had happened between them in Coyote Ridge, Z knew RT was being overly cautious.

Slowing his bike so they could pull down the narrow road that led to the beach house, Z glanced over at RT. Yeah, this was going to get interesting.

The second they stepped onto the front porch five minutes later, Z knew someone had been inside since they'd left. It was a sixth sense he had, one that hadn't failed him yet.

Backing up against the wall beside the door, he pulled his gun. RT did the same, on the opposite side, responding to the same eerie feeling that Z had.

"Someone brought our things by," RT informed him in a rough whisper.

"Doesn't mean that's the person inside."

"True," RT agreed, reaching for the door handle to see if it was unlocked. As he twisted the knob, RT looked to Z.

Well, what do you know? It was unlocked.

When RT nodded, pushing open the door and allowing it to swing inward, they both stepped inside, Z behind RT. A quick glance in the rooms on either side of them didn't give them much to go on, so they progressed toward the living room.

"What's up, fuckers?" Colby Trexler greeted from his perch on the sofa, a huge grin plastered on his pretty-boy face.

"You could've gotten yourself shot," RT told his brother, lowering his gun to his side.

"Could've, sure. But you're not *that* good," Colby joked.

Z chuckled.

Oh, they *were* that good. So good, in fact, that their ability to quickly assess a situation was the only reason Colby was still upright and not in a puddle of blood on the floor. Then again, Colby knew that.

"Whose dick did you suck to get this place?" Colby questioned, glancing around with wide eyes.

"Fuck off," RT grumbled, a strangled laugh escaping him.

Colby lifted his hand, showing them the beer he held. "Y'all know you got cold ones in there?"

Without being told twice, Z slid his gun back into its hidden holster at his back and then headed to the kitchen. He returned less than a minute later, handing over a cold Corona to RT.

"Thanks." RT took the beer and then headed outside, never making direct eye contact with Z.

"So, seriously, what's up with this place?" Colby asked, not talking to anyone in particular as he followed RT outside.

"It's a job," RT answered, his voice fading as he stepped out of the house.

"So why's there a picture of Dad on the mantel? That's just creepy, bro."

Z didn't join RT and his brother, choosing to take a breather while he watched the two men. He liked Colby. Along with all the Trexlers and Kogans, the guy was solid. And Colby and RT were close. As close as two men who generally spent weeks on end in other parts of the nation, sometimes the world, handling jobs that Sniper 1 Security was famous for could be.

"Where'd you go, Tavoularis?" Colby hollered. "Get your giant ass out here."

Z grinned as he sipped his beer. Colby was the only one who called Z by his last name. Z's parents had learned early on that his name was more than a mouthful. Hell, even his last name was more than most people could pronounce. Put them together and most people stumbled. That was the reason his father had nicknamed him Z and it had stuck. Everyone called him Z.

Everyone except Colby. When Z's best friend, Trace, had asked Colby why he called Z by his last name, the guy had said he liked the way it sounded.

Fair enough.

"Gotta watch my fair skin," Z informed him as he joined the two men outside, once again ducking to keep from nailing himself in the head with the doorjamb.

Colby laughed. "Right."

"Somethin' you wanted to talk about?" Z inquired when it was clear Colby wasn't just there to hang out.

"Nope. Hopped a ride on the jet to bring your stuff. Y'all are worse than a coupla chicks, the way you pack. I left your shit in the garage, by the way. Y'all can haul it up to the house if you need it that bad."

Great. What the hell had Kira sent down there?

"So why're you still here?" Ryan cast a bored look in Colby's direction.

"Waitin' for my ride."

"Your ride? How'd you get out here?" Z asked, propping himself against the cement railing.

"Cab."

"Who's comin' to pick you up?" RT questioned.

"Wouldn't you like to know?" Colby teased.

"Damn, bro. You got a chick down here, too?" Z joked, tipping his beer bottle to his lips.

Colby merely smiled. "At least one."

And they called Z the playboy.

The sound of a horn honking drifted on the breeze, causing Colby's eyebrows to dance upward. "That's my ride. You two be safe. If you need me, holler."

"Will do," Z assured him. "Now go catch her before she comes to her senses and ditches your ugly ass."

With that, Colby headed into the house.

RT didn't turn around, still choosing to stare out at the water. Z wanted to move up behind him and press his hips against RT, to wrap his arms around him. The guy always looked as though he needed a hug.

A full-body one.

With lots of skin-to-skin contact.

"You up for a swim?" Z offered instead, riding the wave of heat that crashed through him.

RT peered over his shoulder at Z, his sunglasses shielding his eyes. "Sure. Why the hell not."

Z's thoughts exactly.

"Ocean or pool?" Z was already pulling his shirt off after depositing his gun on the table, gripping the collar and shedding it in one swift move.

Ryan had to look back at the ocean. Looking at Z, remembering the guy's suggestion that they act like a couple for the sake of the operation, thinking about what had happened between them... It was too much.

If he gave in, agreeing to the farce, it wasn't going to be smooth sailing for Ryan. He knew Z was a playboy, knew the man had his fair share of lovers at any given time. He wasn't any different than Colby, save for the fact Z preferred men.

Hell, since the night they'd spent together in Coyote Ridge, Z hadn't said a word about it. At least not to Ryan. He didn't even act as though he remembered, but Ryan was pretty sure he did. After all, Ryan could see the interest in Z's eyes.

But Ryan wasn't like Z. He couldn't write these things off so easily. Sure, it had been a mistake, and the best thing for both of them would be to forget it ever happened, but still. Why hadn't Z acknowledged it? Had he already moved on to someone else? More than one, maybe?

Ryan frowned.

The thought of Z with another man didn't sit well with him. Not at all. He didn't want to think about another man having the opportunity to put his hands on that phenomenal body, or spending a night with those strong arms wrapped around him, laughing with him, soaking up his incredible wit and intelligence.

Fuck.

Reining in his thoughts once more, Ryan remembered Z's question. "We've got a pool back in Dallas," Ryan told Z simply, needing his thoughts to get back to something more appropriate, such as the case.

"Gotcha," Z replied.

Knowing he had to get his shit together and pretend that Z didn't affect him, didn't make him crave something he hadn't had in far too long (if ever), Ryan turned to face the other man.

Z was toeing off his boots, then tugging off his jeans.

Fucking hell.

Standing before him was six foot seven inches of prime alpha male, wearing nothing but a pair of black boxer briefs and a gorgeous grin.

Ryan's mouth dried up like the Sahara Desert.

"You goin' in like that?" Z asked, pointing at Ryan by tipping his beer bottle toward him.

It wasn't as though he could go inside and grab his swim trunks. That'd make him look like a pussy next to Z. Without saying a word, Ryan proceeded to undress, checking his gun and setting it on the table, then tossing his discarded clothes in a pile, all while ignoring the heat of Z's stare. When he was down to his boxers, without a glance back at Z, he went right for the stairs.

As he was heading down to the sand, Z mumbled behind him. Something that sounded very similar to, "Dayum."

Or at least that was what Ryan thought he heard Z say.

For the first time in a long time, Ryan blushed.

Two hours later, after a shower to wash off the sand and salt water, Ryan ventured back downstairs and found Z sitting on the couch in front of the big screen mounted to the wall in the main living area, flipping through channels with a bottle of water in his hand.

After a quick trip out to his bike to retrieve the files he'd brought with him, Ryan went right for the kitchen, coming to stand at the breakfast bar after grabbing a beer from the fridge. Z joined him a minute later.

"That the file?" Z asked, grabbing his own beer.

"Yeah," Ryan relayed. "I thought maybe you could look it over while I call Bryce."

Z nodded, then took the file and spun it around to face him.

Ryan grabbed his cell phone and headed outside. He didn't want Z to hear the conversation he intended to have with his father.

As he stared out at the water, the same peace he'd experienced earlier washed over him. It sure as hell beat the view of the concrete jungle he was familiar with. This...yeah, this he could get used to. It was a surreal feeling. He hadn't been at peace in far longer than he cared to admit. His life was about work, ensuring that the bad guys were taken down, the good guys were protected, and most importantly, he worried about his own enforcers, wanting to keep them safe from the danger that lurked in every corner.

He knew that the people who worked for him—most of them family or close friends of the family—were more than capable of taking care of themselves, but that didn't mean Ryan didn't worry. He figured he'd picked that up from his father over the years. Both Bryce and Casper had done their level best to keep the members of Sniper 1 safe at all costs while still being effective.

Granted, that didn't always work out the way they wanted. Two years ago, they'd lost one of their own. Conner's wife had been gunned down just outside the Sniper 1 offices. It had been a day that changed their lives forever. Although Conner didn't discuss what had happened, Ryan knew that the unfortunate incident wasn't simply the result of a cartel coming back for a little retribution. No, Conner's wife had known something. What, Ryan wasn't quite sure, but he intended to find out. It was an ongoing investigation that Ryan was overseeing himself. He knew that Conner was also seeking answers, but Ryan feared vengeance was more of what Conner had in mind. Although Ryan wouldn't mind putting a few bullets in the brains of the men who'd killed her, he knew that wouldn't solve anything.

Then, of course, there was Ryan's sister, Marissa. She'd spent years running from a man who'd wanted to silence her, and they'd all opted for the easy way out—stashing her rather than finding the man responsible. Ryan knew he'd failed her on every count. If it hadn't been for Trace Kogan and his desperate need to protect Marissa, she would likely still be on the run. Or dead. Thankfully, with a little help from Max Adorite, the leader of the Southern Boy Mafia and now the husband of Trace's sister, Courtney, they'd managed to take the bastard down. And the death of that double-crossing ATF agent didn't cause Ryan to lose a minute of sleep.

Dialing his father's number, Ryan bent over, resting his elbows on the wooden railing that separated him from the sand several feet below, and put the phone to his ear. While listening to it ring, he thought back to swimming with Z in that big ocean earlier. It'd been…interesting.

Sort of.

If it hadn't been for Ryan's unflagging desire for the man, he probably would've said it had been relaxing.

"Hey," Bryce greeted in a fatherly tone. "Everything good?"

"So far," he replied. Then he got right to the point. "Was there somethin' you forgot to mention about this place? Like the fact that you own it?"

Bryce chuckled. "It was...a recent acquisition."

Leave it to his father to make buying a prime piece of beachfront property sound like a business deal.

"For?" Ryan inquired.

"Your mother and I thought it'd be a good investment. Something we could all use. What do you think?"

"It's nice." Ryan continued to peer out at the ocean. "Really nice."

"Glad you like it," Bryce replied. "So y'all settled in? Ready to get to work?"

"Yeah. We're settled in. Anything exciting happenin' up there?" It was difficult for Ryan not to be in the thick of things, but he relied on his father and Casper to fill him in when necessary.

Ryan should've been sharing the reins of Sniper 1 Security with one of Casper's offspring, but unfortunately, the Kogan clan didn't seem to be as keen to take on the task as Ryan was.

Ryan didn't have the luxury of shirking his responsibilities, which meant that left him and him alone for the time being, and truth was, he was fucking tired. As much as he wanted to tell the Kogans he could certainly use the help, that wasn't in his nature. Instead, he continued to plow forward, taking it all on himself. Eventually he'd burn out, but until then, he didn't have time to think about it.

"Hunter's back for good," Bryce told him now. "He's gonna settle back in."

Ryan stood up straight. "Is he gonna take over?"

"No," Bryce answered solemnly. "But Casper and I are gonna talk to Conner again. It's time they address this one way or another. Casper and I can't fully retire until you're comfortable."

Ryan knew better than to argue with his father. The Kogans were as much his family as his own brothers and sister, but that didn't mean Ryan wasn't irritated with their lack of enthusiasm when it came to running the family business. But if Bryce wanted to address the issue again, who was he to stop him?

"Anything else?"

"Not yet. What about you? You discuss the case with Z yet?"

"I've got him goin' over the file, hoping he can pull something out of there that I didn't. Something that'll help us get an in with Ardent."

He didn't bother mentioning that he'd already caught on to Bryce and Casper's plan. Putting Ryan with Z *wasn't* the smartest move—for personal reasons. At least as far as Ryan was concerned. Either his father knew the attraction that Ryan had for the man or he was merely playing with fire. Not that it mattered. Ryan knew that this stunt wouldn't work.

When Z had mentioned that he was all for the plan—pretending to be a couple—Ryan had been surprised. It wasn't a completely *terrible* strategy. It merely wouldn't work. Yes, in theory, if he and Z could establish a cover as a couple interested in art, perhaps they could get close enough to figure out a way to get the original painting out of Ardent's possession. They wouldn't pose a threat, and if they could befriend the guy, not only pretending to work for him, they had a chance of pulling this off.

"What does he think about it? He give you any input?" Bryce asked, a subtle hint reflected in his tone.

"A little," Ryan lied. They'd discussed it thoroughly, and Z was already on board, but he told his father, "We're still tryin' to work it out."

"Well, what if…"

"What if what?" Ryan asked his father, knowing exactly where this conversation was headed.

"What if you and Z were to pretend to be a couple?"

And there it was. Rage stirred in Ryan's veins. He hated that his own father had set him up like this. Biting back the immediate retort, Ryan managed to maintain his composure. "Not a good idea."

"Why not?" Bryce countered, sounding genuinely confused. "It's not like you haven't played a role for a job before."

Ryan caught the slight edge of irritation in his father's voice.

"Not to mention, the two of you appear…compatible."

"What the fuck does *that* mean?" He couldn't hold back any longer. "Compatible? Because we're both gay? It doesn't work that way."

Bryce was silent for a moment, but then Ryan's father's voice filled his ear. "That's not what I meant and you know it. Sure, it's not a secret that you're gay. So is Z. But I'm not some misguided dumb ass who thinks that simply because you have that in common you should be together. Jesus, Ryan. Give me a little fucking credit."

Ryan didn't respond.

"I'm heterosexual, kid, in case you hadn't noticed. So is something like ninety-six percent of the population. Doesn't mean I'm attracted to them. I didn't have some foolish agenda here. I didn't make the suggestion merely because you're gay."

A wave of guilt crashed over him. Deep down, Ryan had known that.

Ryan had always had the support of his family. He knew a lot of people who wouldn't be having this conversation with their parents because their parents didn't support them, hadn't come to terms with the fact that they were different than the norm. His family wasn't bothered by the fact that Ryan was gay, never had been. Not even when he'd come out to them when he was fifteen years old. For that, he was grateful. And maybe he took that for granted.

Truth was, he didn't believe his father and Casper had made the suggestion for that reason alone. But he damn sure wasn't going to confirm to his father that he was attracted to Z and that this setup could very well be a disaster. The last thing Ryan wanted was for things to go bad between him and Z, their past mistake notwithstanding. His family's company was at stake. They couldn't afford to lose Z, and when—not *if*, because it was inevitable—they had a fallout, it would be a disaster of epic proportions.

Ryan had no misconceptions on the matter. First, it was a job. Second, he knew that Z wasn't long-term relationship material. The guy disappeared every night and every weekend, sometimes not coming home until it was time to go to work. It was a subject that Trace had ridiculed Z about for years, which was the only reason Ryan knew of Z's extracurricular activities.

Ryan wasn't looking for a one-night stand, despite the fact that he knew if he and Z did get together again, it'd be just as explosive as the last time. That was a given. There was an undeniable chemistry between them, but that didn't mean it was right.

Which was why Ryan opted to tell his father exactly how he felt. "Face it, Dad," Ryan said. "I'm a good actor because that's part of my job, but when it comes to a situation like this—pretending with Z—I'm not sure I'm that good."

And Ryan wasn't talking about pretending to *want* to be with Z. That was a no brainer.

No, he was referring to his inability to pretend that it wasn't real, when he knew without a doubt that he would wish it were, from the very first touch.

But Ryan decided to let his father decipher that statement however he wanted.

ELEVEN

The following morning, Z was up before the sun. Not wanting to bother RT, he ventured out to the pool. Because it was dark, he ditched his underwear and slipped into the warm water naked, his gaze continuing to stray to the horizon, where the faintest hints of the sun were just breaking free, brightening the otherwise inky black sky.

Desperate to burn off some of his pent-up energy, Z began swimming laps. He didn't bother to count, wanting simply to outrun the thoughts that had plagued him for most of the night.

Face it, Dad. I'm a good actor because that's part of my job, but when it comes to a situation like this—pretending with Z—I'm not sure I'm that good.

Z hated the fact that RT's statement had hurt him so much. He would've preferred not to hear the words at all, rather to go forward without knowing how against the idea of pretending to be with Z that RT was.

But he couldn't undo it now.

And it wasn't as though he could confront RT because Z hadn't exactly been invited into the conversation. Still, he had allowed those words to get to him.

What the hell had RT meant? Was he seriously contemplating the ruse? Pretending to be a couple the way Bryce had evidently intended? It really wasn't a bad idea. Not that they necessarily needed an in with Jericho—the man had hired Sniper 1 for a job—but it could make the guy feel more comfortable. Then again, they hadn't even met Jericho yet, so they could very well be jumping to conclusions.

So what had RT meant? That he didn't think it would work? Or that he couldn't even fake it for the sake of the op?

Z knew without a doubt that he'd seen interest in RT's gaze on more than one occasion.

Like *that* night.

And yesterday.

In RT's office.

At lunch.

In the ocean.

Slowing to turn, Z used the wall to propel himself forward, the water sluicing over him as he began another lap.

RT thought he was good at disguising his feelings, but he wasn't. As far as actors went, RT wouldn't win any awards. Not when it came to pretending *not* to be interested. But Z knew RT. If he continued to tell himself that, there was no way Z would ever get close to him. The man locked up his feelings and kept them close to the vest. Better than anyone Z knew. In fact, RT's emotions were like a steel wall surrounded by concrete, then encased in diamonds. Damn near impenetrable.

Surely the guy wanted to find a man, fall in love...be happy.

Not that Z was that man.

But they'd never know until they tried, right?

Turning once more, Z dove beneath the water, kicking his feet, propelling himself forward.

Z wasn't dreaming of a white picket fence and babies, but he wasn't interested in a brief fling with RT, either. He'd had plenty of those over the years, though far fewer than Trace gave Z credit for. No, his best friend didn't even know the goings-on in Z's life, and Z intended to keep it that way.

But here…in this secluded place, Z recognized there was an opportunity that he simply couldn't pass up. Things had fallen into place, giving him the chance to pursue RT the right way, to show him just how good happiness could be.

And what better way to do it than by setting it up ahead of time? That was the way RT's brain worked. He needed structure and this would provide that. From there, they could see where the cards fell. Wasn't that the way it worked?

Breaking the surface of the water, Z sucked air into his lungs and scrubbed the water off his face with both hands.

Would he pressure RT? Nah.

Hell, he wouldn't even know how to do that.

But that didn't mean he wouldn't take advantage of the situation.

As far as plans went…pretending to be a couple in order to get close to the principal…this was good. It was as good a plan as any, honestly. And if RT would give in, Z also knew there wouldn't be any pretending involved. However, getting the stubborn man to agree… That wouldn't be easy.

After three more laps, Z stopped at the end of the pool facing the horizon, resting his arms on the infinity edge and watching as the world broke into brilliant color. The sound of seagulls nearby combined with the gentle crash of waves down below lulled him into a sense of peace, erasing the irritation he felt from the entire situation.

Z could so easily get used to this. The early morning swim, the view, the peace and quiet. This moment, right here, right now, was one Z would never forget for the rest of his life.

The whooshing sound of the glass door being propelled open pulled him from his euphoria.

"You're up early," RT called out.

Glancing over his shoulder, Z saw RT walking his way, dressed for the day in snug-fitting jeans and a black T-shirt. God, he looked good.

"Problems sleeping?" RT inquired.

If he only knew.

When Z hadn't been thinking about RT's statement last night, he'd been envisioning himself slipping into RT's room, sliding into bed with the man, and wrapping his entire body around him, claiming his mouth, then his body...

"Not too bad," Z finally said, shaking off the thought. "You?"

"I'm usually up early."

Z knew that about RT. The man was dedicated to the job, spending endless hours working and worrying. All work and no play. Z was pretty sure that particular proverb had been created to describe Ryan Trexler to a T.

"I wouldn't complain if I could wake up to this every day," RT muttered absently, staring out at the ocean.

Though he knew RT wasn't talking to him, Z responded anyway. "Me, either." But Z was referring to more than the ocean view.

Turning back to face the sun, Z watched as the small waves crashed along the shore, the water reflecting the orange and pink from the lightening sky.

Stunning.

Twisting around, Z rested his elbows on the wall behind him, keeping himself above water as he faced RT, something else equally stunning to look at. "So what's the plan for today? I doubt you're gonna say we'll be playin' the role of beach bums."

RT smiled. A real smile. Z longed to see those, probably because they were so infrequent. It made his body harden instantly. That was when he remembered that he was naked and the sun was coming up. In a few minutes, RT would see Z in all his glory.

He wondered if RT could see the smirk that tilted his lips. The thought of RT seeing him naked again…

No, Z wasn't modest.

"I thought we'd get breakfast, then meet with Jericho. I emailed him last night, told him we were in town. He'll need to show us the painting, let us know what we're working with."

"Works for me," Z said, pushing off the wall and swimming to the shallow end. "I just need to shower, then I'll be ready to go."

Without looking behind him to see if RT was watching, Z took the steps leading out of the pool. After grabbing his discarded underwear and the towel he'd stashed on a chair, he proceeded to dry off—slowly—before going into the house.

As he was closing the sliding glass door behind him, Z glanced over at RT.

Z smiled.

There, with a dumbfounded expression on his handsome face, was RT blatantly staring.

Nice.

God had been in a good mood on the day he created Z, that was all there was to it.

Ryan couldn't turn away from the incredible view of Z's naked body, even when he saw Z looking at him. Yeah, he'd been staring at a very impressive, very naked Z, and while he had been transfixed by Z's perfection, his dick had stirred to life.

Thankfully, Z went inside.

Memories of the night he'd spent with Z rushed him, overwhelming him with their intensity. Although he had spent the last couple of weeks blaming that incident on the alcohol, Ryan had been sober when he'd taken Z. And he'd been sober every single day since when he replayed that night over and over in his head. Despite knowing better, Ryan wanted a replay, and seeing Z naked... It didn't help his desire to get him in bed once more.

Ryan was tempted to jump in the water to cool off, but he doubted that would help. Plus, he'd just taken a shower before coming downstairs. When he'd woken up, he'd expected Z to still be asleep, so finding him outside, staring out at the morning sun as it crested over the horizon, had been unexpected. He wondered whether Z saw the same thing Ryan did when he viewed the world like that.

It wasn't often that Ryan allowed himself time to slow down. He preferred constant motion. It offered him less time to dwell on his personal life. Something that had been seriously lacking before he and Z had...

Not the right time to think about this.

Which was another reason the temptation of Z wasn't a good thing right now. As it was, Ryan was thinking of nothing else. He was pretty sure he'd never wanted to blow off work and enjoy some down time until now, until Z.

Ryan's cell phone buzzed and he pulled it from his pocket. Hitting the button to turn on the screen, he nearly swallowed his tongue when he saw the text message he'd received.

Did you like the view?

Aw, hell.

Z was known for his mischief. People loved him because…well, because he was so loveable. And fun. And now it seemed he'd turned his wicked charm on Ryan.

Knowing there was no way to defuse Z, Ryan purposely pretended to misunderstand, texting back with: **The sunrise was nice, yeah.**

Within two seconds, another text came in.

Sure was. But I think you liked the moon better.

Ryan couldn't help but laugh. What was he going to do? There was no way he could resist Z if he turned that charm on him for long. Hell, as it was, he was hard-pressed to maintain a professional relationship with the guy.

Not wanting to fan the flames any more, Ryan sent another text, telling Z he'd be waiting out front on his bike, before pocketing his phone and heading through the house.

Another text came right on the heels of his, which had him fishing his phone out once again.

Did that say bike or bed? I think I got chlorine in my eyes.

Ryan grunted a laugh then locked up the back door and headed out front. He opened the garage door and got situated on his bike, waiting for Z, his thoughts wandering in directions he knew they shouldn't. He could still see Z's naked body, all rock-hard muscle and sinew, his perfect ass, his thick cock...

Fucking hell. This was not going to be easy.

As it was, he'd spent most of the night contemplating the notion of pretending to be Z's boyfriend for the foreseeable future. He still wasn't completely on board with the idea, but for the first time in a long fucking time, Ryan hadn't been able to come up with a better plan. His father had set these dominoes in motion, and now Ryan had no way of stopping them.

It made sense.

Unfortunately.

In most situations, pretending to this degree wasn't necessary, but in this case, they needed to befriend Jericho Ardent in order to deceive him, despite the fact that he was technically the client. Getting close to him was prudent if they intended to steal the painting. As it was, Ryan had no idea what Jericho wanted from them.

"Ready?"

Ryan's head snapped around, his gaze coming to rest on Z, fully clothed this time. His faded Levi's hugged his muscular thighs, and the white polo made his bronze skin glow.

"Let's go," Ryan grumbled. He was losing his fucking mind, and they'd be better off getting down to business before he did something stupid, like strip Z naked again and cover him with his body.

"I hope like hell you're plannin' to feed me first," Z said, his tone light, his eyes dancing with mischief.

"Sure." Ryan didn't see the harm in that.

"Where're we goin'?" Z inquired as he mounted his bike, his long legs straddling the magnificent machine, the muscles in his arms flexing as he pulled his helmet down over his head.

Ryan took a deep breath, but he didn't answer Z's question. He couldn't find his fucking voice, so he opted just to ride. He'd figure it out when they found a place.

Half an hour later, the hostess at Cracker Barrel was seating them. Truth was, Ryan wasn't all that fond of down-home country breakfasts, but it was on the way, and he happened to know that Z liked the place.

Not that Z's preference had factored into Ryan's decision at all.

At least he pretended it hadn't, anyway.

"What can I get you boys to drink?" the older woman with the puffy white hair, dark glittering eyes, and a quick smile asked.

"Coffee and water," Ryan and Z said at the same time.

"Comin' right up."

Once again Ryan found himself sitting across the table from Z, preparing to have a meal together. Alone.

"So I was thinkin'," Z began, his eyes perusing the menu in front of him. "This notion of pretending we're a couple..." Z's eyes lifted briefly. "It could work."

"I know," Ryan admitted. When Z's gaze met Ryan's, he found himself trapped in Z's intense stare, and he couldn't seem to look away.

"Do you now?" Z asked, sitting up straight and watching Ryan curiously.

"Yeah," he said, sighing. "The whole point is to get close to this guy, make him trust us. From what Bryce told me, he's guarded. He keeps his friends close, trusts very few people, so we need to make nice."

"You're serious?" Z asked, obviously perplexed by Ryan's reluctant agreement.

"Yeah. I've given it a lot of thought, and I can't come up with another plan. It's not a simple situation. If we were merely guarding the painting, that'd be one thing. We're expected to..." Ryan hated what they were expected to do.

"Steal it," Z finished for him. "Not exactly the most ethical thing we've ever done, but not the worst, either."

No, it wasn't. And based on the information he'd read, it was an issue of national security, something Sniper 1 Security took very seriously.

"How'd Bryce find out about the painting, anyway?" Z regarded him inquisitively. "If Jericho called to hire us, how does it come up that we've got a bigger issue?"

"My father's paranoid," Ryan admitted. "When he found out about the painting, he had Dominic dig into it, told him to find out the real value."

"That makes sense."

It was one of the reasons people regarded Sniper 1 Security with such high esteem. Ryan's family wasn't interested in taking jobs for the sake of taking the job. They had more than they could handle as it was, so they prioritized. Anything to do with a child, they took regardless. Missing persons, high on the list. Everything else, they assessed to determine the probability of success.

"So there's a database, or what?" Z questioned, his dark eyes glinting with humor.

"Somethin' like that," Ryan told him, leaning back when the waitress returned with two small white steaming mugs and two glasses of water.

"Have y'all decided?" she asked, nodding toward the menu.

Z met Ryan's eyes and Ryan nodded. Z proceeded to rattle off his order: eggs, bacon, pancakes, sausage, ham, hash browns, biscuits and gravy. The guy's stomach must've been lined with steel.

"And you, hon?" she asked, glancing over at Ryan.

"Oatmeal," he told her simply.

That earned a beaming smile from the waitress. "Sure thing."

When she left the two of them alone, Ryan looked at Z, finding him staring back at him with a stunning grin.

"What?"

"Nothin'," Z said simply.

"Not buyin' it," Ryan countered. "Why're you smilin'?" Ryan held his breath as Z leaned closer.

"I'm not sharin' my food with you."

Ryan smirked. He hadn't known what he'd expected Z to say, but that wasn't it. Yet it settled the churning in his gut.

Although he could pretend all day that this was merely a job, Ryan knew deep down that there was something else going on here. Something that wasn't simple or easy.

Or pretend.

TWELVE

Z wasn't sure what had caused RT to agree to the plan, but he had no intentions of jinxing it. If the guy was on board, Z was content with that.

Granted, neither of them knew how this would play out, but until they met Jericho Ardent face-to-face, they wouldn't, either. As much as Z wanted to take RT back to the house, strip him slowly, and show him that this wasn't pretend, that wasn't an option.

An intriguing idea but not an option.

"Do we know anything else about Jericho?" Z asked, hoping to ease some of the uncomfortable tension that had joined them at the table.

"Single, never been married, no kids, rich as fuck... What else is there?"

"What is it that he does? You know, besides collecting ugly paintings." Z still refused to call it art.

"He's a venture capitalist," RT explained. "Well, that's the hobby he's taken up recently. Apparently investing in others has paid off for him lately."

"Like Shark Tank?" Z loved that show. He got a kick out of seeing those people presenting their dreams to the "sharks" who could make them or break them. Of course, he enjoyed the positive ending to the other, but it didn't always work out that way.

"You watch a lot of TV?"

"When I can," Z told him. He didn't bother to tell Ryan when and where, because that would be too much information for Z to share. But yeah, he had the opportunity to watch television more often these days.

Their food was delivered, and for the next few minutes, neither of them said anything, peering around casually, doing everything except looking at one another. The tension continued to ratchet up until Z could hardly stand it.

"All right, if we're gonna do this..." Twirling his fork around as though that explained what *this* was, he continued, "We should probably know a few more things about one another."

"Like what?" RT asked, his eyes wide with concern as he looked up for the first time in a few minutes.

"Okay..." Z hadn't given much thought to where the conversation would go, but he was good at thinking on the fly. "What's your favorite color?"

RT looked perplexed by the question.

"It wasn't that difficult," Z said softly, unable to hold back the grin.

"Blue," RT blurted.

"Blue? What color blue?"

"*What?*"

"Come on, it doesn't get much easier than this. Navy? Teal? Aquamarine?"

"Blue," RT said firmly.

Okay, so that was going nowhere.

As he tried to come up with something else, RT surprised him by tossing the same question back at him.

"Silver," Z told him.

"Silver's not a color," RT told him, his eyebrows quirked.

"Sure it is," Z offered, holding up his fork.

That must've stumped RT because he didn't respond.

"Fine," Z finally said. "I'll tell you what I know about you." He forked eggs into his mouth. "We'll go from there."

RT lifted his coffee mug to his lips.

Z set his fork down and ticked off each thing on his fingers as he listed them. "Born November third. Thirty-two years old, six foot three inches." Angling his head slightly, he regarded RT momentarily. "Roughly one-ninety, possibly two hundred pounds. Father, Bryce, mother, Emily. Started working at Sniper 1 Security when you were fifteen, cleaning the offices because your ol' man thought it'd be a good introduction to the way things work. Became an enforcer at eighteen, opted not to go to college in lieu of taking over the world."

Surprisingly, that earned Z a smile from RT.

"That's all you got?" RT asked.

"I can keep goin' if you'd like." Z took a drink of his water. "Favorite color is blue—just blue. You're obsessed with the Mission Impossible movies and saw the first one at least eight times."

RT laughed. "Okay, I get it."

"Now your turn," Z told him.

RT set his coffee mug down on the table. He looked as though he was gearing up for the challenge. "Born June second. Just turned thirty-one. Six foot seven inches, although your driver's license says six foot six. Why is that, anyway?"

"People look at you funny when you say six seven, why, I don't know." Z laughed.

"Got it." RT wrapped his hands around his coffee mug and continued, "Two hundred forty some odd pounds, played football in high school. Mother, Cindy, father, Thomas. Wanted to be a Navy SEAL, but a birth defect held you back. Came to Dallas right out of high school, showed up at the Sniper One office when you were twenty-one, looking for a job."

"Not bad—"

RT continued. "Your father was in a car accident four years ago. Your mother had him transferred up here for better doctors. She moved here not long after."

Z didn't say anything, but he managed to hold RT's gaze. Did he know the whole story? Did he know that Z spent...?

"You're a serial dater," RT continued, his eyes narrowing, his voice lowering. "You don't use your real name most of the time, opting not to let the men you're with know the real you, claiming it's to keep your cover."

Z dropped his eyes to the table. Of course RT would believe the rumors. Why wouldn't he? Z had never disputed them, so those closest to him had taken that to mean they knew the truth. And just like all the other times, Z opted not to correct the assumption.

After all, what difference would it make?

Instead, he forced a smile and then thanked his lucky stars when the waitress came over with their bill.

"Looks like it's time to get to work."

With that, Z snatched the slip of paper and headed to the front without waiting to see if RT would follow.

A short time later, after a rather abrupt ending to their breakfast that had left Ryan's head spinning, and then after they'd stopped for gas, Ryan and Z were walking into Jericho Ardent's not-so-modest home. Figuring with real estate values what they were, the man made more in a minute than Ryan made in a year. Then again, the guy was a self-proclaimed multibillionaire whose hands were dipped in multiple business ventures.

"Mr. Trexler. Mr. Tavoularis. Thank you for coming. Mr. Ardent is expecting you."

"Sure," Ryan replied, following the older woman—a housekeeper, Ryan presumed—down a wide, marble-floored hallway.

"Mr. Ardent is waiting for you in his library."

Not the study, not his home office. The library.

The woman opened a door, and Ryan stepped inside a room larger than Ryan's entire house, and he understood instantly why it was referred to as a library. The walls, at least twenty feet tall, were lined with dark wood bookcases, all filled with books. There was a ladder hooked to a rail that ran horizontally across the wall, likely so that the books on the much higher shelves could be reached.

A freaking library. In. His. House.

Wonders never ceased.

"So good of you to come," Jericho Ardent—a short, slender man with reddish-gold hair, emerald green eyes, and cheeks covered with freckles—greeted cheerily, making his way across the room and holding out his hand for Ryan to take.

He was a lot shorter than Ryan had anticipated.

Ryan returned the gesture, firmly shaking Jericho's limp, smooth hand. Z did the same, and when Jericho turned away, Z shot Ryan a smirk, widening his eyes as though to say, "Seriously?"

Ignoring Z, Ryan moved farther into the room, joining Jericho in a plush seating area. Oversized leather furniture, strategically placed to face the enormous fireplace, sat atop a brightly colored rug with random geometric patterns. A glass-topped steel table pulled it all together.

"Have a seat, gentlemen," Jericho urged, guiding them with his outstretched hand to a small love seat across from him.

Ryan sat down, fully expecting Z to take the chair. He managed to hide his shock when Z took a seat directly beside him. Or at least he hoped he had.

And by direct, Ryan meant damn near on top of him.

They touched from knee to hip. As though that wasn't enough to throw Ryan off, he felt a tsunami of sensation course through him when Z casually stretched his arm across the back of the love seat, his thumb brushing along Ryan's shoulder. His muscles tensed, the air in his lungs seized momentarily, and a tremor shot down his spine.

Not good. Not good at all.

"Can I get you something to drink?" Jericho offered, his eyes darting between the two of them before a smile broke out on his lips. Instead of waiting for them to answer, Jericho clapped his hands as though the sight of them together was the greatest thing since virtual data storage. "How long have the two of you been together?"

Ryan said, "It's a relatively new thing," at the same time Z said, "Two years."

Jericho's head tilted to the side, seemingly confused.

"What I *meant*," Ryan clarified, tentatively placing his hand on Z's thick thigh, "is that it still *feels* new. But technically, we started dating two years ago."

Ryan tried not to notice the way Z's thigh muscle bunched from his touch.

"Very nice. I'm always excited to see an open couple. You'd be surprised how many same-sex couples are reluctant to let the world see how happy they are. And you two...mind if I say...yum. Let me get those drinks. What's your pleasure?"

Eccentric, that was the word Ryan would use to describe the man standing before them.

"Water's fine," Ryan told him with an answering smile.

When Jericho turned away, Ryan purposely pinched Z's thigh. Hard.

Z grunted a laugh. "Careful. Or I'll kiss you right here and show him just how *happy* we truly are."

Before he could pull his hand from Z's thigh, Z startled him, gripping his wrist and casually pulling his hand higher, Ryan's pinky finger brushing along the ridge of Z's... Oh, hell, Z was hard, his erection pressed against Ryan's hand.

Fuck.

Thankfully Jericho was facing away when Ryan snapped his hand free of Z's grip, swallowing hard.

Desperate not to think about how hard Z was, or laying the man out on the sofa and kissing him until they both needed air, Ryan turned his attention on the man in the process of pouring their drinks.

So Jericho Ardent certainly wasn't what Ryan had anticipated. The shrewd businessman who came across very different on the telephone had...flair.

Okay. He was flamboyant.

"And what about you, Mr. Ardent?" Z called out as Jericho was putting ice in three glasses. "Are you currently in a relationship?"

"Oh, please, call me Jeri. And yes, I am. My dear Amahn is the love of my life."

Jericho spoke eloquently, every syllable distinct and ringing with a colorful note.

When Jericho's gaze strayed to the far side of the room, Ryan's followed. There on the wall was an oversized painting of a man. A man Ryan assumed was Amahn.

"And how long have the two of you been together?" Z continued to carry the conversation.

Jericho placed all three glasses on a small tray and brought them over, setting two on the glass table between them, depositing the tray there as well, and keeping one glass for himself. "Two months." Jericho's eyes lit up. "He moved in here with me nearly six weeks ago."

They'd been together for two weeks before they moved in together?

Ryan's training had him taking a mental snapshot of that information and storing it for later. From what he remembered from the file, Jericho had mentioned that the painting—the fake—had been stolen within the last two months. Obviously Z was thinking the same thing, if the way he squeezed Ryan's shoulder was anything to go by.

In an effort to put some distance between him and Z, Ryan got to his feet, taking the glass of water as he walked over to the painting.

"This is nice," he said, not thinking as much. He wasn't much into art, nor could he ever imagine a life-sized painting of his significant other hanging on his wall. It was a little creepy, those nearly black eyes peering back at him, seeming to follow his every move.

"Thank you," Jericho replied, pride dancing in his voice. "It was Amahn's idea. He wanted me to always think of him."

Of course it was.

"So tell me about you two. How'd you meet?" Jericho urged.

Knowing how the game was played—a cover needed to resemble as much of the truth as possible—Ryan answered. "Work. Z's been working at Sniper 1 for a decade."

"How convenient," Jericho replied, sitting down and crossing his legs at the knees. "Must be nice to always see one another."

153

Not wanting to go into detail or give Jericho the wrong impression, Ryan asked, "Does work take Amahn away?"

"Oh, yes. He's so dedicated to his job."

"And what is it that he does?" Z asked, downing his glass of water in one gulp before setting it back on the table.

"He's the curator for the gallery," Jericho explained.

Ryan tried to once again hide his surprise. Was Jericho so blinded by...lust, love, whatever...that he couldn't see how all the pieces seemed to fall together?

"Has he worked there long?" Z asked.

"Three months," Jericho said with a smile.

Holy fuck. There was no way this was a coincidence.

"Tell us about the painting," Z urged, his eyes sweeping over Ryan slowly.

For the next few minutes, Jericho went into a long, boring story about how he'd acquired the painting from a gallery in New York, having stumbled upon it before understanding its true value. From what Ryan gathered, Jericho wasn't aware of the coded information. He seemed genuinely proud of the piece.

"So why keep it at the gallery?" Ryan asked when Jericho was finished with his story.

"It was originally here," Jericho explained, waving his well-manicured hand as though encompassing the room. "But Amahn said it deserved more attention. He suggested that it be kept at the gallery." Jericho's tone hardened. "Now I might seem naïve to you, but I assure you, I haven't made billions by doing rash things. So, I agreed, but the night before the painting was to be taken to the gallery, I replaced it. With a fake."

So, like the file said, Jericho didn't trust easily. Duly noted.

"Is it worth a lot of money?" Ryan probed.

"I take it you haven't heard the story behind the painting?" Jericho asked.

Knowing that this was going to be another long, drawn out story, Ryan knew he would have to sit back down.

A quick glance at Z told him that Z was looking forward to fucking with him some more. Unfortunately for Ryan, there wasn't much he could do about that.

So he sat.

THIRTEEN

Z was pretty damn proud of himself. He'd ruffled RT to the point the man couldn't sit still. For the past ten minutes, RT had fidgeted and paced, looking at everything except for Z. And now here he was, his ass planted back on the cushion beside him.

Evidently RT had realized Jericho was about to launch into another story, and he'd retaken his seat beside Z rather than risk falling over from boredom. Of course, Z had taken advantage of the situation. Since Jericho now expected them to be open, he figured he'd go for broke. Why the hell not?

Taking RT's hand, he linked their fingers, keeping RT's hand firmly in his and resting it on his thigh, which was, yes, pressed right up against RT's.

"Malcolm Jones was a starving artist for most of his life," Jericho explained. "When he met his wife, Jenny, they fell in love and settled down in northern Pennsylvania. It wasn't until they married that Malcolm's work began getting noticed. Speculation was that his pieces were simply lifeless until he met the love of his life."

From lifeless to ugly. Great.

Z wasn't sure how this set Malcolm Jones apart, but he pretended to be interested in the story, keeping his full attention—or at least his eyes, anyway—on Jericho. He was actually very aware of RT's hand in his, the way RT's knuckles brushed ever so slightly against his leg.

"I know, I know," Jericho said with a smile. "Boring, right? Well, that's not the interesting part. Jenny worked for the CIA, had for nearly a decade before she met Malcolm. During her tenure, *after* they were married, she'd gone deep cover once or twice. On the last of those missions, Jenny was kidnapped, taken during an assignment in Iraq. Friends of Malcolm say that he went crazy at that point."

"Crazy?"

"He was a conspiracy theorist. Thought that the US government was working to kidnap American citizens, ship them off, and purposely place them in the hands of the enemy. Staging it, I guess you could say."

"How would that benefit the US?" RT asked, genuine curiosity in his voice.

"According to Malcolm, they were using these kidnappings as validation for launching attacks on their enemies. Anyway, he believed that's what happened to Jenny."

Z wouldn't say as much, but it helped to explain the codes that were supposedly in the painting. If Malcolm believed the US government was working against its own citizens, he could've stolen national security secrets in an effort to barter for his wife's life.

"Jenny was gone for eighteen months and Malcolm believed she was dead. Oh, did I mention? Not only was he an artist, he was also a hacking genius."

And clearly a loon, but again, Z kept his thoughts to himself.

If this was going where Z believed it was, then there was no way Jericho didn't know about the codes.

"He hacked the government systems, stealing information in an effort to find where his wife was, believing wholeheartedly that they'd taken her. Apparently he'd unearthed quite a bit of information, some relevant, some not. For a solid year, he became obsessed, writing to newspapers, magazines, anyone who would listen to him. Granted, he wasn't a terrorist, so he wasn't looking to sell the secrets he'd uncovered; however, he wasn't above using them to get information.

"Surprisingly, after all that time, Jenny came home. Yes, she'd been kidnapped, and it had been legitimate. Some small terrorist cell in Iraq had snatched her along with a journalist she'd been talking to. By the time she'd come home, Malcolm had already begun transferring the information he'd relieved the government of to his paintings. He continued to do so, refusing to believe Jenny's story. In fact, he dragged her into his conspiracy theory, claiming she'd been sent back to the US to kidnap *him*, hence the murder-suicide. The man wasn't well. And to this day, no one seems to know how to decode the information in the paintings."

"There are more?" Z asked.

"Two others, but from what we know, they're in the hands of the government."

That would definitely make Jericho's painting worth quite a bit.

"So this painting…it has a secret code?" RT asked, the astonishment in his tone sounding authentic.

Okay, so maybe the guy could be a good actor, when he wanted to.

"That's the rumor."

"In the paint itself?" Z questioned, still trying to understand how someone would accomplish this.

"That, I don't know. Anything's possible, I guess."

"So it's worth—"

"A fortune," Jericho interrupted. "Far more than what I paid for it, which was why I had a fake—two, actually—made after I acquired it. I wasn't going to risk it being stolen."

Two fakes? Interesting.

"Where are you keeping the original?" RT asked bluntly.

For the first time since they'd stepped into the room, Jericho Ardent wasn't forthcoming with an answer.

"Mr. Ardent," RT continued, "we won't be able to protect your piece if we don't know where it is."

"Call me, Jeri, please," Jericho said more insistently. "And the thing is, the painting is safe. But as I explained to Mr. Kogan and Mr. Trexler, one of the fakes has been stolen. And I'm pretty sure the thief realizes he didn't get the painting he was after."

"So you believe the thief is a man?" Z questioned.

"No, not necessarily," Jericho answered quickly. "I don't know, just a turn of phrase. Anyway, this means the original is still safe, as long as it remains where it is. Only I'm up against a wall. In a few days, I have to place the real thing in the gallery. And that's the very reason I hired you."

"And what's the draw of replacing the stolen painting?" Z asked. "I mean, why would they believe that you suddenly changed out the fake for the real thing when they already know they stole a fake?"

"There's a big show coming up this weekend. Huge." Jericho's animation made Z smile. He was undoubtedly excited about his art. "We've got some of the best art experts across the world coming in to assess the gallery. The original will have to be there."

"Does Amahn know about this?" RT asked.

Jericho studied RT for a moment before he answered. "Of course. I had to tell him that the painting that was stolen was a fake. He was desperate. It's his name on the line. He wanted me to collect the insurance, to try and recoup my loss. I had no choice but to tell him."

Wow. And still it didn't seem that Jericho suspected that Amahn was likely the very instigator of all this bullshit.

"Does he know where the real painting is?"

"No," Jericho said. "And I don't intend to tell anyone until it's time to transport it to the gallery."

Well, it looked like they had their work cut out for them. Jericho Ardent—rightfully so—didn't trust anyone with the real painting. Which meant stealing it to turn it over to DHS was going to be damn near impossible. On top of that, it was highly likely that whoever had attempted to steal it would be back. And that meant Z and RT would have to exert some serious stealth if they planned to pull this off.

"Mr. Ard—I mean Jeri," Z began. "I think it's incredibly important that we're all on the same page here. You've hired Sniper 1 Security...*us*...to keep your painting safe."

"Yes," Jericho replied.

"Does anyone else know that you've hired us?"

"No."

"Amahn?" RT asked.

"No."

"Good," Z said. "It'd be beneficial to keep our identities hidden. We'll simply be...I don't know... maybe friends of yours? Just not your hired security. And that means we'll need to hire some rent-a-cops to handle the security at the gallery. We'll gladly help you transport the painting—"

"No," Jericho snapped. "I have that covered. I won't need assistance in that matter. I simply need you to watch the painting while it's on display for the night. Once the show is over, I'll have it transported back to its safe location, replacing it once again with the second fake."

Great. Definitely not going to be easy.

"Fine," RT said, sounding as disappointed as Z felt. "But we'll be undercover while we guard the painting. Does that work for you?"

Jericho studied them for a moment before responding. "You want to pretend to be my friends?"

"Yes," RT confirmed.

"The thing is…I don't allow many people to get close to me. And I'm in the public eye quite a bit. Especially when it comes to who I rub elbows with. How will I explain the two of you showing up out of the blue? No offense, but…look at you. You're clearly the king and queen of the Alpha Gay Squad, to which I don't have a membership." His smile brightened.

"Who's who?" Z questioned, chuckling.

"What?" Jericho and RT asked at the same time, obviously thrown by Z's question.

"Which of us is the king? Which is the queen?"

Jericho grinned, his perfect teeth flashing. "You're the king, my dear. Of that I'm certain."

Glancing over at RT, Z said, "You hear that? Me, king. You…queen."

RT fought his smile and Z's chest expanded.

"I find it hard to believe that we'd have anything in common," Jericho noted. "Other than our sexual preferences."

"Well," RT said solemnly, his fingers tightening on Z's hand, "that's certainly a start."

Never Say Never

By the time Ryan returned to the beach house, his nerves were fried. He'd spent less time thinking about Jericho and his painting and more time trying to fight his body's reaction to Z's touch.

Which was why, on the drive back, Ryan had vowed to himself to ignore his personal feelings about Z and focus solely on the mission at hand. He'd even gone so far as to produce the memories of the last time he'd ventured into a romantic relationship with someone who worked for Sniper 1. Kevin Fischer. The end result hadn't been pretty, and Ryan promised himself that he'd remember that, not allowing himself to get caught up in the moment.

After parking his bike in the garage beneath the house, Ryan made his way inside before sending an email to Kira, requesting that she send some additional clothes over. As a way to get closer to Jericho and to be formally introduced to Amahn, Ryan had reluctantly accepted an invitation for dinner tomorrow night. He and Z would be introduced to Jericho's other half, and Jericho had promised them a personal invite to the gallery showing on Saturday. He figured that jeans and T-shirts weren't approved attire, which meant they'd need more than what she'd already sent down.

Of course, as though dinner and the gallery weren't enough, Z had mentioned to Jericho they were having a get-together on Thursday night, which required Ryan to shoot off a mass email to the Sniper 1 team, looking for anyone within driving distance who was willing to attend.

"I'm goin' for a swim," Z announced when he walked inside, sidestepping him as Ryan continued tapping out a quick text to his father on his phone. "Join me?"

Ryan looked up. "In a minute."

The naughty smirk Z shot him didn't do much for Ryan's vow to keep his personal feelings out of it, but he pretended not to be affected, instead turning away from Z and heading into the kitchen.

As soon as he'd perched on one of the stools near the breakfast bar, Ryan's phone rang.

"Hey," he greeted his father.

"What's up?"

"Casper there with you?" Ryan inquired.

"No, but he's in his office. I can get him."

"Do that."

The discordant sound of Muzak replaced his father's voice when Ryan was put on hold. Putting his own phone on speaker, Ryan leaned back in his chair and watched Z as he stepped out onto the deck. Shirtless.

It was a crime for a man to have a back that damn sexy. All hard muscle and sleek lines. And his ass...

"All right, I'm here with Casper. What's up?" his father bellowed when he returned to the line.

Ryan jerked his eyes away from Z, embarrassed that he'd been gawking at the man. Clearing his throat, he regained his composure. "Z and I went to see Jericho today," he told them before going on to explain everything that had transpired. Neither man said anything as Ryan proceeded to give them the details of the painting's origin, as well as the status of the theft.

"So he's hiding the original. I take it he suspects this Amahn person as well?" Casper inquired gruffly when Ryan was finished.

"I'm not so sure. I'd like to believe he thinks it's possible, but the guy's seriously infatuated with him."

"But *you* think it's Amahn?" Bryce asked.

"He seems the likely suspect. I find it odd that all of this started once Amahn came into Jericho's life."

"Based on what you told us, I'm inclined to agree," Casper said. "What's the plan now?"

"We're having dinner with Jericho and Amahn tomorrow night, before the informal gallery showing. Then, as you know—I assume you got my email—Z's promised a get-together on Thursday night. Aside from the small gathering at the gallery, the actual show is on Saturday, and that's also the day the real painting's being transported to resume its rightful place on the wall. Z and I aren't privy to its current location, but we're hoping to figure that out between now and then."

"You mentioned there's a second fake?"

Ryan laughed without mirth. "Yeah. Jericho is seriously paranoid. He had two fakes created once he took possession of the painting. One of them was stolen."

"So it's safe to assume he knows the value of the painting?" Bryce asked.

"Definitely. Though, according to him, no one seems to know how to decode, which helps us some."

"What's the plan?" Casper questioned.

"Z and I are still working on that. I think we're gonna have to call in Trace or Clay, see if they want to lend a hand."

"Doing?" Bryce asked.

Ryan didn't say anything for a moment.

"Oh, hell," Casper grumbled.

"I think it's best if I don't share the details with you," Ryan admitted. There was no reason to make Casper and Bryce an accessory should things go to shit.

"I agree," Casper stated firmly. "Just do what needs to get done."

"We will," Ryan assured them both. "As of right now, we're building the relationship with Jericho. I need him to trust us, then we'll know how to proceed."

"Do you think you'll have it wrapped up by Saturday?" Casper was the one to speak that time.

Ryan peered out the window. He could see Z standing in the ocean. "That would be nice," he lied. "But I don't think that'll be feasible. I don't think we'll learn much of anything until we actually get a glimpse of the real painting. Once we know where he's keeping it, we can—"

"Don't continue," Casper interrupted. "Like you said, it's best we don't know. I think it's a good idea to pull in Clay or Trace. Either one. You can probably build a more solid cover if you get Trace. He can bring Marissa to the beach, which'll explain why he's there."

"Agree," Ryan said. "But..."

"But what?"

"I might not need Trace. I learned last night that Ally Shaffaer has a condo down here."

"The girl who owns Percolation?"

"Yeah."

Not only did Ally own the coffee shop on the first floor of the Sniper 1 building, but she was a writer. Apparently, according to his sources, she liked to disappear from time to time to write. He hated that he might have to interrupt her, but she could prove quite useful. On top of that, she was well known, so adding her to their cover would likely get them closer to Jericho.

"So you'll get Clay then?" Bryce inquired.

Everyone knew that Clay had a thing for the sweet coffee shop owner, which made him the best candidate. "Yeah."

"Smart," Casper agreed. "It sounds like you've got it all figured out. If you need anything, holler."

Ryan wasn't sure about the first part, but he knew if he needed them, they'd be willing to help. "Will do."

"Go enjoy some time outdoors, Ryan," Bryce said. "You deserve it."

"Right. Talk to y'all later."

Ryan disconnected the call, his eyes still tracking Z where he moved in the water. As much as he wanted to join Z, he wasn't sure that was a great idea. The more time he spent alone with Z, the more of a temptation he was.

As much as Ryan wanted him, he knew better.

Not to mention, he had a company to run, and this assignment wasn't the only one going on at the moment.

Instead of giving in to the lure of Z, Ryan resigned himself to checking in with all of his agents, leaving Z alone.

For once, he would've preferred to ditch work, but in the end, it would be best for them all if he simply remained focused on the task at hand.

FOURTEEN

As the saying went, patience was a virtue, right?

Z knew that, but he was having a damn hard time believing it. After the interaction between him and RT back at Jericho's, it wasn't as easy to stay away from RT as it had been before—not that he was bragging about his own willpower, because it hadn't been all that easy then, either.

But now... Hell, he'd felt the man's touch, which had reignited everything he'd experienced during that one night they'd spent together. How was he supposed to go forward and pretend he hadn't?

However, during all the emotional back-and-forth, Z couldn't forget what RT had said to him that morning at breakfast.

You're a serial dater. You don't use your real name most of the time, opting not to let the men you're with know the real you, claiming it's to keep your cover.

As he paced through the waves, allowing the water to crash against his calves, Z clenched his fists, trying not to let that frustration from earlier get to him.

Serial dater.

Right.

Because that was what he'd been doing for the past few years. Fucking random guys and pretending to be someone else.

That wasn't the case at all.

Then again, the rumor was his own fault, because rather than share a critical piece of his life with those who cared about him, Z had allowed everyone to make their own assumptions. He'd known all along that he would eventually regret that move. Like now. With RT. The last thing Z wanted was for RT to have the wrong impression of him, to think Z was the one-night-stand type.

He wasn't. Not by a long shot.

His thoughts veered back to when he'd held RT's hand, the way RT's fingers had felt against his skin. As he stood in the surf, letting the sun beat down on his head, Z imagined what it would've been like to kiss RT again, to feel the warm press of his lips against his own. It brought an onslaught of memories from the night in Coyote Ridge...

His body was on fire, his blood surging through his veins. Whipping out his dick and jacking off wouldn't have put a dent in his boner. Not with so many fantasies running loose in his head.

It looked more and more as though he wouldn't be making headway with RT at this point. When they'd arrived back at the house, Z had instantly noticed the shift in RT. He was back to business as usual, once again pretending nothing had happened between them. Nothing out of the ordinary, anyway.

Yet it had.

Z had touched RT, something he'd thought he'd never get the chance to do again. He'd held his hand, felt the warmth of his skin.

Releasing a heavy sigh, he looked up at the sky. There were a few clouds hovering above and more rolling in. He figured it would rain soon. He'd heard that was a phenomenon that occurred on the coast quite often. Rain wasn't unusual for whatever reason, even though the sun was still shining.

He was tempted to sit down in the water and weather it, allowing himself time to devise a plan. If he intended to seduce RT, he wouldn't be able to wing it this time. RT was smart, he was cautious, and above all else, he was hell-bent on ignoring whatever this was between them.

This was a job. An important one, at that.

Still, Z knew what he wanted, and he wasn't sure he could continue to pretend otherwise.

When the raindrops began to fall, Z turned around and trudged toward the stairs. Instead of going inside, he dropped into one of the lounge chairs shaded by the house, closed his eyes, and allowed the water to pelt him from above.

He heard the glass door slide open, but Z didn't open his eyes.

"It's raining."

Z smirked. "Is that what that is?"

RT didn't respond, but Z didn't open his eyes, either. He could feel RT staring, likely taking him in the same way he'd seen RT do a thousand times over the last couple of years. It was the same way Z looked at RT, but neither of them had copped to it.

Z figured it had to do with his extracurricular activities. Trace had assumed Z was out with men, and that was a rumor that had started long ago. Little did they know, but Z hadn't been with a man in... Damn, it'd been six months? Seven? He wasn't quite sure, but the last relationship he'd been in had been a while ago. Even then, he'd dated the same guy for almost three months before they'd parted ways. Apparently Z's job was too dangerous, and most of the men he ended up with couldn't handle the fact that Z put his life on the line for other people.

But there was someone who appreciated what Z did, and he'd been spending a lot of time with him over the years. Only no one knew, and he didn't intend to share that information.

"What're you thinkin' for dinner?" RT called from just inside the house.

As though prompted, Z's stomach growled. They'd skipped lunch, so an early dinner sounded perfect.

Turning his head to the side, he glimpsed RT standing in the doorway just over his shoulder. "Doesn't matter. You gonna cook?"

"I can," RT replied, sounding very unsure of himself.

Z laughed, turning back to face the sky. "I've heard the Trexlers can't cook. Isn't that the reason y'all have Lilah?"

Lilah Snider was the Trexlers' longtime housekeeper. She'd been with the Trexler family for something like thirty years.

"I can cook," RT said defensively.

"Yeah? Then show me your mad culinary skills." It was a dare, one he knew RT would take. It really didn't matter to Z who cooked. Or, hell, they could go out for burgers again. He didn't much care, just as long as he ate.

"Any suggestions?"

"Food," Z replied. "Hot food."

RT grunted, but then the glass door slid closed. Z peered over his shoulder once more to see that RT had gone inside. Just as well. The tension between them was potent enough to set the water ablaze.

Z realized he must've fallen asleep when the scent of food roused him and he noted the shade from the house blocking out the sun had nearly enveloped the entire deck. Getting to his feet, he stretched and then headed inside to where RT was rummaging through the kitchen.

"What're you makin'?" he asked, stopping on the other side of the island.

There was food…everywhere. And dishes. The place was a mess, and he couldn't help but laugh as RT stood there looking completely at a loss.

"So it's safe to say the rumor's true?" Z joked as he moved around to stand next to RT, staring down at the blackened food in the skillet. "What *was* that?"

RT glanced over at him, his blond eyebrows downturned. "Chicken."

Z snorted. "Maybe you should stay outta the kitchen." Flipping off the burner, Z took the skillet, tossed the chicken in the trash, and went to the phone.

"What're you doin?" RT questioned.

"Ordering pizza."

A small smile tugged at the edges of RT's lips, but he didn't give in to it completely. Z proceeded to place an order for pizza, not bothering to ask what RT wanted because, yes, he knew the guy well enough that he already knew RT preferred all veggies on his pizza. As far as Z was concerned, it was practically a sin to exclude meat, but Z didn't condemn the guy for it. He simply ordered two pizzas, one with only veggies, the other doused in meat—double meat.

Two minutes later, dinner was ordered, and Z helped RT clean up the kitchen.

"I called Clay," RT said after he finished rinsing the final dish and drying his hands on a towel.

"To help out?" Z already knew they were going to need a third person. It was the only option to get inside the gallery and Jericho's house. He'd made the suggestion as they were heading out of Jericho's that afternoon. If they could get a man on the inside while they busied their new "friends" at dinner tomorrow night, they could possibly locate the original painting.

"Yeah. He'll be down tomorrow."

"What did he say when you told him that Ally has a place down here?"

RT looked up and grinned; this time it wasn't forced. "I didn't."

"Smart man." Z chuckled. "He's got a hard-on for that woman, no doubt, but she makes him nervous. Have you seen him around her? He always looks constipated. And I don't think he says three words."

RT nodded. "I figured it was safer to let him figure it out when he was already here."

"I like it. And she's famous. Maybe our good buddy Jeri reads as well."

"That's what I'm hoping," RT agreed. "I'll reach out to her in a bit, see if she'd be willing to help out."

Neither of them spoke for a moment; they merely stood there, less than a foot apart, staring back at one another. RT, with his blond hair and glittering blue eyes, was one of the hottest men Z had ever encountered. He had a hard edge to him, yet a boyish face, which, Z assumed, was why so many people trusted him.

Feeling bold, Z took a step forward, closing the gap between them, never taking his gaze from RT's face.

"Y-you...you know this can never happen again, right?" RT stuttered, his voice soft, nearly a whisper.

Z pretended to consider that for a moment. "You know what my motto is, right?"

"What's that?" RT asked, his eyes briefly darting down to Z's mouth and then back up to meet his eyes.

"Never say never."

Never say never.

Ryan didn't know how to respond to that. As it was, he could hardly keep his eyes on Z's, wanting desperately to lean up and close the distance between them completely, to put his palms on Z's bare chest. They were so close a breath could hardly fit between them. Ryan's body was vibrating, eager to feel Z's touch again, to taste him, learn every inch so that it was burned in his memory forever, but his brain wasn't on board.

This was a bad idea.

It was one thing to pretend for the mission. But here…alone…

The temptation was far too great, and reliving the past was never a good idea.

"Why do you think so much?" Z asked, his voice low, sexy, a smirk on his perfect lips.

"Habit," Ryan answered.

Z's hand lifted, his big palm sliding over Ryan's jaw.

Damn it.

He fought the urge to lean into the touch. Before the incident with Z, it'd been a long time since he'd had a lover. Not that he suspected his reaction to Z was due to his abstinence as of late, because he remembered that night, knew how fucking good it had been. He'd been attracted to Z for a long time, but he'd always known it could go nowhere.

Z's thumb brushed against Ryan's lower lip, and he hated that he was about to give in. If Z leaned in, took control, Ryan would be hard-pressed to resist. Not that he would ever say as much, but Ryan longed for someone— namely Z—to take control, to show Ryan what it meant to submit, to allow someone else to lead.

"One of these days, I'm gonna put my mouth here again," Z whispered, his thumb still gliding over Ryan's lip. "And I'm not gonna stop there."

Ryan sucked in a sharp breath. He'd never heard Z talk like that. His deep voice was rough and sensual, but it was the take-charge tone that Ryan found himself reacting to. He'd always been the one in control, the one calling the shots. It had become second nature for him to lead, so the fact that Z was exerting his dominance... That was fucking hot.

"And you won't want me to stop," Z added, leaning forward enough that Ryan could feel his warm breath against his mouth.

Just when he thought he would get the chance to feel Z's lips on his once more, the big man moved back, his hand falling to his side as he smiled back at Ryan with a mischievous gleam in his eyes.

"But I'll let you come to terms with that a little longer."

Ryan nodded. He had no idea what he was agreeing to.

Z's cell phone rang, breaking the spell. While Ryan stood there, unable to speak or move, Z grabbed the phone, peered at the screen, and met Ryan's eyes once more.

"One more thing," Z said with a sexy grin. "Don't be surprised when it does happen again. Because it will. Of that, I'm absolutely certain."

Ryan stood there, still speechless as Z answered the call and disappeared back out onto the deck. Thrusting his hand through his hair, Ryan tried to catch his breath.

This was more than he'd anticipated, and he didn't know how to move forward from there. When he was with Z, he felt alive, normal even. He felt as though he could be himself and not be judged. The fact that he really couldn't cook hadn't seemed to faze Z one bit. Instead of bitching that the chicken was ruined, he'd called for pizza.

God, what was he going to do?

He thought back to Kevin and his stomach churned.

He and Kevin hadn't been exactly happy when things had gone to shit, but they'd been trying. More accurately, Ryan had been trying to make it work. They'd even talked about moving in together, but that had been put on hold because they'd been fighting so much.

And then, Kevin had done the unthinkable. He'd blown Z and Trace's cover, nearly getting them, as well as their client, killed in the process, and Ryan still wondered if it had been intentional. A way to get back at Ryan because things weren't going his way. That fuckup had cost Kevin his job and ultimately was the demise of their relationship. But Kevin had taken it a step further, accusing Ryan of sexual harassment. Claimed that Ryan had seduced him, then told him if he didn't sleep with him, he'd be fired. Kevin had even gone so far as to state the only reason that Sniper 1 had fired him was because he'd ended the relationship with Ryan.

None of it was true, but it had tarnished Ryan's outlook on relationships.

Only he'd entertained the notion of being with Z for at least three years now, and no matter how many times he told himself that business and pleasure didn't mix, he was having a damn hard time believing it. Especially after…

Fuck. He had to stop thinking about that night. It was a waste of time.

He could deny himself all day long, but the truth was, he wanted Z. Only he couldn't have him. Not permanently, anyway. There was no way Ryan could risk something like what had happened with Kevin. That damn lawsuit had been a nightmare. It'd been the result of a perfect storm, one Ryan still didn't quite understand.

Ryan paced, his hands still gripping his hair.

But this was Z. He'd been around during the Kevin debacle. He'd stood by Ryan and the Sniper 1 team through it all. Surely he wouldn't...

This was stupid. Ryan knew he shouldn't be contemplating the idea of sleeping with Z again. Briefly or otherwise.

But what he wouldn't give to be able to give in, take what he wanted, enjoy Z while he had him, and then walk away. They could still be friends at the end. Maybe. And if not, then he could still be Z's boss.

Couldn't he? Lightning didn't strike the same place twice, right?

With a rough growl, Ryan turned away from the window and grabbed a beer from the refrigerator before heading into the living room. He needed a distraction. And not the prime, no-holds-barred, alpha male who was tempting him beyond reason, either.

So he'd just have to settle for some television.

FIFTEEN

God, he hated these stupid fucking sit-down dinners. Couldn't the rich bastard do anything half-assed? Seriously, did there have to be so many people invited? There was no special occasion. It was just dinner.

"They're really cute together," the rich guy said, his usual flamboyant animation causing the others to grin and smirk.

Smiling when appropriate, he kept a close eye on Jericho while stirring his food around his plate, pretending to be interested when the only thing he wanted to do was get up and go. He wasn't hungry. Not anymore, anyway. Mostly because he had no idea why he had to come to this stupid dinner.

For the last half hour, the loony bastard had gone on and on about a couple of friends he'd met with earlier that day. The king and queen of the Alpha Gay Squad, Jericho had said, giggling mercilessly at his own joke. When anyone had tried to get backstory on who these guys were, Jeri had provided limited information, which had only raised his hackles.

Now was not the time for Jeri to be getting cozy with friends from his past. He needed him to stay focused. At this point, he'd already invested too much, and he wasn't interested in Jeri's personal life. As it was, he shouldn't have been there, sitting down at this table with all these people, pretending as though he actually liked them. The plan had been to convince Jeri to put that damn painting in the gallery, and then the next step was to steal it.

How freaking hard was that?

Sure, after a little prompting, Jeri had moved the painting to the gallery as suggested, or so he'd thought. Except that fucking painting he'd put in the gallery had been a fake.

A fucking fake that could very well get him killed if he attempted to pass it off as the real thing, which he'd almost done. It still boiled his blood to think that he'd been duped. By Jericho Ardent, no less. Seriously, the guy was...a freak. He walked around this ostentatious mansion like it was his castle, ruling the world from behind his desk, controlling every damn thing.

And to think the crazy fuck had pulled one over on him.

Sad thing was—despite how crazy Jeri seemed—he actually liked the guy. Jeri was nice when he wanted to be. It wasn't a hardship to use him, that was for sure. But he had a plan, and it wasn't going the way he'd anticipated.

He still remembered the day he'd stolen the painting right off the wall in the gallery. It'd been easier than he'd anticipated, but mostly because no one suspected him. Fortunately, rather than sell it to the highest bidder instantly, he had waited, wanting to see what Jeri's reaction would be to its disappearance, all while pretending not to know what had happened. And he'd never forget the look on Jeri's face when he'd come down to the gallery to see the empty space on the pristine white wall where the painting had originally been.

"Good thing I replaced it with a fake," Jeri had said, throwing him completely off his game.

A fucking fake. Where the hell was the original?

When the news had sunk in that he had stolen the wrong one, he'd come up with the idea of getting the insurance company to pay them off. Dropping a little hint had been easy. Or so he'd thought. Again. He'd quickly learned that Jeri actually had a conscience, and insurance fraud wasn't on his list of priorities.

Damn shame, too. It would've been something, at least.

Jeri's voice brought him from his thoughts.

"We're meeting them for dinner tomorrow night."

The others at the table seemed to be happy about that. Why, he had no fucking clue.

"It'll be good to spend time with some of your friends," someone said politely. "Any ideas on where you'll go?"

"I'll make the reservations," Jeri said politely. "I don't want anyone to have to worry about anything. There's too much going on right now."

"Are you still planning to replace the painting?" he asked Jeri directly, ignoring the glances from the others.

"Of course," Jeri said, looking up and meeting his gaze.

There were times—like now—that he got the impression Jeri was on to him.

"I wouldn't let the gallery down," Jeri added. "But I won't have it transported until the day of. And this time, I'm hiring security to guard the painting while it's on display at the gallery."

"That makes perfect sense," another of the pretentious assholes said.

No, it didn't. If Jeri put security in place, that would only make his job harder.

Jeri smiled sadly. "It's not that I don't trust—"

"We get it," one of the old guys said, interrupting.

"It makes sense," he added, inserting a significant amount of sympathy in the words, watching Jeri and the others closely. "We let you down."

Sure, he was laying it on thick, but he wanted to believe that in the past two months since he'd started this bullshit attempt to acquire one of the most valuable pieces of art he'd come in contact with, he had learned what buttons to push to get his way.

But just when he expected to receive the reaction he was after, Jeri surprised him.

Instead of placating him and telling him that everything would be all right or possibly sharing the details of where the painting was currently located, Jeri simply nodded. Then he pushed back his chair, stood, and left all of them staring after him.

Shit.

That wasn't the way it was supposed to go.

SIXTEEN

Z had spent the last hour sitting out on the deck watching the water as the sun descended behind the house. After dinner, he'd taken a phone call, retreated to his room for a shower, then returned to sit outside and watch the evening sky turn dark.

The view wasn't as intriguing as when the sun came up over the water, but it was nice, nonetheless. Now that it was dark, he found himself debating whether or not he should go to bed. He wasn't tired, but tomorrow would be a long day, so if he were smart, he'd take advantage of the downtime.

Finally resigning himself to turning in, Z got to his feet, grabbed the empty bottle of water from the table, and went inside. After locking the door and turning off the lights downstairs, Z ventured up to the second floor. As he passed RT's room, he stopped suddenly, drawn to the sight before him. There, sitting on the edge of the bed, was RT, staring out the window. His blond hair was still damp from his shower, and Z could see small droplets of water on RT's naked back.

Z had the sudden urge to lick the water off RT very, very slowly.

When RT didn't move after several long minutes, Z stepped into the room, clearing his throat to announce his presence. "You okay?"

RT's head snapped around as he jumped to his feet.

"What were you thinkin' about?" Z inquired.

Rather than answer, RT shook his head, his eyes never leaving Z's.

Whether it was an outside force that propelled him forward or his own stupidity, Z found himself moving closer, eliminating the distance between them. And when RT didn't back up or attempt to get away from Z, he couldn't resist the urge to touch him.

Ever so slowly, Z placed his hands on RT's towel-covered hips, sliding them upward, grazing the hard planes of RT's stomach. His skin was warm and smooth, causing Z to continue trailing his hands over him. He wasn't thinking about what he was doing; his body had a mind of its own.

"We can't," RT breathed roughly, his eyes locked with Z's.

Z had known that would be RT's answer, but there wasn't any conviction behind the words, which was why he didn't pull away. Dragging his fingers lightly over RT's skin, Z took another step closer until their bodies touched, from knee to chest.

"We can do whatever we want," Z told him softly. "There's no one here to stop us."

Z allowed his lips to hover over RT's, trying to hold back but desperate to kiss him, to taste him again. For two weeks, he'd thought of that night, of the way RT had driven Z to madness by fucking him like a man possessed. Z had made himself crazy, desperately hoping for more, all while knowing RT would do his damnedest to keep that from happening.

Except RT wasn't pushing him away now.

"Z…"

Rather than listen to RT's excuses, Z covered RT's mouth with his. He didn't press for more, simply made RT aware of what he wanted. RT's breath shuddered in his chest, but still he didn't pull away. Allowing his hands to slide up RT's arms, Z cupped the back of RT's neck and pulled him closer, their lips pressed together.

"I want you," Z whispered. "More than I've wanted anything in a very long time."

"You had me," RT muttered.

"No," Z clarified. "*You* had *me*. There's a big difference."

RT pulled back, his eyes widening as he stared up at Z. There was no way to discern what the man was thinking, but Z didn't budge, waiting to hear what RT's excuse would be.

"It was one night, Z. It was a fucking mistake." RT's tone was harder than before. "And don't try and tell me you weren't as into it as I was."

Z was confused. "Of course I was."

RT didn't respond to that.

"But it wasn't a mistake. Not for me, anyway. It was a long time coming."

RT took a step back and Z released him.

"It should've never happened."

"Maybe," Z agreed. "Not the way that it did, anyway. But it was inevitable."

"I was drunk," RT countered.

"The hell you were." Now Z was getting angry. They hadn't talked about that night, but now that they were, Z wanted to clear the air between them. "You were as present in that fucking hotel room as I was. I watched your face."

"It was sex, Z!" RT exclaimed. "One fucking night. You of all people should be familiar with that."

Z felt as though RT had sucker-punched him. He wanted to argue, to tell RT he was wrong, but he couldn't find the words.

"What makes me different from any of the others, Z? Why can't you just walk away?"

Taking a deep breath, Z found his voice. "Because I never fucking walk away! That's not who I am, but you wouldn't know that because you won't give me a fucking chance."

"A chance? I'm your boss. Or did you conveniently forget that?"

No, he hadn't. RT was always there to remind him of that fact. Maybe not in so many words, but when things got too difficult for RT, he hid behind his job, used it like a suit of armor.

RT's eyes glittered with heat. Z wasn't sure if it was lust or anger, but he wasn't going to walk away until he knew for sure.

"This is something better left alone, Z. Now, if you don't mind…" RT started to move around Z, heading for the door.

Unwilling to let him get away that easily, wanting to clear the air between them, Z grabbed RT, pushing him into the wall and crushing his body against him. Before RT could shove him away, Z grabbed his wrists, holding them down at RT's sides before crushing his mouth over RT's.

The moan that escaped RT's chest had Z pushing for more, thrusting his tongue into RT's mouth, seeking, searching. He wanted more; he wanted everything. And he wanted it all from RT. Z was so tired of this cat-and-mouse game they'd played for the past few years. He'd always allowed RT to be in control, to make the decisions, but he couldn't sit by and allow RT to keep him at a distance.

Not after what had happened between them.

RT's hands gripped Z's thighs, yanking him closer, and only then did Z release RT's wrists. Grabbing RT's head, Z sought a better angle. The kiss was full of heat and need, but Z could still feel RT's hesitation.

He battled with himself, not sure whether he should walk away or pursue RT. The decision was taken from him when RT slid his hand into Z's shorts, gripping his cock firmly.

"Oh, God," he groaned against RT's lips. "Don't stop. Please don't stop."

Without a word, RT stroked Z's cock, making his body sway from the pleasure that assaulted him. His knees were weak, his breathing labored as his release bore down on him. It wasn't right, not like this, but Z couldn't seem to stop it. He was torn, wanting RT with a desperation he didn't even understand but knowing it would likely backfire in his face.

Once again, the decision was stripped from him when RT released him suddenly, but their bodies remained together, Z's hands still cupping RT's head.

"We can't do this," RT acknowledged softly. "I'm sorry, Z. So fucking sorry."

"You mean *you* can't do this," Z clarified, adjusting himself and ignoring the painful throb between his legs. "Because I damn sure don't have a problem with it." Pulling back, he kept his hands on RT's head, staring into his eyes. "You can't let your past dictate your future," Z told him, his own frustration apparent.

RT didn't have a comeback, but his fury radiated from him. Pissing him off was the last thing Z wanted, but he'd obviously pushed a little too far. When RT shoved Z away, he relented, moving back and letting his hands drop to his sides.

"It was a mistake," RT spat. "Now let's fucking leave it at that."

Z didn't want to leave him, not like this, but it was clear RT had come to a final decision. Since it wasn't in Z's nature to argue when it was pointless, he gave RT exactly what he wanted.

He walked away.

What the fuck was he thinking?

Ryan wanted to punch the wall. He wanted to do some serious damage, but he managed to hold himself back.

Watching Z walk away... It was harder than he'd thought it would be. The whole thing had been his fault. When Z had appeared in his room, Ryan had been fighting the urge to go to him. It was as though Z had read his mind, showing up when he had.

And the kiss... Fucking hell. Ryan could still feel Z's lips on his, the rough stubble on his jaw abrading his skin. The velvety-smooth length of Z in his hand.

Goddamn. Why the hell did he let shit like that happen? He was supposed to be stronger than that, better equipped to resist things that weren't good for him.

What the fuck did you expect?

Fuck. He hated that goddamn voice in his head. The one that reminded him he couldn't throw caution to the wind or he'd be back in the same boat he'd started out in after Kevin.

Plopping down on the edge of the bed, Ryan dropped his head in his hands.

What he wouldn't give to take Z into his arms once more, to take the time to explore him slowly. If he did give in, Ryan damn sure didn't want it to be quick this time. He wanted to savor Z, explore every inch of him, to learn everything about him.

And maybe that was what bothered Ryan the most. He didn't want a one-night stand with Z. If he could do it all over again, he wouldn't have snuck out the next morning, but facing Z... He didn't know how to do that. Didn't know how to accept responsibility and admit that he wanted more.

Instead, he was here in this house, alone with Z, wanting something he couldn't have. It had been what he was thinking about when Z walked into his room in the first place. He'd been contemplating the consequences of his actions, trying to predict the future, wondering if there was even a remote chance for him to be happy.

Because if he could be happy with anyone, it would be Z. They were polar opposites in many ways, and Ryan could accept that they complemented one another. For years, Ryan hadn't thought about spending the rest of his life with anyone, but if he allowed his thoughts to get away from him, Z was always there, a reminder of what true happiness could be.

But then Ryan had gone and been an ass, just as he always was. As much as he wanted to regret sending Z away after instigating that, Ryan also knew it was for the best. Not only was Ryan in a position of authority at Sniper 1, but they were also on a job. What precedence would that set if people were to find out that Ryan was fraternizing with employees? Or taking advantage of them when they were on assignment?

Sighing, Ryan fell onto his back, covering his face with his arm.

Why did things have to be so difficult?

More importantly, why couldn't he just get past this? It wasn't as though Z were the first man to tempt him since Kevin.

But he's the only man who matters.

Great. And now the voice was back. Just what he didn't need.

SEVENTEEN

Wednesday evening

Z tugged at his tie, hating every second that he had to wear the damn thing. Since he was only an hour into a very long night, Z wasn't sure he was going to survive without ripping it off and tossing it to the floor.

The suits he owned were purchased with only the job in mind. When he wasn't working, he preferred jeans and a T-shirt. Simple. Casual. Easy. This—the dark suit, white shirt, and colorful tie that Kira had retrieved from his closet and had delivered to the beach house—this shit was for the birds.

Had it not been for the fact he couldn't simply buy a suit off the rack due to his size, he could've picked out his own attire for the evening. Instead, he was wearing the one suit he preferred the least because apparently Marissa was quite fond of it, or so Kira had informed him in the note that had come with the delivery.

"Quit fidgeting," RT muttered as they made their way through the fancy restaurant, following the hostess.

"I hate this shit." Z spoke out of the corner of his mouth, keeping a smile plastered on his face.

"You look good, so…"

Z smiled—no longer forced—when RT trailed off. He doubted the man had meant to share that compliment with him, but he'd take it. Hell, he'd take anything RT wanted to dish out. After their heated discussion last night, quite frankly, Z hadn't been sure he'd ever receive a positive comment from RT again. He'd consider this progress.

With those words still echoing in his head, they approached the table where Jericho and Amahn sat. Both men stood, holding out their hands in greeting when Z and RT came to stand beside them.

"So glad you could make it," Jericho said enthusiastically.

Amahn didn't say anything as he eyed both RT and Z when Jericho introduced them, though he only used their nicknames, which was smart. Taking his seat, Z kept a cautious eye on Amahn. The man looked exactly like the creepy painting in Jericho's library, only not as two-dimensional. Or creepy. He was older than Jeri, that was clear. By about fifteen years, from what Z remembered. Black hair, styled perfectly, smooth chocolate skin, and nearly black eyes, Amahn Chopra was a rather attractive man. Based on the background they'd pulled up, Z knew he was a US citizen, raised by his parents who had come from India nearly forty years ago, and when Amahn spoke, his definitive accent confirmed his Indian heritage.

"It's a pleasure to meet you," Amahn said confidently. "Jericho has told me so much about you."

Z doubted that, but he understood the pleasantry. Figuring RT wanted to take the lead on this particular meal so that they didn't contradict one another, Z sat idly by, listening and waiting.

"So what is it that you do?" Amahn asked after the server had poured wine.

Z stared at the glass, wondering what the hell he was supposed to do with it. He didn't drink wine, didn't even *like* wine. He needed a beer.

As though reading his mind, Jericho laughed, lifting his hand and calling the waiter back. "What's your pleasure?" Jericho asked.

Z looked up at the waiter. "Corona?"

The man narrowed his eyes at him.

"Heineken?"

No response.

"Fine, no import?" The man again didn't respond. "Right. Then bring something domestic on tap. Both of us." Apparently the waiter understood that, nodding and disappearing back toward the kitchen.

"We're...entrepreneurs," RT told Amahn. "We dabble in a little of this, a little of that."

Z knew it was imperative that they kept their identities on the down low if they expected this to work, but based on Amahn's inquisitive gaze, that wasn't going to be as simple as it sounded.

"And you're down here on business?" Amahn probed.

"Pleasure, actually," RT answered. "We've got a house on the beach. Unfortunately we don't get to visit as often as we'd like."

Z leaned back in his seat, casually resting his elbow on the back of the chair. Yes, he was aware he lacked some of the decorum necessary to reflect wealth and status, especially in this...whatever this place was. A French restaurant of all places. He didn't even know what French food was. He doubted French fries counted.

But even as he sat there surrounded by well-dressed people assembled around fancy, white-linen-covered tables with flickering candles as a centerpiece, Z refused to be someone he wasn't. It was one thing to pretend to have a certain job or come from a particular area, but Z wasn't going to fake it when it came to who he really was on the inside. He definitely wasn't one of these pompous assholes whose closet consisted of three-dozen neck nooses to go with their Armani suits.

"RT's two favorite things are the beach and art," Z lied through his teeth when it appeared Amahn was looking for more detail. "So, I thought it'd be nice for an extended vacation. He gets the sand and the sun, I get the water, and thanks to our good friend here, we get art. Our interest was in meeting with a few collectors while we're here."

"That's why we sought out Jeri," RT tacked on, his eyes glued to Z's face, clearly stymied by Z's blatant misrepresentation of the truth.

Amahn's lips pursed slightly, likely surprised at the casual reference to his lover. It hadn't eluded Z that Amahn had referred to him as Jericho a few moments ago. "And I hear you're having a get-together tomorrow night. Will anyone we know be in attendance?"

Yes, Amahn was suspicious; there was no doubt about that.

"You'll have to come and find out for yourself," RT said teasingly. "Shall we?" he asked, nodding toward the menu.

"Yes. Of course." Jericho's laugh had an edge of anxiety to it. "Let's order. That's why we're here. We can continue the interrogation over the meal."

Right. And Z figured that wasn't very far from the truth. It was obvious that Amahn didn't trust them. But that went both ways. Z's first impression of the guy was that he was a snake. He was after something and he had to assume it was the painting. That or Jericho's money.

Either way, he was going to be someone they would definitely have to keep their eyes on.

Turned out that the questions at the beginning were the highlight of the meal. For the past hour and a half, Z had endured endless explanations regarding what Jericho and Amahn did for a living, including boring details about the art at the gallery.

He was surprised he hadn't fallen asleep.

With three beers under his belt, Z was feeling better than good, although he was hardly buzzed. Thankfully they'd taken a cab over, which meant he didn't have to worry about driving home. But he did have to worry about groping RT when they were alone. The beers had relaxed him enough that he could deal with eating the fancy meal that tasted like cardboard, but they hadn't helped ease his desire to put his hands all over RT.

As it was, Z had focused most of his attention on RT. Watching him interact with Jericho and Amahn...it was no wonder the man had taken Sniper 1 Security to new heights since he'd taken on more responsibilities in recent years. The guy was phenomenal. He spoke eloquently yet still appeared casual and approachable.

And sexy as fuck.

RT reminded Z a lot of Jessie Pavelka, the fitness expert/television host. Well, except that RT was taller.

And right now...as RT sat talking art with Amahn and Jericho, Z was pretty damn sure the man had never been hotter. He rocked that light gray suit and that dark blue tie like no one's business.

"Well, I think it's time we move on to more interesting things," Jericho said. "I know you've got to put finishing touches on your party, which we will definitely be at, by the way, so what do you say we head out?"

Z got to his feet before the others, but they quickly followed suit. RT shot him a questioning look, but Z merely smiled, then placed his arm around RT.

Yep, that's right. I'm touchin' you.

RT didn't pull away, which only encouraged Z. As they headed for the door, he maintained a position close to RT, his hand on RT's back as though guiding him.

After Jericho and Amahn climbed into the sleek black car that had been waiting for them, Z asked the valet to hail a cab.

It wasn't until they were in the cab that RT turned to him.

Z fully anticipated a scolding for something he'd possibly done to screw shit up tonight, but that wasn't what he got.

"We're meeting them at the gallery," RT informed him, heat blazing in his eyes.

Right. Gallery.

Fuck.

No, he definitely didn't get a scolding, nor did he get anything else from RT. What he got...was a stupid reminder that the night wasn't over yet.

They'd taken a cab to the gallery, and during that short trip, Ryan could've sawed the tension with a chainsaw and still not cut completely through. His vow to keep distance between him and Z was failing miserably, mainly because he found he enjoyed Z's company, more so than he'd anticipated. More so than he *wanted*.

Ryan had managed to talk himself around in circles when it came to Z. Last night, before he'd finally dozed off, he had committed himself to keeping things professional between them. That was a hell of a lot easier to do when he wasn't around Z. Pretending to be a couple... It wasn't helping. Ryan found himself hoping, sometimes convinced that he could manage a relationship with Z if he'd just give it half a chance.

But then he remembered what happened if it all fell to pieces. And that was the equivalent of being doused in ice water.

Now, as he stood next to Z, he could feel the man's overwhelming presence. Once again, he drew attention from those in the room, many eyes slowly perusing him. Ryan knew what he was feeling couldn't possibly be possessiveness, but he didn't know what else to call it, so he pretended not to notice all the people looking their way.

The gallery was just as Ryan had expected. Sterile, white, and cold. Since he wasn't much into art, the colorful, abstract paintings on the wall and awkward sculptures were lost on him. Z as well, if his expression was anything to go by.

But the floors were nice. Odd thing for Ryan to notice, but he appreciated the stained concrete. The charcoal color flowed throughout and offset the bright white walls. There weren't any ceilings, only a variety of lighting that hung haphazardly from the rafters in an obvious attempt to once again highlight the main focus of the place.

A waiter cruised by, his gaze rolling over them briefly. Apparently they didn't look like the champagne type because he didn't bother to stop. Not that Ryan minded. He simply wanted to look around, and he was in no way referring to the art.

They needed to identify the offices, see if they could get in to sneak a peek of what was inside. Maybe find a clue. Anything that might lead them to the stolen painting now that they knew the original was off in some secret location. In all honesty, Ryan still strongly believed that Amahn had something to do with it. Which meant the gallery was a good place to start looking.

"I'm gonna head to the little boys' room," Z announced, a little louder than necessary.

Ryan glanced over, and when he met Z's gaze, he realized the man had said the words at that unnecessary decibel for a reason.

Ryan nodded his understanding and then moved toward Jericho and Amahn, who were standing in a corner with an older woman. They were talking softly, the woman apparently interested in one of the pieces on the wall. Not wanting to interrupt but hoping to divert the pair if they ventured off, Ryan pretended to peruse the pictures on the wall.

"I hope you don't mind me saying, but you don't look like the artsy type."

Ryan glanced over to see a pretty young woman stepping up to his side.

"Looks can be deceiving," he told her politely.

"This one, it's rather... I don't know what the word is."

"Confusing?" Ryan questioned, smiling. "The odd use of color draws the eye in different directions."

The woman smiled up at him. "You're right, looks *can* be deceiving."

Ryan smiled back at her.

"Cassandra Chapman," she said by way of greeting, holding her hand out to him.

"Very nice to meet you. You can call me RT." He gave her hand a gentle shake. It was crucial that he kept a low profile, and since the Trexler name was well known in certain circles, Ryan felt using his initials was good enough. Just to be safe.

"God-given name?" she teased.

"What my friends and family call me," he replied with a small smile.

Another waiter came by, this one actually stopping to see if he wanted something. In order to fit in, Ryan took a glass and pretended to sip. He shot a quick look across the room to find Jericho and Amahn still conversing with the older woman, so he turned back to the painting.

"And what are your thoughts on this one?" Cassandra asked, nodding at another painting.

"Not exactly my taste," he said, referring to the blurry images painted on the canvas.

Ryan feared if he talked too much, he'd give away the fact that he hadn't the slightest clue about art.

For the next half hour, he allowed Cassandra to lead him around the room while he kept an eye on Jericho, making sure the man stayed within sight. He was scanning the room when Z reappeared, a sigh of relief escaping him when he noticed the big man walking toward him.

Z's eyebrows lifted when he approached, his eyes darting to Cassandra.

"Cassandra, I'd like you to meet Z, my—"

"Boyfriend," Cassandra interrupted with a huge grin. "I should've known. As the saying goes, the good-looking ones are either married or gay."

"Nice to meet you," Z replied, taking her hand and gifting the woman with his signature grin.

She stared at them both for a moment, apparently contemplating her next question. Ryan was glad he hadn't been taking a drink when she finally spoke.

"I don't suppose the two of you are interested in a threesome?"

Z laughed as though the question was perfectly natural. Ryan inhaled sharply.

"Ma'am, trust me, if we swung that way, you'd be the first one in our bed." Leave it to Z to flirt ruthlessly in an art gallery.

The response seemed to placate her, for which Ryan was grateful. It was the next thing that happened that threw him off.

Before Ryan could contribute to the conversation, Z turned to him and pressed his lips right on Ryan's. It stole the breath from his lungs and nearly caused him to drop his champagne. He was saved from utter embarrassment when Z's big hand wrapped around his, keeping the glass from falling to the floor.

Figuring Z was going along with the ruse, Ryan managed to control his response.

Barely.

Swallowing hard, he glared at Z when he pulled back, a promise of retribution in his eyes.

They needed to get the hell out of there. And fast.

"It was so nice to meet you," Z told Cassandra. "But if you don't mind, I need to steal him away for a bit."

"Not a problem," she said, still eyeing them as though they were an after-dinner mint—of the chocolate variety.

Ryan allowed Z to lead him away, his legs feeling slightly unsteady as he followed him. "How'd it go? Find anything?"

"There're a couple of offices, but they're locked," Z informed him.

"And that stopped you?"

Z smirked. "Not at all. However, while I was snooping, someone went into the other, so I had to make like wind and scatter. There's a desk in Amahn's office, but it's locked. I need to get back in there."

Ryan shook his head. "Not tonight. We'll send Clay back over when he gets down here. See if he can find something."

Z didn't seem happy with the response, but like usual, he didn't argue.

"Find anything else?"

"One of the file drawers was unlocked, and I found a picture. Several, actually."

"Of?"

"Amahn's family."

"Family? Like, his parents?"

"No," Z said, his eyes hard. "Like…his wife and kids."

"What?" Ryan turned to peer across the room. Amahn had his hand on Jericho's arm. The pair looked cozy, and strangely, they did look like a couple in love.

"Wife and kids," Ryan muttered before glancing back at Z. "How old do the kids look?"

"Grown. In their early twenties at least."

That was an interesting twist. One Ryan would need to toss around for a bit.

EIGHTEEN

While the two of them stood in the middle of the gallery, a handful of people milling about, Z couldn't seem to take his eyes off RT. He was still imagining that kiss...and wishing like hell he'd added a little tongue.

Hindsight and all that.

It'd been interesting to throw RT off course so easily, but it hadn't been his intention. Merely an attempt to keep up the charade, pretend to be a couple for the others around them. Especially since he'd nearly been caught snooping in Amahn's office just a few minutes ago.

Not that he intended to tell RT that. What the man didn't know wouldn't hurt him.

But now Z was ready to head out.

Z inched closer to RT, keeping a smile plastered on his face as he got close to RT's ear, inhaling the sexy, spicy scent of him as he said, "Please tell me you're ready to get outta here. I think I'm allergic to this place."

When another waiter scooted by, RT placed his champagne on the tray.

Good sign.

When RT took Z's arm casually, he pretended that an influx of sensation hadn't hijacked his nervous system. Focusing on putting one foot in front of the other, Z allowed RT to lead him over to Jericho and Amahn. He hated to head out too early, but he worried that spending too much time in that place might cause him to break out in hives.

Jericho's eyes widened and a smile tilted his lips. "RT. Z. Are you gentlemen enjoying yourselves?"

RT nodded, returning a polite smile. "We are, but we need to be going."

"So soon?" Amahn eyed them skeptically.

"We've got to put some finishing touches on that party," Z said, mirroring Jericho's words from earlier.

"Well, we look forward to seeing you tomorrow night." Jericho nodded toward them.

"Likewise," Z added. He was, of course, lying, but in his line of work, that wasn't necessarily a bad thing. Not always, anyway.

When they finally climbed into a cab a good fifteen minutes later, Z yanked at his tie, loosening it.

"Will you quit fidgeting?" RT hissed.

Z glanced over, studying him for a moment. The guy was stressed, but Z wasn't sure why. As far as RT knew, the gallery excursion was a success. After all, RT didn't know that Z's acting abilities had been put to the test when one of the gallery employees had caught him coming out of Amahn's office.

"What were you doing in there?" the man asked sharply. "You're not supposed to be back here."

Knowing he couldn't very well deny being in Amahn's office, Z offered the other guy a grin. "Sorry, man. You know how it is." Leaning in conspiratorially, Z continued, "The john was otherwise occupied. Figured it wouldn't hurt if I borrowed a private one. If you know what I mean."

Thankfully, the topic of bathroom habits flustered the guy, because he rolled his eyes. "You need to go back that way. And don't let me catch you back here again."

"Gotcha, bro," Z agreed with another smile.

It hadn't been the most compromising position Z had ever found himself in, but he didn't want the gallery employee to go tell Amahn, so he'd slipped him a twenty in agreement for keeping it between them.

"Somethin' wrong?" Z inquired now, still studying RT.

Instead of answering, RT turned to face him, and the next thing Z knew, his world had been tipped on its axis.

Ryan was at his tipping point.

It'd all started when Z had appeared from his bedroom wearing that damn suit, looking…fucking edible.

The guy wasn't known for dressing up; then again, none of them were. Over the years, Ryan had seen Z in almost everything—and yes, even naked—but in that particular suit…Ryan hadn't been able to take his eyes off of him.

And then through dinner, Z had held his own, pitching in when necessary but allowing Ryan to carry most of the conversation. He was so damn smart, and he'd apparently done his research prior to the meeting. Enough that he'd even awed Jericho and Amahn a time or two with his tidbits of information on art history.

However, through it all, he'd still been Z. Relaxed, cool, witty.

Then, at the gallery…

Well, Ryan could go on and on, but his brain was misfiring, and he wasn't sure what to do about it. Needless to say, he was turned on to no end. And he knew that resisting Z—right, wrong, or indifferent—was no longer an option. Not tonight, anyway.

Now, as they got in the cab to head back to the beach house, Ryan waited until the cab pulled away from the curb before he turned to Z. When the other man's eyes widened slightly, Ryan knew that Z was aware of what was about to happen.

Electricity crackled in the air between them.

Leaning in, Ryan kept his eyes locked with Z's until he was too close to see him. It was then that he moved in until his mouth brushed Z's. Lightly at first, but Z modified that instantly. His big hand came around to cup the back of Ryan's head possessively, pulling him closer, melding their mouths together as Z's tongue slid across the seam of Ryan's lips.

The world exploded in brilliant, unfathomable sensation. Ryan's body lit up like a pyrotechnics finale when his tongue met Z's. It was…cataclysmic. Devastating. Earth-shattering.

And Ryan never wanted it to end.

Aching to touch Z, Ryan slid his hands inside Z's jacket, finding rock-hard muscle beneath the soft cotton of his dress shirt. He wanted skin to skin, but considering where they were, that would have to wait.

The kiss seemed to go on forever, deepening, growing more and more out of control by the second. It took everything in Ryan's power to remain cognizant of their surroundings. They were in the back of a cab, after all. They couldn't pursue more until they were in the privacy of the beach house.

Z's rough growl sent shockwaves of pleasure through Ryan, making his dick throb, longing for Z's touch.

Finally, Z pulled away. Or maybe Ryan did. He didn't know for sure, but they didn't remove their hands, Z's still cupping the back of Ryan's head, his fingers latching on to Ryan's hair, tugging slightly while Ryan gripped Z's waist firmly.

"We need to do that more often," Z said breathlessly, his voice low enough only Ryan could hear. "A fuck of a lot more often."

Ryan couldn't contain his smile. The look on Z's face was priceless and so damn sexy. His eyes were hooded, his lips wet and slightly parted, as he appeared to be processing what had just happened.

When the cab came to a stop, Ryan realized they'd made it back to the house. After handing money over, he exited while Z did the same on the opposite side. His body was revved to go, desperate to pick up where he and Z had left off just as soon as they got inside the—

"Son of a *bitch*," Z rasped as he came to stand beside Ryan.

The cab disappeared into the night, leaving them both standing there, staring at…

Clay's motorcycle parked in the driveway.

"Has anyone ever mentioned that your brothers have horrible timing?"

Ryan choked out a laugh. No, they hadn't, but he couldn't help but agree with Z.

Clay's timing sucked.

"Is he stayin' here?" Z questioned as they made their way up the stairs to the porch. "Please tell me he's just pillaging the fridge and he's sleeping in a tent on the beach."

Honestly, Ryan hadn't thought about it.

Shit.

Then again, maybe this was a sign. Maybe Clay showing up and effectively putting a halt to whatever had been about to transpire between Ryan and Z was a sign.

One Ryan shouldn't ignore.

Stepping inside, Ryan pulled off his tie and shrugged out of his jacket.

"Hey," Clay called from the living room. He had his booted feet propped up on the coffee table, his ball cap turned around backward, a baseball game on the television. "Don't y'all look spiffy?"

"Shut it," Z said good-naturedly before disappearing upstairs, probably to change.

"How'd it go?"

"Not too bad," Ryan said. "You?"

"I scoped out the house after they left. Security's tight."

"So no luck?"

Clay grinned. "You don't give me enough credit, big brother. Keep in mind who we are."

Ryan waited for Clay to continue.

"With Dom's help, I got in. We disengaged the alarm temporarily. Twelve thousand square feet is a lot to cover, especially with Ardent's staff there, but I managed to check out the most obvious places. Nada. I don't think the painting's there."

Ryan hadn't figured it would be.

Clay tipped his beer to his lips, his eyes locked on Ryan.

"You look...different. What's up?"

Ryan fought the heat that infused his face, as well as the urge to flatten his hair. If he had to guess, he probably looked as though he'd just been thoroughly kissed by a sexy giant. Which he had.

Memories of that kiss flooded him.

"Tired," he lied, glancing over at the stairs. "I think I'm gonna call it a night."

Clay didn't move, other than to hold up his phone. "I got your text. I'll make a midnight run to the gallery."

"Not alone," Ryan insisted.

"Not much of a choice," Clay said, peering around the room. "No one else here."

"Fine," Ryan huffed. "But have Dom or Austin on the phone with you in case you run into problems. They'll be able to help virtually."

"Will do."

Slowly heading to the stairs, Ryan suddenly wished his brother would find other accommodations for the night. A tent on the beach wasn't a bad idea. He really wanted to be alone with Z.

"Oh, before I forget," Ryan said, stopping on the stairs. "Ally's got a place down here. 'Bout five minutes away, actually. She'll be here tomorrow night, too."

Clay showed the first signs of life, sitting up straight, his feet dropping to the floor, and putting his beer on the coffee table. "Ally? Ally Shaffaer?"

"The one and only," Ryan confirmed, watching his brother's interested expression.

"Does she know I'm here?" There was a hint of uncertainty in Clay's tone.

"Yeah. She said she'd be more than willing to be your date tomorrow night and at the gallery on Saturday." She hadn't really said that, but since Ryan had played matchmaker with Ally in order to convince her to come, he figured what the hell. Might as well expand on it.

"Really?"

Ryan moved up a couple more steps. In for a penny, in for a pound. "Yeah. She likes you. You stayin' here tonight?"

"Thought I would," Clay said, his gaze straying up to the second-floor landing. "That a problem for you?"

Yes. "No. Not at all. See you in the mornin'."

Clay nodded but thankfully didn't say anything.

And with that, Ryan snuck upstairs, his heart pounding in his chest, and it had nothing to do with the climb.

NINETEEN

After changing out of his suit, Z had stopped in the hallway, listening to the rumble of voices from below. He couldn't make out what they were saying, but he wasn't ready to interrupt. Because his night had taken a sudden turn backward, he was biding his time, hoping for a little alone time with RT but not wanting to give RT too much time to start thinking again. The man was on the verge of giving Z whiplash with his frequent mood swings as it was.

Which was why Z was waiting for RT when he reached the top of the stairs.

Using his hand to cover RT's mouth, Z jerked him closer, then pressed him up against the wall, smirking at the shock that registered on RT's too handsome face.

Lowering his hand, Z replaced it with his mouth, crushing himself up against him, his hands sliding into the cool strands of RT's blond hair. RT didn't try to pull away, which only sparked another flame, causing Z to ignite beneath the sensual onslaught.

RT took control, pushing until Z was the one against the wall, their tongues dueling, neither of them giving up control but both of them desperate to maintain it. When RT's rigid cock slid against Z's—the only thing that separated them was their clothing—he couldn't stop the rumble that came from his throat.

Then it was RT's turn to pull back and slam his hand over Z's mouth. Their eyes met, locked, but neither moved. There were numerous unspoken questions between them.

Did they continue this?

If so, where?

But the biggest question…should they?

As far as Z was concerned, this moment had been inevitable. No matter how hard RT tried to hold himself back, Z still felt that connection, that need for more. However, he knew that Clay was just downstairs, and honestly, the next time Z was with RT, he didn't want to have to hold back. And he had no intention of rushing things, either. Call him old-fashioned.

"I'm gonna say this again," Z whispered. "Your brother has horrible timing."

RT leaned up and kissed him softly, stunning Z with the sweetness of the gesture. He didn't linger, though. "Well, he won't be here forever. But until then…"

Z knew how that sentence ended. He didn't like it, but he understood. Rather than dwell on the fact he was on the verge of imploding, he slid his thumb over RT's bottom lip once again, then stepped away. "I've waited this long," Z told him. "What's a little longer?"

Instead of lingering in the hallway and making things more difficult for both of them, Z headed back downstairs, leaving RT staring after him. Z passed Clay on his way.

"Where're you headed?" Clay questioned.

"Swim," he said tersely.

He knew he shouldn't harbor any ill feelings toward Clay, but he had to admit to being disappointed. The man was there on assignment; it wasn't his fault he'd interrupted probably the single most important night of Z's life thus far. The night he would get another chance to prove to RT how fucking good they could be together.

Before heading out, Z grabbed a bottle of water. Setting it on the edge of the pool, he stripped out of his T-shirt and climbed in, this time leaving his shorts on rather than going in naked. It wouldn't do for Clay to come outside to find Z in his birthday suit.

Although, if RT wanted to join him...

He sank under the water, keeping his eyes open as he tried to relax. When he managed to calm himself somewhat, he started swimming laps until he was tired, which took longer than he'd expected, given the way his hormones were rioting.

Z had no idea how long he'd been out there, staring up at the inky black sky, counting stars while the warm breeze fanned his face and the sound of the waves crashing in the distance soothed his frayed nerves, when he heard the sliding door open.

He turned, catching a glimpse of RT standing in the doorway, wearing only a pair of loose-fitting shorts. Z's body instantly stirred to life once again. He hadn't expected RT to come out there. In fact, he'd expected the man to find a way to withdraw entirely, yet there he was.

Neither of them said a word. RT closed the door, then joined Z in the water, keeping a safe distance between them. Z maintained his position against one wall, his arms spread wide along the concrete edge. He never took his eyes off RT.

Long minutes passed before RT finally spoke. "What you said earlier..." RT dipped down, submerging his shoulders and moving his arms in the water, still keeping several feet between them. "That you'd waited this long. What did you mean by that?"

There was a distinct insecurity in RT's voice. Z found it hard to believe the man had a vulnerable side, but if he wasn't mistaken, it was coming to the surface.

"You didn't think this was spur-of-the-moment, did you?" Z replied, keeping his voice low.

"It had crossed my mind," RT said.

Of course. RT was under the impression Z was a playboy, sleeping with endless men on a nightly basis. Z had to wonder whether RT would call him on it. Thankfully, he didn't. Z certainly didn't want a replay of their conversation at breakfast. It'd hurt to know that RT truly believed the rumors, more so that he didn't have a problem throwing them in Z's face in order to keep his distance.

But that wasn't important right now. RT had come to him.

Z finally said, "I've noticed you for years, Ryan. *Many* years. And I'm pretty sure you know that."

His statement seemed to surprise RT. That or the fact that Z had referred to him by his name again, rather than the nickname he'd been given. Either way, Z liked the response, the way one golden eyebrow cocked, his mouth partially open while he stared back at Z, obviously at a loss for words.

"Why now?" RT suddenly asked.

"Why *not* now?" Z countered.

"I'm your boss."

"Not out here you're not," Z informed him firmly. He wasn't going to allow RT to play that card. As far as Z was concerned, they weren't at work.

More silence lingered between them, until finally Z spoke again. "Come here."

And when RT didn't hesitate, Z knew his night was about to take a turn back in the right direction.

At the gruff command of Z's voice, Ryan moved toward him. He didn't hurry, but he managed to eliminate the distance between them without hesitation or second thought.

Z still stood with his arms spread wide, his broad, bare chest glistening in the moonlight. Ryan's fingers itched to touch him, to trail over the hard muscle covered by smooth, bronze skin.

When he was within inches, Ryan stopped, looking directly into Z's dark eyes, waiting.

"You want to touch me," Z stated.

It wasn't a question, and the blunt statement threw him for a moment.

"Yeah," Ryan finally agreed. "I do." *Everywhere.*

"What are you waiting for?"

Casting a glance at the house to make sure Clay wasn't watching from the living room—which he wasn't—Ryan then placed his hands palms down on Z's broad chest. A slideshow of memories flashed in his head, all from that night in Coyote Ridge. Z naked. Z with Ryan's cock in his mouth. Z willing and eager, begging while Ryan impaled him over and over, fucking him hard.

Holy fuck.

The big man hissed in a breath, pulling Ryan from the memories as a flurry of adrenaline pumped through Ryan's body. For as dominant as Z was being, the man melted beneath Ryan's touch, which was strangely empowering. Sliding his hands over Z's wet skin, Ryan didn't do anything more than memorize the hard planes, the rigid grooves of his abs while he continued to stare back at Z.

Z's stomach muscles contracted beneath his palms. Ryan was tempted to slide his hands lower, wanting to feel Z's cock, to know just how hard he was. But he refrained. For now.

"I want your mouth on mine," Z growled, a sexy, throaty rumble that had Ryan's cock hardening even more than it already was.

Throwing Z's words back at him, Ryan said, "What are you waiting for?"

"You," Z said easily. "To kiss me."

Z was undeniably good at this alpha, controlling thing.

Unable to resist the incredible lure of the man, perhaps because he'd done so for so long, Ryan leaned in and pressed his mouth to Z's softly. Z kissed him back, their lips sliding together gently until Ryan slid his tongue over Z's bottom lip, then captured it with his teeth.

Another growl, but Z still didn't move. That encouraged Ryan to take what he wanted. With his hands on Z's sides, his thumbs making circles over smooth, wet skin, Ryan gently bit Z's lip, then slid his tongue into Z's mouth.

Again, Z didn't move, allowing Ryan to have complete control. In an effort to maintain that control, Ryan tilted his head, offering him a better angle as he explored Z's mouth, his body catching fire when Z's tongue moved against his own. The kiss was sensual, with an underlying intensity that neither of them released entirely.

It was like the first time Ryan had kissed a man when he was sixteen years old, finally understanding what he'd been holding back. An exploration. A defining moment in his life, proving to him that this was what he wanted.

When Z started to move, Ryan instantly grabbed his forearms, keeping him from reaching for him. "Stay there." Moving closer, so that their torsos rubbed against one another, Ryan deepened the kiss, moaning his pleasure as he did.

Ryan's palms glided down Z's arms until their hands touched. Z linked their fingers, stealing Ryan's control when he moved his arms, forcing Ryan's behind his back, effectively holding him prisoner.

"Much better," Z groaned against his mouth.

Without the use of his hands, Ryan had to get his fill using his mouth, which he did. The kiss shifted from an exploration to something much, much hotter, significantly more potent. A brutal, brilliant mating of tongues and lips and teeth. It stole Ryan's breath. He was overcome by sensation. The warmth of Z's lips, the smoothness of his chest, the ridge of his erection pressed between their bodies.

When Ryan tried to break his hands free, desperate to touch Z again, Z held firm, keeping him pinned in place.

"Let this be enough for now," Z whispered, his lips grazing Ryan's.

Ryan was confused. He wanted more, he wanted to feel the impressive length of Z's cock against his palms, he wanted to taste Z's skin against his tongue. He didn't want limits.

"More," Ryan returned gruffly. "Need more."

"We've got plenty of time. But for now, this is enough."

Ryan pulled back, peering into Z's eyes, seeking answers as to why Z was insistent on halting this. Acting as though they were inexperienced teenagers.

Z evidently read his mind because his response answered Ryan's questions.

"When the time's right, I'll be here," Z said. "But not tonight. Not yet. I want you to myself when that time comes."

Ryan's head was spinning. He'd had plenty of lovers in his lifetime, but never—at least not since high school—had any of them been content with a heated make-out session that didn't go further than first base. Hell, even when he'd been with Z the first time, they'd moved right into the intercourse stage, no hesitation.

But he had to admit, despite the fact that he wanted to feel Z's hands on his entire body, this was erotic. Allowing Z to take control, that was a first for Ryan, something he'd never encountered before but something he'd dreamed about. He'd always preferred to top because it came natural. There'd been plenty of times he'd wondered what it would be like to be on the receiving end, but he'd never had the opportunity. Or maybe he had and he hadn't taken it.

Not that he was now, but it just seemed…right. Like the pieces were falling into place naturally, without effort, without thought.

Another first for Ryan.

And that was the reason he decided to give in, to take the pleasure Z was willing to give without question. Tightening his fingers around Z's, which were still holding Ryan's hands firmly behind his back, he leaned in and kissed Z again.

Content for the first time in a hell of a long time.

TWENTY

Thursday

Z should've known that the Sniper 1 team would make what should've been a casual get-together into one of the biggest parties of the year—at least from an internal perspective. They didn't do anything half-assed.

Casper and Elizabeth Kogan had come down with their Escalade packed full of decorations. Casper's son Trace and Trace's wife, Marissa, had arrived with tables and chairs that they proceeded to set up along the beach down below. RT's parents, Bryce and Emily, had had the good sense to bring food and drinks—an endless supply of wine, beer, and liquor to go with the hamburgers and hot dogs that Evan had agreed to cook. And yes, because Evan was a Trexler, they were all leery about the outcome and had no qualms about telling him so.

Hunter and Conner, along with Conner's fourteen-year-old daughter, Shelby, came to set up the fire pit, while Clay and Colby merely stood around directing people who didn't need directing. RT's aunt and uncle, Stephanie and TJ, hired a DJ, as well as put together a rather impressive guest list. And a handful of others had come along to simply provide warm bodies for the party. In total, around forty-five people were in attendance with just a day and a half notice. Pretty impressive.

It didn't look like a spur-of-the-moment shindig, that was for sure.

For the past hour, the guests had arrived, many of them employees of Sniper 1 Security, but there were quite a few VIPs who were close to Casper and Bryce as well. Seemed everyone appreciated a good party.

On top of that, Courtney came with her husband, Maximillian Adorite—a freaking gangster who had his hands in quite a few business ventures, most of them illegal, though he'd never been convicted of a single crime. Apparently they didn't travel light, either, because along with Max and Courtney's security team—an apparent necessity when you had the sort of enemies that the Adorites had—they also brought Max's sister, Ashlynn, and her bodyguards. And from what he'd overheard, it wouldn't be a party without the second-in-command of the Southern Boy Mafia, so that was why Max's previous right-hand man and now underboss of the organization, Leyton Matheson, was also in attendance. Z wondered whether or not he was the only one who'd noticed the way Leyton eye fucked Ashlynn at every opportunity.

Not that it was any of his business.

From his perch on the veranda, Z was overseeing the final setup as well as the interactions of the people when RT approached, coming to stand beside him. RT leaned casually against the wall, a beer in his hand as he kept his eyes focused on the others, the same way Z was.

"Jericho and Amahn just arrived," RT said unceremoniously, not looking directly at Z.

Ever since last night's make-out session in the pool, RT hadn't been looking at him. Not directly, anyhow. Z wasn't sure why that was, but he didn't have time to worry about it, either. Throughout the day, they'd pored over the blueprints of Jericho's house as well as the gallery, looking for a secret hiding place, to no avail. Clay had shot down every nook and cranny they had identified, confirming he'd searched it. Aside from the servant's quarters, it appeared Jericho's mansion wasn't a viable place to store an expensive painting that you didn't want anyone to find.

And now, the guests of honor had just arrived, and that meant they needed to entertain them while Conner and Colby headed over to the gallery to see what they could find out, at the same time Hunter and Trace went back to Jericho's. They still hadn't identified where the original painting was being held, and it looked as though they wouldn't actually get up close and personal with it until its arrival at the gallery. However, they refused to stop searching, desperately seeking that one piece of evidence that would lead them to the treasure they sought.

Not the way they'd hoped things would go. But the overall objective of the night was to rub elbows and chat it up with Jericho and Amahn while the others handled the tactical recon. If they didn't find that painting tonight, their hands were pretty well tied until Saturday night. At that point, they'd have to come up with another plan on how to steal it and replace it with the fake they had yet to locate or acquire. All while hoping the thief didn't get his hands on it first.

Thank God most of their missions didn't have so many unidentified variables. This was easily turning into a fiasco. Oh, and they couldn't forget the fact that RT and Z were supposed to be playing a part—one that required them to be rather intimate amongst their guests.

"So, how's this supposed to go?" Z asked, glancing over at RT, hoping he could provide a solution to get through this with their covers in tact.

"How's *what* supposed to go?"

"Well, we've put on a show for Amahn thus far; he thinks we're a couple. As does Jericho." Z glanced around at the people he considered family. "They're gonna ask questions."

RT didn't say anything, and Z had to wonder whether he'd given it any thought. The idea of a party was great. Get Jericho and Amahn there, distract them while they tried to locate the painting, but Jericho and now Amahn expected Z and RT to be out and proud, a loving, touchy-feely couple. Kind of hard to do when it was all subterfuge.

"What do *you* suggest we do?" RT inquired, his voice low enough that only Z could hear.

"I say we keep up the charade," he told him truthfully. "I doubt anyone's gonna out us here."

Then again, it was quite possible that the women might make a big deal out of it. It wasn't a secret that Z and RT were gay. No one questioned that. However, seeing the two of them acting as though they were together... That would likely produce some smiles and encouragement from the women.

He knew these people. They were family, a close one at that. They supported one another, and though they focused a majority of their lives on their company, family still came first for them.

And Z didn't particularly mind who noticed. It was RT he worried about.

"Then we'll go with that," RT said, his voice not as firm or cold as it had been throughout the day.

Z jerked his head over to look at RT. "Seriously?" A seductive smirk turned up the corners of RT's mouth, and Z was tempted to kiss him. Right there in front of everyone. Then again, maybe… "You want me to kiss you, don't you?"

RT's eyes widened, but the smile didn't disappear.

"Be careful what you wish for, Ryan," Z said, purposely using his first name again.

"I like when you call me that," RT responded, surprising Z.

"That right?"

"Yeah."

Well, then. Z wasn't sure what to think about this. He'd figured, based on his actions throughout the day, that RT had decided to run and hide, but looking at him now, the man looked ready to combust.

Good to know.

"RT, so good of you to invite us."

The spell between them was broken when Jericho and Amahn wandered over.

Remembering the ruse, Z moved closer to RT but didn't put his arm around him. He used his beer as an excuse, holding it in his left hand, which prevented him from wrapping RT in his grasp.

"We're glad you could come," RT said politely. "How's the setup for the gallery showing?" he asked Amahn directly.

"We've got most of the items in place," Amahn said, his eyes darting back and forth between RT and Z as though he was still trying to figure them out.

Z didn't doubt that he was. That was what guilty people did. And as far as Z was concerned, Amahn was still the prime suspect in the theft of the fake painting. He had opportunity, sure. But the one thing Z had yet to figure out was what his motive was, other than money. But even that didn't fit. The guy would surely fare better simply by being with Jericho.

Hopefully tonight, with the help of their strategically placed guests, they would get some answers. After all, that was what the party was for.

Hunter kept close to Trace as they hugged the wall of Jericho's ridiculously large house. Upon his arrival at the party, Hunter had been informed by RT that his assistance was needed. Never one to turn down a job, he had agreed only to learn that he was being sent to break into a house that was occupied while everyone else got to enjoy the party.

As far as he was concerned, he got the better end of that deal. Then again, he wasn't feeling all that sociable as of late. Not with everything going on in his life.

But it was good to be back. He'd missed his family while he'd been attempting to outrun his demons.

"Earth to Hunter?" Trace whispered. "You ready?"

"Waitin' on you," he informed his brother.

Although Jericho—their client—and his lover, Amahn, were at the beach with the others, his entire staff was still at the house, roaming about as they normally did. Hunter wasn't all that comfortable breaking into an occupied residence, but it wasn't as though he hadn't done it before. It required a little more stealth than usual, especially one with the type of security Ardent had, but it was doable.

"Dom?" Trace said into the transmitter he wore to communicate with their IT genius, who was back in Dallas, manning the fort.

"I'm here. Just say when."

Trace started moving toward a door at the back of the house and Hunter followed.

"Give me a minute to pick the lock," Trace told Dom.

"Sure thing. When I say go, you'll have fifteen seconds to get in and close the door behind you. Then the door alarms will be reengaged, but I'll leave the motion sensors off. I've temporarily disrupted the security cameras, so the guards on duty will see everything on a loop. Good?"

"Yeah," Trace said. "As long as Hunter doesn't keep draggin' ass."

Hunter stared at Trace, unable to hold in the laugh. It'd been a while since Trace had given him a hard time. "I promise, Grandma, I'll do my best to keep up."

"You ready, Trace?" Dom asked.

"Two seconds," Trace told him, twisting the metal tool, then turning to look at Hunter as he smiled. "We're good on this end."

"All right, boys…" The sound of a keyboard clacking was heard, followed by, "Go."

On Dom's command, Hunter followed Trace inside the house, half expecting the alarm to sound, but fortunately, they were greeted by the lonely sound of silence. Closing the door behind him, Hunter stuck close to the wall while Trace moved across the room and peered out the door.

Trace motioned with his hand for Hunter to follow.

So follow he did.

TWENTY-ONE

After a brief conversation with Jericho and Amahn, Ryan mingled with the other guests, keeping his eye on the pair as they merrily interacted with everyone at the party. He noticed they were both social, but Amahn appeared...curious. Or perhaps cautious was a better word. Amahn's gaze continued to stray to Ryan throughout the night, and he figured Amahn was still trying to figure out how Ryan and Z played into all of this. The man wasn't stupid. It wasn't a coincidence that they'd dropped into Jericho's life when the painting had suddenly become a hot commodity, and it was clear Amahn suspected something.

Knowing the other man's eyes were on him, Ryan purposely interacted with everyone, finally making his way over to Ally Shaffaer.

"Hey," she greeted, drawing out the single word with a twinkle in her eye.

Ryan hugged her briefly, then stepped back. "Thanks for coming."

"Thanks for inviting me."

He glanced around. "Where's Clay?"

"I was hopin' you could tell me," Ally said with a chuckle. "I think I make him nervous."

"He bailed?" Ryan couldn't help but laugh.

"Technically, no. He was going to get us some drinks. That was ten minutes ago."

Ryan smiled down at her. "Don't worry, I'm sure he's trying to work up the nerve to come back."

"I don't mind," Ally said. "I'm just grateful to be around people. I've been cooped up for three days now, and it can get quite lonely."

"The solitary life of a writer?" Ryan inquired. Ally had told him that there were times she could go a week at a time without interacting with another human. According to her, the fictional characters in her head were quite adept at keeping her company.

"Something like that," she answered with a smile.

"You come here often?" he asked, knowing it sounded like a line. "To the beach, that is."

"When the characters are chatting and I need some space, yes. Maybe three or four times a year."

"And it helps?"

"Most of the time. More so because it eliminates the distractions. I don't have to worry about the coffee shop, and I can't come up with a million other things to do." Ally glanced back at the beach house. "Nice place, by the way. I was talking to your father. He said they just purchased."

Ryan laughed. "Apparently. That was news to me a couple of days ago."

"So you're here on assignment?" she questioned in a conspiratorial whisper.

Ryan nodded.

Ally peered up at him, a question burning in her gaze. "Is Clay working, too?"

"He is. That's the reason we needed your help," Ryan told her. "I'm hoping the two of you can offer a distraction while we attempt to get some things taken care of."

"Put me to work," Ally laughed. "I'll consider it research for a book."

Her eyes scanned the area around them briefly.

"He'll be back," Ryan assured her.

"That obvious, huh?" Ally snorted. "He's mastered the art of disappearing when I'm around."

"Not this time. He... Clay likes you."

"He's a nice guy," Ally stated, sounding as though she were closing a door on that particular topic. Ryan knew when to take a hint.

"Until he comes back, do you wanna go chat with Jericho and Amahn? If you hear anything you might think is important, just let me know," Ryan said, nodding toward the couple standing near the bonfire with the others.

"Sure. But it'd help if you told me what I'm tryin' to find out."

"I don't know, and that's the problem. We're tryin' to find a hiding place, I guess you could say. Something that'll lead us to a piece of art that Jericho has stashed."

"Got it."

Ryan's phone rang as he led Ally toward the bonfire, where Z and the others had begun to congregate once the sun had slipped lower and lower in the sky, leaving darkness in its wake.

"Excuse me a minute," he told Ally, then hit the button on the phone to answer the call. "What's up?"

"Nothin', man," Conner grumbled roughly. "And that's the problem. We managed to make it inside—their security's a joke, by the way—but nothin'."

"Did you check Amahn's office?" Ryan inquired, pivoting on his heel and heading in the opposite direction, seeking privacy. "Z said the desk was locked."

Ryan watched as Ally approached Amahn and Jericho, who'd been intercepted by Kira.

"Scoured it from top to bottom," Conner said. "Nothin' to be found other than a few personal items and an inventory list. You sure he's the one?"

"No, not positive. But it makes sense," Ryan told Conner.

Amahn might not be the one after the painting, but he was overly suspicious, which raised the hair on the back of Ryan's neck. He wanted to know what the man was up to.

"Well, bro, it looks like this is a dead end."

"Shit." Ryan knew they were running out of time to come up with a plan to intercept the painting before the show. If they couldn't get their hands on it sooner, they'd have no choice but to attempt to steal it when it was on its way to the gallery or after. Either way, they still had to get their hands on one of the fakes to replace it with.

"Did you hear from Trace or Hunter?" Conner inquired.

"Not yet," he told Conner. "I doubt they'll find anything, either."

Going back to Jericho's was a long shot, but Trace was convinced there was something to find, and he was hell-bent on locating it. When it came to matters of national security, they all sweated a little. They loved their country, most of them having served in one branch of the military or another. So when someone threatened the place they had put their lives on the line to protect, they took it personally.

"Hold up," Conner grumbled roughly.

Ryan scanned his surroundings, making sure no one was within earshot while he waited for Conner.

"Colby found somethin'. Looks like your good buddy Amahn's got a storage unit not too far from here."

"Check it out," Ryan instructed, hoping like hell it'd provide them with something.

"Will do. We'll get back to you."

Ryan disconnected the call and placed his phone in his pocket. He had hoped he would hear from Trace or Hunter by now. He needed some good news, like they'd found a storage unit for good ol' Jeri and the painting was now safe and secure and ready for transport to DHS.

Unfortunately, things didn't seem to be working in Ryan's favor.

As far as the assignment, that was.

His gaze strayed to Z, who was laughing at something Casper had said.

Ryan remembered Z's kiss from the night before. Well, more accurately, it'd been a make-out session that had put any of his teenage rendezvous to shame. Didn't matter that he was thirty-two years old, Ryan had felt like a damn hormonal kid when they'd been in that pool. Especially afterward, when he'd climbed into his bed alone, his dick in hand. The hand job had eased the ache in his balls but not much more than that.

Tonight wasn't much different, but he'd been trying to refrain from jumping Z at the first opportunity. First, it wasn't professional, and second, his entire family would be there to witness should he lose his self-control.

Sure, he knew he'd appeared standoffish during the day, but he had to continuously remind himself that they were here for a reason. A mission. One that couldn't go by the wayside because they couldn't fight their hormones. Plus, Clay had been there, eyeing them warily at every turn.

Granted, Ryan was ready and willing to give in just as soon as Z said the word. Why Z seemed to be the one who was hesitant now, Ryan hadn't yet figured out. From all the stories he'd heard... Like the one about...

Okay, so they hadn't so much been stories as they'd been statements. People claiming Z was promiscuous. Wild. Now that he thought about it, he had no actual proof of that, only what his gut told him. Still, he'd never seen Z with a man, and they all tended to hang out together when they had the chance. Z wasn't in the closet, not by a long shot. So why wouldn't Z bring his partners with him when they got together if he had been seeing someone?

He's never home. And I'm starting to think he's got a secret life. You know…one where he has a husband and kids stashed somewhere. Every night at eight, he disappears. Sometimes he comes home before sunup, but more often than not, he doesn't come home at all.

Those were his sister's words. Ryan had overheard a conversation between Marissa and Courtney one day in the office when Z hadn't arrived as they'd expected.

If he wasn't out playing house, where *did* he go?

As he sipped his beer, Ryan continued to watch Z, realizing he didn't know all that much about the guy on a deeply personal level. Other than the pertinent information such as his medical history, where he'd grown up, what his parents' names were. He also knew that Z was loyal, dedicated, and honest to a fault.

His thoughts drifted back to their conversation over breakfast. The one that Z had reacted quite badly to.

"You're a serial dater. You don't use your real name most of the time, opting not to let the men you're with know the real you, claiming it's to keep your cover.

Ryan had been hoping, somewhere deep, deep down, that Z would refute the statement, tell Ryan he was out of his mind for believing that. Unfortunately, Z had appeared angry when he'd clammed up, then told him it was time to go to work.

Since then, Ryan had thought about Z's reaction numerous times, but he'd yet to find an opportunity to bring it back up. As a rule, Ryan had never jumped to conclusions, but it dawned on him—especially after Z had gotten angry—that he'd done exactly that where Z was concerned. He'd listened to the rumors—rumors that Z had never tried to deny—and made a shitload of assumptions.

"Whatcha hangin' out in the shadows for?"

The sound of his cousin Kira's voice yanked Ryan from his thoughts. He downed the rest of his beer and shot her a quick look. "Took a call."

"Yeah?" Her smile lit up her face. "Was that while you were ogling Z from afar?"

"*What*? No. I wasn't—"

"Don't bother to deny it," Kira interrupted. "We've all seen it. But it's cool. So how's it goin'? The assignment?"

Grateful she dropped the subject of Z, he said, "It's gonna fizzle out fast if we don't get a lead on the painting."

"That's why I'm here," she said with a huge grin. "I was talking to Jericho and Amahn—he's kinda overprotective, by the way. Amahn, that is. Anyway, when Ally showed up, they started chattin' about her condo on the beach. Turns out, Jericho's got one, too. Not far from here."

Ryan's full attention turned to his cousin. "Damn. Why hadn't I thought of that?"

"Because you're too busy tryin' to get in Z's pants?"

Kira's offhanded remark wasn't helping Ryan focus.

"Kidding," she said with a giggle. "I gotta get back."

With a short wave and another face-splitting grin, Kira left him standing there, thinking about what she'd said.

Jericho had a condo on the beach.

Did Amahn know about it? Obviously he had to if Jericho had mentioned it.

Knowing they had a little time left, Ryan shot a quick text to Kira's brother Dominic.

I need an address. All properties in the area owned by Jericho Ardent. Send to Trace.

After that, Ryan shot off another text. This one to Trace, informing him he'd be receiving an address shortly and to check it out as soon as possible.

And now, the only thing Ryan could do was wait for more details.

Which meant he had no excuse to keep his distance from Z.

As he slogged back through the sand, Ryan realized that he was looking forward to spending some time with Z.

A lot more time.

TWENTY-TWO

"Are you serious?" Jayden questioned, giggling. "You really did that?"

Z grinned against the lip of his beer bottle as he scanned the faces over the flames from the bonfire. He scooted over so that RT could join him on the bench he was seated on. "Not me, no. But the twins were always pulling one prank or another."

For the past half hour, they'd been pulling stories about the Walker brothers from him. It'd all started after his trip down to Coyote Ridge to help out Brendon Walker. When he'd come back, Z had shared a few stories with the ladies in the office, and since, they'd been interested in hearing more about his rebellious childhood.

So he gave them what they wanted.

"An ice machine in the cafeteria?" Jayden confirmed. "Did they get caught?"

"Them, no," Z explained. "But their brother Zane took the fall 'cause his brothers had too many marks. They would've been expelled, but Zane was a straight-A student."

"But you're the one who set it up?"

Z smiled, not answering. He'd been wild as a teenager, and he blamed it on the guys he'd kept company with. The Walker brothers had been known for their mischief, so yeah, maybe Z had picked up a few things from the twins.

Or vice versa. Who knew?

"So, I've got a question." All eyes turned to Courtney. She was sitting on a bench beside Marissa, elbows propped on her knees, a beer bottle dangling from her fingers. Her husband was standing a few feet away, talking to Leyton and Ashlynn. "Where do you disappear to at night?"

Z hadn't expected the question, and he tried to hide his discomfort, glancing around at the others. All those eyes had turned to him, clearly anticipating an answer.

"We've decided you've got a secret life," Marissa added, excitement buzzing in her words. "Possibly a husband and kids tucked somewhere."

Thankfully, Jericho and Amahn were up near the stairs, talking to Ally and Clay, out of earshot. That offhanded remark would've easily blown their cover. Or made Z look like a cheating bastard.

Z laughed. The notion of him having a secret family was absurd, but he should've expected Marissa and Courtney to come up with something like that.

RT shifted, catching Z's attention. Glancing over, he saw that he was anticipating an answer. An answer Z wasn't ready to give.

"Are you a stripper?" Jayden asked bluntly. "I bet that's it."

"Magic Mike," Kira added. "I can so totally see that. And I bet Evan's a stripper, too."

"Is Evan even old enough to be a stripper?" This time Casper was the one with the question.

"Whatever," Evan snorted with a laugh. "I'm definitely old enough." His face reddened. "But I'm not!"

Z exhaled, grateful they'd shifted the attention off him, the teasing turning on Evan. Downing what was left of his beer, he peered over at RT to find him still looking his way. Curiosity glowed in his ice-blue eyes.

Luckily RT's phone rang, and he snatched it from where it rested on his thigh. From Z's position next to him, he could see by the caller ID on the screen that it was Trace.

"Yeah?" RT spoke into the phone.

Z couldn't hear the other half of the conversation, but the pleased smile that lifted RT's lips told him it was good news.

"Perfect." *Pause.* "No. Don't do anything yet." *Pause.* "Okay, good. See you soon."

RT's gaze shifted to Jericho and Amahn. The pair was still deep in conversation with Ally and Clay.

After disconnecting the call, RT leaned over, his mouth dangerously close to Z's ear. "Trace and Hunter found a painting in Jericho's beach house. Trace doesn't think it's the real thing, but at least we know where the other fake is."

"Beach house?" Z questioned. Obviously, he'd been out of the loop on this particular aspect of the mission.

"Kira mentioned it to me a little while ago. Dom pulled the address, and Trace and Hunter went to check it out."

RT's warm breath against his neck was giving Z chills. He pulled away slightly, not wanting his body to give him away in front of all these people. "It's about time we got some good news."

"Yes, it is."

"So no luck on the real thing?" Z asked.

"No. Conner and Colby found a storage unit key in Amahn's office. They're over there now."

Z knew that the only thing they'd possibly find—if anything at all—would be the fake that was originally stolen. And now that they knew the whereabouts of the other, they didn't necessarily need it.

234

"What do we do now?" Z inquired, a surge of relief coursing through him.

"We enjoy the night."

The way RT said the words had Z thinking about something other than the party. Something more private. A *lot* more private. Turning to look directly into RT's eyes, he attempted to see whether RT had meant it the way it sounded. Based on the flare of heat that ignited in those icy blue orbs, it looked as though they had plans for later.

Hopping to his feet, Z was tempted to tell everyone to go the hell home.

Instead, he smiled down at RT. "You want another beer?"

"Sure."

"Be right back."

Ryan watched as Z trekked through the sand to the stairs that led up to the house. Thanks to Courtney's intrusive inquiry—the one that Z had dodged—his mind worked overtime trying to figure out what Z did at night when he went out. It'd already been a question he'd been pondering, but even more so now. Ryan was beginning to doubt it was due to Z's salacious dating life. It no longer felt right.

Not based on what he'd learned about Z recently. Rather, the way Z acted around him. He was confident and sure of himself, but the fact that he hadn't wanted to rush things with Ryan was making him question those assumptions.

Their argument from the other night came to mind.

What makes me different than any of the others, Z? Why can't you just walk away?

Because I never fucking walk away! That's not who I am, but you wouldn't know that because you won't give me a fucking chance.

And that was the real problem. Ryan hadn't given Z a chance; he'd allowed his own insecurities, his own fears, and his own assumptions about Z's personal life to overshadow his decisions.

Though he now doubted Z's promiscuous lifestyle, Ryan still believed Z was hiding something. He just didn't know what. Obviously it was important to Z, because Ryan had noticed the slight flutter of his eyes when Courtney had called him on it. He didn't want to share, whatever it was.

Casper moved to sit beside Ryan, pointing toward the fire as though saying something about it, but his words didn't match the action. "Any news?"

"We've located one of the fakes," Ryan answered, pretending to be paying attention to the others. "Conner and Colby are checking out a storage unit. We should know something soon."

"Good. And them?" Casper jerked his chin in the direction Amahn and Jericho were sitting.

"They seem to be fitting in well."

"And I'm sure by now Amahn has figured out who you are," Casper acknowledged.

Yeah, that was the downfall of this party. Amahn wouldn't think it was a coincidence that he'd been invited to a party put on by the leading security company in the nation. He would figure it out, which why Ryan had hoped they'd have the original painting in their hands before the night was over. Looked like they would have to resort to another plan. If only Ryan knew what that plan was.

Z rejoined the group a moment later, handing Ryan a beer before taking the seat beside him once more.

"Keep me updated," Casper whispered, then got up and trudged across the beach to where his wife was now chatting with the guests of honor.

And once again, Ryan found himself completely captivated by Z. More so now than ever.

For the next couple of hours, Ryan spent the majority of his time beside Z, talking to his friends and family. When Trace, Hunter, Conner, and Colby finally returned, it felt like they were whole once again. Nothing could be done until tomorrow, and though they were now down to the wire if they expected to do something prior to the gallery showing on Saturday, Ryan was managing to push work away and enjoy the brief reprieve.

Z did that for him and it surprised Ryan. Relationships had never been his thing. Sure, he'd dated randomly, but nothing serious since Kevin. As much as he wanted to pretend that work was his main reason for avoiding men, Ryan knew that wasn't the whole truth. The fact of the matter was, he'd been hung up on Z for quite a while. So long that this...the easy interaction between them...just seemed normal.

It was after midnight before most of the guests finally left, but the house was still full by the time everyone decided to call it a night. As much as Ryan wished he and Z would have the place to themselves, he couldn't very well send his parents away considering they owned the place. And Casper and Elizabeth were staying, as well.

The next thing Ryan knew, all six bedrooms had been filled—Trace and Marissa in one, Elizabeth and Casper in another, Bryce and Emily took the master, Ryan's brothers, Clay, Colby, and Austin camped out in the room with bunk beds, while Max and Courtney surprisingly opted to take the last available room. Conner had made a pallet on the floor downstairs, his daughter, Shelby, was taking the couch, and Hunter had staked his claim on the media room.

That had left Ryan without a room because he'd insisted that Z not give up his own.

Sure, he could've crammed into the room with his brothers or slept in one of the recliners in the media room, but the truth was he didn't want to. Instead, he'd remained outside by the pool until the lights in the house went out and all was silent.

The sound of the glass door opening and closing had him glancing over his shoulder.

Z.

"What're you doin' out here?" Z questioned, his voice a notch above a whisper.

"Not tired."

"Liar," Z countered, moving up close to Ryan's side.

The warmth of Z's muscular arm pressed against his own was comforting, and he didn't bother to move away.

"You know, you can always share a room with me. I'll be a gentleman," Z offered, a smile in his voice.

Ryan tossed around the idea for a moment. He'd actually been thinking the same thing. Well, except for the gentleman part.

"I promise to keep my hands to myself, Mr. Trexler," Z crooned against his ear. "Mostly."

That made Ryan smile.

For fear his voice would fail him, Ryan didn't say a word, just turned to Z and nodded.

It was all he could do.

TWENTY-THREE

The house was full of people. Like, to capacity.

And that was the only reason Z had managed to keep his hands to himself when the only thing he wanted to do was to wrap RT in his arms and lose himself.

After he and RT snuck back to his room and locked the door, the sexual tension returned. That ever-present, stifling desire that made it damn hard to breathe. And though they had some privacy, it wasn't nearly enough.

As Z had told RT before, when they were together again, they'd be alone. And clearly that wasn't happening tonight. But that didn't mean they couldn't sleep in the same bed.

When RT started fidgeting, Z found the action cute. Something he hadn't seen from RT before. So rather than put a spotlight on what was (or wasn't) happening, Z crawled into bed and then raised the blankets for RT to join him.

Neither of them said a word.

It didn't take long—if a couple of tense minutes could be considered not long—before RT finally relented and crawled into the bed alongside Z. Never the one to play games or pretend something wasn't what it was, Z inched closer and pulled RT to him, sliding his arm beneath RT's head.

Damn, it felt good to hold him, to feel the warmth of his body alongside him. As horny as he was, Z was content to simply lie there with RT in his arms. Hell, he'd be happy if holding RT every night while they slept was all he could have for the rest of his life.

RT's body twitched beside him.

"I promised," Z whispered into the blackness.

"I know," RT replied, sounding somewhat disappointed, which made Z smile.

They lay there for the longest time, neither of them talking, but not going to sleep, either.

Z's body was as hard as stone, the thick ridge of his cock tenting his shorts beneath the blankets. Had he been alone, he would've slid his hand downward and taken care of the problem. With RT there, that wasn't possible.

After all, he'd promised.

Just when he started counting down from one hundred, something he did when he couldn't fall asleep, Z felt RT's warm lips against his collarbone.

He bit back the moan that the slight touch triggered.

Turning his head so that he was facing RT, though he could hardly see him in the darkened room, Z held out hope, wishing that RT would kiss him. It wouldn't be enough, but like last night, it would be enough for now.

The bed shifted and RT's solid weight moved closer, and that was when Z felt RT's rigid dick pressing against his thigh.

"This is a lot fucking harder than I thought," Z told RT as quietly as he could. His voice was rough with the ache quickly building inside him.

"A lot harder," RT agreed, his hand sliding along Z's thigh until it rested on the ridge of Z's erection. RT's hips moved, his cock sliding against Z's leg.

"Ryan." There was no way Z would be able to resist him if he continued, and overpowering RT—as hot as that idea made him—didn't seem like the appropriate response.

"Shh."

Shh? How the fuck was Z supposed to be quiet when RT was sliding his warm hand—*son of a motherfucking bitch*—beneath the waistband of Z's shorts.

RT's heavy thigh slid over Z's, his rough palm gripping Z's cock firmly, skin to fucking skin. Z sucked in air, unsure how he was going to survive this. He'd had plenty of fantasies about being with RT—some far more erotic than this—but never had he thought it would happen again. Not this soon, anyhow.

Of their own volition, Z's hips began to buck, his cock sliding back and forth in RT's fist. The fragile grip that he still had on his control slipped another notch. Z twisted to his side, continuing to grind his dick against RT's palm, then slamming his mouth over RT's.

It sucked that he had to hold back the moans that were desperate to escape, but he had no idea how thin the walls were, and he certainly wasn't interested in having company in the middle of the best fucking hand job he'd ever received.

RT's tongue thrust into Z's mouth, mimicking the smooth motion of his hand. Air was quickly becoming scarce, and Z had to pull back, panting as his body soared from the pleasure of RT's touch.

Suddenly RT stopped, Z's cock slipping from RT's grip, and Z nearly cried. The bed shifted once again, the blankets disappearing from his body before his shorts were being tugged down his hips, his dick springing free from the confining cotton.

"Ryan," Z pleaded in a rush. "We can't..." That thought quickly died when RT's mouth encircled the sensitive head of his dick. He grunted as his hips jerked forward, driving him into the sweet cavern of RT's mouth. "Oh, fuck... Oh fuck... Oh fuck... Ryan... Oh fuck." Somehow—he had no idea how—he managed to keep the words so soft he doubted RT even heard them.

RT's lips were wrapped perfectly around his dick, his tongue gliding expertly along his shaft while his fingers kneaded his balls in a way that had Z damn near swallowing his own tongue. He wanted to come. He wanted to hold off. He fucking *wanted*. That was all there was to it. The thought of returning the favor and drawing RT's cock into his mouth had him huffing, his chest rising and falling, his heart pounding.

His hands slid into RT's soft hair, holding him steady as Z did his best to hold himself back. With a soft pop and no warning, Z's dick sprang from RT's mouth, and he sucked in another breath.

"Come for me," RT whispered, his warm breath fanning the head of Z's dick. "Come in my mouth, Z."

Nodding like a freak, Z closed his eyes, dug the back of his head into the pillow as RT's skilled mouth went to work on him again. He tightened his grip on RT's hair, knowing he was likely causing RT pain but unable to help it. He couldn't cry out, which meant he was wound so tightly, his body coiling in on itself as his balls drew up against his body, his insides tingling, his abs contracting.

Breath rushed in and out of his lungs as he held on for as long as he could, but then he hit the point of no return when RT took him to the root, his throat gripping the sensitive, swollen head of Z's cock.

Z came in a rush, his body jerking uncontrollably while he kept a firm hold on RT's hair, forcing him to take all of him, though he knew RT wasn't trying to pull away.

Still attempting to regain some semblance of himself, Z urged RT toward him, locking his mouth on RT's when he was close enough. The kiss was languid and unhurried, though Z's heart was still trying to beat its way out of his chest.

When he got himself under control once more, he pulled back from RT, peering at him, though it was still too dark to see him.

"I promised," Z whispered, feeling somewhat guilty for letting things get so out of control.

"But I didn't," RT replied.

Well, Z couldn't very well argue with that logic, now could he?

Ryan hadn't exactly planned for that to happen, but the moment he was in bed next to Z, he'd been desperate to touch him, to taste him, to see what else it took to send the man over the edge. The only thing he'd had to go on was that one incredible night a couple of weeks ago, and it wasn't nearly enough. There was so much more of Z he wanted to explore, so many things he wanted to do to him. And Ryan wanted to learn his breaking point.

And now he knew.

He lingered against Z's mouth, kissing him as the hard thump of Z's heart beat against Ryan's chest. But when Z tried to reach between their bodies, apparently in an attempt to return the favor, Ryan shifted his hips away.

"Nuh-uh," Ryan whispered.

"Bullshit," Z growled against his mouth, the sheer strength in Z's arm too much for Ryan.

When Z's firm hand clasped Ryan's aching dick, he inhaled sharply. There was no pain, only pure, undiluted pleasure that gripped him in the same way as Z's physical touch.

"My turn," Z informed him, keeping his voice low.

"You promised," Ryan returned, smiling in the dark, his eyes rolling back in his head as he indulged in the gratification that came from Z's hand stroking him.

"That was before you gave me the best blow job of my fucking life."

Ryan wanted to argue, but Z began shoving Ryan's shorts down his hips, and the idea of Z touching him was more than he could resist.

Climbing off Z, Ryan managed to shed his shorts, tossing them aside while Z continued to fumble with Ryan's dick in the dark. When he was naked, Z surprised the hell out of him, jerking him forward, causing Ryan to lose his balance as he reached for the headboard, managing to keep himself from falling only to find that he was hovering over Z's chest, his cock plunging past Z's exquisite lips before he could take his next breath.

Fuck.

Ryan prayed the strangled cry was only in his head, but he wasn't sure that was the case. Z repositioned him so that Ryan was straddling his head as he willingly fed his dick into Z's eager mouth. With a firm grip on the headboard, Ryan gave himself over to what was happening. He didn't want Z to stop, so fighting it wouldn't benefit either of them.

Lifting his hips and planting one foot beside Z's head, Ryan adjusted the angle of his dick, sliding it past Z's lips, the delicious friction making his head spin. Z kept a firm grip on Ryan's hips, pulling him forward until Ryan's cock was stuffed deep into Z's mouth. Z worked his tongue and teeth along the rigid length, then teasing his glans, driving him absolutely mad as Ryan continued to white-knuckle the headboard.

Ryan shifted again, pumping his hips, fucking Z's mouth more forcefully. He was vaguely aware of Z's hands moving, Ryan's cock briefly stilling in Z's mouth as a finger dipped inside, sliding alongside his shaft. Then Z was pulling Ryan's ass cheeks apart, wrenching his hips forward, his cock tunneling in and out again while Z pressed his spit-slicked finger against Ryan's asshole, gently fucking him with the single digit.

Oh, fuck. It was too much. It wasn't enough.

Suddenly not giving a shit where he was or who was on the other side of the wall, Ryan gave in to the overwhelming pleasure, fucking Z's mouth while Z fucked his ass with that thick finger. Ryan grunted, biting his lip to keep from crying out as his orgasm detonated. He came in a rush, his dick throbbing and pulsing as he flooded Z's mouth.

Falling to the bed, Ryan tried to catch his breath. The mattress dipped and then Z was gone.

While he willed his heart to slow, he heard the sound of water from the adjoining bathroom, then the sound of the toilet flushing. A minute later, Z joined him in the bed once more, pulling Ryan into his arms.

It was then that Ryan gave in to the exhaustion that had consumed him, falling asleep—naked and sated—next to the man he'd vowed to stay away from. He now knew that was no longer a possibility.

TWENTY-FOUR

Never in his adult life had Z slept so soundly, but when his eyes opened, roaming the room slowly to find the clock, it took him a moment to remember where he was. When he noticed the sexy, tousled blond lying next to him, he instantly remembered.

He wasn't alone in the bed.

Z smiled to himself.

It was ten o'clock and RT was still there, still sleeping. A damn good sign.

Remembering what had happened the night before, Z's gaze strayed to the door. He listened but heard nothing from outside the room. Had everyone left? Or were they wandering around downstairs or possibly out by the water?

"Please, please, please, let them be gone," he muttered to himself, sliding out of bed and pulling his shorts on. Because it was possible that someone was downstairs, Z also grabbed a T-shirt.

Leaving the room as quietly as he could, Z snuck down the hall and peered over the railing to the floor below.

Nothing.

Turning back, he noticed that all of the bedroom doors were open, which meant they'd likely been cleared out as well. With his heart beating with anticipation, he flew down the stairs, practically ran through the rooms, glimpsed out the back door, and then darted to the front.

There weren't any people or cars in sight.

When he turned to go back upstairs, he looked up in time to see RT standing on the second-floor landing, wearing only his shorts and a smile.

"They're all gone," RT informed him, holding up his phone. "Bryce sent a text letting me know they cleared out."

Z couldn't find any words.

They were alone.

Finally.

Stalking up the stairs, Z didn't care that he looked like a madman. He was finally alone with RT, and no one was going to interrupt them.

"I need to—"

Z cut RT off with a look. Before RT had a chance to convince (or order) him to do something else, Z made his way closer, not stopping until—

RT suddenly turned and bolted down the hall.

"Where are you going?" Z questioned, surprised.

"To brush my teeth!" he called out over his shoulder.

It took a second for RT's words to process, but then Z laughed.

Brush his teeth.

Good idea.

While RT slipped into the room he'd originally taken, Z went back to his own. After a quick brush and a swig of mouthwash, Z practically tripped over his own feet in his haste to get back to RT. He knew the guy. Give him a chance to rationalize his own actions and this wouldn't be happening.

Since RT wasn't in Z's room, Z traipsed across the hall, fully expecting to find RT in the bathroom, hesitating.

That was *so* not what he found.

There, lying prone on the bed and utterly, completely, beautifully naked was RT. Again words eluded him as he stared unabashedly at the sexiest man he'd ever seen laid out like a feast beckoning him.

When his brain flickered online briefly, Z thought to close and lock the door—just because no one was there now didn't mean they wouldn't come back.

In a flurry of motion, Z ripped off his T-shirt, then shoved his shorts down his legs before joining RT on the bed. His eyes continued to rove over RT's exquisite form, slowly sliding back up to meet his eyes.

"In a hurry?" RT asked.

"Maybe." No, he wasn't, but he was desperate to get close to RT. He wanted to touch him, to taste him, to relive what they'd experienced on that one remarkable night that seemed so long ago.

While Z was on all fours, moving toward him, RT gripped his arm, yanking him close, causing Z to fall over, practically crushing him. RT let out a surprised "oomph," but Z quickly silenced him with a kiss, reversing their positions so that RT was over him.

Gripping the back of RT's head, Z slipped his tongue past RT's lips, colliding with him from mouth to knee. The sweet taste of mint exploded on his tongue. So fucking good. While he sealed his lips to RT's, Z's other hand roamed RT's back, feeling the muscles flex and bunch beneath his touch.

Z smiled against RT's mouth. "You look so damn good on me."

RT laughed, some of the tension Z had sensed vibrating through him slowly fading.

"I happen to like you on me," RT muttered. "But this works, too." With a gentle tug, Z pulled RT's mouth back to his.

Z loved the way RT's hands slid over his face, lazily exploring as he cupped his head gently. The kiss robbed him of all sense, made him delirious with need. After a few minutes fused to RT's lips, tasting, teasing, exploring, Z pulled back, staring up at him, cupping his head. "Tell me this is real."

RT's expression turned serious. "It's real."

"Thank God." With that, Z pulled RT's mouth back to his, kissing him as though he'd been starved for the man for a lifetime. Sometimes it'd felt that way, especially over the course of the past few days. Z wanted RT with a passion he'd never experienced before.

With so much back-and-forth between them, Z hadn't known what to expect, but that hadn't stopped him from hoping. And now that they'd seemingly moved past all the issues between them, he wanted to claim RT as his.

Not just sex, either.

Something much, much deeper than the superficial joining of their bodies.

"I want to feel you," RT whispered.

"I'm right here," Z muttered, sliding his mouth down RT's jaw. "Right here."

"No, I mean…"

When RT trailed off, Z looked up at him once again, studying his face. "Tell me."

"I want to feel you," RT said softly, never breaking eye contact. "Inside me."

"We're gettin' there," Z assured him.

"That's not what I meant. It's just… I mean…" RT swallowed hard, his Adam's apple bobbing in his throat. "I've never…"

Studying him for a moment, it didn't take long for Z to read between the lines. Z's cock throbbed as all the blood in his entire body pooled in his groin, as he comprehended the full meaning behind RT's words. "You've never? Like, *never* never?"

A small smile flirted with RT's lips, his crystal-blue eyes sparkling. "You sound surprised."

"Well…" Z hadn't given it much thought, really. Z would've figured RT, at thirty-two, had experimented with his sexual desires, figured out what worked and didn't work for him. He found it a little hard to believe that RT had never been on the receiving end. Then again, as far as Z was concerned, top, bottom, it really didn't matter. Personally, Z was pretty damned flexible.

RT's brow furrowed. "Never mind."

"*No.* No, no. Not never mind. We need to…explore this. I'm more than happy to show you what you've been missin'." Z grinned. The idea of being RT's first was the equivalent of the first rush from a drug in his system.

"Okay, too much talking," RT groaned, falling over onto his back.

"Nope." Z was instantly on him, covering RT's thigh with his own, propping his upper body over RT's chest. "Don't run from me now. I've finally got you naked."

"Talking's not supposed to be part of the deal."

Those words hit a sore spot inside Z, but he attempted to mask his reaction. As far as he was concerned, talking was a huge part of this "deal." Intimacy wasn't merely two bodies joining, it required mind, body, and soul to play an active role. And this wasn't just sex for Z. Not this time.

Definitely not this time.

As soon as the words left his mouth, Ryan knew he'd said the wrong thing. It'd sounded a lot different coming out than it had bouncing around in his head. Truth was, he was nervous.

And it was true, most of the time conversation wasn't part of the sexual experience for him, and certainly not a topic like this one. That was what a date was for. Dinner, casual conversation, getting to know someone. But in the privacy of the bedroom, Ryan didn't want to talk, only it was clear Z had other plans.

"Is that what you see this as?" Z finally asked, his expression masked. "A deal?"

"No," Ryan stated firmly, wrapping his arms around Z, fearful that he'd try to escape. "I'm just…" It took him a moment to gather his thoughts, but he finally did. "I'm not good at this. The intimacy part."

"You're much better than you give yourself credit for," Z told him, his eyes trailing down to Ryan's mouth briefly.

"The idle chatter…it's not my thing. Usually."

"Then what is?"

Leave it to Z to drag more words out of him when he didn't want to talk at all. At a time when he wanted Z to be buried balls deep within him, the man wanted to have a heart-to-heart.

Ryan wanted to distract him, but based on the gleam in Z's stunning brown eyes, it was clear that this aspect of the encounter was important to him. And above all else, Ryan really did want to give Z what he needed. He wanted to please him, to make him happy, to earn one of those heart-melting smiles. All while getting a chance to have the whole man to himself.

He trailed his palms up Z's thick arms, rounding his big shoulders and then cupping his neck. "Feeling. That's my thing. I just need to feel."

Z appeared to understand based on the short jerky nod he offered moments before his mouth grazed Ryan's. Within seconds, the room heated several degrees, their naked bodies gliding against one another, hands roaming, mouths claiming. Ryan was left desperate for more when Z trailed his mouth downward, over his chest, his stomach, then hovering precariously close to Ryan's dick.

He thought he'd known what to expect after last night, but the warmth of Z's mouth on him was the equivalent of an electrical shock, sending nearly painful impulses to all of his nerve endings, the pleasure threatening to overwhelm him.

Z applied exquisite suction, taking him deep, teasing the oversensitive head with the flat of his tongue while cupping Ryan's balls firmly. Unlike last night, there was no rush, nor was there a reason to. Z seemed to know that.

"You've really never...?" Z licked Ryan's balls, the warmth of his breath making Ryan's dick twitch.

"Never."

"So, I'll be your first?"

The hair on Ryan's arms stood on end, too many sensations coursing through him as Z licked him from root to tip. "Yes."

"You want to feel me here?" Z asked, using the tip of his finger to tease Ryan's anus.

"Yes," he rasped. More than he could express. It was true, he'd never bottomed before, but not because he was against it. He'd merely always been the more aggressive lover.

Z's big body hovered over him once again, his nose close to Ryan's. "I don't wanna hurt you."

The sincerity in Z's tone shocked him. "But I thought…" Ryan hadn't misjudged Z, had he?

"That I'm usually a top?" Z smiled. "When it comes to you, I'll take you any way I can have you, as you already know. But yes, your assumption was accurate." Z's deep voice lowered. "Trust me, I have every intention of fucking you until you beg me to let you come. I still don't wanna hurt you."

Ryan's mouth went dry. This wasn't going the way he'd planned. This wasn't the way it had been that first time. That had been a quick fuck, both of them giving in to the irresistible lust. It was supposed to be spontaneous and dirty, quick and fun. This felt far too intimate.

Then again, this was Z. He wasn't a random lover or a guy Ryan had just picked up at a bar. He was a friend, someone Ryan had come to respect—not to mention care about—over the years. Still, this was new and he wasn't sure how he felt about it yet.

"Quit thinking," Z growled. "I'm not askin' you to marry me."

Ryan forced a laugh, but there was no amusement in it. He was nervous, that he couldn't deny.

The next thing Ryan knew, he was flipped over onto his stomach, Z's heavy body crushing him into the mattress, Z's hard chest flattened against Ryan's back, his thick cock grinding between Ryan's ass cheeks.

"Yes," Ryan pleaded. This he understood.

"I take it you thought ahead for this, right?" Z asked, his mouth pressed against Ryan's ear.

"Condom and lube…in the drawer," Ryan forced out, barely able to breath beneath the glorious weight of Z.

But then Z was gone, and there was the sound of the drawer being opened then slammed closed.

As he looked at him now, Ryan realized Z was far larger than he'd anticipated. Sure, he'd managed to take Z in his mouth—not easily, but he'd managed—but the mere thought of Z fucking him with that monster made his asshole clench. Ryan focused on breathing as he watched Z swiftly open the condom and roll it over his thick, heavy erection before uncapping the lube, then positioning himself over Ryan again.

"You're gonna have to—" Ryan was quickly cut off when Z nipped his shoulder, hard enough to send a bolt of pleasure-pain ricocheting down to his balls.

"I know what I'm doin', Ry. Relax for me." Z's words were soothing and gentle, a clear attempt to keep Ryan from panicking.

It wasn't as simple as clearing his mind, though. Ryan was overly aware of every place where Z's body touched his own, the sound of Z's breathing, the way his leg hair brushed against Ryan's calves.

But he wasn't afraid. No, this was more like anticipation that kept his body humming. He was desperate to feel Z, but he didn't know how to express himself. It seemed that when he opened his mouth, the words that came out sounded far crasser than he intended.

So he kept his mouth shut.

Or tried to, anyway.

"Oh, hell," he said on a breathless moan. Z's tongue trailed straight down Ryan's spine—an erogenous zone he hadn't been aware of until now—his big hands cupping Ryan's ass firmly, kneading the muscle. It was impossible to focus on only one sensation, so his brain strained to determine which was more potent.

"Yes," Ryan breathed. "God, yes."

Z's tongue dipped along the crack of his ass, sliding lower until he was rimming him, driving Ryan crazy with his tongue over the sensitive flesh. Unable to help himself, he rocked back against Z's invading tongue, random pleas spouting from his mouth as Z proceeded to tongue-fuck him gently. Z's tongue was replaced by something cool, the sensations once again warring with one another. But when Z's finger penetrated him, Ryan's dick—currently trapped between him and the mattress—jerked in anticipation.

"Tell me it feels good," Z insisted, his tone firm.

"Yes," Ryan confirmed.

"Tell me," Z demanded, driving one finger in deep a few times, followed by two, and then twisting until Ryan damn near flew from the bed.

"Holy fuck! Too much, Z. Too… Oh, fuck, yes."

Z continued to massage Ryan's prostate, driving him higher and higher until he thought he would soar right over the edge. Clearly, Z had other plans, because his fingers disappeared, and his knees forced Ryan's legs farther apart as he positioned himself so that the head of his cock brushed Ryan's anus.

This was it.

Closing his eyes tightly, he awaited the pain he expected to come, but nothing happened. Not until Z's body once again covered him, Z's mouth close to Ryan's ear.

"You sure this is what you want?" Z whispered. "To feel my dick in your ass?"

"Yes." A tremor of desire raced through him, tightening his muscles as his body prepared for the pleasure he knew would come.

"I want you right here with me, Ryan."

The way Z said his name, it did strange things to him. It made him want this to be something more.

Z shifted, the head of his cock pressing against Ryan's ass, gently breaching the muscles. Ryan managed to relax, sliding one hand over Z's, the other reaching around to grab Z's thigh. It became glaringly obvious that Z was trying desperately not to hurt him, so when the thick head of Z's cock passed the ring of muscle, Ryan pushed his hips back, the air rushing from his lungs as his body took more of Z.

"Oh, hell," Ryan huffed. The pain was brief but intense.

"Relax, Ry." This time Z sounded as though he was begging, his mouth trailing over Ryan's shoulder. "So fucking tight. I need to go slow."

Ryan didn't want slow, but he was still trying to catch his breath, so he nodded, allowing Z to lead. Long seconds ticked by until finally Z was lodged deep inside, his breath fanning Ryan's neck as he remained still.

"Fuck me," Ryan begged. "Need more, Z. Need all of you."

"We'll get there." Z retreated slowly, then thrust back inside. "Aww, fuck. So good, Ry. So fucking good."

Z's weight disappeared, but firm hands gripped Ryan's hips, pulling him back as Z began fucking him slow and deep, hitting that perfect spot, making Ryan's entire body tingle.

He had no idea how much time passed, but time no longer mattered when Z began fucking him, thrusting harder, faster, deeper. His hands kept a firm grip on Ryan's hips while Ryan forced himself back against Z, taking all of him.

Then Z shifted, pulling Ryan up so that the backs of his thighs were pressed against Z's, his back to Z's chest, the change in position causing Ryan to be impaled on Z's dick.

"Fuck me," Z commanded, his words coarse in Ryan's ear.

The position was somewhat awkward, but it allowed Ryan to lift and lower himself on Z's cock while Z took Ryan's dick in his firm grip, stroking him roughly.

"Fuck," Ryan breathed. "Keep...doin' that...and I'm...gonna come."

Z leaned in and nipped Ryan's earlobe. "Ride my cock, Ryan."

Oh, hell. The gruff command had Ryan seeing stars. He continued to rock up and down, taking Z's dick in his ass until the head of his cock felt as though it would explode in Z's hand.

"I'm close," Ryan warned.

"Come for me, Ry. I won't come till you do." Z sounded as though he was trying desperately to hold back. Ryan envied the man's control, but there was no way he could outlast him.

Z's free hand gripped Ryan's hip securely as he began thrusting forward, driving himself deep until Ryan's breath lodged in his throat, every muscle in his body went rigid, and his dick pulsed. He peered down his own body as he came in Z's hand, the sight far more erotic than he'd anticipated.

"Fuck yes." Ryan groaned.

The next thing Ryan knew, he was on his hands and knees again, and Z was pounding into him again and again. Several demanding thrusts later, Z stilled, his fingertips digging into Ryan's hips as he felt Z's dick pulse in his ass.

He couldn't breathe, much less think, but there was one fleeting thought he couldn't dislodge: when it came to Z, Ryan definitely didn't know the man as well as he'd thought he did.

But he was undeniably interested in learning everything about him.

TWENTY-FIVE

"What's on the agenda for the day?" Z asked after they'd showered—together—and made their way downstairs to find food.

Figuring RT wasn't interested in a repeat of the chicken incident from the other night, Z took the lead, pulling out eggs, bacon, sausage, and biscuits. He made a mental note to find out who had stocked the kitchen, because they deserved a raise. Based on the amount of food, it appeared as though they'd personally stocked it for Z, which he greatly appreciated.

"Nothin'," RT answered, climbing up onto one of the barstools and watching Z as he moved around the kitchen. He had his cell phone in hand and continued to scroll through the screen, doing whatever it was that RT did.

"A day off?" Z met RT's gaze. "How the fuck did that happen?"

RT returned Z's smile briefly. "We're between a rock and a hard place. Since we can't find that damn painting, we're dead in the water."

"Is that a game?" Z glanced at RT over his shoulder as he cracked eggs into a bowl.

RT's golden eyebrows narrowed down.

"The cliché thing. See how many you can use in one conversation?"

RT rolled his eyes, making Z laugh. Turning back to his task, he continued to prepare breakfast.

"I'm just stumped that we can't find that damn thing," RT continued, his eyes once again riveted on his phone. "Where the hell does a rich guy stash a painting when he doesn't want anyone to find it?"

"Wherever he wants," Z replied, though he figured the question was rhetorical.

"But why put the other fake at his beach house? I'd have to assume he hasn't taken Amahn there or the man would know about it already."

"What if Amahn's not the one who's tryin' to steal it?" Z questioned, playing devil's advocate.

"I've considered that, too. My brain tells me there's too much of a coincidence."

"It is pretty damning that the problems started around the same time Amahn showed up, but it's not conclusive." Z still wasn't entirely certain that Amahn was behind it. From a logical perspective, sure, it fit. But after seeing Amahn and Jericho at the party, he wasn't feeling it anymore.

"Your brain's workin'," RT said. "What're you thinkin'?"

Z shrugged, pouring the eggs into the skillet. "I don't have a theory. Yet."

"Well, when you get one, be sure to share it with me." RT chuckled.

Z turned his head once again to look at him. It made him feel good that RT looked so relaxed. He'd probably smiled more in the last half hour than he had in the last year. Z wanted to believe that he was partially responsible for it.

Twisting back around, he focused on the food. He multitasked, placing the bacon in one pan alongside the eggs, the sausage in another. When all three were going, he slid the biscuit can and a baking sheet toward RT. "I don't think you can mess this up."

RT laughed. "You'd be surprised at what I'm capable of messin' up."

For a moment, it sounded as though RT was talking about something other than the mundane task of putting biscuits on a pan. Rather than invite trouble when there wasn't any, Z let it go.

"Okay. So we'll have breakfast. Then what?" Z asked, continuing to juggle the three pans on the stove.

"I need to check in with the others, make sure they're good."

"Is that what you do every day?"

"Among other things," RT said. "But yeah, I reach out to all of them to check in. Their safety's important to me. *Your* safety."

"So, it's not really a day off?"

"I never get a day off, Z. Not entirely, anyway."

"You could, you know."

"How do you figure?" RT didn't sound at all pleased with the conversation, but Z didn't drop it.

"There're others you could put in charge of certain tasks. You don't have to handle it all yourself."

"If the Kogans would step up to the plate—"

Z interrupted. "You can't blame them for the fact you work more than you should and you know it." How they had gotten to this point, Z wasn't sure, but he finished his thought. "If the Kogans don't want to handle it, there are others who would. I'm just sayin'."

RT didn't respond, so Z turned back around.

"Look, I'm sorry," Z added. "It's not my place to tell you how to handle your job."

"You're right, it's not."

That verbal punch hit Z square in the solar plexus. He took a deep breath, nodded his head, and turned back to the stove. He hadn't meant to start a fight with RT. It wasn't the way he saw this day going. Not after...

"Okay, fine. We'll do something. After we eat."

"What'd you have in mind?" Z questioned, still leery.

When RT didn't immediately answer, Z twisted to look at him. That was when he saw the playful gleam in RT's bright blue eyes.

"Oh, yeah?" Z asked, widening his smile. "If you're thinkin' what I think you're thinkin', then count me in."

A day off with RT—perhaps naked again—sounded like a damn fine plan.

"Well, I didn't figure I could do it all by myself," RT said, and Z's dick instantly jumped to attention.

Breakfast first. Then on to the fun.

Two hours later...

"This is definitely *not* what I had in mind," Z told RT as they slipped around to the back of Jericho's beach house, peering in windows in an attempt to make sure the place was empty.

"What *did* you have in mind?" RT asked, his attention elsewhere.

As soon as RT had finished breakfast, he'd been back in work mode. When Z had attempted to interrupt, RT would silence him with, "One minute." That one minute turned into one hundred twenty, and now they were no longer spending a day off together, they were fucking working.

"I was thinkin' that gettin' you naked was a good plan," Z admitted, keeping his voice low. "Not sneakin' into Jericho's beach house."

Clearly RT wasn't capable of taking a day off or they'd be back at their own beach house, lounging by the pool, or even better, Z would be flat on his back with RT—

"I don't think anyone's here," RT said, interrupting Z's wandering thoughts. "Dom's about to disengage the alarm system."

"Great." Z hoped RT heard his lack of enthusiasm.

"Let's get in and get out."

"That was my plan," Z mumbled under his breath, "but it involved you naked."

"What?"

"Nothin'. Get in and get out. Good idea."

Sticking close to RT, Z kept an eye on their surroundings, fighting the urge to retrieve his gun from its holster. They were the ones breaking and entering, not the other way around, so being armed wasn't necessary. He just had to hope they weren't busted, because the charges would likely be steeper than a simple B and E because they were carrying.

Resigning himself to getting this over with so hopefully he could show RT what it meant to work in an entirely different way, Z followed RT inside once RT had successfully picked the lock on the back door. Neither of them spoke for a few minutes while they crept through the house. Thankfully the place wasn't nearly as overwhelming as Jericho's mansion, but it wasn't necessarily small, either.

Half an hour later, they'd come up empty. Well, except for seeing the other fake—just as ugly as the picture he'd seen on RT's iPad—that Trace had already located last night, hanging right there in the living room. Although he wasn't particularly fond of the painting, Z was still confused as to how everyone seemed to know that it wasn't the real deal. One was just as ugly as the other, so he had to take RT's word on it.

"Are we gonna take it?" Z inquired. "The painting?"

"No," RT whispered. "Not yet."

"So we're done here?" He prayed RT said yes.

Unfortunately, just before RT could answer, the sound of a key in a lock alerted them that someone was there.

"Shit." RT snuck down the hall that led to a bedroom. Z remained close behind.

Shit was right. The alarm system had been disengaged, which meant…

"I know, Fred. I heard you the first time. Don't worry. No one knows where it's at, and I plan to keep it that way until tomorrow night. Security'll be in place, but even they don't know. I only need them there to keep an eye on it for a little while."

Waiting for another voice to respond, Z realized the man was on the phone when Jericho spoke again. "Look, I've gotta go. Amahn's meeting me in a few minutes. I'll call you tomorrow before the show."

Jericho's tone wasn't as chipper as it had been the few times Z had spoken with him. In fact, he sounded stern and not at all happy. The distinct sound of an alarm code being entered echoed, making Z's heart beat faster.

Figuring Jericho was about to realize the alarm was off, Z held his breath. Peering over at RT, Z raised his eyebrows in question. What the hell were they supposed to do now?

As though understanding the nonverbal question, RT shrugged, his back tight to the wall as he kept his gaze trained down the hall.

Z turned his head when he heard footsteps going up the stairs, then released his breath when he realized they weren't going to need to make a run for it. Yet.

Glancing over at RT, he willed the man to come up with a plan to get them out of there without being seen. They couldn't stand there forever. Who knew when Amahn would arrive. At that point, getting out undetected wouldn't be quite so easy. Z waited for RT to give him a signal. He felt his eyes beginning to bulge from lack of oxygen to his brain, when he realized he'd been holding his breath again. By the time RT finally nodded toward the living room, the room that led to the back door they'd come in through, Z was feeling a tad light-headed.

With a quick nod, Z nudged RT forward. He didn't need to wait around any longer. This was ridiculous. They'd broken into the home of their client. Explaining that would be damn near impossible, so they had to get out while the getting was good.

The creak of a door opening had Z ducking behind one of the oversized chairs, pulling RT down with him.

"Jeri? You here?" Amahn's clipped tone rebounded through the downstairs, followed by the click of the front door closing.

"Up here, love."

Z's head darted over to RT. Seriously? Two minutes ago, Jericho sounded as though he was ready to string someone up and now...well, now he sounded like a man getting ready to romance his better half.

He internally shivered, trying to block the mental image of Jericho and Amahn because...that was not an appealing thought.

"Oh, before you come up here, can you grab the wine from the kitchen?" Jericho called out.

Definitely not what Z wanted to be witness to. They had to get the hell out of there.

"All right," Amahn replied.

When Amahn made a detour, passing directly by the spot where Z and RT were hiding, Z practically plastered himself to the floor, praying Amahn didn't glance their way. The chair they were using for cover wasn't that damn big.

The sound of a drawer being opened and closed followed by returning footsteps had Z once again holding his breath. At this point, he was going to fry some brain cells from lack of oxygen.

Amahn suddenly stopped, his shoes the only thing Z could see from his hiding place. He was directly in front of the fake painting, which meant he was well aware of the fake. There went their theory that Amahn was the master thief.

The shoes that had paused started to move, followed by a creak in one of the stairs leading to the second floor. Thank God, they were alone again. Without waiting for RT to give him a signal, Z urged RT forward, climbing back to his feet and rushing them both out the door, closing it silently behind him.

They took the stairs down to the sand at a fast clip and didn't stop until they were behind a row of plants that ran parallel with the house.

"Amahn knows about the fake painting," RT told him when they were safely hidden from the house.

"Looks that way." Z was still trying to calm down as they started toward the road they'd left the bikes parked on.

"What does that mean?"

"It means Amahn didn't attempt to steal the painting," Z told him. "Other than that, I don't know what the hell it means."

Neither of them said anything during the five-minute hike.

Once they reached the motorcycles, Z's heart rate had resumed a steady pace.

"I think we need—"

Z immediately cut RT off. "*I* think it's safe to say you're not making any more decisions today." Z pulled his helmet from the bike, not bothering to look directly at RT.

"No?"

"No. Someone should've taught you that a day off means no sneaking around and breaking into houses. It's a day to do nothing."

"Well, I was thinking that we *could* do something." RT's mischievous tone had Z glancing over at him as he straddled his motorcycle.

"See," Z said, pointing at RT with a frown on his face. "That tone right there. I hear promises of sex when you talk like that." Z nodded his head back in the direction of where they'd narrowly escaped from without being seen. "Then I find myself breaking into a house."

Ryan yanked his helmet over his head, kicked the engine over, and followed Z back to the beach house, laughing most of the way. He wasn't laughing *at* Z, per se. Just Z's reaction.

The fact that Ryan found it amusing that Z would prefer to get naked and sweaty again rather than work was a testament to the fact that what had happened that morning truly had been as good as Ryan remembered.

And yes, he was anxious to get Z naked again. And soon.

But work was work, and no matter how hot and bothered Z made him, Ryan couldn't easily turn the switch off. They had an assignment, and with one day left before it could all come crashing down around them, the outcome was not looking good.

As a matter of fact, after overhearing Jericho's telephone conversation, Ryan was beginning to believe that had been Jericho's plan from the beginning. Did he know that DHS was looking to acquire the painting? If so, putting Sniper 1 Security in place to guard the currently nonexistent thing was the perfect plan. They seemed to be chasing their own asses, and Jericho was pulling all the strings.

Several minutes later, Ryan was ascending the stairs behind Z, going back into the beach house. He was trying to figure out what they could do for the rest of the day, something that would convince Z to forgive him for derailing their attempt at a day off, when all thought came to an abrupt halt. The instant he stepped inside, Ryan found himself plastered up against the wall, Z's huge body crushing him.

"No more work today," Z whispered, his big hand cupping Ryan's jaw firmly.

"But—" Ryan truly didn't have a rebuttal, but the retort came naturally.

"No buts," Z insisted, his fingers grazing Ryan's cheek. "Unless we're talkin' 'bout somethin' else entirely."

"Well, when you put it that way…" Ryan wanted to smile, but it was no longer an option when Z's mouth came down over his, stealing the air from his lungs.

Slow and seductive at first, Z's tongue coaxed Ryan's lips apart, making him relax into the warm body pinning him to the wall. A mad crush of lips ensued, leaving Ryan clinging to Z, desperate to get closer. Years of avoidance and Ryan suddenly wanted nothing more than to spend the rest of the day lodged inside him.

Z's words from earlier resounded in his mind. *When it comes to you, I'll take you any way I can have you, as you already know.*

So yes, being buried inside Z sounded like a hell of a plan. Ryan had spent years imagining what it'd be like to take Z, never expecting it to actually happen, yet if things went the way he hoped, he was about to have the honor a second time. There was no denying that he'd thoroughly enjoyed being fucked by Z, but Ryan still craved that control, even if he wanted it stripped from him from time to time.

"Oh, fuck," Ryan hissed, sucking in air when Z reached down and cupped him through his jeans, grinding the heel of his hand against Ryan's rigid erection. The next thing he knew, his jeans were unbuttoned, the zipper lowered, and the warmth of Z's bare palm was gently sliding up and down his dick.

"I need to touch you," Z muttered. "I can't stop thinking about you."

Ryan gripped the back of Z's head, pulling his mouth back to his, thrusting his tongue past Z's lips, stealing his kiss, taking everything he wanted from the man. When Z's grip tightened around Ryan's dick, he had to pull his mouth away, letting his head thump against the wall while he succumbed to the pleasure.

The slick warmth of Z's mouth suddenly replaced the calloused grip of his hand, making Ryan's hips thrust forward as he looked down to see Z kneeling before him. Unlike last night, when he'd been straddling Z's head, held in place by Z's strong arms, Ryan had control this time, and he took it. Sliding his hands into Z's thick, dark hair, he gripped him gently while Z swallowed his dick, sucking him all the way to the root.

"Fuck. You're good at that." The words escaped on a moan as he rolled his hips forward. "So good."

When Z hummed his response, the vibration shot straight up Ryan's cock and settled in his balls, making his body tense. He would not come yet, but fuck, he wanted to.

Holding Z's head, Ryan began fucking his mouth, going slow and deep, watching the way Z's lips wrapped tightly around him, every so often, Z's tongue darting out to lick him. Before long, Ryan was fucking Z's face at a steady pace, his body coated in a fine sheen of sweat as he let the pleasure overwhelm him.

"Stop," Ryan cried out, pulling his dick from Z's mouth as his chest heaved. "Don't wanna come yet."

Almost instantly, Z was back on his feet, his mouth on Ryan's, the kiss ruthless and sweet at the same time. Ryan held on to him, thrusting his tongue against Z's, trying to devour him.

Ryan reached for the button on Z's jeans at the same time Z took Ryan's dick in his hand again, stroking firmly. All thought fled, and his arms fell to his sides once again as he allowed Z to skillfully jack him. Just when he thought he was the one in control, Z proved him wrong.

Z's mouth shifted, sliding over Ryan's jaw, then lower, Z's breath fanning his neck. "I could make you come just like this."

Ryan grunted, knowing it was true.

Z's lips trailed up his jaw then brushed the outer shell of Ryan's ear. "But I'd rather have you fucking me when you come."

Another rumble burst from Ryan's chest, his cock throbbing in Z's hand. Opening his eyes, he met Z's hungry gaze.

"Upstairs?" Ryan asked.

"Right here." Z stepped back, reaching into his pocket and retrieving…

Ryan laughed. "You come prepared."

"I'm prepared to come." Z smirked.

"Naked," Ryan insisted, retrieving the condom and small packet of lube from Z's fingers before shedding his own clothes and rolling the latex over his cock.

When Z was naked, his big hand gliding up and down his thick cock, Ryan found himself transfixed for a moment. Zachariah Tavoularis was the most beautiful man he'd ever laid eyes on. But not only that, he was so much more than a great body and an attractive face. He was sexy and funny and…

Ryan shook off the thought, not wanting to turn this into something more than it was. Right now, right here, this was spontaneous sex, something they both needed. Ryan wasn't supposed to be conjuring up feelings for Z.

"Come here," Z commanded, somehow still in control, though Ryan should've been.

Moving forward, Ryan kept his eyes trained on Z's hand stroking up and down his thick cock. "Turn around," Ryan commanded, flicking his eyes upward to meet Z's.

Z turned. Slowly.

"Put your hands on the sofa."

Z did as Ryan instructed, bending forward, his legs spread wide, an open invitation if there ever was one. Unable to resist, Ryan pressed up against Z's back, resting his lips on Z's smooth skin, sliding his hand around and jacking Z's cock a few times, relishing the way the man moaned in response.

"You like that?"

"So fucking much," Z groaned.

After coating his fingers with lube, Ryan resumed stroking Z's cock with one hand while he teased Z's anus with his fingers, pushing one inside, then two. He fucked him slowly, gently. It wasn't long before Z had spread his legs wider, begging Ryan to fuck him deeper. He continued, scissoring his fingers in Z's ass before pulling out.

He couldn't hold back any longer, needing to feel Z's body clamped around his dick. Ryan coated his latex-covered cock with lube and lined up to Z, guiding himself in slowly.

"Ry... Oh, fuck yes," Z whispered, bending over farther, giving Ryan better access. "Don't be easy. I don't need easy."

Wanting to give Z what he wanted, Ryan thrust his hips forward, lodging his cock halfway before pushing in all the way, his hips pressed up against Z's ass.

"Aww, yes. Fuck me. Hard," Z growled.

Gripping Z's hips, Ryan pulled back, thrust his hips forward, pulled back again. Shallow at first, then deeper until he was pounding into Z, his fingers digging into Z's flesh as he focused on the point where their bodies joined. Ryan was mesmerized by the carnal sight of his cock tunneling in and out of Z's ass, rocked by the intense sensation, his skin feeling as though it were too tight for his body.

"Jack yourself off," Ryan insisted. "Stroke your dick hard and fast, Z."

Z released the edge of the couch and took his dick in his hand, furiously stroking himself while Ryan continued to drive deep into Z's body. Neither of them spoke other than rough growls and groans as Ryan fucked Z against the sofa.

It felt as though hours passed, but was only minutes as Ryan drilled his dick into Z's ass, fucking him harder and harder until they were both sweating. Ryan hit the point of no return, his eyes crossing, lost in the ecstasy of Z's body. He cried out at the same time Z did, both of them groaning as they came.

He was weak and tired, but Ryan managed to pull his cock out of Z, stumbling until his back met the wall, his lungs working double time in an attempt to suck in air.

"Now that's what I consider a damn good day off," Ryan rasped, unable to tear his eyes off Z.

Z's gaze found Ryan's and he smiled. So beautiful.

"I'd have to agree with you there," Z huffed. "Best damn day off I've had…ever."

TWENTY-SIX

"Tell me about your dad."

Z peered over at RT from beneath his sunglasses, wishing he'd heard him wrong but knowing he hadn't. They'd been relaxing in the sun for the past hour, jumping into the pool when they were hot, drinking beer and watching the waves crash below, but apparently the silence had been too much for RT.

"What about him?" Z asked, trying to prepare an answer that would be sufficient for RT.

"Tell me about the crash."

Z hated talking about the accident that had put his father in a coma for the past four years, but it was much easier to discuss that than the rest of it, so Z told him. "He'd been on a business trip to Houston. On the night he was comin' home, there was a bad storm. The police say that visibility was minimal on the highway, so they suspect that he didn't see the lines on the road, possibly crossing over into the other lane. An eighteen-wheeler was coming right at him, so they believe my dad swerved to get back into his lane but overcorrected and ended up going off the road and hit a tree head on.

"A woman with her two children were behind him when it happened. Thankfully she stopped, because they said it could've been a while before anyone would've noticed him due to the rain."

"What about the eighteen-wheeler? He stop?"

"No." Z had long ago stopped blaming the trucker who hadn't bothered to stop and render aid, though the witness said there was no way he wouldn't have known what had happened. Regardless, Z knew deep down that it wouldn't have changed the outcome if he had. "He was lucid for a bit, but after they rushed him to the hospital, he was unconscious. He's still in a coma," Z added sadly.

"Any change in his condition?" RT asked.

"Not yet." Yes, Z still held out hope that his father would one day open his eyes, despite the fact that four years had passed since the accident.

"Do you visit him often?"

Z didn't look at RT when he answered. "Every chance I get." What he didn't tell RT was that he spent every single night in the long-term care wing of the nursing home when he was in town. He hated that his father was alone in that place, although he knew the medical staff was looking after him. Z didn't want to think that his father could possibly wake up one day and he wouldn't know where he was, how he'd gotten there, or even who was there—and that was if he had all his faculties, which the doctors weren't sure would be the case, even if he did regain consciousness. It didn't matter to Z; he wanted to be by his father's side as much as he could.

"And your mom? How's she doing?"

Happy to change the subject, Z uncurled his hands, realizing he'd been fisting them at his side. "She's doin' well. She's been workin' at an elementary school in Plano since she relocated." Glancing out at the water, Z resigned himself to telling RT the rest. "She recently met someone."

"A man?"

Z nodded. "They met in a support group for grieving spouses. She's still having a really hard time with it all. My dad's been in a coma for so long. They've stated there's a ninety percent chance he'll never wake up, and if he does, he'll have significant brain damage. She's put her life on hold in the hopes he'll wake up."

"What do you think about that?" RT didn't sound judgmental, which made Z feel marginally better.

"I want her to be happy. She didn't intentionally start dating, so meeting this man was happenstance, but he knows what she's goin' through, so that helps." Z knew that his sister was encouraging their mother to keep living her life, which he understood, but it was still a hard thing to wrap his mind around.

"Is it serious?"

"Yes." Much more serious than Z had expected. "She loves him."

"Do you think they'll get married?"

"No," Z answered immediately. Although he wasn't even sure how that would be possible. She would have to divorce Thomas in order to do so, which seemed complicated and...wrong. "Jensyn mentioned that and my mother nearly lost it. She's insistent that she will remain by my dad's side because she takes those vows seriously."

"What does this new guy think about that?"

Z wasn't exactly sure. He'd met the man a time or two, and he seemed nice enough, even supportive, but Z was still leery to trust him.

Z stared out at the water, watching dark clouds roll in from afar. When RT didn't say anything more, Z felt both relief and disappointment. He liked that RT had asked him about his family, that he had wanted to know more.

No matter what RT would say, Z knew that it meant there was more of a connection between them than RT would be willing to admit.

And that was the bright spot in an otherwise gloomy conversation.

Ryan didn't move from his position on the lounge chair, although he wanted to go to Z, to offer him physical comfort. He'd heard the devastation in Z's voice when he talked about his father, and it was apparent that the situation weighed heavily on him. It didn't surprise Ryan that Z went to see his father whenever he could. From what he'd heard over the years, Z was very close to his family, even though they'd been mostly separated since Z and his brother and sister had grown up and started to make their own way in the world.

But that was the type of man Z was; anyone who knew him knew that. He supported everyone he came in contact with. Never one to judge or belittle, always finding a way to help if he could. Another quality Ryan found so damned appealing.

"Are you ready to go in?" Z finally asked after a few minutes of silence.

Ryan sat up. "I was thinkin' we could take a walk."

Z peered back at him, nodding instead of saying anything. They headed down to the beach, and once they made it to the water, Ryan took Z's hand in his, unable to resist.

For a brief moment, Z's hand was tense, as though the action had surprised him. Ryan knew how he felt, because he'd surprised himself. But after a few minutes of walking, holding Z's hand, it felt right, almost as though this was the exact place they were supposed to be at this particular moment in time.

The feeling was incredibly confusing considering Ryan was both scared and content. He didn't know what he was supposed to feel, and he wasn't sure whether this was real or temporary. Because they were alone here on assignment, paired together for an undetermined amount of time, Ryan feared they could very well be leaning on one another as a way to pass the time.

As much as he wanted to believe this was real, this was something that might possibly go somewhere in the future, his doubts still outweighed his hope. Then there was the mission, which was not going well, could very well fail because of their lack of focus. That wasn't something he wanted to think about, because he would never forgive himself if he put his feelings above the importance of the job.

Now, as he peered over at Z, he wondered what he was thinking about, but he couldn't bring himself to ask. Whether or not that was because he didn't want to know the answer or simply because he couldn't bear to think about what would happen after this assignment was over, Ryan didn't know.

And for now, he was going to have to be content with that.

TWENTY-SEVEN

Saturday evening

For most of the day, while they got ready for the gallery show, Z felt as though he were walking around outside his own body. Every time he glanced at RT, he pictured him spread out before him, taking Z's cock deep in his ass, begging for more, and then... Then Z would remember the way they'd lounged around the house yesterday, swimming in the pool and the ocean before climbing into bed once again and making love. Afterward, RT had pressed up against Z's side while Z trailed his fingers leisurely up and down RT's back until they both had fallen asleep.

By far, best day of his life. Up to this point, anyway.

And ever since, it hadn't been easy to disguise the constant hard-on he sported, but now that he and RT were walking into the art gallery, Z knew he would have to put more effort into not thinking about what had transpired between them over the last forty-eight hours.

Easier said than done, that was for sure. His brain was on the fritz, constantly trying to decipher what was to come, what could possibly happen between him and RT when they returned to Dallas after the assignment was over, whether they would still be able to see one another. Most importantly, whether or not Z would find himself slamming headfirst into that emotional brick wall RT normally kept between them if it came out of nowhere.

There was always that possibility, but he was trying his best not to think about that.

Once they had finally crawled out of bed that morning, they'd showered together again—something Z could quite easily get used to—then headed for the kitchen. Z had made breakfast, and RT hadn't complained, though it hadn't been quite as intimate as the day before, because RT was once again in full-out work mode. The fantasy had been completely shattered when Clay had showed up, insinuating himself in between them in order to work.

For most of the day, RT had been on the phone with Austin and Dominic, both of Sniper 1's tech geniuses, attempting to locate how Jericho Ardent was moving his painting since they'd failed at locating its whereabouts beforehand. After hours of hacking, they'd come up empty. It was clear to all of them that Jericho was serious about protecting his treasure, and for the first time in a long time, Z had to wonder whether they were going to be able to successfully complete this mission.

Granted, Jericho had hired them to protect the painting while at the gallery, and RT had done as he'd told Jericho he would, hiring a handful of rent-a-cops for appearances, so technically the mission was still a go. Colby, who'd been called in to help, had suggested that they bring in their own people as a decoy, hoping for a better chance at retrieving the painting before Jericho could whisk it off to safety once again, but that was shot down immediately. It would've been a good idea prior to Jericho and Amahn having seen most of their agents at the party on Thursday night, but now, not so much. There was no way they could pull it off, so RT had opted to go with the original plan.

"What happens if we don't get our hands on this painting?" Z asked RT now as they roamed the perimeter of the room, surveying all the people who'd arrived. The place was packed, everyone dressed in formal attire, including him and RT, as well as Clay and Ally.

The tuxedo Z had been told to wear was again one that Kira had shipped down to them. It wasn't Z's favorite, that was for sure, but he preferred it to the other suits he owned. Tonight he knew he had no choice but to be on his best behavior, so he refused to fidget in the penguin suit. This was the critical moment, the time when they would either make or break this assignment. Protecting the painting for Jericho was second to acquiring it and handing it over to DHS, but until they had a clear opportunity, they'd agreed to act as though their only intention was keeping an eye on it.

Rather than explain the repercussions if the assignment went to the shitter, RT scowled back at him, his lips a hard, thin line.

"Got it." Z didn't need an explanation.

It wasn't typical for them to fail. In fact, it rarely happened. But they weren't perfect, and no plan was guaranteed to be a success. At this point, Z could only hope for an unexpected twist that would work in their favor.

While keeping a smile planted on his face, Z followed RT around the large, open room, giving the art a cursory glance while taking note of the people he recognized and those he didn't.

"Update?" Trace's terse tone rang in Z's earpiece.

For a moment, he'd forgotten that Trace and Colby were sitting on Jericho's beach house, ready to go in and grab the fake painting that they'd previously located and reconfirmed a short time ago was still in the same place. They would need it. Eventually.

RT turned to face Z, smiling as he spoke. "Original painting's in place. A lot of interest."

"Not from me," Clay noted, and from where Z stood, he could see Ally peering up at him confused. She'd been warned they would be wearing earpieces, but he doubted she'd expected to have Clay randomly blurting things out.

Z smiled back at RT, nodding in an attempt to join in on the ruse, hoping others would think they were having an intimate conversation.

"We're bored," Trace complained via the earpiece, making Z chuckle.

"Jack yourself off," RT muttered.

"Don't need to," Trace instantly answered. "I've got a wife now, remember? Oh, that's right, she's your sister."

"Fuck you, Kogan," RT grumbled, his piercing blue eyes meeting Z's momentarily.

Z couldn't help but laugh. Trace had taken to tormenting RT regarding the fact that he'd married Marissa. Granted, those taunts didn't usually involve details of their sex life, and he could tell RT wasn't amused.

"We've got incoming," Z told RT when he caught Jericho and Amahn moving their way.

RT turned, greeting the two men with a handshake and a smile.

That was when Z noticed another man, this one a spitting image of Amahn, only younger. The same young man Z had seen in the picture in Amahn's office.

"I'd like you to meet my son, Amit. Amit, this is RT and Z."

Amit's dark gaze scanned them both briefly, clearly unimpressed, but the only greeting he offered was a curt head nod. He didn't appear happy to be there.

"Amit." RT acknowledged him but didn't bother with further pleasantries. "Are you into art?"

"I work here." Again Amit's face was stony as he responded tersely.

Z's brain turned over that information. Perhaps...

"Well, we better mingle with the others," Amit announced, evidently in a hurry to get away from them.

"Glad you could make it," Amahn said politely, appearing somewhat apologetic for his son's brusque response. Amahn glanced back and forth between RT and Z before taking Jericho's hand and leading the man to another couple standing close by.

"Was that introduction as weird as it sounded?" Trace's deep voice grumbled in Z's ear.

"Most definitely," RT concurred. "Get Dom to find out everything he can on Amit Chopra. ASAP."

"Roger that."

Z met RT's questioning gaze.

The son worked there? "Are you thinkin' what I'm thinkin'?" Z questioned.

"What are y'all thinkin'?" Colby asked, his tone giddy, as though this was the most excitement he'd had all night. Then again, if he was confined to a car with Trace, it probably was.

"Keep an eye on him," RT instructed Z, taking a glass of champagne from a passing waiter before venturing off, leaving Z standing there.

"Right," Z mumbled beneath his breath.

Something was off with RT, but Z didn't know what. Gone was the laid-back guy he'd briefly glimpsed in recent days, and in his place was the no-nonsense workaholic. It was evident the assignment wasn't going as planned. In fact, it looked more and more like they'd be going home empty-handed, which meant...

Fucking hell.

Z sighed, then downed a full glass of champagne in one chug, his nostrils flaring from distaste. Yep, he still hated champagne.

Remembering he was at work, Z set the glass down on a table in the corner, vowing he'd spend the rest of the evening focusing on what was important and not the potential outcome of this endeavor.

Should the mission go to shit, RT would likely hold Z responsible for the failure. Well, maybe not him personally, but RT would definitely blame the circumstances, finding some absurd excuse such as their personal interactions interfering with the outcome.

And right now, that was something Z definitely didn't want to think about.

Ryan needed to put some distance between himself and Z. It was clear he'd allowed his emotions to cloud his priorities, and now they were down to the wire, about to risk an entire assignment because... Fuck. Because Ryan had been fucking horny.

Goddammit.

Why the hell hadn't Ryan thought about Amahn's son being the one responsible for the theft? It made so much damn sense considering Amit would've come around at the same time Amahn had. He would have access because he worked at the gallery, and if Ryan had to guess, he was likely staying at Jericho's with his father.

"Shit."

"Something wrong?"

Ryan peered over to his left to find the woman from the other day, Cassandra Chapman. "No, sorry. Just..."

"Fight with your husband?"

"Oh," Ryan sputtered, surprised by the statement. Following Cassandra's gaze, Ryan glanced across the room to see Z standing there, glaring back at him. "No. No fight." Turning back to her, he added, "And he's not my husband."

"Right. Boyfriend." Cassandra's green eyes twinkled knowingly. "Well, he certainly looks like a man scorned. What'd you do to break his heart?"

Break his heart? *Z?* Ryan doubted Z's heart could be broken. The man was invincible.

Chuckling to himself, though he didn't find the thought at all comical, Ryan turned his attention to the painting in front of him. Jericho's painting, to be exact. "What do you think of this one?" A change of subject was definitely warranted right about now.

Cassandra laughed softly. "Message received. I promise not to pry anymore."

Ryan spared her another glance, forcing a smile.

"As for this painting, I find it oddly appealing, but I don't think it's the artist's brush stroke or use of color that fascinates me."

"No?" Ryan studied the painting again, still not understanding what anyone found fascinating about any of it. Z was right; it was ugly.

"No. It's the backstory about the artist that's compelling. Then again, a lot of famous artists were off their rocker, right? I mean, it's rumored that Van Gogh cut off his own ear."

"Wasn't that recently disputed? That his ear was actually cut off in a fight with a friend?" Good thing he'd had Kira pull up some facts prior to this engagement or Ryan would be lost.

"Yes, but who really knows? It's also said that Van Gogh suffered from schizophrenia, and Michelangelo was said to have obsessive-compulsive disorder. You get the idea. So it's not farfetched to think that Malcolm Jones was a conspiracy theorist and suffered from severe paranoia."

"No, I guess not," Ryan acquiesced.

"The notion that someone could code national security secrets into art... That's what's appealing about this particular piece."

Ryan didn't respond. He didn't know what to say.

"Well, it was nice to see you again," Cassandra said sweetly. "I better mingle with the others so your boyfriend'll quit giving me the evil eye."

Across the room, Z remained in the same position he'd been in, scanning the room smoothly, homing back in on Ryan periodically. Ryan didn't think Z was giving anyone the evil eye, but sure, he could see it from Cassandra's perspective.

"Nice to see you, as well," Ryan answered courteously. "I'll go talk to him."

"Good idea."

Ryan didn't return to Z immediately, although he did cast glances in Z's direction a time or two. It wasn't until Amit came over to talk to one of the rent-a-cops standing a few feet away from Jericho's painting that things started moving. The rest of the patrons of the gallery seemed oblivious to the fact that a theft was likely in the works right there in their midst.

"Dom got the info. Wanna hear it?" Trace's voice reverberated in Ryan's head. Because he was standing alone with several people around him, he whispered an affirmative.

"Born and raised here in the states. Twenty-three years old, never enrolled in any university. Worked some odd jobs until he started here at the gallery when his father transferred. Visits his mother regularly, and based on his social media accounts, he's not all that fond of the fact his father left his mother and is now hooking up with a man."

"So he's doin' this to get back at his father?" Clay questioned from somewhere within the gallery.

"Could be," Colby confirmed. "Or he knows the value of the painting. According to Dom, he's used the Internet to seek interest from potential buyers. And not for its visual appeal, if you know what I mean."

Just fucking great. As it would seem, Amahn's own son was attempting to steal the painting as payback but looking to be financially rewarded for his efforts. At least they knew that Amit was aware of the value and the reason it was valuable, which would make him even more determined.

"What do we do now?" Trace asked.

"We'll sit on the gallery until the show is over," Ryan told them after moving to a more private location. "That's our only option."

"So you do want us to snag this one?" Colby inquired, referring to the fake painting at Jericho's beach house.

Ryan took a deep breath, scanned the room again. Amit was definitely attempting to lure the guard away from the painting. If he had the other fake, he could easily pull off what Ryan had been hoping to do himself. Replacing the original with the fake when no one was expecting it wasn't as easy as it sounded, but at some point tonight, Ryan figured it would be possible. And since Amit would be armed with the fake he'd stolen, he'd easily be able to do it.

"Yes. Get the painting, then get your asses over here and watch the gallery." Ryan didn't think they'd need it. Unfortunately. But he'd rather be safe than sorry.

Since pulling the stunt off looked less and less feasible with every passing minute, Ryan had to figure out a way to throw Amit off long enough to replace the original with the fake they had, and then they'd be home free.

That or they'd have failed miserably, and Ryan wasn't sure how he felt about that.

TWENTY-EIGHT

Amit couldn't believe those assholes were back.

Friends of Jericho's. Uh-huh. They were fucking security guards, that's who they were. And they were there to keep an eye on the stupid painting, right alongside these idiot rent-a-cops who thought they were so fucking tough.

This was not going the way he'd planned, and he had Jericho's paranoia to thank for that. Then again, Amit felt rather accomplished since he'd managed to put everyone on high alert. It confirmed for him just how much that painting was worth. And since his bank account had just accumulated a very large sum of money in the last couple of hours, Amit was going to reap the rewards before the night was over.

The only thing he had to do was replace the original painting with the fake he'd stored in the back room, and then he'd be home free. He'd spent the last half hour getting acquainted with one of the guards, hoping to gain his trust, possibly lower his guard. Worst case, Amit knew he only had to toss the guy a little money. Turned out that rent-a-cop number one—James something or other—was the perfect man to do what Amit needed. He had four kids and a wife, and his job as a police officer didn't pay enough, which was why he took shitty jobs such as this one to supplement his income.

It wouldn't take much to get him to look the other way.

But for now, Amit needed to bide his time. The show would last for a few more hours, and until the place cleared out, he wouldn't be able to get his hands on the painting.

His phone buzzed in his pocket.

Amit retrieved it, then glanced at the screen.

I expect delivery by first thing tomorrow morning.

Yes. Delivery. Great.

Amit had promised the buyer that he'd deliver the painting by tomorrow, which was why Amit had insisted on half of the money up front. That half was enough to keep him living in the lap of luxury for quite a few years, but the rest would be icing on the cake. At that point, Jericho Ardent would never be able to look down his snooty nose at Amit ever again.

However, Amit did have to find a way to get those big assholes out of the way. He'd never have a chance as long as they continued to watch him.

And that was where James came in.

TWENTY-NINE

The night progressed exactly as Z had feared it would. RT was purposely keeping his distance, and based on the fact the place was officially clearing out, it didn't appear as though they were going to get their hands on the painting.

Fucked up all around, if you asked him.

They'd made a valiant effort to keep Amit's grubby paws off of it for the past few hours, so there was that. The kid wasn't happy that Z had become his shadow, but Z could say the same. Having spent most of his time following Amit around, listening to his childish ramblings while attempting to make conversation with the uptight little prick wasn't Z's idea of a good time, either.

In fact, he'd prefer to be plucking his own nose hairs with a pair of rusty pliers.

If it hadn't been for James, the head guard from the security company they'd used, they very well could've been chasing their own asses. In circles. Turned out that James was a solid guy, a Corpus Christi cop who couldn't be bought, although from what Z had heard, Amit had tried to lure him with a rather large sum of cash. Five grand wasn't bad bank for a night's work. Too bad for Amit, not all men could be bought.

That didn't change anything, though. Z was still hovering over Amit, keeping him close like a baby bear cub, while RT stuck close to Jericho.

"What's the plan?" Trace huffed in Z's earpiece. "I finished readin' the dictionary. Need somethin' to do."

"Shut up," Colby bellowed. "You were readin' the label on your Gatorade. Not quite the same thing."

"We're still sitting on the painting," Z told him, watching as RT continued to speak with Jericho and Amahn, doing a damn good job of pretending there weren't voices chitchatting in his ear. All three men—Jericho, Amahn, and RT—were keeping one eye on the painting at all times, as though it would vanish in thin air.

If only it were that easy.

When RT finally peered over at Z, the expression on his face didn't give Z a warm and fuzzy feeling.

"Oh, hell," Colby grumbled in Z's ear.

"What's wrong?" Z asked, keeping his eye on RT.

"Did you ever see that movie where the guy killed his boss and stole the money they'd stolen from someone else? The one with that super-tall hot chick who cracked safes for a living... What's her name? Charlene something or other, I think."

"Charlize Theron," Trace corrected. "Damn, she was hot in that movie."

"Dude, she's hot in *any* movie," Colby countered. "Even that one where she was the psycho crazy bitch."

"She was a fucking serial killer, Colby. Only you'd find that hot," Trace countered with a snort.

"Get to the point," RT muttered.

"Right. Sorry," Colby said. "Well, we've got three armored trucks pulling up near the front doors, three more along the back entrance. If my math's correct, they're about to play an advanced version of the shell game with us."

"Shit." RT's expression went from upset to downright pissed.

Shit was right.

"Want us to follow?"

RT shook his head but didn't speak as he approached Z.

"If you ask me," Colby continued, "I think it's in our best interest to ensure that painting stays with Jericho for now. As long as Amit doesn't get his hands on it, we'll have another opportunity."

"Eventually," RT said, sounding as though he agreed but wasn't completely on board with the plan.

"Your call, boss man." Trace didn't seem put off by the plan, based on his tone.

"Let's do that," RT stated. "We'll keep the rent-a-cops in place, Z and I'll ensure the painting gets into one of the trucks while the two of you stand guard outside. For now, it's all we can do."

"Roger that."

The transmitter went silent, and Z waited for RT to take his wrath out on him, but to his surprise, RT didn't. What he did was much, much worse.

"Stick close to Amit," RT instructed when he approached. "Then you get a ride with Clay and Ally once the painting is out of here. They can take you back to your bike. I'll be heading back to Dallas tonight. Feel free to stay at the beach house till morning if you need to."

Son of a bitch.

Just as he'd thought, RT was holding him responsible for this bullshit, though they'd known going in that this would be the likely outcome.

But being brushed aside as though what had transpired between them meant absolutely fucking nothing was what pissed Z off the most. And when he got pissed off, he didn't do what a lot of men did. Z didn't pick a fight or instigate an argument. He shut down. It was easier than dealing with the repercussions of the emotional fallout.

He should've known, damn it. He should've known better than to give in, to go after what he wanted. RT was good at shutting people out. Damn good. So much so that Z didn't have the energy to try to claw his way past those walls again.

"Got it," he told RT curtly.

RT looked up at him momentarily. For an instant, Z thought he saw remorse in that clear blue gaze, but it was masked quickly.

Rather than push, because in the end, the outcome would undoubtedly be the same, Z did as instructed—he turned and walked away.

Two hours later, once again wearing jeans, a T-shirt, and his protective gear, Ryan crouched low on his bike, watching the lines on the highway pass by at a blurring speed. He had stopped by the beach house long enough to change and get his bike, but he hadn't run into Z. He had hoped he wouldn't, but Ryan had to admit he was slightly disappointed.

He couldn't stop thinking about Z, about the way he'd looked when Ryan had told him that he'd be going back to Dallas tonight.

It wasn't as though Ryan had a choice. This thing between them, deep down they'd both known it was temporary. Sure, he hated that he'd put that look on Z's face, but he had to get his head back in the game. He'd fucked up royally.

Not Z. Ryan.

He'd allowed himself to get sidetracked and they'd failed. Jericho still had the painting, Amit was still lurking, but at least the kid hadn't been able to steal it yet. So they hadn't failed Jericho completely, but in the end, they hadn't really helped him, either. They'd been working against him the entire time, and still Jericho had managed to outsmart them, keeping the painting in his possession with a few extra eyes on the prize in the interim.

Regardless, Ryan had let Sniper 1 Security down. He'd been distracted, and in the end, he'd let the mission become second, rather than first as it should've been all along. The only positive was that this hadn't been a life-or-death situation or he very well could've been responsible for a grizzly outcome.

Damn it.

Whipping around a slow-moving car, Ryan focused on the road. Although it was closing in on two in the morning, he wasn't the least bit tired. Adrenaline still pumped furiously through his veins, anger radiating from his pores.

How had he let himself be manipulated by so many people? Going into this assignment with Z had been a mistake, and he'd allowed his father to pull the strings. He should've known better than to think there was a happily ever after in his future, but there for a few hours, it had seemed within his grasp. What had happened between him and Z... Ryan hadn't wanted it to be temporary.

It was clear that when he allowed himself to be distracted, he lost his edge and he came up empty-handed. On all fronts. Now, not only did Ryan have to deal with the guilt of failing, he also had to deal with the guilt of hurting Z. That was the last thing he'd intended, but clearly Ryan couldn't handle Z *and* running a multimillion-dollar company at the same time. At this rate, if he continued down this path, he would let everyone down, and Ryan couldn't allow that to happen.

Unfortunately, letting one person down—Z—was a hell of a lot easier than disappointing everyone.

Or so he wanted to believe.

THIRTY

Two months later – October

"Hey, Dad," Z called out to his father as he walked into the bright, cheery room. The blinds were open, the setting sun peering in and highlighting the tan walls. The television was on, set to the travel channel as Z had instructed it to be at this time of day.

For all intents and purposes, it looked like a room someone would want to spend their days in. There were knickknacks on the dresser, a couple of pictures on the wall, small framed photos on the table beside the bed, even a comfortable recliner Z had brought to furnish the room. The only thing that was off was the unconscious man who'd spent far too many days and nights inhabiting the room without ever saying a single word.

There on the hospital bed—some fancy, specialized model that was filled with air, to aid with circulation—was Z's father, lying on his back, eyes closed, surrounded by machines that kept track of his vital signs and brain activity. Thomas Tavoularis was in a perpetual state of sleep. Aside from the fact that he didn't open his eyes, had to be fed through a gastrostomy tube—or G-tube—in his stomach, and had lost a significant amount of weight over time, he still looked like the resilient man Z had admired for his entire life.

"The nurses tell me you're doin' well, Dad. Sorry I haven't been here in a couple of days. Had another assignment. This one took me to Oregon. Easy peasy, though. Got back as soon as I could." Z took a seat beside his father's bed as he had done every night when he was in town for the past four years.

The doctors continued to tell them that his father could still wake up, though the prolonged coma would likely leave him mentally altered. Since he was breathing on his own and didn't require any type of life support aside from the feeding tube and IVs, they had put him in a nursing home that catered to long-term care, where he could be monitored around the clock. While Z's mother visited once or twice a week, Cindy had had no choice but to get back to a normal life. As normal as it could be, anyway.

Which was the reason Z had started visiting, staying with his father overnight.

"Z! You're here. So glad to see you."

Z shifted in his chair, glancing over at the door to see Buddy Stallone standing there, eyes wide with excitement.

"Hey, Buddy. Come in. Have a seat."

Buddy ambled in, slow-moving now that he was closing in on his eighty-fifth birthday in just a couple of months.

"I was telling Dad about my trip."

Buddy's grin widened as he gingerly lowered himself into the extra chair.

"Have you had dinner yet?" Z asked the elderly man.

"Not yet. I was hoping you'd be here."

"Well, I'm here. Maybe we could go down and eat together."

"I'd like that. I've been talkin' to Tom." Buddy glanced over at Z's father. "Tellin' him about your last assignment. The one with the painting."

"Yeah?"

"I'm sure he's so proud of you."

Z's chest tightened as he watched the rhythmic rise and fall of his father's chest.

While his friends assumed he was out with different men, Z had spent the last four years right there in the nursing home. He'd become an honorary member of the staff due to the many hours he spent there, not only with his father but talking to Buddy and several other patients who resided there. They would share meals, watch television, sit outside under the stars. Z looked forward to spending time there. All in the hopes his father would wake up one day. Z wanted to be there when he did, not wanting Thomas to wake up confused. And yes, even after all this time, Z still held on to that hope.

"Hey, Dad," Z said, smiling over at Buddy. "I'm gonna take Buddy down to dinner now. We'll be back and I'll tell you all about Oregon. Okay?"

Z got to his feet, helping Buddy up as he did.

"Oregon, huh?" Buddy inquired as they slowly made their way down the hall toward the cafeteria.

"Yeah. Nothing exciting, really."

"Everything you do is exciting, boy," Buddy told him. "Everything."

During the years Z had been coming to the nursing home, he'd become close to Buddy. The man had no children, and his wife had passed away nearly a decade earlier. He lived there, in another wing of the building, due to his deteriorating health brought on by age, and he was one of the many who actually enjoyed being there. They'd talked at length about how Buddy had been living alone with no one to talk to, so having so many people around eased Buddy's mind, gave him something to look forward to.

They'd become friends, and Buddy was always eager to hear about Z's latest assignment. The man was quite intrigued by it, always asking questions, encouraging Z to talk, sometimes even when he didn't want to.

"What's for dinner tonight?" Z asked as he helped Buddy into a chair at one of the many tables.

"Lasagna," Buddy told him, looking up at him with so much happiness on his face.

"Your favorite. I'll be right back, okay?"

"Don't forget the lemon cookie."

Z leaned in close. "If you don't tell anyone, I'll get you two."

Buddy's smile made Z's chest swell, some of the anger and hurt he'd been experiencing for the past couple of months easing. It'd been difficult since he'd parted ways with RT in Port Aransas. They hadn't spoken much, and even then, their conversations were restricted to work only.

RT had stopped including Z in assignments that would allow them to work alongside one another, but Z hadn't bothered to express his resentment of that. It was easier to smile and accept his fate.

"Hey, Barb," Z greeted one of the ladies who worked in the cafeteria.

"Zachariah!" The smaller woman came over and hugged him, her graying hair stuffed into a hair net. "Have you seen Buddy yet?"

"I have. I'm here to grab his dinner."

"Will you be eating?" Barb inquired.

Z nodded. "Of course."

"Perfect. Let me grab you a few things while you get Buddy's."

"Thanks, Barb."

After taking the small plates with predetermined portions already on them, Z returned to the table where Buddy was waiting for him.

"Where's yours?" Buddy asked.

"Barb's makin' it."

The twinkle in Buddy's brown eyes reflected his amusement. "She knows you so well."

That she did. Barb knew that Z couldn't live off the small portions of food they served to the residents, so she always seemed to have something special on hand. They knew to expect him, because at most, he would be gone for four, maybe five days. If he had an assignment that would be longer, he always made sure to inform the nursing staff as well as the center's director. Since they checked in with him every single day, he felt it was important to keep them apprised of his whereabouts.

When Barb called out to him, Z held up one finger to Buddy, letting him know he'd be right back. After grabbing the tray, piled high with chicken breast, broccoli and cheese casserole, two rolls, and a huge slice of cherry pie, Z returned to the table.

"I remember when I could eat that much," Buddy told him.

"That was last week, right?" Z teased.

"It feels like it. So tell me again about the painting. Then, I'll get to hear about Oregon when you tell your father."

Z smiled, feeling almost normal once again as he proceeded to tell Buddy, the man he considered as much family as his own, the same story he'd told him at least five times now.

A loud noise had Ryan jerking his head up in time to see Trace heading down the hall toward his office. It was late on a Saturday, so Ryan hadn't expected anyone to be there, certainly not Trace Kogan.

"What are you—" Ryan didn't get the question out before Trace was slamming Ryan's office door, staring down at him with fire burning in his almost eerie white-gray eyes.

"You're a fucking asshole, you know that?"

Leaning back in his chair, he considered Trace, taking him in. His posture was defensive, arms crossed over his chest, jaw set, mouth a thin line—mad-dogging, he'd heard Z refer to that look. The guy was angry, no doubt about that. Based on that comment, Ryan didn't have to guess at whom.

"Why now?" Ryan asked for the hell of it.

"What the fuck did you do to Z?"

That got Ryan's attention. "Is he okay?"

"Not since the two of you fucking came back from Port A. What the hell did you do to him? Why're you treatin' him like a leper?"

"What the hell are you talkin' about?"

"I'm the one askin' the questions," Trace demanded.

"And I'd answer them if I knew what the fuck you're in here bitchin' at me for."

"Why'd you send him to Oregon?"

Ryan tried to rein in his anger, but it wasn't as easy as it used to be. Ever since he and Z had spent time in Port A, the failed mission, Ryan had been hanging by a thread. His emotions were all over the damn place, and he had no idea why. This confrontation with Trace wasn't helping. "It's not your place to question where I assign my people."

"*Your* people?" Trace snapped.

"Yes, *my* people," Ryan hissed, launching to his feet and slamming his hands down on his desk. "I don't see you or your brothers stepping up to help out."

It appeared Trace didn't have an immediate response to that.

"So don't come in here hoping for a pissing match. In case you haven't noticed, I'm in charge here. I'll send people where I think they'll do the most good."

Trace's eyebrows shot upward. "Is that right? And you thought that Z was the best fit for a fucking babysitting job? In *Oregon*?"

"Someone's got to take the jobs, Trace." He had no idea why Trace was in there questioning his authority. It was so unlike him.

"Better suited to follow some big-mouthed exec around than, say, to help with the missing person case here?"

"Yes," Ryan lied. Trace had him there. Z had been needed on the case Ryan was currently working, but Ryan found it too difficult to work directly with Z. Two months had passed since their...whatever it was...but Ryan still couldn't look the man in the eye.

"You are such a fucking liar," Trace growled. "I used to think that you had everyone's best interest at heart. That you actually fucking cared. Your recent actions have me doubting that."

"Fuck you," Ryan snapped. "Fuck you and the goddamn giant white horse you fucking rode in on, Trace."

"You're lettin' your own selfish motives lead you around."

"It's better than bein' led around by my dick," Ryan yelled, instantly slamming his mouth shut.

Trace's posture softened somewhat, his voice lowered. "Is *that* what happened? You and Z?"

Ryan refused to answer the question, forcing himself to calm down.

"Did Z do something?"

"No," Ryan immediately answered. "He didn't do anything. I did. I fucked up."

Trace stared back at him as though he'd lost his mind. These days, Ryan felt as though he had. Ever since the fuckup with the Jericho Ardent case, Ryan had started doubting everything he did.

Taking a deep breath, Ryan met Trace's gaze once again. "I'm sure Z understands."

"No, you *think* he does. You're not fucking sure of anything."

"Get to the point, Trace."

"Turns out, your sister is quite the investigator," Trace told him, pulling up a chair and dropping into it.

"What're you talkin' about?" Ryan stood up straight, crossing his arms over his chest as he waited for Trace to elaborate.

"Apparently, Z's extracurricular activities have been making her crazy. No one knows what he does, and everyone's just assumed…"

"I don't wanna hear about it." There was no way Ryan could sit there and listen to Trace tell him that Z had moved on with his life, resumed his late-night trysts, when Ryan did nothing but think about that one perfect day in his life when he'd had Z all to himself.

"That's the thing. You do. Z's not the slut everyone's accused him of bein'."

"Playboy," Ryan corrected. He did not like the idea of someone calling Z a slut.

"And the difference is?" Trace lifted an eyebrow.

Ryan pinned Trace with an irritated look.

"Fine. Call it what you will. But Z's not out with different men every night. He's out with the *same* man."

"Trace, I don't—"

"His father," Trace interrupted. "Z goes to the nursing home where his father has been for the last four years. Every. Single. Night. The man's still in a coma, but his loyal son spends every night there when he's in town. Most of the time he even sleeps there. They've practically adopted him as one of the staff members."

Ryan's heart thudded painfully in his chest. He remembered Z's answer when Ryan had asked if he visited his father. *Every chance I get.* It wasn't as nonchalant as Ryan had suspected it was. And he certainly hadn't expected to hear that Z went every night he was home. It explained so much, though. Z spending his time with his comatose father answered every question Ryan had ever had about him. It also confirmed his suspicions that Z wasn't the playboy Trace had accused him of being.

"And you've been sending him off on these random assignments, rather than keeping him local. You're not only putting your own selfish needs in front of everyone else's, you're takin' Z away from people who need him." Trace got to his feet, a frown still marring his face. "Z's my best friend. And you're like a brother to me, but I can't sit back and watch you hurt him because you're too fucking scared to admit that you care about him."

Ryan swallowed hard. "It's not that simple."

"From where I sit, it's exactly that simple. Z is *not* Kevin. Not even fucking close. You need to remember, we've all been hurt in this life, but what we do with that pain is what counts. We can harp on it for as long as we want, but it doesn't change anything. In the meantime, while you're tryin' to protect yourself, you're ignoring everyone else. And isn't that our motto...protect by any means necessary?" Trace's hands dropped to his sides. "I'd like to think that applies to the people we care about, too."

Ryan didn't get a chance to refute anything Trace said, because he was suddenly alone in his office once again, hating himself more now than he had already.

Yet he still had no idea what he was supposed to do about that.

THIRTY-ONE

At eight o'clock, Z resumed his post beside his father's bed. Most of the residents went to sleep early, or retired to their room, at least. That gave Z time to spend with his father, something he always looked forward to.

For most of his life, Z had used his father as his sounding board. These days, he still told his father everything, even if the man couldn't give him any advice. He wanted to believe that his father could hear him, knew that he wasn't alone.

"What d'ya wanna do tonight, Dad?" Z asked, flipping through the channels on the television as he got settled into the recliner he'd brought from his own house, giving him a comfortable place to sleep without taking up too much room. "We could watch the history channel, but it doesn't look like there's anything good on." Glancing over at his duffel bag that he'd placed on the dresser, Z remembered the other items he'd brought. "I've got a new Guinness Book of World Records book I could read to you."

"I think he'd like that better."

Z's head jerked toward the voice at the same time he launched himself out of his chair. "Jensyn. What're you doin' here?"

There, looking as pretty as always, was his kid sister. His heart leapt as he hurtled toward her, lifting her into his arms and squeezing her tightly.

"You're crushing me, Z," Jensyn whispered.

"Sorry. It's just... God, it's good to see you." He managed to keep his voice down, despite the excitement that churned through him. Z hadn't seen Jensyn since Christmas, due to both of their busy schedules. "Have you talked to Reese? Does he know you're here?"

Jensyn moved farther into the room, closing the door a little to give them some privacy. "He's comin' up tomorrow. I came right from the airport, so I'm exhausted. I've only got a couple of days, but I wanted to come see Dad before I crashed for the night. And you, of course."

Z's sister looked sad as she moved closer to their father's bed.

"Hi, Daddy," she said softly. "I'm here. I just stopped in for a minute, but I'll come back tomorrow, spend the day with you."

Z watched his father closely, wishing for a sign of life. Had Thomas Tavoularis been awake, he would've pulled Jensyn to him and crushed her the same way Z had.

Jensyn leaned down and kissed Thomas on the forehead before standing up straight and facing Z once more. "I can't stay long. I need to get a hotel room."

Z frowned. "You can stay at my place. It's empty."

"Are you sure?"

Rummaging through his gym bag, Z found his house key, sliding it off the ring and handing it over to Jensyn. He wasn't going to give her any other options. "Positive. You'll have it all to yourself. I'll call Marissa so she can get you past the security." Z nodded toward the recliner. "I'm gonna stay here tonight."

"If it's not an imposition," Jensyn said seriously. "I really appreciate it."

"Tomorrow mornin' we'll have breakfast?"

"Sounds like a plan." Jensyn hugged him once more before slipping out of the room.

"Did you see that, Dad?" Z stared at the doorway. "Jensyn's here. And Reese'll be here tomorrow." Turning back to his father, he continued to smile. "That means you better rest up. You remember how it was when the three of us got together."

By the time Ryan got home, it was after midnight, and he was exhausted. The only way he found he could sleep these days was to work nonstop until his body practically gave up on him. Tonight, though, his brain was running amuck. He'd spent countless hours since their trip to Port A thinking about Z, but more so tonight after his conversation with Trace.

The information Trace had relayed—the fact that Z visited his father every night—was something Ryan couldn't stop thinking about. He couldn't imagine how painful that must be for Z, yet the man was always quick to smile, never pushing his own pain and suffering on anyone else. From the outside looking in, no one would know that Z wasn't living the high life, doing everything he'd ever wanted to do. Instead, he was taking care of his family, spending time with the people most important to him.

And here Ryan was, wallowing in his own self-pity and letting his life be dictated by work. That was one of the major ways he and Z differed, although Ryan knew Z was dedicated to his job. However, it would appear that Z had other things that he juggled at the same time.

Stripping out of his clothes, Ryan crawled into bed, lying on his back with his hands linked behind his head, staring up at the ceiling, the only light coming from the red glow of the numbers on his alarm clock.

What was Z doing right then? Was he watching television with his father? Reading to him? Or simply talking? Was he lonely?

And what gave Ryan the right to care? He'd walked away from Z. The look on Z's face was still etched into his memory. Part of him had wanted Z to fight for him, but that hadn't happened. Not that he'd deserved it.

Trace was right, Ryan had been acting like a first-rate prick for the last couple of months. He'd been self-serving in his decisions, doing what would be easier for him, not thinking about anyone else.

But they hadn't failed another assignment. That was a good thing. It only went to prove that Ryan didn't have time to focus on anything other than Sniper 1 Security. When he allowed his attention to stray, things went to hell.

Forcing his eyes closed, Ryan breathed deeply, imagining Z, thinking about the last time they'd been together at the beach house. As he finally drifted off, he felt the same guilt stab into his gut, a painful reminder that getting close to someone only ended badly.

THIRTY-TWO

The following morning, Z met Jensyn at a small diner close to the warehouse where he lived. He'd been surprised to find Trace and Marissa had also come along, offering to drive Z's sister rather than force her to take a cab. Seeing the three of them together made Z a tad bit nervous. Okay, it made him really fucking nervous, but what could he do?

"She's much prettier than you are," Trace told him after they'd all taken a seat in a booth near the back.

"I'd hope so," Marissa chimed in. "No one's ever accused Z of bein' pretty."

"No," Jensyn agreed. "But he's had some pretty boyfriends in the past."

"Thanks for sharing that," Z grumbled facetiously, studying the menu, fighting his smile.

"How's your dad?" Marissa inquired.

"He's..." Z glanced between Trace and Marissa, somewhat puzzled by the question. He felt a pang of guilt that he hadn't bothered to share the fact that he spent the majority of his time with his comatose father with his closest friends, but he got the impression Marissa knew more than he'd thought she did. "He's good."

Jensyn spoke up, as though sensing Z's discomfort with the subject. "He's good for a guy who's been in a coma for four years. For the most part, he's healthy, besides his body's natural deterioration. I'd like to think that Z's the reason he keeps fighting to come back to us."

"So the doctors think he'll wake up?" Marissa looked directly at Jensyn.

Yep, Marissa definitely knew more than he'd thought.

"The prognosis was better in the beginning," Jensyn replied, looking at Z briefly as though trying to understand why his closest friends were asking something so basic. "He's suffered immeasurable brain damage, but we've refused to give up on him until we know for sure. He's not bein' kept alive by machines, other than the feeding tube, so it's one of those things where we're hopeful."

"Is that why you spend the night there every night?" Marissa inquired.

Okay, this conversation was definitely not going the way Z had hoped.

"I wish you'd've told me," Trace inserted, watching Z closely.

Yeah, well.

Rather than reprimand him for not being an open book, Jensyn glanced at Z briefly, then turned back to Trace and Marissa. "No matter what it looks like on the outside, my brother's a really private person. Trust me, he doesn't tell me everything, either." Jensyn laughed. "And I try to pry all the time."

"I wish you'd have talked to me before telling them," Z told Jensyn softly.

"What? *Me?* I didn't tell them. They—"

"My wife's nosy, Z. You know that. I've tried to stop her from snooping, but she actually dug this up on her own."

"Figures." Z smiled at Marissa, feeling somewhat relieved that the secret was now out. "I should've known."

"It's a good thing, though," Marissa added, reaching over to pat his hand. "Now we can be there for you when you need us. And Trace can stop spreading rumors that you're a man whore."

"Thanks for that, by the way." Z had long ago given up on trying to stop the steady flow of rumors.

"You're welcome. It's only made you a legend." Trace laughed.

The waitress arrived, taking their order quickly and then hurrying off.

"I'd appreciate it if you'd keep this to yourself, though," Z told Trace and Marissa. "I don't need everyone at the office asking about my personal life."

Trace instantly frowned and Z knew that look.

"Shit, man. I'm sorry."

Z prayed Trace had not told Ryan, but the way Trace's frown deepened, he knew he couldn't be so lucky. "Great."

"What's the big deal?" Jensyn asked. "You always said the people you work with are like family. Wouldn't they want to know?"

The most important person, as far as Z was concerned—RT—already knew. Well, most of it, but not about him spending all his nights there. Regardless, Z clamped his mouth shut. RT didn't deserve to know anything. He had yet to get over the pain RT had inflicted the last time they'd talked, back when he'd sent him on his way without so much as a thanks for the hot sex speech.

It was hard to believe that so much time could pass without either of them speaking directly to one another. At least nothing more than a few text messages pertaining to work, anyway.

Marissa and Trace traded a look. Z wanted to change the subject more than he wanted the triple stack he'd ordered, and his stomach was already attempting to eat itself, he was so hungry.

"There's somethin' more between you and RT, isn't there?" Jensyn's tone was sympathetic.

"No," Z insisted. "Not at all."

"Come on now, Z. You're a lot of things, but a liar ain't one of them."

"Can we talk about somethin' else? Please. Anything but this." Z had had enough of the conversation.

"Fine, let's talk about—"

Before Marissa's suggestion made it out of her mouth, Trace's cell phone rang, the familiar ringtone announcing it was RT on the other end of the line. That strange twinge of hope swelled in Z's chest, along with a small measure of jealousy that RT wasn't calling him. He ignored both.

"What's up?" Trace answered sternly, his arm casually sliding around his wife as he leaned back in the booth. "What? Seriously?" Trace sat up straight once again. "Yeah. Okay. I'll be right there."

Z waited to hear where Trace was off to, but the answer wasn't forthcoming. At least not immediately.

"We've gotta go." Trace kissed Marissa on the lips, confusing Z. If they had to go, why did it look like Trace was kissing *her* good-bye?

"Come on, Z. Take me by the warehouse so I can get my bike. I'll leave the Escalade for the ladies." Trace tossed three twenties onto the table along with his car keys. "We've got an assignment. I'll call you as soon as I know what it entails. You good?"

Marissa nodded, then winked at Jensyn. "Yep. I can always use a little girl time."

Z glanced at his sister. "You're good?"

"Sure. No plans for the day except to visit Dad, so once I'm done there, I'll hang out at your place until Reese gets here."

Reese. Right. Shit. "Tell him I'm really sorry. I'll call when I know more."

"Go protect the world. We'll be fine."

Z had no idea what he was going to protect the world from, but he figured he'd soon find out.

Ryan was waiting in the conference room, everything set up and ready to go when Clay arrived. Rather than wait for Trace, he proceeded to give his brother the high-level details, promising to go in depth when the third member of the team arrived.

Exactly forty minutes after they'd ended their call, Ryan looked up to see Trace stepping into the room, a frown on his face.

Ryan's gaze slid right past Trace to land on…

Schooling his features, Ryan pretended not to be surprised that Trace wasn't alone. Z, in all his beautiful, dark-haired glory, was standing in the doorway, watching the scene before him, looking as baffled as Ryan felt.

"We only need the three of us," Ryan told Trace, hating himself for treating Z like shit, but it'd become a self-preservation instinct.

"Bullshit." Trace stabbed a finger in Ryan's direction, his face darkening with anger. "Now shut the fuck up and tell us what's goin' on."

Ryan bit his tongue, refusing to get into it with Trace while Z and Clay were there, but he made sure Trace saw his answering fury.

"I can go," Z stated, his deep voice drawing Ryan's attention.

"Sit," Trace commanded. "This assignment needs you more than any of us. He's just bein' a jackass."

Ryan ignored Trace's snide remark, even if it was true. "You didn't tell him?"

"Nope. You're the boss. That's your fucking job."

Okay, so Trace was definitely pissed, and it sounded personal, which meant he still harbored some anger toward Ryan regarding what had transpired between him and Z. Made sense. Ryan was pissed at himself as well, but he wasn't good with apologies. However, this definitely wasn't the time or place to drag those skeletons out of his closet.

Ryan motioned for Z to take a seat at the table, refusing to look at him, rather staring at the computer screen. "I got a call from Jericho Ardent a short while ago. Amahn's son, Amit, has disappeared."

"With or without the painting?" Trace questioned.

"Without," Ryan explained. "According to Jericho, the night of the show, he had suspected that Amit was the one who'd attempted to steal the painting. In order to spare Amahn any heartache, he'd decided to talk to Amit himself, hoping to handle the issue without causing a problem between father and son. He thought that had worked, but he continued to have Amit watched."

"If he hired his own security, why's he callin' us?" Clay asked.

"Amit quit his job at the gallery shortly after the show and told Amahn that he was going to spend time with his mother. Amahn received a phone call from her yesterday letting him know that Amit hadn't been home in two days and wanting to see if he'd gone back to Amahn's. After several attempts to get in touch with him, Amahn started to panic."

"And they're sure he disappeared?" Clay inquired.

"They are now," Ryan confirmed. "I had Dom hack the kid's bank account, and there was a large sum of money deposited into his account on the same day as the gallery show. It's slowly been disappearing a little at a time, and it appears Amit's been spending it."

"He took payment for the painting," Z muttered, staring down at the table. "Without having the painting to give in return."

"That's what I think, too," Ryan confirmed.

"You think he tried to pass the fake off as the real thing?" Trace glanced between the three of them.

"More than likely. Probably to buy himself some time until he could get his hands on the real thing." Jericho had given Ryan as much information as he had, but Ryan knew it wasn't enough. "I've got Dom digging to see what else he can find. Told him to trace where the money came from."

"What're we supposed to do?" Clay did not look at all happy.

"We're going to find Amit."

"Fuck," Trace huffed. "If he's a thief, aren't they better off without him?"

Ryan glared at Trace.

"Okay, fine. You're right."

"Where was he last seen?" Z asked.

Ryan met Z's gaze for the first time since Z had stepped into the room. A strange churning erupted in his gut. "Dom's tracing the GPS in his phone. If I'm right, Amit'll try to convince whoever this is—presuming it's the buyer—that Jericho will hand over the original or pay up."

"What if this guy only wants the painting? Will Jericho hand it over?" Z kept his eyes locked with Ryan's.

"Yes. He told me he was willing to do whatever it took to get Amit back safe." Handing over the original painting wasn't something Ryan would allow—at least not unless he had to—but Jericho didn't know that. "That's where we come in. Our only job right now is to find Amit."

Ryan's phone rang, interrupting him. He glanced down at the caller ID. Dom.

"Hey, what'd you find?" Ryan asked, putting the phone on speaker.

"Good news. Sort of… If he's still got his phone on him, and I hope that's the case, then Amit's here in the Dallas area. I've narrowed it down to close to where Courtney lives. I've contacted her to help me out."

Great. Just what Ryan needed, his mafia-wed sister involved in this. Remembering the last time Courtney had gotten Max involved in a case, Ryan looked up at Z. Courtney had sought Max's help in locating a missing girl whose father had abducted her. Thanks to Max, that little girl had been found and delivered back to her mother unharmed. Maybe getting Courtney involved wasn't such a bad idea, after all.

Ryan's cell phone beeped, signaling another call. The number on the screen was Jericho Ardent's. "Lemme call you back, Dom. That's Jericho."

"Sure thing."

The line disconnected, and Ryan hit the button to switch to the other call. "Jericho? I've got Trace, Clay, and Z with me now. Dom's already tracked Amit's cell phone to our area."

"That's good," Jericho said, sounding out of sorts. "I just got a call from a blocked number. The guy said I had six hours to get the painting to him or he'll kill Amit."

"That's actually good," Z said calmly, talking toward the phone. "He'll have to give us a location to deliver to."

"He did," Jericho said, then rattled off the information he'd received.

"We need that painting," Ryan told Jericho. "It's no longer an option."

"I know," Jericho said hurriedly. "I've got my private jet waiting. As soon as I can give him a delivery point, he'll be en route."

It was Ryan's turn to provide information, giving Jericho the address for their private airfield near the compound.

"Please keep me updated." Jericho's voice shook with the instruction.

"Absolutely," Ryan confirmed. "I'm gonna have Dom call you so he can set up a trace on your phone. Give him whatever information he needs. We'll keep you apprised, but we've gotta get boots on the ground first. Give me a couple of hours."

"Thank you."

Jericho disconnected the call, and Ryan grabbed his phone, getting to his feet. "I'll have Dom send the coordinates for the house he's located," he told Trace. "Verify it's the same address Jericho provided, then go get that fake we acquired. Z, come with me. We need to get to the airfield and wait for that painting."

Z nodded, and that was when Ryan realized what he'd done. He would spend the next hour alone in a car with Z because he didn't have a choice.

Why the hell had he done that?

Hoping he didn't appear as uncertain as he felt, Ryan grabbed his laptop and left the three men in the room.

Was he crazy? Or maybe—something that bothered him more than the question of his mental state—he'd paired himself with Z on purpose.

Not that he had any time to think about that.

Never Say Never

Not yet, anyway.

THIRTY-THREE

Walking out to the Escalade, Z made a promise to himself that he would not engage in personal conversation with RT no matter what. He would not let hope take over, either. Seemed his entire life was based on hope these days.

He hoped his father would wake up and be the same man he was before his accident.

He hoped Reese would decide to come work with him, so he'd get the chance to spend more time with his brother.

He hoped Jensyn would graduate early and then decide to move to Dallas to start her career, so, yes, he could spend more time with his sister.

He hoped his mother would find happiness and be able to live her life to the fullest.

He hoped RT would tell him that he was sorry and that he'd made a mistake.

Hope.

Sure, Z was optimistic by nature, but this was a little ridiculous.

Without asking RT's permission, Z climbed into the driver's seat, needing to drive so that he didn't fidget on the way to the airfield. The last thing he wanted was for RT to think he was still affected by him.

Although there was that.

Even when they'd been in the conference room, Z had been overwhelmed by RT's presence. The slight musky scent of his cologne, the sexy hard edge to his jaw as he fell into the role he was born to be in—leader. The attractive way his blond hair curled slightly at the nape of his neck.

It was all making Z crazy, and the last time he'd allowed himself to get distracted by RT, he'd gone and fucked up a good thing. At least before, they'd been friends. RT had been punishing him ever since, forcing him to do remedial tasks or take assignments that should've been handled by junior agents.

But through it all, Z had kept his trap shut, not arguing, not asking why.

Truth was, he didn't *want* to know what RT was thinking. He didn't want to know that RT regretted what had happened between them.

Neither of them spoke for the first ten minutes or so of the drive, to the point the silence was beginning to grate on Z's already frayed nerves. In order to alleviate the itchiness that the tension was causing, Z turned on the radio.

"Walking Away" by Five Finger Death Punch erupted through the speakers.

Walk away. Make it easy on yourself.

Okay, good suggestion, but not what Z needed at the moment. He hit the button for another channel.

"Want to Want Me" by Jason Derulo came on. Z sighed.

Great.

You're the one I want to want me.

Nope. Not helping.

Z jabbed the screen again. Another channel.

"Only Wanna Be With You" by Hootie & The Blowfish.

Okay, seriously. What the fuck?

With his eyes on the road, Z hit the button again. Maybe country music would be better.

"Bottoms Up" by Brantley Gilbert.

Z choked on a laugh. That conjured images better left alone.

Once more.

Ah. This would work.

"Kick the Dust Up" by Luke Bryan.

Yep. He could deal with that.

"Are you okay?" RT asked.

Z glanced over at him quickly. "Never better. You?"

RT didn't answer.

Z turned up the music.

RT instantly turned it down.

"Look, Z, we need—"

"To talk?" Z adamantly shook his head. "No, we don't."

RT twisted slightly in his seat, and Z felt the intensity of his eyes on him. He didn't want RT to look at him. He preferred that RT ignore him as he had for the last two months.

Liar.

"Once this is over..."

Z felt a stab of anger pierce his chest. "Don't make promises, RT. I get it. Fun while it lasted, right?"

With a jerk of the wheel, Z took a hard right after exiting the highway.

"Fuck." RT gripped the handle on the door.

Z gritted his teeth, watching the speedometer climb. Taking a deep breath, he tried to relax. They had a job to do. This wasn't personal. In fact, as far as Z could tell, it'd never been personal for RT. Right place, right time, and all that fucked up, stupid-ass, bullshit.

Yep. Anger. Not helping, either.

"Z—"

"No!" Z exclaimed, slamming his hands on the wheel.

"Z! Goddammit. Slow the fuck down or pull over and let me drive."

He peered down at the speedometer. Whoops. He'd hit ninety-seven. In a fifty-five. Slowing down was probably a good idea. Z couldn't get his foot to listen to his brain. He kept at the same speed, barreling toward the airfield.

"Z." RT slammed his hand down on the console. "I said—"

Z smashed his foot on the brake, the Escalade coming to an abrupt stop, throwing them both forward with the momentum. The only thing keeping them from hitting the windshield was their seat belts.

But the good news, they were at their destination. Without waiting for RT to lecture him, Z ripped off his seat belt, threw open the door, and jumped out, slamming the door behind him. He took a deep breath, emotion lodged in his chest, choking him.

Why had he thought he could endure even a few minutes alone with RT? Every memory he had from that trip to the beach came roaring back, battering and bruising his mind with their intensity. He didn't want to think about it, didn't want to think about RT.

"What the fuck is your problem?" RT yelled, stomping around the truck and coming to stand directly in front of Z.

Z ripped off his sunglasses and stared back at the man he'd fallen head over fucking heels in love with. The same man who'd tossed him aside like last week's garbage.

It took a moment to realize he was breathing hard, like he'd run a mile, the emotion sending his blood pressure soaring.

Not the time or place, he reminded himself.

"Look, Z." RT took off his own sunglasses. "I know you're angry."

Z took a step forward, his fingers itching to touch RT. Unable to contain the beast that threatened to break free, Z growled. "You don't know the fucking half of it."

As soon as the words were out, RT surprised the shit out of him, his hand coming up to wrap around Z's head, pulling him forward and crushing his mouth to Z's.

Instinct. Pure instinct drove what happened next. Z spun them both around, his arms banding around RT as he slammed RT's back into the side of the truck, his mouth fused to RT's, the kiss hard, desperate.

Two months worth of misery, fear, anger... It all came rushing to the surface as he plundered RT's mouth with his own. He grabbed for RT, his hands roaming over him, holding him, needing more. His touch, his taste. Z couldn't get enough.

He could feel RT's fingers digging into the muscles of his back, pulling him closer while he attempted to control the kiss.

A warning bell echoed in Z's brain. He tried to ignore it, but it got louder and louder until he could no longer focus. He jerked back, ripping his lips from RT's as he stared back at the man.

"Z."

The way RT said his name was as though he were trying to calm a wild animal. But that kiss... RT had instigated that. Not Z. He was not to blame for this one.

"Don't," Z hissed, turning away from RT. "Don't bother telling me—"

RT's hand gripped Z's arm, jerking him back around to face him.

Z stood there, momentarily speechless as he looked into those crystal-blue eyes that haunted his dreams.

"What the hell do you want from me, Z?" RT exclaimed, the muscle in his jaw flexing.

Z considered that for a moment. He'd endured so much at the hands of this man. He'd been tossed aside so many times he felt as though he'd been playing a vicious game of tug-of-war and RT had finally let go of the rope, sending Z careening into despair.

"Tell me, Z!" RT yelled. "Tell me what it is you want from me."

"I want you to love me," Z said simply, swallowing hard. He couldn't believe the words had come out of his mouth, but based on the stunned look on RT's face, they definitely had.

RT took a step closer, the warmth of his fingers sliding over Z's jaw and him feeling that dull pain erupt in his chest again, right there where his heart was. He could hardly breathe.

"I'm sorry, Z," RT bit out. "I'm so fucking sorry."

"You're sorry? For what? For fucking with me? For kissing me? For making me think there might be—"

RT pressed the palm of his hand over Z's mouth, effectively silencing him.

"For walking away," RT whispered, his eyes glassy.

Z was confused. He suddenly didn't know which way was up. He'd let the emotion get to him and he didn't want it. He didn't want to deal with the pain again. No one had hurt him the way RT had. Z had never let himself get that close to a man, but with RT...he'd let down his guard.

RT cupped Z's jaw again, his eyes locked on Z's. "We have to talk. It's no longer an option. But we have to get through this job first."

"Right. Job." Z pulled away. "So let's wait until after the job is over, just in case I fuck it up. That way you'll know how that conversation ends, right? Yeah. No thanks."

With his heart in his throat, Z put some much-needed space between him and RT.

Ryan deserved Z's wrath. He knew he did.

So much for keeping things professional between them. He'd given in to the longing he'd shoved aside for the two months since they'd shared the most unbelievable moments together. But that was the problem, wasn't it? Ryan didn't want moments. He wanted days, weeks, years. He wanted Z. For the rest of his life.

It was difficult to accept responsibility, but Ryan was at fault. He'd blown the mission, but he no longer gave a fuck about that. He'd fucked up with Z. Somehow the man had come to mean more to him than any job. Only he didn't know how to express himself.

Which was why he'd kissed Z.

And Lord have mercy on him. That kiss... It'd reminded Ryan of everything he'd ever wanted, everything he'd ever dreamed of.

Everything he'd ever lost.

Z had given all of that to him. Optimism, anticipation, something to look forward to.

The man who wouldn't bother to look at him held all of it in the palm of his hand, and he doubted Z had any idea how easily he could crush Ryan. And maybe he deserved that, too.

The sound of a plane engine drew Ryan's attention away from Z and over to the hangar. Taking a deep breath, Ryan willed his heart rate to slow. He needed to get control of himself and this assignment.

"Z. Can you at least look at me?"

Z turned around, his face stony, as though he'd shoved everything down deep.

Ryan understood that. He'd done it for longer than he cared to admit.

Closing the gap between them, Ryan got up in Z's personal space once more, refusing to give up. He'd learned his lesson, and now it was time to move forward.

I want you to love me. Z's words echoed in his mind.

"We've got a job to do," Z whispered harshly.

"Yes. We do. But afterward"—Ryan held up a hand before Z could interrupt—"we're going to talk. Or I'll talk and you can listen."

Z didn't say anything. That wasn't what Ryan was expecting, but again, he couldn't fault Z for being angry. Ryan was acting like an idiot, doing exactly what he'd insisted had caused the problem in the first place. Allowing his emotion to interfere with the job.

"Let's get the painting, then go get Amit. After that, if you want to tell me to fuck off, you can." Not that he was hoping for that particular outcome, but this wasn't the time or place. "Deal?"

Z nodded.

That was enough for now.

Twenty minutes later, with the real painting in their possession and Ryan behind the wheel, they headed to Courtney and Max's house. It was the location Dom had told them to go, advising that Trace and Clay would meet up with them there.

Aside from talking to Trace on the phone, Z hadn't said a single word. Ryan now understood what it must have been like to be Z for the last two months. Ryan had done the same thing to him, and he was riddled with guilt, but for now, he promised to keep his focus.

Once they arrived at Courtney's and got through the ridiculous amount of security the Adorites had, Ryan, Clay, Trace, Z, and Courtney met in Max's office to put together a plan. While Max, his sister Ashlynn, and the Southern Boy Mafia underboss, Leyton, stood at the back of the room watching them, Dom was on the phone, providing the information he'd learned.

"Guy's name is Thurston McElroy."

"Thurston? Seriously?" Clay's face reflected his amusement. "Who names their kid Thurston?"

Ryan shook his head, quieting Clay for now.

"Anyway," Dom continued, "after I identified what account the wire had come from, I was able to get all the information we could ever want on this guy. And it looks like Amit's GPS is still active, because the address I located for Thurston is, in fact, the same location the signal is coming from. Provided Amit is alive, we should be able to get in and get out, no problems."

"The guy's expecting the painting," Ryan explained. "I have no intention of handing over the original unless it comes down to life or death. The plan'll be to use the second fake as a decoy until we can get Amit out of there."

"Who's gonna hand it over?" Trace inquired.

"I am," Ryan told him, looking at the others in turn.

"Alone?" It was Courtney's turn to chime in.

"No," Z inserted, his tone leaving no room for argument. "I'm goin' in with him. We'll distract Thurston while the rest of you find a way to get Amit."

"What if he's got Amit with him?" Courtney inquired.

"Doesn't matter," Ryan said. "The objective is still the same. We get Amit out unharmed."

"Hold up a minute," Trace stated, drawing all eyes to him. "What's to keep this guy from goin' after Amit again once this is over? We can't just hand over a fake painting and expect this guy to shrug it off. He paid Amit two mil up front—half of what he'd been intending to pay. That's a lotta fuckin' cash."

"And he's cautious," Dom added. "The reason he hadn't paid Amit the remaining money was because he was having the painting assessed. I hacked his email and found an email thread between him and some expert. One week after taking possession of the painting, Thurston was informed it was a fake. He's been hunting Amit ever since."

"That explains why Amit went to his mother's house."

"Regardless," Ryan inserted, "I'm not handin' over the original. Four mil ain't shit compared to what'll happen if this painting gets in the wrong hands."

"I've got an idea." Courtney waved her hand to get everyone's attention. "I'll talk to him."

"Talk?" Clay huffed. "You think that's gonna make him forget the fact he lost two mil?"

Courtney's eyes narrowed on Clay, but the voice that sounded did not belong to her.

"He will if I talk to him."

Max Adorite.

All eyes moved to Max as he came to stand behind his wife. Impeccably dressed in a suit and tie, the guy looked as though he should've been in a boardroom.

Unfortunately, Max very well could *talk* to Thurston and likely get this resolved without injury. Most people feared the Adorites, and Ryan couldn't exactly blame them. He'd seen firsthand just how ruthless Max could be.

Ryan shook his head. "Your help always comes with a price."

Max smirked and his sister laughed.

"Thanksgiving dinner," Courtney inserted.

Ryan frowned. "Huh?"

"Thanksgiving dinner. Here. At our house. That's the price."

Max chuckled from behind her. Ryan had no fucking idea what he was supposed to say to that. "You want *me* to spend Thanksgiving at your place? That's what it'll cost me?"

"Not just you. Everyone," Courtney clarified.

"Fine," Trace stated. "Done. Can we get on with this?"

"How do you propose we do this then?" Z asked Max directly.

While Max broke it down step by step, Ryan listened, but his attention continued to stray to Z. Part of him was glad to have Max's interference, because at this rate, Ryan's distracted state was likely going to get them all killed.

THIRTY-FOUR

In order to be an effective member of the team, Z took a moment to clear his mind. As with all missions, the end result was all that mattered. Not RT. Not the fact that they were working with the mob to break in some rich fucker's house and extract an art-stealing asshole.

Nothing.

It all came down to getting Amit out of the house and to safety. The rest would be left up to RT and Max. They'd decided to go in together to confront Thurston, creating a diversion more than anything.

Which was where Z came in.

His one and only responsibility was to work with Trace and Clay to get Amit out.

Standing at the sliding glass door of the enormous fucking mansion, Z waited for a signal as he peered inside, trying to make out what was what. Trace and Clay were on the east side of the house, looking for a way in, as well. This part was child's play considering what they'd just endured. The first obstacle had been to distract the two Dobermans they'd encountered as soon as they'd stepped on the property.

Granted, Z was all for dogs, but not when they were baring their teeth and ready to rip muscle from bone. No thank you.

That was where Clay came in.

For whatever fucked up reason, RT's brother had anticipated that issue, and Z had been floored when the guy had pulled dog treats out of his pocket.

Fucking dog treats.

As odd as that was, it had done the trick.

From where Z stood, nose pressed to the glass, he couldn't see RT and Max inside the house, but he could hear them thanks to the transmitter that RT wore. The drone of conversation sounded in Z's earpiece, and he listened carefully, waiting for the go-ahead.

He needed some action, something to help burn off some of the excess anger that simmered in his veins. This would certainly accomplish that if they'd stop rattling their lips and give him something to do.

Maybe.

Knowing Max Adorite, the guy would give ol' Thurston the evil eye, threaten to decapitate him and his family, toss them in the river with a new pair of shoes made of cement, and it would all be over.

Not exactly what Z had in mind, but then again, after his confrontation with RT, Z wasn't feeling all warm and fuzzy toward anyone, so if the mob boss wanted to fuck someone up, more power to him.

"Z, you ready?" Trace's raspy whisper pulled Z from his thoughts.

"Ten four," he replied, glancing behind him to ensure no one had snuck up on him.

"Looks like Amit's bein' held in one of the second-floor bedrooms," Trace informed him. How he knew, Z didn't know or care, but he appreciated the heads-up.

Z looked up at the yellow glow coming from one of the second-floor windows, but that proved futile. Apparently he'd left his superpowers in his other jeans, which meant he wasn't going to be able to scale the wall, and unfortunately, there wasn't anything he could climb even if he wanted to. Not that he was much of a climber, but he was willing to give it a shot if it would get the kid to safety.

"I'll go in through the back door," Z said softly.

"Roger."

"Hold up," Clay demanded. "We've got company."

Company? What the fuck?

"You got some friends comin' to help you out?" RT asked Thurston, the information being broadcast through the microphone RT wore.

"Figured you'd have help. Why shouldn't I?" The man's tone was snooty, reflecting far too much money and not nearly enough sense.

"Shit, guys. This don't look good," Clay said. "We've got...I'd say a dozen dudes dressed in black walking right up to the front door like they live here. They don't move like SWAT, so I'm guessin' hired guns."

"Stand down," RT announced, the words hardly heard in Z's ear.

What the hell was he doing?

Z tried to get a better look inside, but he was still blind, thanks to the walls that obscured his view. Rather than wait for the shit to hit the fan, Z decided to invite himself inside. Crouching low, he eased around to the west side of the house, finding a single window down low.

Interesting. Most houses in Texas didn't have a room below ground, but it appeared good ol' Thurston had given Z the perfect opportunity to drop in unannounced.

"What the fuck?" RT declared. "I thought we were workin' a deal here, Thurston?"

"As long as it goes my way, we can work any deal you want. But first, I want the painting. Then we'll chat." Thurston sounded oddly calm. "Oh, and call off your dogs."

"You don't wanna do that," RT growled, sounding as though he was talking to someone within close proximity to himself. Obviously he wasn't referring to calling off the dogs.

Z's blood pressure spiked; adrenaline fueled him when he heard the rustling sound that followed. Even without eyes on the situation, he could tell someone had just put his hands on RT.

"Sit!" a deep voice grumbled. Not Thurston, so there must've been someone else in charge of this band of merry mercenaries. "And hand over the weapon."

"Let go of me and I'll think about it," RT retorted.

That shit wasn't going to fly with Z. No sir.

"Round up the guys outside," the same deep voice ordered.

Rather than wait for someone to give him a personal invite, Z shoved his boot through the window, kicked aside the glass shards, and propelled himself inside.

No alarm, no dogs. He was met with silence. This Thurston guy was kind of an idiot. Then again, he had hired some thugs to protect him, so maybe not.

The room he landed in appeared to be some sort of glorified laundry area. Commercial-grade machines greeted him without sound, along with ugly paintings with even uglier frames lining the walls. With money did not necessarily come taste, clearly.

Rather than find himself cornered, Z didn't waste time looking around. With his Sig in hand, he twisted the knob and pulled the door open, peering into the hall to find it empty, as well.

He slipped out, keeping to the wall in the darkened hallway. He passed two additional doors on the opposite side before he arrived at a set of stairs that led up to what Z assumed was the main floor.

"All right, bro," Trace growled deep inside Z's head via his earpiece. "If you're gonna feel me up, my wife ain't gonna be too happy."

Fuck. They had Trace.

335

Not that Z was worried just yet. In order to give Thurston what he wanted, they would've had to give someone on the outside up.

"Where's the other one?" Z heard the inquiry from an unknown through someone's transmitter, but he didn't know whose.

Either they didn't know about Z or they didn't know about Clay. Either way, that helped.

"Right here," Clay announced. "I'm comin' willingly, so keep your fuckin' hands to your goddamn self."

Clay did not like to be touched.

"Take 'em upstairs with the kid."

The bad guys might've thought they were doing the smart thing, getting everyone in one place so they could keep their eyes on them, but what they didn't know was that putting Trace and Clay in with Amit only gave them opportunity to get the kid to safety. By now, Z knew they were aware he'd slipped inside.

"Where the fuck is Max?" a female voice sounded in Z's ear.

Shit. Courtney did not sound happy, but the beep preceding her question meant she was using the transmitter to talk to them, not lurking somewhere inside the house. Yet.

"I want all four of you to check in right now, dammit," Courtney declared.

Z clicked his transmitter, signaling he was there, as he slowly ascended the stairs, keeping to one side until he could get a visual of the next floor. No one was guarding the area, so Z continued. He peered around another wall but jerked back quickly when he saw two guys dressed in black talking to one another.

Three more clicks sounded in his ear, accounting for RT, Trace, and Clay. At least they still had their earpieces in and were in a position to respond.

"I'm bringin' backup with me. Be there in two," Courtney informed them.

Great. Z was all for backup, but he had a feeling Max was going to lose his shit once he realized his wife was walking into this shit storm. So the sooner they got this wrapped up, the better off they'd be.

Before he could peer around the wall once again, a man appeared, surprising Z but not keeping him from hitting the guy hard enough to knock the wind from him. Z grabbed him from behind, putting him in a choke hold long enough to knock him out temporarily.

"Have a good nap," he whispered, lowering the body to the floor and glancing in the hall once more.

All clear.

Z maneuvered his way through the enormous house, having to duck only twice to avoid being seen by two of the men who'd obviously been called in to protect Thurston. Only one of *those* men was now incapacitated, along with the first guy Z had encountered—two out of twelve wasn't bad—but it wouldn't be long before both would wake up, so Z knew he had to get on with it.

Glancing up the stairs, he weighed his options. With Trace and Clay with Amit, there was no need for Z to go up there just yet. They would be able to handle the situation themselves. If they couldn't, they would've said something.

So Z made a decision.

First, he'd find RT. Then, they'd figure out how to get out of this goat fuck of a mission.

This was fucking bullshit.

Ryan sat in a straight-back chair watching Thurston pace the floor, Max seated to Ryan's left, looking as calm as he'd ever seen him. They each had one hand cuffed to the chair—their right hands—they were sitting in, and they'd been relieved of their weapons.

"Your wife's on the way," Ryan informed Max, muttering beneath his breath so that Thurston couldn't hear.

Max's dark eyebrows arched upward, his eyes narrowing on Ryan. Clearly he wasn't happy about that.

"She's bringin' the cavalry."

"Tell her to sit tight," Max ground out.

"No can do," Ryan told him. "Unless you've got a better plan. She's good at what she does and you know it."

One of the men pacing the room stopped to glare at them. Ryan smiled. All teeth.

"Where's the painting?" Thurston inquired, coming to stand a few feet away but not too close.

Ryan let his gaze rake over him, taking in every nuance. Thurston McElroy was a stout, well-dressed man in his mid to late fifties, muddy-brown eyes, snow-white hair, and an impressively sized house decorated with too much red and gold for Ryan's taste. It was clear based on the décor that the man was an art collector, and Ryan had to wonder how much of the stuff had been acquired through channels such as this, rather than legitimately. He had no qualms paying a ridiculous amount of money for art, but that didn't mean he wasn't up to no good. The fact that he had a team of mercs on his payroll was also telling.

"Sir," one of the men in black interrupted before Ryan or Max had to answer Thurston's original question. "We've got…a woman at the front door. She's got the painting with her, or so she claims."

"Is it in her hands?" Thurston asked, his gaze locked on Ryan and Max.

"No, sir."

"Have her take you to it," Thurston demanded.

"Oh, you don't wanna do that," Max grumbled softly.

No, he didn't, Ryan thought with a smile. Courtney was smart. She'd have figured they would want her to take them to the painting. Even if there were two or three of them accompanying her, she'd be able to disable them easily, and that was if she was alone, which he seriously doubted.

"Who's her backup?" Ryan asked Max, keeping his voice low, his eyes on Thurston as the man retreated toward the door.

"Everyone was at the house," Max muttered. "My brothers, my sisters, Leyton. So I'd say with their security detail, we've got enough."

"Good."

"Damn right. You got your boys captured," Max growled.

"That's what *they* think." Ryan knew without a doubt that unless they'd knocked Trace and Clay out or bound them from head to toe, they weren't going to contain them. And for whatever reason, Thurston hadn't yet restrained Ryan or Max completely—probably figuring that taking their weapons was sufficient—so he presumed the guy thought he had the situation handled.

He should've never underestimated Ryan's team.

The messenger disappeared, and Ryan continued to watch Thurston pacing the floor and apparently waiting for an update. He doubted one would come quickly, but Ryan had been surprised more than once today, so he wasn't going to get cocky yet.

Minutes ticked by, and his earpiece was silent, which he hoped meant his team was devising a plan or, better yet, already out the door with Amit in tow. The end goal was to get Amit, round up the team, and then get out of the house without any casualties. With Max Adorite there, Ryan was a little concerned about the latter, but he didn't figure saying anything would matter. Max would do what Max wanted to do, regardless.

"Four men disengaged," Z's voice sounded in his ear.

"Three out here," Courtney added.

"I counted twelve," Clay noted.

"We've got two standing guard outside the room up here," Trace volunteered.

"Two more keeping an eye on RT," Z said.

If Z could see the two guards standing outside the room, that meant he was close.

Ryan peered over at his gun, which Thurston had relieved him of but hadn't bothered to take out of the room. The guy truly was an amateur at this, but Ryan figured he felt secure with the team he'd acquired to come in and take over the situation. The guy should really be more careful.

"Where's the woman with the painting?" Thurston yelled out into the hallway, his eyes still pinned on Ryan and Max.

"I'll check," one of the remaining guards said.

A scuffle ensued, a shout, and then nothing. Ryan couldn't see a damn thing outside the room. Rather than sit around, he decided to put an end to this bullshit once and for all.

Getting to his feet and dragging the chair with him—though it was much heavier than he'd anticipated—he advanced on Thurston, but the man turned quickly, a look of panic on his face as he realized Ryan was coming toward him.

Unfortunately, Ryan hadn't thought things all the way through, didn't consider the fact that Thurston was merely a businessman with more money than sense, and the Walther P99 he was wielding did not have a safety.

"Sit down!" Thurston yelled, the gun trembling in his hand.

"Don't move," Z commanded, his tone harder than Ryan had ever heard it.

"I'll shoot him," Thurston argued, glancing over at Z.

"That'd be stupid," Z told him. "We didn't come here to hurt you. We came to get the kid."

"Where's my painting?"

"Face it," Max injected. "You aren't gettin' the painting. And if you wanna walk away from this without bein' dead, I suggest you put the gun down."

Two more people walked into the room, both of whom Ryan had seen at Max's house. Backup.

Z took a step toward Thurston.

"Don't come any closer. I want my goddamn painting. That little asshole stole my money."

"You'll get your money back," Ryan ensured him.

"I want the painting."

Of course he did. No way would this snotty bastard make this easy on them. It should've been a simple plan, come in, get Amit, leave without Thurston being any wiser. Instead, they were engaged in a standoff in the middle of the atrociously decorated living room.

"Put the gun down," Z instructed. "The cops are on the way."

Ryan wasn't sure that was the truth, but he decided to keep his mouth shut. With Max there, he doubted they'd engaged the police, but again, Ryan wouldn't be surprised at anything at this point.

Okay, maybe he spoke a little too soon.

With his eyes locked on Thurston, Ryan realized the instant things went to shit. The world seemed to explode around him. One minute they were all standing there, trying to defuse the situation calmly, the next…

A gunshot rang out, and fire burned through Ryan's left arm. Instinct had him grabbing for the wound instantly, but he was pulled up short thanks to the zip tie holding him to the chair. All hell broke loose when Z scrambled deeper into the room, diving on top of Thurston and taking him to the ground at the same time Max retrieved his gun, spinning around and pointing it directly at the two jumbled bodies on the ground.

"No!" Ryan yelled. "Don't fucking shoot him!" He was referring to Z, but he didn't bother to clarify. Let Max think what he wanted.

For half a second, his heart had lodged in his throat thinking that Z could take a bullet. When Z's eyes slid over to Ryan, he noted concern. "Flesh wound, Z," he said, hoping that little white lie would suffice for the moment.

He'd forgotten that he had his mic still on, and the sound of gunshots rang out from somewhere else in the house, followed by more yelling. Minutes ticked by slowly while chaos ensued, Ryan's heart pounding dangerously hard against his ribs as he waited for each of his team to check in. It wasn't until everyone had been visually inspected that he gave himself over to the pain.

What he'd thought was a mere flesh wound…well, it wasn't quite that simple.

And that was the last thing Ryan remembered before everything went black.

THIRTY-FIVE

Z paced the long, white hallway, waiting for the doctor to come out. The rest of the team, along with RT's family, Courtney, Max, and Max's brother, Victor, as well as Jensyn and Reese, were in the waiting room, anticipating the same thing. They'd been there for three hours, and with each passing second, Z's anxiety level was rising to the point he wondered if his heart could actually pound out through his ribs.

RT had been shot.

He could still see the image in his head, feel his heart constricting with fear as he watched the gruesome sight.

"Hey, man," Trace said, coming to stand in front of Z, forcing him to stop pacing.

Z didn't say anything, simply met Trace's gaze.

"He's gonna be fine. It was little more than a flesh wound." Trace grinned.

Right. Flesh wound. If that were the case, RT wouldn't be in surgery to have pins put in his elbow to repair the damaged bone. Granted, all in all, it really wasn't that serious—normally an outpatient procedure, the doctor had assured them—but Z was still freaked. He couldn't help it.

Z appreciated Trace's need to reassure him, but until he could see RT for himself, hear his voice, touch him, he wasn't going to believe it. After all, Z's father had been conscious for a brief time after his accident, and look where he was now.

No, Z didn't need anyone to placate him. He wouldn't be able to relax until RT was awake and looking at him.

"Let's get somethin' to drink," Trace said firmly, touching Z's arm.

"I can't—" He was going to say leave, but Trace lifted an eyebrow, stopping him.

"There's a soda machine right there." Trace pointed behind Z.

Rather than argue, he allowed Trace to lead him the few feet to the alcove that held a Coke machine and a vending machine full of junk food. While Trace put in some cash and got two bottles of water, Z continued to peer out into the hall, not wanting to miss the doctor when he came back.

Trace nodded toward a bench in the hall.

With a bottle of water pressed into his hand, Z took a seat, but his eyes continued to stray toward the waiting room.

"He really is gonna be fine, Z. And when he wakes up, you'll be the first person he wants to see."

Z turned to face his friend. "Why me?"

Trace smiled. "Because he loves you."

"What the hell would make you think that?" Z could not believe they were having this conversation.

"Um, hello? I've known the guy my whole life. It's so fucking obvious when he looks at you."

Z shook his head. "I wouldn't go that far." He refused to get his hopes up. He had already been anticipating that conversation RT had promised after the assignment was completed, and yet here he was, inhaling the acrid smell of disinfectant and who knew what else while the man he loved was in surgery because he'd been shot.

Z dropped his head, staring down at the water bottle he held between his splayed thighs.

"I know the two of you have some shit to work out," Trace said, his voice soft. "And you will. There's no doubt in my mind that RT loves you. I've never seen him look at someone the way he looks at you. Not even that crazy fuck, Kevin."

Z had to keep his hands from fisting and crushing the bottle at the mention of RT's ex. He hated that bastard.

"Trexler family."

Z launched to his feet at the deep voice that sounded within the waiting room. The doctor had returned, and Z wasn't about to miss what he had to say, no matter how much he appreciated Trace's need to reassure him.

"He did perfectly," the doctor explained when everyone had closed in around him. "No issues, and I expect a full recovery. He'll need some physical therapy once he's healed."

"Thank God it wasn't his shooting arm," Clay muttered, causing the doctor's eyebrows to lift.

"Can we go in to see him?" RT's mother asked.

"The nurse will be out in a few minutes to bring you back. He'll be in recovery for a bit, but after that, he'll be moved to a private room."

"He won't wanna stay," Bryce told the doctor. "He'll insist on goin' home. Is that possible?"

The doctor considered that for a moment. "As long as he doesn't have any issues with the anesthesia, he can go home. But not alone."

"Thank you," Bryce said gruffly, holding out his hand for the doctor to shake.

Everyone started talking to one another, but Z only heard a jumble of words as he peered around at the people he considered family.

Speaking of family…his eyes drifted over to his sister, who was… No. Fucking. Way.

There, smiling up at Max's younger brother, Victor, was Jensyn. Surely she wasn't thinkin'—

"Feel better now?" Trace asked, cutting off Z's view of his sister when he stepped in front of him.

Nodding, he forgot all about his sister conversing with the mob, his thoughts returning to RT. Z breathed a little easier now that he knew RT was out of surgery, but still, he wouldn't be able to get rid of the boulder sitting directly on his lungs until he saw RT for himself.

And he prayed that would be soon.

Ryan hated the groggy feeling the pain meds left him with, but he was grateful that the fire in his arm was no longer there. Then again, he couldn't move his arm thanks to the device they had him in. He'd been awakened by a kind woman with big blue eyes and a sweet smile and then left alone shortly thereafter when she'd promised to go get his family so they could see him.

He had managed to refrain from telling her to get Z for him. He figured his parents would want to see him first, but the only person he cared to see was Z.

"Hey, you're lookin' good."

Ryan looked up to see his mother and father standing just beyond the curtained area he was in.

"I wouldn't go that far," Bryce teased. "He looks like he's been shot."

"Thanks," Ryan muttered, though he could hardly feel his lips. His eyes kept wanting to close, but he refused to give in to sleep until he could see Z. "Where's Z?"

Ryan's mother smiled. "He's in the waiting room."

"Can I see him?"

"Of course," Emily said softly, moving closer. "Just forgive your ol' mom for wanting to see you first."

Ryan nodded, his head still fuzzy from the drugs they'd used to put him under. He briefly remembered the nurse telling him that the surgery to repair the shattered bone in his elbow had gone well and he'd be back to normal in no time. Ryan wasn't sure that was the case, but for now, he was glad to know it was over.

Emily stepped up to his side, leaned over, and kissed him on the forehead after brushing his hair back.

"Please get Z," he said roughly, not sure how much longer he could stay awake.

"Sure thing, honey," Emily said. If she was hurt by his request, she didn't show it. "We'll be back to see you before you leave."

"How long do I have to stay here?"

"The doctor said you can go home in a couple of hours."

Well, that was good news. He'd thought for sure he'd have to argue with the doctor to let him go home.

"But someone has to stay with you tonight," Emily explained. "We thought you could come stay with us."

Ryan shook his head. He wanted to go home to his own bed, and he wanted Z there with him. Granted, if Z refused, then Ryan wouldn't have much of a choice, but for now, he wasn't going to explain that to his parents.

Staring up at them, Ryan willed them to go get Z.

"Okay, okay," his mother said with a laugh. "We'll go get Z."

When they left the room, the same nurse from earlier stepped in, checking to make sure he was all right. When he nodded, she strode toward the machine by his bed, punched something in, then disappeared once again.

Ryan's eyes grew heavy, sleep threatening to overtake him once more, but then...

"Z," he whispered when Z appeared.

"Hey," Z murmured back, stepping into the small area and closing the curtain behind him.

Ryan could've sworn he saw tears in Z's eyes, but as Z moved closer, he thought maybe the drugs were causing him to hallucinate. Unable to take his eyes off him, he continued to stare into Z's beautiful face, words escaping him as his chest filled with emotion. He prayed like hell he didn't break down and cry. If the stupid pain meds made him gush like a fucking girl, he'd never forgive that damn anesthesiologist.

Z took Ryan's good hand, squeezing it gently as he leaned closer. "How're you feelin'?"

"Like I've been nailed back together," he forced out, still unable to look away from Z. "I..." God, the words were right there, but his brain wasn't functioning well enough for him to string the sentence together.

"It's okay, Ry," Z said softly. "You need to get some rest."

"Will you take me home after?" he asked, his eyes growing heavier by the second.

"Is that what you want?" Z sounded surprised.

"Yes. Only you."

"Then yes, I'll take you home after."

"And you'll stay with me?"

"Of course."

Ryan couldn't open his eyes as sleep took over, but the last word he managed to utter was, "Forever?"

He didn't get to hear Z's answer.

THIRTY-SIX

At RT's request, Z managed to get him home after he'd been released from the hospital. Having talked with Emily and Bryce, Z had partially expected RT's parents to want him to come home with them, but they'd both smiled when Z said he would be happy to get RT settled and stay with him for the night.

Clearly they knew something was going on.

Although RT had appeared to be coherent during the drive, mumbling from time to time and offering his driving expertise from the passenger seat, Z had watched him drift off more than once. But now that they were inside, it appeared the patient had regained all of his faculties. Especially his verbal skills.

"We need to talk," RT told him from his spot on the couch, where his gaze continued to trail Z around the small kitchen.

"After we eat," Z informed him as he rummaged through RT's kitchen, trying to find something to piece together. The man's refrigerator was barren, his pantry equally so. The only thing Z could find were three TV dinners in the freezer, so he managed to combine those and make a relatively filling meal.

After they ate—both of them sitting on the couch in front of the television—Z knew that the conversation RT had promised was inevitable. That hope he'd been fighting for so long was back. Had been ever since RT had asked him to stay with him, tacking on the word forever just as he was giving in to the pain meds, which had been keeping him hovering on the edge of consciousness.

For that reason, Z had tried not to think too much about what RT had said. There was no guarantee that the conversation they were about to have would end the same as it had earlier.

The television clicked off and Z glanced over to see RT holding the remote.

"Are you ready to listen?" RT asked.

Z leaned back against the cushions and crossed his arms over his chest. Turning his head to look at RT, Z smiled. "I am," he began, "but honestly, I'd prefer we pick this up tomorrow after we've both had some sleep."

It was late, and though RT had been sleeping for some time now, he still needed his rest. He'd been shot and then pinned back together over the course of the last few hours. The last thing he needed to do was have a lengthy conversation that could possibly end badly for both of them.

RT seemed to be considering what Z had said. He finally nodded, but he didn't get up. Instead, he edged closer to Z, his good arm sliding behind Z's neck.

"We'll do this your way," RT whispered. "As long as you stay with me tonight."

"I'll stay here," Z said, patting the couch beside him but keeping his eyes locked on RT's. "I can sleep right here."

"No," RT said adamantly. "I want you in my bed."

Z swallowed hard and looked away. His heart ached in his chest, fear of reliving the hell of the last couple of months once RT decided this wasn't what he wanted. Sometimes Z felt as though he'd been caught in a cyclone that he could never seem to escape, and the longer he was involved, the more battered and bruised he ended up.

Now that he knew RT was safe, recovering nicely from the surgery without any permanent damage from the bullet, he knew he would've been smart to put that boundary back between them, to distance himself from the pain.

Was he over RT? No, not by a long shot. But Z knew he couldn't take much more before he broke completely. He had fallen in love with RT long ago, and spending time with him had only sealed Z's fate. Having to walk away again wasn't going to be easy.

RT's arm moved from behind Z's neck. "Look at me."

Z drew in a deep breath and turned his head once again.

RT's mouth touched his gently, sweetly. And that single touch nearly had Z breaking down. When RT pulled away, Z didn't know what to expect, but the words that came next certainly hadn't been it.

"You told me earlier that the only thing you wanted from me was for me to love you."

Shit. Z did not want to rehash this now.

"Well, the truth is, I do love you, Z," RT said softly. "And before you get defensive, it's not the drugs talking."

Z's throat worked as emotion made it impossible to speak.

"I won't push to talk tonight," RT added. "But I had to say that. I had to tell you."

Z nodded.

"Now let's get some sleep." RT got to his feet, wobbling slightly. "Actually, scratch that. I need a shower."

Z got to his feet when RT stumbled once more. "I'll help you."

"I was hoping you'd say that."

351

Ryan managed, with Z's help, to fumble through a shower. If it hadn't been for the pain and the fact he had to keep his arm dry, he wouldn't have been able to control his body's response to Z's nearness. The way Z had been so clinical about everything hadn't hurt, either.

Now, as he lay in bed, staring up at the ceiling while Z slept only a few inches away, Ryan found he couldn't sleep. The additional pain pill he'd taken with dinner was doing its job taking the edge off, but now that the anesthesia had worn off, he was no longer tired. And his brain was working overtime, replaying the events of the day.

Z shifted, rolling onto his side facing Ryan. "What're you thinkin' about?"

"I thought you were asleep."

"Tryin'," Z mumbled groggily.

"Am I keepin' you awake?"

"It's your bed," Z admitted.

Ryan turned to look at him, making out his profile in the darkened room. "Not comfortable?"

"Too comfortable."

They stared back at one another for a minute, heads turned toward one another on their respective pillows. Ryan couldn't believe Z was there with him. He'd thought about this moment for so long, never figuring it would be feasible considering all the hell he'd put Z through, but like always, Z had come through for him.

"I love you," Ryan admitted again, unable to keep from telling Z. He wished he could hear the words back, but that wasn't the reason he said them.

Z lifted his head, then leaned closer and pressed his lips to Ryan's. Ryan raised his good arm, sliding his fingers into Z's hair, holding him in place so he could kiss him back. A shudder ran through Z, but he didn't push for more. When the kiss finally broke, Z continued to look down at him.

"I don't want this to be the drugs talkin'," Z said, sounding sad.

"It's not," Ryan told him. "It's all me, Z."

"Why now?"

Ryan sighed as he pulled Z's head down to his shoulder. He ran his fingers along the smooth skin of Z's back. "I've been an idiot. Selfish and worried about only myself for so long. After..." This conversation had seemed like a good idea a couple of hours ago, but now Ryan was having a hard time with the words.

"After Kevin?" Z inserted.

"Yes."

"I get it."

Ryan pressed his lips to Z's forehead. "Do you?"

"Yes. I understand the pain, the fear of being hurt again."

"Someone hurt you?" Ryan hadn't heard about any of Z's former relationships, and he wasn't sure he wanted to hear them now, but he wanted to talk to Z, to find a way to make that connection again.

"Is that so hard to believe?" Z questioned.

"Who?"

For almost a minute, the room was silent, and Ryan figured Z wasn't going to answer him. "Never mind," Ryan whispered. "Get some sleep."

"You," Z stated.

"Me? Me what?"

"*You* hurt me."

353

Ryan swallowed past the lump that formed in his throat, blinked rapidly to hold back the tears. He hadn't expected that at all.

"I can't go through it again, Ryan."

He had no idea what to say to that, so Ryan simply held Z close to him, gliding his fingers over his back, thanking God for this moment and praying it wasn't going to be the last. Because, yes, Ryan understood all too well about being hurt, being fearful of the future, not wanting to endure the heartache ever again. What he'd been through in the past still left him leery, but Ryan knew one thing with complete certainty.

What he'd felt before had nothing on what he felt for Z. And this time… This time he might not survive.

It didn't matter that he'd be the one completely responsible because he'd been stupid enough not to snatch Z up when he'd had the chance.

THIRTY-SEVEN

Three days later – Thursday night

"You've really got to head back?" Z asked Jensyn as he walked his sister out of the nursing home. A cab was waiting at the front doors, and the sight of it had Z's heart hurting. He hated that his sister had to go back to California, but he understood.

"It was good to be back. And it won't be long now." Jensyn turned to face him.

"So you're still plannin' to move back when you graduate?"

"Why wouldn't I?" she questioned with a smile.

"Oh, I don't know. I thought maybe Cali was growin' on you."

"It's not, I promise. Yes, I like it there, but home has always been where my family is."

Z pulled his sister in for another hug as he peered over at the cab. When she pulled back, she was still smiling.

"Tell Dad I love him every day. And let him know I'll be back as soon as I can."

"Will do," he told her. "Be careful."

"I should be telling you the same." She laughed. "I'm not the one out tryin' to save the world."

"Right."

Jensyn turned away, wheeling her suitcase behind her. The cab driver climbed out of the car and walked around to load her luggage into the trunk while Jensyn climbed into the backseat.

"Oh, hey," Jensyn called, one foot still hanging out of the car. "Do me a favor."

"Anything," he said, placing his hand on the top of the door.

"Tell RT how you feel. I know you don't wanna hear it, but he really does love you."

Z's brows furrowed. "He called me," she admitted. "I'm guessin' because you've been puttin' him off?"

Z had been trying to gain some perspective, to convince his heart that RT was worth the risk, so yes, he hadn't been answering RT's texts. At least not at length. He'd responded, but until Z was convinced that RT's feelings weren't drug-induced, he hadn't wanted to accept them.

"He's a good guy," Jensyn said. "And you're the best thing that's ever happened to him."

"I wouldn't go that far," he told his sister.

"Those were his words, Z. Not mine."

Z nodded but didn't respond. He wasn't sure what to say. In a moment of weakness last night, after Reese had gone back to Coyote Ridge, Z had broken down and told his sister about RT, not realizing she'd spoken with him.

"I'm serious, Z. He deserves to know."

"I'll think about it," he told her, forcing a smile. He had actually already made up his mind to tell RT how he felt. He merely hadn't decided when.

Jensyn's eyes softened. "The sooner the better. Don't let him get away, Z. He's stubborn, like you."

"Thanks for that."

"Sure thing. What're sisters for?"

"Go on or you're gonna miss your flight." Z waited for her to get situated in the car before closing the door behind her. He waited there, watching until the yellow cab was out of sight. When he turned back around, he found Buddy standing in the reception area, waiting for him.

"Hey," he greeted when he joined the elderly man.

"Your sister's a smart lady." Buddy turned slowly, and they headed back to the double doors that would lead to the patient rooms.

"She is," Z concurred.

"So, when're you gonna tell this fella how you feel?"

Z peered over at Buddy, smirking as he did. "You heard that, did ya?"

Buddy tapped his ears. "I haven't lost all my senses yet. But you can't change the subject that easily, sport."

The two of them walked the long corridor that led to Buddy's room. "I'm not tryin' to, I promise."

"I think you should go tell him tonight."

"Do you now?"

Buddy stopped, turning to face Z fully. "Have you learned nothing since you've been here?"

Z scrunched his forehead in confusion.

Buddy placed his hand on Z's shoulder. "Son, life is short. If you want something, go after it. If you let it slip away without giving it everything you've got, that's on you." Buddy squeezed Z's shoulder lightly. "You can't have it both ways. If you try to always protect yourself from emotional pain, you'll never know true love."

Z swallowed hard and nodded. He didn't know how to refute that. He loved RT; there was no debating that. He wanted to spend the rest of his life with the man, but having to deal with the back-and-forth, it was tearing him up inside, and Z wasn't comfortable with the emotions RT managed to invoke.

"Life's short, Zachariah," Buddy said softly. "Too short to run away from what's important." Buddy let his hand drop. "Now, go tell your father good night, and go talk to that man of yours."

"He's not mine," Z said defensively, the words spewing forth before he could stop them.

"Oh, but he is. You've just got to claim him." Buddy smiled. "Good night, son. I hope to see you here tomorrow. Maybe you can tell me about the stolen painting case again."

"Why do you like that case so much?" Z inquired. It seemed every time Z saw Buddy these days, the man always wanted to hear that story over and over again. For years, Z had shared the details of his assignments—what he could, anyway—but never had Buddy been as interested as he was in that particular one.

Buddy's face lit up. "I guess I'm just a romantic at heart."

"Romantic?"

"Don't get me wrong," Buddy explained, "I love the suspense, but with that one, it's the underlying love story that keeps me wanting to know more." With that, he turned and hobbled to the door to his room, offering Z one last wave before disappearing inside.

Contemplating that, Z went to his father's room and dropped into the recliner. He peered over at his father briefly.

"I wish you could tell me what I'm supposed to do, Dad." Z sighed. What he wouldn't give to have his father open his eyes and tell him the same thing Buddy had, that he shouldn't waste a minute, that life was too short.

As he stared at his father, his heart clenched, emotion swamping him. And that was when it hit him. Life *was* too short. His father was proof. Thomas had been taken from them far too soon. Even though he was physically there, he wasn't there. Had his father done and said everything he'd wanted to do before the accident? Did he have any regrets? Anything he wished he could've said?

Getting to his feet, Z grabbed his keys from the dresser. After kissing his father on the forehead, Z practically ran out of the room, nearly plowing over the night nurse in his haste.

"Something wrong?" the young man asked, concern creasing his forehead.

"No. I just… I gotta go talk to someone."

"We'll be here when you get back," the man said with a smile.

"Thanks. Keep an eye on him, would ya?"

"Absolutely."

Without wasting another second, Z hightailed it out of the nursing home.

Ryan was flipping through the channels on the television when a knock sounded on his door. Figuring it was his father coming back to check on him, Ryan hollered that it was unlocked.

When the door opened and Z stepped inside, Ryan's heart lurched in his chest. He'd only seen Z briefly the past couple of days when he would come to make sure Ryan was recovering and to bring him food since he'd insisted Ryan was not capable of feeding himself without anything in his refrigerator. Never did he stay for long, though, and he hadn't come by late at night, either.

Although Ryan had attempted to text Z, trying to keep that connection open, it'd been obvious Z had been brushing him off. Which was why Ryan had called Jensyn, after getting Dom to find her phone number. Fear had driven that conversation—fear that Ryan had lost Z forever, fear that he would never know that kind of love again—and Ryan had ended up spilling his guts to her. It had helped to get it out in the open, but he hadn't actually expected Z to return.

"Is something wrong?" Ryan asked, dropping his feet to the floor and sitting up. He'd removed the sling from his arm because he'd felt too restricted, and the quick movement sent fire shooting from his elbow.

Z closed the door behind him and stalked toward Ryan, his face steely and intent. Had something happened?

Before he could get the question out, Z dropped to his knees in front of Ryan.

"Z?" Now he was really concerned.

"I love you," Z blurted.

Ryan knew he hadn't misunderstood, but he couldn't help but be surprised by the words. He'd been hoping to hear them, trying to come up with a way to show Z that he was worthy of his love, but hadn't been able to figure out how.

"Z—"

Before he could finish his sentence, Z reached for him, being careful not to jar his elbow as he wrapped his arm around Ryan's neck, pulling him closer and pressing his lips to Ryan's.

"I love you," Z whispered against his mouth. "I'm sorry I didn't tell you before."

Ryan cupped Z's cheek, pulling back and meeting his dark gaze. "I know." Ryan smiled. "But I'm the one who should be apologizing."

"No, you sh—"

Ryan quieted Z by placing his finger over his mouth. "I should. And I am. God knows I don't deserve you." Ryan swiped his thumb over the stubble lining Z's jaw. "But I can't give you up. The only thing I can do is prove to you that I'm worthy."

"I like the sound of that," Z said with a sexy smirk. "I definitely like the sound of that." Z laughed. "Again, when you talk like that, I hear sex."

Ryan couldn't help but smile. A surge of emotion flooded him. Love, lust, hope, anticipation. It was all there, threatening to choke him up, but of course Z was there to lighten the mood, to give Ryan something to cling to.

"I love you, Ryan," Z whispered, once again kissing him lightly.

"I never thought I'd get to hear you say that," Ryan told him. For the past few days, he'd feared he had lost Z forever.

"I told you, never say never."

"Your motto."

Z nodded. "My motto. I knew you'd figure it out sooner or later."

"Better late than never," Ryan stated.

"There you go with the clichés again."

Ryan pressed his lips to Z's, talking between kisses. "Well, I can think of one way to get me to be quiet."

"Bedroom?" Z asked.

"Right here," Ryan said. "Right now."

Z nodded toward Ryan's elbow. "You sure you're up for it?"

"I'm up for anything you can give me."

"Why does it feel like we've had this conversation before?" Z asked, mischief gleaming in his dark eyes.

"Naked," Ryan ordered.

"You sure?"

"I've never been more sure about anything in my life."

"Okay," Z said, climbing to his feet. "I'll be right back."

When he disappeared down the hall, Ryan called after him. "Where're you goin'?"

"To brush my teeth!"

"Seriously?"

Z stuck his head back in the room. "No. I'm goin' to get the lube."

"I figured you had some in your pocket," Ryan joked.

"Not this time, but trust me, that's not a mistake I'll make again." Z turned away, leaving Ryan staring after him.

Ryan glanced at the couch, then back at the hall. Rather than wait for Z, Ryan got up and trailed him back to his bedroom. He found Z in his room, rummaging through the nightstand. Shutting the door behind him, Ryan adjusted his sweat pants. He only had one functioning hand, so getting undressed wasn't going to be all that easy, even though he'd gone without a shirt after fighting with the damn thing for five minutes trying to get it on without hurting his arm.

"I love when you strip for me," Z told him, his eyes glittering with heat.

"Maybe you should help," Ryan said, trying to force his pants down his hips with one hand.

"My pleasure."

Once again, Z was on his knees before Ryan, this time pulling his sweat pants down his legs, allowing Ryan to step out of them.

"Sit," Z commanded, nodding toward the bed.

His body tensed with anticipation. Ryan would never tire of Z taking charge. "Do you realize what a turn-on that is?" Ryan asked as he took a seat on the edge of the bed.

"What?" Z asked, moving closer, his hands sliding up the insides of Ryan's thighs.

"That take-charge thing you do." Ryan's voice cracked as his cock thickened.

Z leaned forward, kissing the head of Ryan's dick, the gentle touch sending all the blood in Ryan's body straight to his groin. Z's mouth was gentle, as was his touch. He kissed and licked Ryan's cock until it was hard and aching, but never giving him enough.

"Z." Ryan slid the fingers of his good hand into Z's hair, pulling him forward and sinking his dick into the warmth of Z's mouth. "Oh, God, yes."

Z never hurried, never used his hands, simply bobbed up and down on Ryan's cock, laving him, sending shards of pleasure coursing through him until the ache in his arm disappeared entirely. When Z stood, helping Ryan to lean back on the bed and stripping out of his clothes, Ryan wasn't sure he'd be able to wait much longer.

Once he had rolled the condom on and coated his cock with lube, Z gripped Ryan's ankles, pulling him toward him—again mindful of his arm—until Ryan's ass rested on the edge of the mattress.

"Don't move," Z told him, adjusting his position by placing his knee on the mattress while keeping his eyes locked with Ryan's.

Ryan nodded. "Don't worry. There's no place I'd rather be than right here. I'm not running anymore, Z."

Z teased Ryan's anus with two fingers briefly before taking his dick in hand and guiding it to where Ryan needed him most, still never taking his eyes off Ryan's. It was intoxicating, being lost in Z's gaze while he entered him slowly, pushing deep but never rushing.

"I love you," Z whispered, holding Ryan's legs as he slid in slowly, then retreated the same way.

This was a first for Ryan, making love like this, both of them captured in the moment, connected not only by their bodies but by something far deeper, far more intense than anything Ryan had ever known.

"I love you, too," Ryan said on a gasp. Z's thick cock filled him so perfectly. "So fucking much."

Z continued to fuck him gently, rocking forward and back, holding Ryan's legs so that he didn't move away from him. When he reached between Ryan's legs and wrapped his fist around Ryan's cock, it was too much.

"Z, it's been too long," Ryan admitted. There was no way he could hold back. His release was rushing upon him.

"Come for me, Ryan. While I'm buried deep inside you, come for me."

The delicious friction continued as Z plunged inside, his movements getting more forceful but never enough to jar Ryan. Z was holding back, that was evident. He was making sure he didn't hurt Ryan, and that alone had Ryan's heart pounding, emotion clogging his throat.

God, he loved this man. And he'd been telling the truth when he'd said he didn't deserve him, but there was no way Ryan wanted to live the rest of his life without him.

"Ryan," Z growled. "Come for me, baby. Oh, God."

As Z stroked Ryan's cock, he gave himself over to the man completely, no longer holding anything back. Z's hips jerked forward, thrusting deep.

"Fuck," Ryan cried out, his eyes closing as his cock swelled and pulsed.

And when Z's hips stilled, his dick pulsing in Ryan's ass, Ryan came in Z's hand, feeling whole for the first time in his entire life.

THIRTY-EIGHT

The next day

"I still can't believe he passed out," Trace said, laughing as he looked across the table at RT. "Strapped to the fucking chair."

Z was tempted to punch his friend, but when RT smiled, he managed to refrain.

The small conference room was filled almost to capacity. It seemed like the entire Sniper 1 team was there—Trace, Courtney, Clay, RT, Conner, Colby, Tanner, Hunter, Dominic, Austin, Evan, Kira, Decker, Jayden, along with Casper and Bryce, who were standing at the front of the room. Even TJ, Steph, Elizabeth, and Emily were in attendance, sitting at the back of the room. All fifteen chairs at the table were filled; more had been brought in for this.

Like the others, Z had no idea what was about to happen. Everyone's previous side conversations had stopped once Trace had started to tease RT, and the tension was increasing as everyone waited.

"You'da thought he'd taken one to the chest," Clay added, laughing alongside Trace.

"Will you two shut the fuck up?" RT said, grinning. "I was *shot*."

Ever since that first night when he'd stayed with RT, Z hadn't been able to sleep much. Until last night, he'd been plagued by nightmares about RT being shot. Sure, the bullet hadn't hit anything major, and it had in no way been life threatening, but witnessing it had fucked Z up good. Not that he'd allowed anyone to know that. Instead, he had retreated to the nursing home, sharing his thoughts with his father.

Watching RT now, Z felt his chest expand, the love he felt for the man making it difficult to breathe. Last night had been…perfect. Better than perfect, actually. Never had he thought they'd make it this far, especially not after what had happened between them, but now, all that hope that had filled him remained, this time reinforced by the fact that RT had told him that he was no longer running.

"Yeah," Clay agreed. "In the fucking arm. You big baby."

Z didn't contribute to the conversation. He was still a little overwhelmed. He'd spent the last few days trying to recover from watching RT take a bullet, from spending the night in RT's bed that same night, wishing like hell he could trust him again, wanting desperately to throw caution to the wind and tell RT how much he loved him. Only to find himself back in RT's bed, every dream he'd ever had where RT was concerned realized.

Although Z had reluctantly taken the week off, helping RT when he needed it but spending most of the time with his father, as well as Reese and Jensyn, who had both remained in town until yesterday, he had been eager to get back to work. His brother and sister had gone back to their normal lives, leaving Z alone again, which was how he'd woken up that morning, as well. Only he hadn't been alone. He'd had RT. But still, Z had been expecting to spend a few more days doing as little as possible. If it had been up to him, he would've spent most of that time naked with RT.

Except RT had called everyone into the office this morning.

"So, why're we all here?" Clay stared at his brother, looking like a man ready to bolt from his seat.

"I've got some news," RT answered.

"Well, if it's about Amit, we know how that ended," Clay noted.

"It's not about Amit," RT said.

Z and the others had already been debriefed about the case. Amit was home safe and sound; he'd returned the money to Thurston that he'd been paid for the stolen painting—the portion he hadn't spent already, anyway. Jericho had loaned him the rest. Thurston had been arrested but released the same day. He was facing charges for shooting RT, but no one figured he would spend any time in jail considering the circumstances, not to mention how much money the loony bastard had. The original painting had been handed over to DHS, and Z hoped they never had to see the damn thing again. And to top it all off, Max had sworn to Courtney that he wouldn't retaliate against Thurston for what he'd done—not that anyone necessarily believed him, but whatever.

"Then what's this about?" Clay grumbled.

Casper cleared his throat. "We wanted to make an announcement."

All eyes turned to Casper.

"We're stepping down," Casper stated, coming to stand at the end of the table and glancing at everyone individually before continuing. "Going forward, Bryce and I will no longer be in charge. We're officially transitioning the control over to where it belongs."

"We'd like to say that we won't be coming into the office," Bryce added, "but we all know how that usually works out."

A few chuckles followed.

Z glanced at RT. Although he knew this was what Casper and Bryce had been working toward, he wasn't as thrilled as he should've been. With RT taking over in an official capacity, he would be even more wrapped up in the job, more intent on staying focused and moving the company forward. Not that Z blamed him. This was his legacy. But that meant Z would have even less time with him than he did already.

"Congratulations," Decker said, nodding toward RT.

"Don't congratulate him yet," Bryce chimed in. "We've known this day was coming for a long time, and though RT has been groomed to take over, and ultimately will remain in charge, at his request, we're making a few changes."

Z's attention shifted to Bryce.

"Everyone in this room knows that this is not a forty-hour-a-week job," Casper said. "Never has been, never will be. We work when we're needed, and we don't stop until the job is complete. And yes, I know there are some of you who insist on fieldwork and couldn't imagine sitting behind a computer all day. Luckily for everyone here, that isn't what Bryce and I have done for the past thirty-five years, either."

More laughter erupted around the room.

"In case some of you haven't noticed, RT is still very much hands-on. He wants to be in the field as much as everyone else, but he can't run this place by himself, and in the coming weeks, Bryce and I will no longer be as available as we once were."

Z glanced over at RT again, noticing he was staring back at him. Bryce's hand squeezed Ryan's shoulder, breaking the moment.

RT got to his feet. "I've been told more than once that I work too much, but it wasn't until someone specific informed me of this that I realized what it meant. Maybe I've been selfish in taking on so much responsibility without delegating to some of you who are far more capable of handling certain things than I am. Or perhaps I was simply trying to ensure everyone had the ability to do what they wanted to do at my own expense.

"Either way, the same man who so bluntly informed me that I work too much also told me that there are other people who would be glad to step up to the plate and help out." RT glanced at Conner briefly, then scanned the room once more. "I've taken certain things into consideration when coming to this decision, but in the end, I'm confident that these changes are what's best for the company. And the reason I brought you all here today is because everyone in this room is a decision maker in some way or another within this company. Your input is crucial to our success."

"Which means...?" Hunter asked.

"It means that I want your support."

Z felt the tension in the room as everyone, including him, hung on every word RT said.

"Starting immediately, Conner will be moving into his rightful place within Sniper 1."

Everyone's eyes shifted to Conner. Z had expected him to bitch and moan, something he'd gotten good at over the last two years.

"RT's right," Conner conceded. "I've shirked my responsibilities for long enough. It's time I do right by him, and you. And I figured if I took over Casper's office, he wouldn't be able to hang around so much."

Z was shocked, but not as shocked as some of the others whose mouths were hanging open at Conner's admission. Or maybe it was his attempt at a joke. Who knew?

"After a lengthy discussion with Conner," Ryan continued, "the two of us also agreed that some additional changes were needed. And we've decided to implement three teams, all with a team leader, who will be responsible for managing the day-to-day of each person within their organization. Due to the fact we're continuing to take on more business, we'll be expanding, hiring more agents and additional office staff.

"This means everyone will be taking on more responsibility, some other positions will be created, some will change to incorporate this additional level. Does anyone have any questions?"

"Who're the team leaders?" Clay inquired, looking none too happy with this.

RT glanced over at Trace. "Trace will handle one of the teams, another will be managed by Courtney."

Z glanced over at Trace, smiling. He knew Trace loved being in the field, but now that he was married, it would give him more time with Marissa, allow him to travel less if he chose that route.

"And the third... The third team will be managed by Z."

The information took a moment to register, and Z's eyes snapped over to RT but not before seeing Trace smile and point in his direction.

"Wait, what?" Z knew his confusion registered on his face as he stared back at RT, not sure he'd heard him correctly.

But if he thought that announcement was the biggest surprise he would receive that day, he was sorely mistaken. The next words out of RT's mouth nearly leveled him.

Ryan watched as Z processed the information. He was the only person Ryan and Conner hadn't talked to after making the decision, but he had hoped it wouldn't be an issue. As far as everyone was concerned, Z was the most qualified, and so incredibly loyal, it had been a no-brainer to put him in that position.

But that wasn't Ryan's only reason for wanting Z there.

Taking a step closer to Z, who was sitting in the chair at the end of the table across from where he'd been seated, Ryan didn't look away as he continued. "You're an integral part of this company. You've proven yourself time and time again, given one hundred fifty percent, and we need you here."

Z didn't respond, but Ryan hadn't expected him to.

"But more importantly," Ryan continued, "*I* need you here. Not only because of your loyalty and dedication, but…" Ryan took a deep breath. "But because I love you."

There were a couple of gasps from behind him, but Ryan ignored them.

"Everyone in this room can attest to the fact that I've spent the last few years with blinders on. I've been single-minded and so focused that I've overlooked the best thing that's ever happened to me. And now that I have it, I refuse to let it go."

Someone clapped, but Ryan held up his good hand to quiet them.

Reaching for the arm of Z's chair, Ryan eased down onto one knee in front of Z, never breaking eye contact. This was the part he'd been rehearsing all morning.

"Zachariah Tavoularis." Ryan swallowed past the lump that formed in his throat. "Will you marry me?"

Based on Z's stunned expression, Ryan had taken him completely off guard. This had been a gamble, he knew. Proposing to Z in front of everyone they worked with, everyone Ryan considered family had been Ryan's attempt to show Z that he didn't want to hide any longer, that, like he'd told him last night, he wasn't going to run from what he wanted anymore.

As he waited for Z to say something, Ryan's hands began to shake, sweat slid down his spine, as fear started to creep upon him with each passing second.

Then Z leaned forward, a smile tilting the corners of his mouth. "You'll never get these guys to believe I'm the chick in this relationship, you know?"

Okay, so not at all what Ryan had expected, but he should've known. This was Z, after all. Smiling back at the man he loved, Ryan said, "Never say never." That seemed to throw Z off, making Ryan and a few others laugh. "Marry me, Z."

In true Z fashion, he grinned wide and said, "Of course, I'll marry you, my queen."

Ryan's heart kicked hard in his chest as the applause sounded, growing louder, followed by whistles and shouts. He peered over at the others in the room, unable to erase the goofy grin he knew was plastered on his face. "He said yes." Laughter ensued, but Ryan glanced back at Z. "I love you."

"I know," Z said with a smirk. "I definitely know."

EPILOGUE

Two months later

"What are you doing?" RT asked when Z wandered into his office, closing the door quickly behind him, then engaging the lock.

It still took Z a moment to adjust to RT's new surroundings since he'd moved up in the world, taking over Bryce's plush office after Bryce had done as promised, retiring and trying to enjoy his time away from the office. The room was much bigger than RT's old office, which Z had taken over with his new promotion. Oh, and it also had a bathroom in it, which proved quite useful for what Z had in mind.

"Just here to make sure you're workin'," Z told him, loving the way RT's eyes narrowed in disbelief.

Z had to admit that he'd come to enjoy his new position within Sniper 1 Security. Particularly the position that he could so easily get himself into when he snuck into RT's office in the middle of the day and locked the door.

"Z, you know we can't do this here," RT said, but he didn't sound at all as though he believed those words.

"Oh, but we can. And we will."

RT twisted in his chair, turning to face Z when Z came around his desk.

"Conner's next door," RT informed him.

"No, Conner has left the building." Unceremoniously dropping to his knees in front of RT, Z reached for the button on RT's jeans. "But Trace is in his office, so you might wanna keep it down."

RT chuckled, but it was strained. "Z, seriously."

"Shh," Z insisted. "Now help me out here."

RT might've been verbally resisting, but at the command, he lifted his hips and allowed Z to easily pull his jeans down his legs.

"Hmm. Commando. I like it."

Leaning forward, Z swiped his tongue over the head of RT's semi-soft cock, peering up at him to watch his lover's face.

"Fuck," RT groaned softly, his hand sliding into Z's hair. "Why do you do this to me?"

Z chose not to answer the question because they both knew why he did it. Because he couldn't keep his hands off RT. Ever since they'd gotten engaged, Z had been making up for lost time, and he had no intention of stopping anytime in the near future. As far as he was concerned, they had a lot of time to make up for.

"Oh, yes. Suck me, Z."

Z worked RT with his mouth, getting him hard before deep-throating his beautiful cock, sucking him firmly as he stroked him with his hand. RT's hips continued to thrust forward with every downstroke, forcing him all the way in. Watching RT fascinated Z; he loved seeing the sensual expressions, the way his eyes closed as he fucked Z's face, his fingers tightening in his hair.

"I wanna fuck you," RT mumbled. "But damn, that feels good."

Z continued blowing RT, waiting for him. One way or the other, Z was going to make him come. Whether it was in his mouth or in his ass, that was completely up to RT.

"Oh, fuck, Z. I don't... I don't... Fuck." RT growled the last word as he pulled out of Z's mouth, opening his eyes. "Bend over the desk," RT ordered.

Z smiled as he got to his feet, quickly unhooking his jeans and shoving them down his thighs. While RT retrieved lube from his top desk drawer, Z assumed the position, bracing himself on RT's desk after grabbing a towel from the drawer on the other side. No sense in making an unnecessary mess.

Ever since RT's proposal two months ago, Z had noticed that his future husband had begun to lighten up significantly. They'd talked at length about so many things and had come to quite a few conclusions. One, they had chosen to move in together, in RT's house for the time being; two, they would dedicate time to the important things in life, like family; three, they would forgo condoms in the future if they both agreed to be tested (which they had); and four, they would keep the lines of communication open between them. Always.

Not only was RT making a valiant effort to delegate some of the workload, he was ensuring that the two of them spent as much time together as possible. And not once had Z been sent on an out-of-state assignment, which allowed for a lot more of *this*, which he knew he would always crave.

RT opened him up using two lubed fingers, making Z growl and plead for more, though he did his best to keep his voice down so as not to draw attention to what they were doing. Granted, he already knew that Trace suspected they were sneaking off for *nooners*, as Trace referred to them, any chance they could get.

Which they were.

"Quit playin' and fuck me," Z encouraged, gripping the edge of RT's desk. "I wanna feel you inside me."

RT's fingers disappeared, replaced by his cock, and Z held on as pleasure assaulted him.

"Ah, God, yes," he groaned. "Just like that."

RT plunged deep, then gripped Z's shoulders, holding him still as he began to pound him from behind. As usual, RT remained silent, likely super aware of others being able to hear them if they were to press their ear to the door.

Z wasn't quite as careful, but he did manage to bite his lip to keep from crying out as RT continued to fuck him hard and fast. Snatching the towel, he reached down and covered his dick, unable to hold back.

"Fuck. I'm comin'," he announced in a harsh whisper, his dick jerking in his hand.

Apparently RT had been waiting for him, because he slammed into Z only twice more before letting go.

After cleaning up, Ryan joined Z on the leather sofa in his office, lying down and resting his head on Z's lap. It was funny how he looked forward to this time they shared together almost as much as he looked forward to sex. It was the peace Z afforded him, just by being close.

"Did you talk to Buddy?" Ryan asked, looking up at Z.

"I did. He was honored that I asked him to give me away."

"I knew he would be," Ryan told him. For the last two months, Ryan had been given the chance to get to know the people closest to Z. Those who Z had kept practically hidden from his friends.

Although Z no longer slept at the nursing home overnight, they did stop by for at least an hour, sometimes longer, every night to visit with Thomas and Buddy. Three nights a week, they had a standing dinner date with Buddy as well. Ryan had noticed from the very beginning just how attached to Z the older man was. He'd practically adopted Z, though Ryan didn't think Z had even figured that out.

"Are you gettin' nervous yet?" Z asked.

Ryan met his gaze. "About the wedding?"

Z smirked.

"Not at all. You?"

"Not yet."

Ryan sat up abruptly. "*Yet?* What does that mean?"

Z smiled, then shifted, crowding Ryan until he was forced to fall onto his back, Z hovering above him.

"It doesn't mean a thing, I just like fuckin' with you." Z kissed him thoroughly.

Ryan sighed. "What am I ever gonna do with you?"

"You're gonna love me. What else can you do?"

Ryan smiled up at Z. He was right, as far as Ryan was concerned, loving Z was the only option. And he intended to do so for a very long time.

♥□□□□♥□□□□♥

I hope you enjoyed RT and Z's story. Never Say Never is the second book in Nicole's bestselling Sniper 1 Security series. You can read more about Sniper 1 Security as well as her other series on her website. Did you know that the Sniper 1 Security and Southern Boy Mafia series overlap? You can find the full reading order at:

www.NicoleEdwardsAuthor.com.

Want to see some fun stuff related to the Sniper 1 Security series, you can find extras and details regarding what's coming next on my website as well. I keep my website updated with the books I'm working on, including the writing progression of what's coming up for the Sniper 1 team.

If you're interested in keeping up to date as well as receiving updates on all that I'm working on, you can sign up for my monthly newsletter.

Want a simple, *fast* way to get updates on new releases? You can also sign up for text messaging. I promise not to spam your phone. This is just my way of letting you know what's happening because I know you're busy, but if you're anything like me, you always have your phone on you.

And last but certainly not least, if you want to see what's going on with me each week, sign up for my weekly Hot Sheet! It's a short, entertaining weekly update of things going on in my life and that of the team that supports me. We're a little crazy at times and this is a firsthand account of our antics.

And, as always, thank you so much for reading. I hope you'll be able to leave an honest review, as this is the best way to share your thoughts about the book with others.

♡▪▪▪▪♡▪▪▪▪♡

About Nicole

New York Times and *USA Today* bestselling author Nicole Edwards lives in Austin, Texas with her husband, their three kids, and four rambunctious dogs. When she's not writing about sexy alpha males, Nicole can often be found with her Kindle in hand or making an attempt to keep the dogs happy. You can find her hanging out on Facebook and interacting with her readers - even when she's supposed to be writing.

Nicole also writes contemporary/new adult romance as Timberlyn Scott.

Website
NicoleEdwardsAuthor.com

Facebook
Facebook.com/Author.Nicole.Edwards

Twitter
@NicoleEAuthor

ACKNOWLEDGMENTS

I have to thank my family first, for putting up with my craziness. From my sudden outbursts when I think of something that needs to be added or when I question why one of the characters did what they did, to the strange hours that I keep and the days on end when I'm MIA because I'm under deadline or just engrossed in a story... Y'all are incredibly tolerant of me and for that, I am forever grateful. I love you with all that I am.

My street team – The Naughty & Nice Posse. Ladies, your daily pimping and support fills my heart with so much love. You are a blessing to me, each and every one of you.

My beta readers, Chancy and Denise. Ladies, I'm not sure thanks will ever be enough. However, not only are you the ones who catch the weird things and ask the bigger questions, you've both become my friends and you keep me going.

My copyeditor, Amy. Punctuation and grammar... well, that's not my strong suit. But it is yours and you are truly remarkable at what you do. You simply amaze me and I am so glad that I found you.

Nicole Nation 2.0 for the constant support and love. This group of ladies has kept me going for so long, I'm not sure I'd know what to do without them.

And, of course, YOU, the reader. Your emails, messages, posts, comments, tweets… they mean more to me than you can imagine. I thrive on hearing from you, knowing that my characters and my stories have touched you in some way keeps me going. I've been known to shed a tear or two when reading an email because you simply bring so much joy to my life with your support. I thank you for that.

By Nicole Edwards

The Alluring Indulgence Series
What's hotter than a Texas cowboy? Seven Texas cowboys.
All with a heart of gold and a sexy, devious side.

Kaleb

Zane

Travis

Holidays with the Walker Brothers

Ethan

Braydon

Sawyer

Brendon

The Club Destiny Series
Come see how hot these powerful men and their lovely ladies
can get. All from the comfort of the infamous Club Destiny.

Conviction

Temptation

Addicted

Seduction

Infatuation

Captivated

Devotion

Perception

Entrusted

Adored

The Dead Heat Ranch Series

*Love cowboys? Love smokin' hot cowboys and the sweet,
sexy cowgirls they love? Come on in and stay a while.*

Boots Optional

Betting on Grace

Overnight Love

The Devil's Bend Series

*Sexy is just the beginning for these down home cowboys.
Add in a little country music, some big dreams and you're in
for a ride.*

Chasing Dreams

Vanishing Dreams

The Devil's Playground Series

*Come hang out at Devil's Playground - the hottest
nightclub in Las Vegas, Dallas and New York! This is a
spin-off series from Southern Boy Mafia, featuring
those who work at Max Adorite's nightclub, Devil's
Playground.*

Without Regret

The Sniper 1 Security Series

*The Kogans and the Trexlers are in the business of
protecting those who need to be protected. And their
motto is: Protect... by any means necessary.*

Wait for Morning

Never Say Never

The Southern Boy Mafia Series
Everybody loves a bad boy!

Beautifully Brutal

Beautifully Loyal

Standalone Novels
Just to spice things up a bit!

A Million Tiny Pieces

Writing as Timberlyn Scott

Unhinged

Unraveling

Chaos

Because Naughty can be oh so Nice®